THE LADY OF ASHES MYSTERIES

Lady of Ashes

Stolen Remains

ALSO BY CHRISTINE TRENT

By the King's Design

A Royal Likeness

The Queen's Dollmaker

STOLEN REMAINS

STOLEN REMAINS

A Lady of Ashes Mystery

CHRISTINE TRENT

KENSINGTON BOOKS

KENSINGTON BOOKS are published by

Kensington Publishing Corp.
119 West 40th Street
New York, NY 10018

ISBN-13: 978-1-61129-257-2

Printed in the United States of America

To the memory of
Barbara Øvstedal, a.k.a. Rosalind Laker,
British historical romance novelist
1921–2012
The dearest and sweetest of women, who was not only
my inspiration for picking up a pen to
scribble out the words for my first book,
but who graciously welcomed this American traveler
into her home and into her life.

and in honor of my English friends
John and Jo Maginnis
Daphne Moon
Susan Keane
Barbara's spirit continues to live in you, much to my great happiness.

ACKNOWLEDGMENTS

There are many people who push and prod me along to the completion of each book, and it is only proper that I acknowledge their contributions to this story.

My appreciation goes to Audrey LaFehr, my editor at Kensington Books, whose idea it was to turn the Victorian undertaker's adventures into a series. I'm also indebted to my agent, Helen Breitwieser, who is not only a consummate professional, but just plain fun.

I extend thanks to Janeen Solberg and Beth Rockwell at Turn the Page Bookstore in Boonsboro, Maryland, for their ongoing support of my books. Ladies, it is always a pleasure working with you.

Jackie Buckler and the entire staff of The Hair Company always allow me to hang around for hours, writing away in the chaotic environment of a busy salon. You're not only marvelous hair professionals, but wonderful friends.

Carolyn McHugh has turned herself into my dedicated (and totally unpaid) research assistant. She is responsible for many historical nuggets of Victorian life in my books.

Diane Townsend spent a lot of time reading my manuscript and providing valuable input.

From beginning to end, this book was truly a family affair. My brothers-in-law, Christopher Trent and Paul Trent, helped me through plot issues in the initial stages of the book.

My brother, Tony Papadakis, also helped with plotting, then returned to edit the book at the end.

Despite many health challenges, my mother, Georgia Carpenter, pores through every manuscript and fixes my grammar (I still have no idea what she means when she tells me to quit splitting infinitives). Maybe that's what moms are for, but I think my mom goes above and beyond the call of duty.

James and Lois Trent are my biggest fans, and always purchase a pile of my books to mail off to friends and family. I am so grateful for such wonderful in-laws.

I am the luckiest of women to be married to my husband, Jon. He helps me plot my books, edits the finished works, takes all of my ideas seriously, lets me collect cats, and builds me all the bookshelves I want. After fifteen years of marriage, I am still in awe of how blessed I am.

Deo gratias.

CAST OF CHARACTERS

VIOLET HARPER'S FAMILY AND FRIENDS

Violet Harper—undertaker with a penchant for stumbling into macabre situations
Samuel Harper—Violet's husband
Susanna Harper—Violet's adopted daughter, living in Colorado
Benjamin Tompkins—Samuel's law clerk, living in Colorado
Eliza Sinclair—Violet's mother
Arthur Sinclair—Violet's father
Mary Cooke—mourning dressmaker and friend of Violet's

THE UNDERTAKERS

Harry Blundell—co-owner of Morgan Undertaking
William "Will" Swift—co-owner of Morgan Undertaking
Julian Crugg—the Fairmont family undertaker

THE VICTIM'S FAMILY

Anthony Fairmont, the Viscount Raybourn
Stephen Fairmont—Lord Raybourn's son and heir
Katherine "Kate" Fairmont—Stephen's wife
Dorothy Fairmont—Stephen's elder spinster sister
Eleanor "Nelly" Bishop—Stephen's younger sister
Gordon Bishop—Nelly's husband
Tobias "Toby" Bishop—Nelly's son
Cedric Fairmont—once the eldest Fairmont child until he was lost in the Crimean War

THE HOUSEHOLD STAFF

Mrs. Peet—Lord Raybourn's housekeeper
Madame Brusse—the cook
Larkin—the valet
Louisa—the new maid

THE DETECTIVES

Pompey Magnus Hurst—Detective Chief Inspector at Scotland Yard
Langley Pratt—Second Class Inspector at Scotland Yard

FRIENDS, ENEMIES, AND BUSYBODIES

Ellis Catesby—newspaper reporter
Adam Farr—a friend of Toby's
James Godfrey—an old wartime friend of Cedric's
Rebecca—the maid from next door

HISTORICAL PERSONAGES

Victoria, Queen of England
Albert, Prince Consort—dead eight years but forever alive in the queen's mind
Albert Edward, "Bertie," Prince of Wales
Alexandra of Denmark, "Alix," Princess of Wales
William Gladstone—Queen Victoria's prime minister
John Brown—Scottish-born personal servant and great favorite of Queen Victoria's
Lieutenant Colonel Edmund Henderson—Commissioner of Police of the Metropolis (London)
Alfred Nobel—inventor of dynamite, founder of the Nobel prizes

STOLEN REMAINS

1

Musafirkhana Palace, Cairo, Egypt
March 1869

"This has been a profitable trip, has it not, my dear?" The Prince of Wales gazed down at his prime acquisition from their tour of Egypt: a mummy, which the seller said dated to Egypt's twenty-sixth dynasty.

What revelations would the twenty-sixth dynasty have for the nineteenth century?

He sipped from his glass of dreadful rosé, wondering if it had been taken from an ancient amphora entombed with the mummies themselves. It tasted like dried wool. The Egyptians had much to commend them, but winemaking was not among their finest talents.

Albert, or Bertie, as his mother Queen Victoria called him when he happened to be in her good graces, was surrounded inside the viceroy's palace by the closest confidants of his entourage on this trip through Egypt: his elegant wife, Alix; the British explorer, Sir Samuel Baker, along with his unconventional wife, Lady Florence Baker; Lord Raybourn, the queen's man, sent along to discuss the canal's opening ceremonies with Isma'il Pasha, the Egyptian viceroy; and Colonel Christopher Teesdale, the prince's equerry, who'd distinguished himself during the Crimean War fifteen years ago.

All agreeable company except for Lord Raybourn. He was too serious and too concerned with the political events in Egypt, remaining locked up with the viceroy for hours at a time, going over the minutiae of the flotilla lineup and what speeches would be given and by whom.

Why did his mother need to send a tedious old peer to Egypt for such donkeywork? Surely some parliamentary bureaucrat could have done it. Was Lord Raybourn's real purpose to serve as his mother's eyes and ears, to report on the Prince of Wales's activities?

To cast a further pall over the trip, there were no interesting women in the traveling party other than Mrs. Baker, whose dramatic life story as a young Hungarian princess, kidnapped and nearly sold into a harem before being rescued by her future husband, stretched credulity a little far. And Mrs. Baker was far too devoted to her husband to consider the prince's affections.

Why wasn't Raybourn working on a private entertainment for the prince, like those involving exotic music and veiled, nubile Egyptian girls that Isma'il Pasha had provided during their cruise down the Nile—rather than worrying about whether the British flag would fly higher than the French one during the opening ceremony?

Bertie looked affectionately at his wife, Alix, who had taken days to recover from the indignation brought on by his visit to meet Pasha's harem. She was a good woman, and patient, but didn't understand his voracious appetite for variety in all things. By God, he wasn't yet thirty years old and there was so much to *experience*. At least he knew that she was loyal despite his weakness for beauty, and would never spy on him for his mother.

Nor would Lady Susan Vane-Tempest. As much as he'd enjoyed Pasha's entertainments, Bertie was yearning for his current mistress. He'd considered bringing her along, but that would have been asking too much of his tolerant wife.

Enough ruminating. After days of nodding approvingly at the progress of tons of dirt being shoveled out of the middle of the desert, Bertie was ready for something interesting, and what lay before him was *vastly* interesting.

The mummy was part of a cache of some thirty mummies sup-posedly discovered together in a tomb. Sir Samuel insisted the mummies couldn't possibly be as old as the seller claimed, but what did it matter? A mummy unwrapping party would be great fun, and Bertie planned to send the rest of the cache to museums throughout England and the world. Maybe he'd even send one to Mother's ostentatious South Kensington Museum, although the British Museum might have a quibble with that idea.

"Who would like to be the first to pull on a bandage?" he asked.

"I'll do it," Florence Baker said, getting up from her chair and approaching the table where the mummy lay. She went straight for the corpse's feet and unwrapped a length of linen from there. "Everyone knows a corpse's smelly feet is the last place the under-world spirits would search for valuables, so there's probably a nice nugget of gold hidden here."

"Flooey, you are just a pip," her husband said, laughing.

Her strip broke free without a trinket appearing.

"Now I'll try," Sir Samuel said. "I'll go for the opposite end, shall I?" He loosened a strip of tattered cloth from around the mummy's head. Again, nothing.

Everyone took turns repeatedly, trying to unravel a strip under which a piece of gold, a precious gem, or other tiny artifact had been hidden for the deceased's underworld journey.

It was Lord Raybourn, though, who had the first success, hold-ing up his trinket for all to see. "What is it? Some kind of amulet?" Raybourn said.

"That's an *ankh*," Sir Samuel said. "It's the symbol for life. May you enjoy the richness of life here and in the afterworld."

"Huzzah!" Colonel Teesdale said, raising his glass. Everyone joined him in the toast, although the prince felt less than enthusi-astic over cheering his mother's spy.

The group continued playing until the final trinket was found, a scarab discovered by Alix in the mummy's hand.

"What happens with our friend here?" Teesdale said, nodding at the table, which now contained the unwrapped body, resem-bling a piece of petrified wood.

The prince considered this. "Keep your linen strips and trinkets as souvenirs, and let's draw straws to determine who the lucky recipient will be to display him in his study."

After a brief discussion over whether a married couple should have two straws or one—and deciding that they should have two—the group pulled straws from Teesdale's hand.

"Ah, Your Highness, you enjoy good fortune," the colonel said. "Where will you display your great find?"

"The princess and I must think carefully on it," he said, but he was already developing a grand idea for it: somewhere prominent inside Windsor Castle, where it would be sure to give his mother apoplexy. Perhaps then she'd quit sending nannies along to watch over him whenever he left England's borders.

Anthony Fairmont, the Viscount Raybourn, was heartily sick of Egypt. The heat, the tourists, the European girls looking for husbands, the shouting in the streets that passed for civilized conversation . . . for God's sake they even had periodic locust plagues, although it was no wonder the Almighty was still trying to get the nation's attention.

How was it that Prince Albert Edward found this place so delightful?

Even Raybourn's stay along the lush area bordering the Nile during the Prince of Wales's tour had been little compensation for his misery. He just wanted to complete his duties and return home to England and what awaited him there.

Instead, he was in conference every day with Isma'il Pasha, negotiating the fine points of what nation would have precedence at November's opening ceremonies, then he endured the prince's activities all night into the wee hours of each morning. Was there anything less dignified than drawing straws over the dusty, mummified remains of some ancient being?

Now this. His meeting with Ferdinand de Lesseps had started amicably enough inside the Frenchman's Cairo villa, although de Lesseps was prickly, as though a dung beetle were running up and down beneath his skin.

"How do you find your stay in Egypt, Lord Raybourn? It ees to your liking?"

"I am impressed with the progress you have made on the canal."

"It ees an achievement *magnifique* for France. And the prince, he ees pleased with his visit?"

Yes, the prince's satisfaction was really the question, wasn't it?

"He is very pleased with the variety of, ah, entertainments he has been provided. Attending the bazaar incognito was an especial pleasure for him."

De Lesseps smoothed his mustache, his nerves momentarily calmed. "*Oui,* I recommended that outing to Isma'il Pasha. But I do not think you are pleased here, Lord Raybourn. Do you have zee wife and children at home you miss? Maybe zee grandchildren?"

Raybourn cleared his throat. This was not a topic he wished to discuss with the Frenchman, no matter how important he was. "My wife died in eighteen thirty-seven, trying to give me another son, who didn't survive. I have three living children and one grandson to remind me of her, though. What of you, monsieur? Is your family back in France?"

De Lesseps spread his hands. "I am as you are, my lord. My wife, Agathe, and my son Ferdinand Victor died within weeks of each other in eighteen fifty-three. I still have two other sons still living, but it ees not the same, ees it?"

"No, although we must bear up and continue on, monsieur."

"*Oui.* It was only when I had the impulse to create the Suez Canal that I was *régénérér,* made new. You understand?"

Raybourn knew exactly what it meant to have the heart and mind return from an early grave, but that was his own closely held secret. Unfortunately, de Lesseps wasn't done probing.

"Do you look for another wife, or at least an *amour,* my lord?"

Raybourn shrugged. "We'll see. What of you? Will you remarry?"

"Ah, for now I am wedded to the Suez Canal. But once it ees finished, maybe I will find another wife. I believe I can make a good case as a husband. I have a long diplomatic career, you know, and have been consul to Cairo, Rotterdam, and Barcelona, among other postings. Of course, right now it ees the completion of the canal that is in some jeopardy, *non?*"

Raybourn didn't like the new tone de Lesseps adopted as he

started pacing in front of him. The insects were active under the man's skin again. Maybe it was better to remain on the topic of marriage.

"It ees my concern," de Lesseps said, "that your Victoria *la reine* and your *parlement* are working against me. They do not wish this project to be successful."

"That isn't true, monsieur."

"Then they do not wish me to have my full glory in it."

Raybourn was silent.

"Aha! I am correct in this. It ees why you have ignored my complaints about the blackmailer who threatens to destroy this project."

"Monsieur de Lesseps, you can hardly expect the British government to—"

But Ferdinand de Lesseps wasn't listening as he paced more furiously, working himself into a righteous lather as he enumerated all of Great Britain's crimes against him.

"This blackmail, it ees an outrage! What will your government do to see to my satisfaction? I am, how you say, *persécuté* by this man. He believes he ees greater than Ferdinand de Lesseps, but this ees not so. I am *le roi*, like a king, here in Egypt. I tell this man, 'Go here,' and he goes here. I say to this one, 'Dig at this spot,' he digs until I say stop. The viceroy ees *mon ami*, will do anything I wish. But he cannot help with what I wish now, which is for this blackmailer to be found and run through with the sword."

Lord Raybourn hoped he was successfully maintaining an interested look, one that was tinged with concern. He badly needed a glass of brandy, but would settle for a cup of Egyptian beer. De Lesseps was too agitated to notice his guest's needs.

". . . You see that the people, they cheer me in the streets for what I am doing for their country and for the world. But this little insect of a man threatens to expose me. It is . . . it is . . . *intolérable*. Why am I so badly treated when you, monsieur, your Mr. Stephenson used corvée labor here not long ago?"

Raybourn shifted uncomfortably in his chair. It was unfortunate that Robert Stephenson, who was responsible for Egypt's first standard-gauge railway being completed in 1854, had used corvée labor, workers who weren't quite slaves, because they were paid, but didn't exactly have the freedom of normal workers, either, for they were paid barely enough for food.

"Monsieur de Lesseps, you must understand that Stephenson was not under as much scrutiny as your canal is. Also, his was a vast construction project that required thousands of men, and—"

"Lies, all lies. The Suez Canal project ees the largest construction project ever in the history of humanity. Stephenson's railroad, pah! Your country uses corvée labor when it suits you, but castigate me for it. Now I have this little blackmailer attempting to ruin me."

"I will telegraph the prime minister and ask him—"

"*Non.* If your government gets involved, your newspapers will get involved. I will have no *notoriété* on this project, not when I am so close to completion."

Lord Raybourn spread his hands. "What do you want from me, monsieur?"

The Frenchman stamped his foot. "I want action! *Immédiatement.* You must find him and prosecute him."

What de Lesseps was asking was impossible. Raybourn might be a peer, but he was not the police. Perhaps he could send a discreet message back to Scotland Yard.

"If you will not do this, I will find another way," de Lesseps said. "But it will be better for you if you take care of it, Lord Raybourn."

After finally escaping de Lesseps's verbal clutches, Raybourn returned to his quarters, where he found a telegram waiting for him. It was well coded, with specific instructions in it. Instructions that suddenly made his life very bleak.

As Isma'il Pasha stood on the dock, extolling Egypt's virtues to him, Bertie positioned himself on the deck of the ship that would take him from Alexandria to other points on his return trip from Egypt: Constantinople, the Crimean battlefields, and Athens. He was especially eager to see Constantinople. Sir Samuel said that the architecture of the Hagia Sophia mosque would remind him of Brighton Pavilion, with its center rounded dome and multiple minarets dotting the complex.

Bertie's great-uncle, George IV, had built the magnificent and ostentatious palace of Brighton earlier in the century, and the prince wondered if the mosque was equally as unrestrained.

Speaking of unrestrained, Lady Florence was looking rather fetching in her garb, some sort of English interpretation of Egyptian concubine dress. Perhaps she really had spent time in a harem.

Bertie wondered if he could sneak a glance at his pocket watch without being noticed. They would never get to Constantinople if the viceroy's speech was to last into eternity. Even Alix rustled impatiently next to him, her hand in the crook of his arm as she kept a smile plastered on her face.

". . . that the idea of a canal, although now to be completed by Monsieur de Lesseps with our help, was originally an Egyptian idea, one rooted in our ancient and glorious culture, an idea of the legendary Pharaoh Sesostris . . ." Isma'il Pasha said, his voice booming so that people crowding around him on shore could hear. The man was in his finest dress, with a red bucket-shaped hat on his head, and his chest covered with bright badges and medals.

Monsieur de Lesseps stood next to the viceroy, his chest puffed in pride over the comparisons between his idea and that of an ancient pharaoh's.

While Pasha talked, the prince thought forward to the rest of his trip. The Crimean battlefields were not much to Bertie's taste—how could touring empty expanses of land and hearing about artillery, military tactics, counteroffensives, and casualty totals be of interest to anyone other than Colonel Teesdale?

". . . but when he found that the sea was higher than the land, he stopped. Later, King Darius also made strides on a waterway passage between the Heroopolite Gulf and the Red Sea. . . ."

But the colonel had been a dedicated servant, so a stop at the battlefields where he'd once risked his life was not too onerous for the prince.

". . . Ptolemy the Second made a trench as far as the Bitter Lakes. . . ."

Athens should prove to be entertaining. Alix had talked of nothing but the Parthenon the past two days in their room, a sign that she, too, was ready to see sights other than the Nile.

"... and even the French conqueror, Napoleon Bonaparte, found remnants of an ancient east–west canal late in the last century...."

Did Bertie detect a note of conclusion in the viceroy's voice? A whistle sounded in the distance, which he hoped was a signal to clear the waterway for his vessel.

"... and so we wish Your Highnesses fair winds in your journey home, with hopes that we will be honored again with your presence at the opening ceremony...."

Bertie nodded regally to the viceroy, while Alix gave a delicate wave to the cheering crowds. Finally, they were off. There was so much more of life to be tasted, sampled, and enjoyed before returning home to England.

London
May 1869

Harriet Peet lifted the saddle of lamb for an expert sniff. "Mr. Litchfield, you cannot possibly mean to tell me you just got this in. Why, it's a week old if it's a day."

"Ah, Mrs. Peet, I don't know how that was left in the case. I meant to send it to the workhouse yesterday. Let me show you another cut. How about this one? So fresh it's practically still bleating, it is."

Harriet took the proffered chunk of meat cradled loosely in paper. She didn't need to smell it to know that it was, indeed, a fresh cut. But she wasn't about to let Mr. Litchfield off that easily.

"You know I'll not tolerate tainted meat. Lord Raybourn's table must be perfect."

"Yes, of course, Mrs. Peet. May I offer His Lordship a discount for your trouble?"

With the wrapped lamb in hand and Lord Raybourn's account not much lighter for it, Harriet Peet went on her way to visit the grocer for a tin of tea. She'd be sure to inspect that, as well, lest he try to slip her used leaves that had been brewed, dried again, and repackaged.

As if any storekeeper could actually slip something past Harriet

Peet, Lord Raybourn's housekeeper these past fifteen years . . . and hopefully soon to become, well, *something more*. A rare smile dared make an appearance on her face as she waited for the tea to be weighed.

Speaking of something more, she should pick up some butter. "Two pounds of cow's butter, too, if you please," she said.

"Yes, ma'am," said the owner's boy working behind the counter. "Shall I have everything sent over to Lord Raybourn's residence?"

"No, don't bother. I'll carry it with me." There was no time to wait for a deliveryman. She needed to return quickly and change into something finer than her regular work dress. Lord Raybourn was returning this afternoon from his diplomatic mission to Egypt with the Prince of Wales, and he had promised to marry her when he returned.

Imagining it again brought a decided warmth to her neck. The Viscountess Raybourn. Lady Raybourn, his children would have to call her. She might expire from pleasure the first time she witnessed his frumpy daughter, Dorothy, spit the title out between her teeth.

"Ma'am, are you feeling well?" the grocer's boy asked.

Harriet realized she'd been laughing to herself. If she wasn't careful, people would start thinking she was a bit balmy.

"I'm quite well, thank you. Please charge Lord Raybourn's account," she said with a wave of her hand as she departed.

She entered Raybourn House, built in the reign of King George IV of shimmering Bath stone, through the servants' entrance, just as she always did at Lord Raybourn's Willow Tree House estate in Sussex. Not for much longer, though. Soon, she'd be something as rare as a silver teapot in a coal miner's house: a lower-class woman elevated to the peerage. Lord Raybourn—Anthony, as she called him in their private moments—was already buying her new dresses and hats and gloves in preparation for the moment, although they were all stored in trunks for now.

Putting away the butter and tea in the larder and keeping the mutton out on the worktable to prepare later, she went up the servants' stairs to her attic room to change into a full emerald skirt with a black jacket edged in the same green, which had spent several months in her trunk. Anthony always said the color showed off her eyes and gave her a feline quality.

A stout feline to be sure, but I still have some appeal left to me.

She hummed contentedly as she transformed herself before her tiny tabletop mirror. As a last measure, she clipped a pair of jade bobs to her ears, turning to one side to admire them against their matching necklace. Anthony would so enjoy setting his eyes on her in this combination after so many weeks away in Egypt.

He wasn't expecting her to be at the train station, waiting for him. She had a momentary bit of discomfort, for Lord Raybourn had taken Madame Brusse and Larkin, his cook and valet, with him, and seeing her dressed this way would broadcast to them what her relationship with their master was.

Anthony had not yet said they could make their relationship public.

Mrs. Peet shrugged. Anthony said they would announce their engagement upon his return, so what difference did it make that Madame Brusse and Larkin would know sooner? They were the ones who needed to get adjusted to it the fastest, anyway, given her elevation above them in the household.

She arrived early at St. Pancras station, after stepping fastidiously past the construction on the Midland Grand Hotel taking place right outside the station. It was difficult to see yet what it would look like when finished, but by the quantity of brick lying about, she guessed it would be magnificent. Rumor had it the hotel would have gold leaf walls and a fireplace in every room. Imagine that! Not even Lord Raybourn could afford so much finery.

She stopped to examine her skirts inside the station. Satisfied that they hadn't been sullied by construction dust, she found the platform where Anthony's train was due to arrive. Many other British subjects had also gathered in the station, which was decorated with flags and bunting to welcome the Prince and Princess of Wales home from their trip.

I am the only one here who doesn't care about the royal return.

As the prince's train came steaming into the station, the crowds began cheering their welcome. The members of his entourage disembarked to polite clapping, followed by more wild shouts of approval when Prince Albert Edward stepped out and gallantly offered an arm to his wife. The public loved the beautiful and charming Alexandra of Denmark, and went rapturous with joy at the sight of her.

The crowds dispersed to follow the prince and his entourage. Mrs. Peet was nearly alone on the platform.

What had happened? Why wasn't Lord Raybourn with the prince? Where was he? She waited through the arrival of several more trains, hoping that perhaps he had been delayed somehow and would be along shortly. But it became evident that Lord Raybourn was not arriving home today.

Or perhaps he'd arrived on an earlier train, and was waiting on her now at Raybourn House. With that encouraging thought, Mrs. Peet returned home by omnibus, again entering by the servants' entrance. How strange it must seem to anyone watching out a window, to see a woman so finely dressed entering through the rear.

Madame Brusse wasn't in the kitchens, but Mrs. Peet didn't stop to consider whether that was meaningful. She went as quickly as she could up the narrow servants' staircase to see if Anthony was in his study or his bedroom.

Best to stop first on the ground floor to see if the postman had dropped mail through the door slot.

There was mail lying on the floor, but it was what else lay on the floor that sent Harriet Peet, a dedicated housekeeper so full of self-control that her employer's children had no idea of her relationship with their widowed father, into paroxysms of terrified screaming, punctuated only by ragged gasps for air.

At the bottom of the stairs, sharing space on the black-and-white-tiled floor with the day's mail, Lord Raybourn lay sprawled in his dark olive smoking jacket, one of his favorite Turkish cigarettes, half-smoked and crushed, lying next to him.

The blood, though. All of the dark, foul-smelling blood emanating from her dear Lord Raybourn's face. She backed away, not

3

E dmund Henderson blotted the words before him and read the document over one more time with satisfaction.

It was an advertisement he planned to submit to the *London Illustrated News*, since they placed their advertisements in far more prominent locations than *The Times*. He was seeking detectives to add to his new, centralized force of elite inspectors. Right now there were only twenty-six detectives and one desk sergeant, not nearly enough for a city of three million. His plan was to increase the force to over two hundred and ensure that he, as commissioner of police, would determine which crimes could be solved by divisional detectives in local police departments, and which were "higher classes" of crimes requiring the investigative abilities of his choice inspectors.

Since taking over the London Metropolitan Police a few months ago, he'd had a free hand in developing what was already known as Scotland Yard, so named for its rear entrance location on Great Scotland Yard. This advertisement was intended to attract men of intelligence and good breeding. Detectives frequently cut their teeth working as police officers in Whitechapel or the East End. But despite the knowledge and experience they had prior to promotion to detective, half those men were practically illiterate, barely able to cobble together reports.

An educated man could learn detection; an ignorant detective could learn little.

There was a rap on his door. "Yes, come in," he commanded.

"Ah, Chief Inspector Hurst, and Inspector Pratt, please sit." The two detectives took seats in chairs whose leather coverings had seen better days. Pratt winced as he sat, a reminder to Henderson that the chair's springs had developed a mind of their own and tended to attack unsuspecting occupants. An updating of Scotland Yard's furnishings was definitely in order.

"What news have you of the baby farmers?" Henderson asked.

"Another little body found, this time along with his mother, Miss Alice Dalrymple of Belgravia."

"Belgravia! Was she the daughter of someone important?"

"Her father has some railway and shipping investments. Mrs. Flood, our key suspect, keeps changing her name, making her difficult to find. She may have left London. We still need to talk to two young women we believe used this so-called midwife. It's hard to catch London's finest at home now that all their parties and goings-on are starting up for the Season, although I expect they'll be accommodating enough once word gets around that one of their own was messily dispatched to the hereafter. The lords and ladies won't be able to resist the opportunity for gossip."

Hurst was one of Scotland Yard's best detectives, but suffered from a colicky case of Harsh Opinion. Henderson scratched at his wide side-whiskers as he contemplated this, noting that Hurst was growing his own set of identical whiskers.

Perhaps Chief Inspector Hurst required a uniform. It was Henderson's observation that detectives got uppity when permitted to work in plain clothes instead of donning a uniform like regular officers.

Hurst wasn't done complaining. "If we could keep the newspapers from inserting their wasplike stingers into this case, we'd be much farther along. It seems as though they are constantly one step ahead of us. You'd think *The Times* was having tea with Mrs. Flood each day and probing her for information, with as much as they seem to figure out."

"I'm sure you are more than capable of besting a simple newspaper reporter, Inspector."

Henderson turned to the meek Langley Pratt, one of those

police-officers-turned-detective that Henderson generally frowned upon. Pratt, though, showed great promise. Very intelligent, just not forceful enough, despite having worked two years in the slums of the East End. He was a second-class inspector assigned to work with—and learn from—Hurst.

"And you, Pratt, have you written it all up yet?"

"Mostly, sir. I'll have it by morning."

"Very good. Once that's done, pass this work on to Inspector Richardson. I have something else for the both of you."

Hurst began to protest, but the commissioner held up a hand. "What I have for you is more important. It's of national interest, actually. We've been contacted by Ferdinand de Lesseps. Do you know who he is?"

Hurst shook his head. "The name sounds familiar, but I can't place it."

"He's a Frenchman, the frog behind the Suez Canal project, which is scheduled to open in November. You are familiar with the canal?"

"Of course, sir."

"De Lesseps is being blackmailed by someone who has been involved in corvée labor on the project, and this man is threatening to expose recent use of these workers to the British public, even though Great Britain had an agreement with de Lesseps that this practice of exploiting the Egyptians will not be tolerated."

"Slave labor? The public will be outraged."

Henderson nodded. "Indeed. Despite Parliament's deep concerns over the French gaining more influence in the Mediterranean, the Suez Canal will be of great benefit to the British Navy and merchants, and even a false perception of the use of corvée labor will result in a public hue and cry that will cripple our ability to leverage what the French have championed. The political and economic consequences are far-reaching. Have to give de Lesseps credit. He telegraphed us about the problem instead of making a big stink in the press or contacting some lowly member of Parliament, which would have caused a stench worse than that of any sewer.

"So that you are aware of the sensitivity of this matter, I have made this blackmail circumstance known to the ear of the Crown and the prime minister."

"What can Scotland Yard do?" Hurst said.

"You will investigate the matter and try to discover who this blackmailer is, so we can arrest him before he follows through with his threat of tainting public opinion, whether real or perceived."

Hurst frowned. "What do we have to go on?"

"De Lesseps says he thinks the blackmailer might move in society, mostly because of how educated-sounding the notes are. It's not much, but there you are. Also, the man may or may not be in London. De Lesseps is a powerful man in Egypt and has expended a great deal in time and men to find the blackmailer, but the cretin uses some complicated system of messaging with boats and lantern signals to get his notes delivered to de Lesseps. He has thus far escaped detection.

"On another matter, I have just learned of a death in Park Street, another of 'London's finest.' The dead man is Anthony Fairmont, the Viscount Raybourn. Coincidentally, he was a member of the prince's entourage in Egypt, and it appears that something may have occurred on the trip that caused him to shoot himself upon his return. I can't imagine that there is any connection to the blackmailing scheme, but best to make sure. Talk to the coroner to verify that it is a suicide, and then report back immediately, as I must keep the Crown informed. Thereafter, investigate the blackmail scheme."

Hurst scratched at his own whiskers. "This is going to be difficult, with so little to go on."

"That's why I'm putting my best inspectors on it."

Inspector Hurst brightened considerably. "You can rely on us, sir."

Henderson hoped so. The queen and Prime Minister Gladstone would be furious to learn that some imbecile was about to ruin such a high-profile diplomatic event as the opening of the Suez Canal.

4

Windsor Castle
1869

Queen Victoria sat and stared over the balding head of her latest prime minister, William Gladstone, wondering when the parade of parliamentary leaders through the government would cease. What had it been? Ten prime ministers during her thirty-two-year reign? And now Gladstone, her eleventh, had taken office last December.

Quite insufferable, he was. Seemed unable to tame or even trim what coarse hair remained on the sides of his head and over his elephantine ears. Breathed fire most of the time, going on and on about his various plans, most of them centered on pacifying Ireland. It almost made her wish for the days of Lord Palmerston's appalling and immoral leadership. Really, the elderly Palmerston's dalliances—with much younger, married women—had been the height of tastelessness and nearly drove Victoria to apoplexy. Yet, that seemed preferable to Gladstone's rants.

Things were so much simpler when dearest Albert was still alive. He would have deftly handled undesirable men like Gladstone. Albert also knew how to groom himself. How unfair it was of the Lord to take her Albert away and leave Victoria to fend for herself.

Gladstone's pacing and droning about this scheme and that proposal reminded her of a swarm of angry bees. Ah, how Albert had loved his beehives, proudly showing them off to her and instructing the beekeepers to ensure the honey gathered was always served at the breakfast table.

She really should check on the state of those beehives. She mustn't let the outdoors staff think they could forget about them. Whatever was important to darling Albert was still important to everyone in the kingdom.

"Ma'am?"

The droning had stopped, and now Gladstone was looking at her, expecting some sort of answer.

"Yes, I'm sure whatever you think is best is—"

A footman, flushed and breathless, entered without knocking. "Yes, what is it?" Victoria said. Even servants were behaving in the most boorish manner these days.

"Begging your pardon, ma'am, but the commissioner of police is here from London. Major Cowell spoke with him, then said I was to bring this note to you straightaway."

If the master of the household had met with the commissioner, something must be very wrong indeed. She hoped a member of the staff wasn't involved in anything too scandalous. Weren't Bertie's peccadilloes enough for one monarch to bear?

She cast aside thoughts of her amorous, wayward son and her bellicose prime minister to open the sealed envelope the footman handed to her on a silver plate engraved with her *VR* monogram. The note was signed by Lieutenant Colonel Edmund Henderson, who had been commissioner of police for just a couple of months, even less time than Gladstone had been prime minister.

So much change all of the time. No one understood how difficult it all was.

Victoria scanned the letter rapidly once, then again more slowly to be sure she had correctly absorbed its contents.

This was impossible. Utterly preposterous.

She realized that Mr. Gladstone was looking at her expectantly. He needed to know this as well, didn't he? She dreaded his response, but what was a queen's lot in life but to endure?

"It would appear that Lord Raybourn is dead."

"What? Dead, you say? It cannot be! When? Where?" Beads of sweat accumulated on Gladstone's considerably wrinkled forehead.

This was a delicate, political nightmare for them both, but Victoria refused to perspire so heavily and obviously over it.

"As near as the commissioner can tell, it happened yesterday late at Lord Raybourn's Mayfair townhome. The coroner believes he committed suicide, but Henderson has his best men interviewing the family quietly to be sure there was no foul play."

"Good man." Gladstone pulled a stained, crumpled handkerchief from his pocket and mopped his brow. Victoria swallowed her disgust.

"Yes, we are grateful for his discretion. The question is what we are to do about it."

Gladstone offered several ideas, one more outlandish than the next. Have the viscount's body whisked to Windsor, indeed! Imagine the public's response to *that*.

"We must not panic, sir. We must think." Victoria once again resumed her stare past the prime minister's moist, messy pate.

Was it possible to keep this news out of the papers? Of course not. *The Times* was probably running an extra edition at this very moment. How could she and Gladstone learn more without raising too much curiosity on the part of the public as to why she had a personal interest in this?

What would Albert do in this situation?

He would involve someone who wouldn't arouse anyone else's curiosity.

Victoria tapped Henderson's note in her hand. Who would that be? Someone who would do the queen's bidding without being too . . . inquisitive.

Gladstone once again interrupted the blissful peace of her own mind. "Your Majesty, if I may, I believe our first concern is to prevent the family from burying the body."

True. Their family undertaker could not be permitted to—

A thousand memories of Albert's funeral flashed through her mind, not all of them entirely unpleasant. Of particular note was the undertaker's assistant, who had been so helpful, and so very distressed at the loss of Britain's cherished prince. Dear Mrs. Morgan.

Except that it was Mrs. Harper now, wasn't it? She'd married some American man and moved off to the U.S. wilderness after their civil war ended, hadn't she? Had she gone away permanently or just to visit? Victoria would assign someone to find out.

"Mr. Gladstone, we believe we have an idea. There is an undertaker with whom we are well acquainted. She took care of the prince consort. Very reliable, very discreet."

"You are proposing that an undertaker investigate this situation?"

"Yes, she has pleased us in the past, and operates with utmost discretion."

Gladstone rubbed his forefinger across the skin beneath his nostrils, as though he'd inhaled a disagreeable odor and was trying to surreptitiously rub it away. It was his telltale sign that he disagreed with her, but was buying time while thinking up a reasonable objection.

"Ma'am, the woman is not only a mere undertaker but, well, a *woman*. I know how you feel about women performing trades. Why do you endorse this one?"

Victoria leaned back in her chair and fixed Gladstone with a steely gaze, the one she usually reserved for her children when they displeased her by, say, forgetting their father's birthday. Or, in Bertie's case, by merely entering a room smoking.

For all of his jittery, sweaty behavior, though, Gladstone was not cowed. In fact, he smiled as though he'd just remembered a secret.

"You're right, of course, Your Majesty. In fact, may I leave it all in your capable hands? Obviously, I shall muck it up if it's left to me. You will be much better at guiding the undertaker's movements properly to ensure she gets to the bottom of things."

That was much more respectful. "Yes, we will deal with the undertaker directly, Mr. Gladstone. I'm sure she will uncover what happened with Lord Raybourn straightaway, and you'll see my idea proved to be the best one."

An idea that must surely work, else some of the queen's best-laid plans would burst into flame before disintegrating into swirling, throat-choking ashes.

She could only pray Bertie was not somehow involved.

After he escaped the queen's presence, Gladstone motioned to a servant. "I need to send a message to Scotland Yard," he said.

The servant nodded and went to fetch writing materials.

Let Her Majesty dillydally about with her undertaker here in London. It would keep her occupied while he worked with Henderson to discover what had really happened. If he solved it, perhaps then the queen might admire him more.

Why was Lord Raybourn dead? Why had he returned early from Egypt, against very specific orders?

What real mischief was being conducted in the Suez?

5

Preston Village, outside Brighton, Sussex

"How was it, Mother?" Violet asked, taking away the bowl of warm broth.

"Very good, dear. I feel much more settled today." Mrs. Sinclair arranged her coverlet for the tenth time and retied the bow on her nightgown once again. "If only I didn't have to lie here, rotting like a bag of potatoes before they are thrown to the pigs."

Violet laughed. "Now I know you are well on the way to good health if you are making jokes again."

"But I'm not joking. I'm not sure how much longer I can endure this inactivity. What I wouldn't give for a stroll on the pier."

"The doctor says it won't be much longer. He just wants to make sure you're strong enough for walks on Brighton Pier."

Eliza pointed to the open window, where a breeze gently sailed in, causing the curtains to flutter in welcome. "It is a perfectly lovely day outside and the smart set have gone to London for the Season, leaving the pier alone and just aching for me to visit."

"Yes, Mother, the pier is in visible pain without you to tread its boards."

Eliza crossed her arms. "You're mocking me."

Violet sighed. The dead were so much easier to manage than the living. "I suppose I am. My apologies. How about if I promise to fetch Dr. Humphries tomorrow and together we'll try to convince him that you're well enough to be up and about. If he agrees, we'll go for a walk on the pier in the afternoon."

"I suppose that would be fine. Not that Dr. Humphries knows anything. I think he enjoys keeping me trapped here like an animal."

"You mean like a bag of rotting potatoes."

"That, too."

Violet carried the empty soup bowl back to her parents' small kitchen. She and her husband, Samuel, had been staying here for a couple of months during her mother's convalescence. When they'd first received word in America that Eliza was gravely ill, Violet had left her undertaking business in the hands of her daughter, Susanna, while Sam turned over his law practice to his assistant, and the two of them had skittered from Colorado to the coast via stagecoach and train, then across the Atlantic in a steamer ship. Their travel had been dangerous and exhausting, but they'd reached Eliza's bedside at the very moment it seemed her mother would not make it another day.

The sight of her daughter must have revived her, for Eliza had been making progress ever since. Her undiagnosed intestinal ailment had left the woman weak and thin, but she was finally eating and drinking.

For the past week, she'd been grumpy at her situation, an attitude most unlike her mother's usual state of contentment.

Violet washed the bowl and spoon and put them away in the dish cupboard, then looked around for what she might prepare for dinner, always her most challenging task of the day. An array of vegetables lay on the worktable. Perhaps she should cut them up and—and—do something with them.

The Sinclairs' day help usually prepared a meal and left it on the table, but Maisie was away visiting family this week. Leaving the household management in Violet's hands was tantamount to disaster. Although she knew exactly what to do with a body overcome by rigor mortis, a pork loin left her baffled.

In fact, anything having to do with domestic affairs she either handled badly or not at all. She remembered having gone through five maids in only two years when she'd lived in London, mostly due to her own incompetence at supervising them.

Fortunately, Sam wasn't troubled by her lack of domestic expertise, and, in Colorado, she and Susanna had gotten by with periodic day help.

Broth. Perhaps she should use a portion of Mother's leftover broth and stir some of the vegetables into it.

Violet took out a chopping knife and went to work attacking the onions, leeks, and parsnips, heaping them in a big pile in the center of the table.

"Viiiiolet," came the plaintive cry from her mother's bedroom. Perhaps if Violet ignored it, her mother might settle down to sleep. She resumed her chopping.

"Tea, dear, I need some tea. Extra sugar, if you please."

Violet put down the knife. Tea was simpler than putting together a meal, anyway. She rose and lifted the kettle that rested on the cast-iron range's burner. Still plenty of water in it. She lit the burner and assembled a tray with teapot, cup, saucer, spoon, sugar, and milk.

She wondered when Sam and her father would return. The two men had escaped early in the morning, ostensibly to visit the Grand Hotel along the waterfront in Brighton. They wanted to see the hotel's vertical omnibus, a hydraulically powered lift. Could she will them to come home and take a turn at her mother's bedside?

Not for the first time, she thought about her undertaking business back in the Colorado Territory. Susanna was competent, and more empathetic with the dead and grieving than anyone she'd ever known, but at twenty years old she was just so *young*. Violet had started in undertaking at the same age, but wasn't running a shop by herself. How was the town taking to Susanna as the proprietress?

Sam had asked his assistant to keep an eye on Susanna. Perhaps he was helping her in the shop, too. Such a nice young man, and so clearly taken with Susanna. Maybe there was even a wedding in their future.

As well as Eliza was doing now, they should be able to go back to Colorado soon enough to determine if there were nuptials in the air.

The kettle was whistling. She poured steaming water into the teapot and carried the tray to her mother. Just as she set the tray down at the foot of the bed, she heard an insistent rapping at the front door.

"Just a moment, Mother." She went to the front door to find an urchin in a telegraph office uniform outside, holding a piece of paper.

"A telegram for you, ma'am."

Curious. The boy tipped his hat at Violet before departing.

She tore it open and read the message, transcribed from a ciphered code in a slanted handwriting by a telegraph operator.

> *Your presence requested at Windsor Castle for an indefinite stay to complete particular funeral arrangements please ask for Major Cowell take the London and South Western train from Brighton to Windsor & Eton station this afternoon a carriage will be waiting for you Victoria R.I.*

Queen Victoria, Regina Imperatrix, wanted to see her. This afternoon? And another royal funeral? Whose could it be? Surely nothing had happened to the Prince of Wales? Violet had to give the queen credit for figuring out where she was. She hadn't seen the queen in four years, since Violet had left England for the United States in 1865.

Prior to that, she had been summoned to the queen's presence periodically after serving as the assistant undertaker for Prince Albert's funeral. Victoria enjoyed reliving her husband's funeral, even though, as monarch, she had not been permitted to attend the service. Instead, she'd called on Violet to provide all of the details over and over in excruciating detail.

Surely the queen hadn't discovered Violet had returned to England, and wanted to discuss Albert's funeral again?

6

M ajor Cowell was courteous, but unwilling to answer any of Violet's questions as to which member of the royal family had died. He told the carriage driver not to unload her luggage, then escorted her through the upper ward and to the queen's apartments. Violet was familiar with Windsor, having worked inside St. George's Chapel in the lower ward for Prince Albert's funeral. Not only Major Cowell, but every male she encountered along the corridors, still wore black armbands in remembrance of Albert. The women had black caps.

The queen's man led her to one of Victoria's private rooms, a place where Violet had spent many an hour describing Albert's calm repose in death, and avoiding any discussion of how terrible his decomposition was, given his long lying-in prior to burial. In fact, the Grenadiers posted at the four corners of his coffin had to be switched out every hour, despite Violet's profusion of lilies all around the coffin and chapel. The odor was intolerable even for military men who had witnessed the horrors of war.

Instead of sitting behind her usual immense mahogany desk, the queen was in her sitting area, perched at the edge of a burgundy velvet settee in close conference with a handsome man whose traditional Scottish dress was spoiled only by another black armband, and who occupied a matching settee across from her. Between them lay an ottoman with oblong cards spread across it.

The man's good looks were obscured by the reek of cigar smoke that emanated from him, reaching all the way to Violet in an invisible, noxious fog. The queen didn't seem to notice it.

Violet approached and curtsied, something she hadn't done once since going to America.

"Your Majesty," she said.

The queen and the man both sat back in their seats. "You may rise. Mrs. Morgan—we mean Mrs. Harper; it is so difficult to remember that you remarried, especially since we continue on in our widowed state, waiting to be reunited with our dearest Albert—we welcome you back to Windsor and are glad to see you returned from America."

Had the queen summoned her here to throw barbs into her chest?

Violet's first husband, Graham Morgan, was morose and inscrutable, but to him she owed her knowledge and passion for undertaking. Graham had inherited Morgan Undertaking from his grandfather and Violet had worked at her husband's side for years. Graham changed, though, eventually getting involved in a gun-smuggling scheme with the American Confederacy during their war of rebellion, and had paid dearly for it.

Violet had almost paid dearly, too. If not for Samuel Harper, she might have long ago been one of her competitors' customers. She subsequently returned with Sam to his homeland and successfully reestablished her undertaking practice there. She'd had no intention of ever returning to England, until learning of her mother's illness.

"Thank you, Your Majesty."

"Mr. Brown, this is Mrs. Harper, the undertaker of whom we spoke to you. Mrs. Harper, this is our ghillie, Mr. Brown. He helps us with our riding and takes care of the wildlife on our estates. We could hardly do without him."

Was Violet mistaken, or was the queen simpering?

"Mrs. Harper." Mr. Brown nodded his head toward Violet but did not move from his position. "Her Majesty speaks highly of your skill and compassion."

"Thank you, sir."

The queen waved. "Do have a seat. No, not there, in the

damask chair right here. Yes, that's it. Do you know the tarot, Mrs. Harper? Mr. Brown gives the most delightful readings."

"No, I cannot say I know it. I've never . . . indulged . . . in the occult." The cards that lay between queen and servant had numbers and caricaturized people on them. She could make neither head nor tail of what the arrangement of them meant.

"Ah, you must let me do a reading for ye, Mrs. Harper," Brown said. "The cards are marvelous at telling the future."

"Oh, they are indeed," the queen said. "Mr. Brown has assured us on more than one occasion that our dear Prince Albert is quite content and is watching over us."

"I see." Was Mr. Brown's smile an expression of pleasure at the queen's compliment, or a self-satisfied smirk? "I should be honored to attend to Your Majesty in whatever capacity you wish, but your telegram indicated that you had a matter of great importance to discuss."

"Yes, of course, of course. Mr. Brown, we will need you after tea to discuss our evening plans."

Taking his cue, Mr. Brown rose and bowed to the queen. He gave Violet a curt nod and left. The queen's eyes followed his retreating figure until the door clicked behind him. Victoria turned her attention back to Violet.

"We need to speak with you regarding a funeral."

"Has someone in the royal family died? I heard no gossip—I mean talk—of it in Brighton, nor on the train."

"No, Mrs. Harper, our children are all well. It is a funeral of someone whose death, both sudden and most shattering, is of particular . . . interest . . . to us."

Please let this not be another funeral I will have to discuss incessantly to the end of my days.

"Of particular interest?"

"Yes. It has come to our attention that Anthony Fairmont, the Viscount Raybourn, has just died. Perhaps a suicide, but quite possibly murdered, at his townhome in Mayfair."

"How dreadful! Has the culprit been caught?"

A childhood memory pushed forward. Arthur Sinclair had once been the estate manager for a Lord Raybourn. He'd moved Violet and her mother into a cottage on the property in Sussex, serving Lord Raybourn for about two years until he obtained a more lucrative—and less strenuous—position managing some of the East India Company's accounts. Violet remembered a secret friendship with one of Lord Raybourn's children. Secret, for a friendship—however innocent—between a viscount's younger son and the estate manager's daughter was impermissible.

A flood of recollections flashed through her mind. Splashing through ponds to collect toads, climbing up trees to serve as lookout as the master's son played at being a highwayman and "robbed" one of the family's hounds, and, in a particularly exuberant moment, wandering into the kitchens for a loaf of rye and a piece of trout before stealing off to their secret location in a grove of oaks and attempting to turn their catch into five thousand loaves and fishes. How disappointed they'd been when it didn't work.

Was her father's employer the same Lord Raybourn the queen spoke of now?

"No one has been arrested yet. Lord Raybourn is—was—very important to our kingdom and we are deeply saddened by his passing. We have decided to provide undertaking services on behalf of the family. As such, we have decided to engage you to attend to Lord Raybourn. We will look to you to comfort family members arriving from Sussex."

Violet's mind whirled. This was surely the Lord Raybourn she remembered. She tried to focus on what the queen was saying. "I'm not sure I understand, Your Majesty. You are providing burial assistance rather than, say, a spray of flowers or a wreath?"

"Yes."

"Instead of giving a gift of gloves to the funeral attendees?"

"Yes, Mrs. Harper."

In all of her days in the funeral business, no aristocrat had ever given a grieving family of fellow aristocrats the gift of a funeral. Now the queen planned to do so? For what reason? Was the Raybourn family so impoverished that they couldn't afford it? And why was she summoning Violet for it? She had a thousand more questions, none of which could be asked.

"I see. I've a friend in London I can stay with while I make the arrangements and—"

"Actually, Mrs. Harper, we have considered your living situation, and have decided we will have you installed at St. James's for the duration of your stay."

"Your Majesty, that is very generous, but I shouldn't be here more than a few days, so I would be happy to just—"

"Yes, well, it may be that your services will require more than mere undertaking. We may require some diplomacy from you."

This was getting stranger by the moment. "I'm sorry? I'm afraid the last thing I'm known for is my diplomatic skill. In fact, I'm really rather tactless at times and I can never seem to—"

The queen's eyes narrowed. "What we mean is that we wish for you to . . . to delay . . . to impede . . ." The queen cleared her throat. "What we wish to say is that you will be required to ensure that Lord Raybourn's burial be delayed for as long as possible. Do something to keep the viscount preserved until things can be sorted out."

"Sorted out? What do you mean?"

"You see, Lord Raybourn was not only a valued peer, but he was recently returned from Egypt. He was with the Prince of Wales to tour the country and witness progress on the Suez Canal. There are certain investigations that must be completed, Mrs. Harper, before Lord Raybourn can be interred."

"An inquest, you mean?"

"Along those lines. For example, our son must be questioned."

"You plan to interrogate the Prince of Wales?"

"No, we do not."

Violet's heart stopped as she realized what the queen was saying. "Your Majesty, you want *me* to question him? I'm not qualified; I wouldn't know what to ask. Shouldn't the police—"

"We will send a message to Marlborough House that you'll be along to question him soon, as it would be entirely too unseemly for the police or the queen to question His Royal Highness. It might suggest that we do not trust him. Ah, but a few curious questions from the queen's undertaker will arouse no one's suspicions, and he will be receptive to a charming woman such as your-self.

"First, though, it is vital that you set yourself off to Raybourn House to visit the family. As we were saying before, lodgings will be made available for you at St. James's Palace. The staff there are prepared for your arrival, and Major Cowell will see to it that you are settled into sufficient quarters. We will expect you to bring us periodic reports."

"Reports of what, Your Majesty?"

"Of anything unusual, of course."

More unusual than a man perhaps murdered in his own home? A man she might have known?

7

Violet was quickly scuttled off to St. James's Palace, to a suite of rooms far more elegant than anywhere she'd ever lived, and permitted a short time to change from her traveling clothes into her undertaking garb. How thankful she was that she'd brought a complement of undertaking supplies with her across the ocean, despite Sam's admonition that she'd never need them, arguing that if Eliza Sinclair died, he would save her the morose familiarity of attending to her deceased mother, and hire an outside undertaker, to permit her to properly grieve. Violet, not wanting to entertain for any longer than necessary the thought of her mother passing, had swiftly argued just as vehemently that a good undertaker never knew when her services might be needed, and, unlike with her lawyer husband, everything she needed was *not* crammed in her head.

After changing, Violet was just as quickly ushered to Raybourn House in Park Street, just a street over from Park Lane, one of the most prestigious addresses in London. The likes of the Earl of Shaftesbury and the Earl of Beaconsfield lived here in Mayfair during the Season for balls, parties, engagement announcements, gambling, and horse races.

Poor Lord Raybourn would experience none of it. When his peers learned of his demise, they would work quickly to demonstrate the appropriate level of sorrow without allowing his death to impact their daughters' debuts into society.

Carrying her black leather undertaker's bag, she climbed the wide steps to the front door as the royal conveyance lumbered off. She paused, set the bag down, and readjusted her black top hat, making sure that the long, ebony silk tails were properly arranged down her back. Smoothing her dull crape skirts, she took a deep breath and twisted the bell handle.

It rang loudly within the house. Violet's policy was to always go to families through the front door, never a rear or servants' entrance. Sometimes she was met by an angry wife or mother who took her for just another tradesman. In Violet's mind, though, an undertaker became an intimate member of a family, even if for a very short time, and family members enter through the front door.

The Raybourn door was opened by a housekeeper, her telltale chain of keys around her waist. She had arresting green eyes that made an otherwise plain face most compelling. The woman held a well-used handkerchief in her hand, and upon taking in Violet in her black hat with tails, unadorned black dress with matching gloves, and undertaker's bag at her feet, the poor servant burst into loud sobs. She buried her face in her handkerchief with one hand while waving Violet in with the other.

In typical townhome style, there were two connecting rooms to her right, a dining room and a drawing room, both much larger than in a middle-class residence such as where she used to live.

Directly in front of her was a tiled hallway, and hugging the wall to her left was a staircase with heavily carved oak newel posts and balustrades. Oil paintings lined the wall up the stairs in a fantastic jumble of opulence probably leading up to two floors of bedrooms and then an attic of servants' quarters.

What lay on the floor was in stark contrast to the décor. Under a blanket lay a human form.

"Is this Lord Raybourn?" Violet demanded. "Why is he still here? Why hasn't someone at least carried him into the dining room?"

The housekeeper snuffled and gulped. "Mister Hurst said that Lord Raybourn was not to be moved yet, not until certain investigations were complete."

"Not to be moved! The poor man has been dead for more than a day. You'll have to help me, Mrs.—?"

"Peet. Harriet Peet."

"I am Violet Harper."

"Are you Mr. Crugg's assistant?"

"Who?"

"Mr. Crugg. The undertaker. He's upstairs with Mr. Hurst right now."

As if on cue, a thin, wiry man, dressed similarly to Violet in solid black and carrying an undertaker's bag, charged down the stairs. He grabbed his silk hat with tails from a coatrack and jammed it on his head, pausing at the sight of Violet. He wagged a finger at her.

"So *you're* my replacement. I've served the Fairmont family for many a year, and I'll not sit idly by while some upstart woman comes along and thieves away my good business and precious reputation."

"Mr. Crugg, that will be enough." A man wearing a cocoa-brown coat over rigidly creased black pants, and sporting thick, curly whiskers on either side of his face, appeared at the top of the staircase. "The queen has honored the family in her own way and there's no sense in insulting Her Majesty's chosen servant."

Servant! Violet was a respectable tradeswoman. She reached into her reticule for one of her calling cards.

Mr. Crugg merely harrumphed, ignored the proffered card, and stepped casually over the remains of Lord Raybourn as he stormed out of the house.

The housekeeper's previously florid, swollen face now went white in disbelief as the front door slammed shut behind the family undertaker. Mr. Crugg obviously adhered to Violet's philosophy on an undertaker's status.

Deaths were difficult for servants as well as for family members, Violet knew, and to have been this long in the house with her dead master lying on the floor must have been excruciating.

"Mrs. Peet, might I have a cup of tea?" Violet asked. "I've traveled extensively today."

"Yes, beg pardon, where are my manners? Everything is just so . . . so . . ."

"Of course it is. Why don't you let me take care of things here? Also, could you cover the dining room table with a cloth? Something dark, if you have it."

Mrs. Peet went down the hall to the servants' staircase, where she disappeared down into the kitchen.

Violet looked up at the man who still stood at the top of the staircase. "Mr. Hurst?" she asked.

The man walked, or, rather, lumbered down the stairs. He was a giant of a man, powerfully built, with neatly clipped side-whiskers on a broad face. His clothing was of better-than-average quality. This was no ordinary policeman.

She handed him her card. He glanced at it only briefly before tucking it inside his coat. " 'Undertaking and embalming services for Golden City, in the Colorado Territory,' eh? You're an undertaker far from home, aren't you? Magnus Pompey Hurst, chief inspector at Scotland Yard at your service . . . Mrs. Harper, is it? We were informed that you'd be undertaking the funeral."

His stature matched his name. He just needed a centurion's cloak and helmet crest, and Violet would swear he was ready to go to battle with Caesar against the Gallic tribes.

"Yes, I have been greatly honored by the queen. However, first I would like to know why Lord Raybourn is on the floor twenty-four hours after his death, then I want you to help me place the poor man on the dining room table so I can properly attend to him. He deserves respect and honor, not to be ignominiously left on the ground like a stricken deer."

Hurst visibly stiffened, his welcoming smile gone. "Excuse me, Mrs. Harper, but I am the detective in charge of this investigation, and I left Lord Raybourn here while certain matters were looked into. From the coroner's report, however, and my own observations, I am convinced this was a suicide."

"I see. Yet still the man lies without dignity on the floor."

"You might have noticed that the family undertaker was already here, but because I was given instructions to wait for you, I turned Mr. Crugg away."

"Nonetheless, from the ugly smears here and over here, it looks as though you've wiped some blood from the floor, so surely you could have found the time and decency to make Lord Raybourn more comfortable."

"He is beyond feeling or caring about anything, Mrs. Harper. Surely you of all people understand this."

"What I don't understand is your attitude as someone who is entrusted with the care of his body."

"Scotland Yard is entrusted with justice and to chase down hardened criminals who perpetrate the most heinous of crimes, ensuring safety for all Londoners."

"A pretty speech, sir. I, too, am entrusted with justice—for the deceased's earthly remains. To ensure its safe and solemn carriage to the grave."

Hurst shook his head and muttered unintelligibly under his breath. "Beg your pardon, madam, but you are a strange one, indeed. Very well, let's fix Lord Raybourn up all dainty and proper. Maybe we'll all take tea with him in His Lordship's study. Mr. Pratt!" he shouted up the stairs.

Violet heard the sound of multiple pairs of feet moving around. To her surprise, three more people appeared at the landing and came down. One was another man dressed similarly to Mr. Hurst except younger, wearing a black jacket and looking more rumpled, in addition to a man and woman around Violet's own age.

The woman was tall, blond, regal, and elegantly dressed enough to tell Violet that she was a family member. The man next to her was . . . Stephen Fairmont. Was this poised, self-assured gentleman the same boy she had once chased in and around the stables at Willow Tree House?

He looked at her quizzically. "Hello, don't I know you?"

Violet proffered a hand in greeting. "You do, indeed. I'm Violet Sinclair, now Violet Harper."

Recognition dawned in his eyes. "Of course. So it is you the queen has sent to care for Father? I'd never have imagined you as an undertaker, of all things. I more imagined you'd have ended up helping your father run an estate somewhere. I remember all of the endless questions you used to ask of the gardener, the beekeeper, the footmen. As though you were trying on each of their positions and deciding which one you'd take. How did you end up an undertaker?"

"I came by it through my deceased husband, and together we enjoyed some success. The queen was pleased enough by my work on Prince Albert's funeral, which I believe is why she summoned me to help you."

"So you are a widow?"

"Not anymore. I married an American by the name of Samuel Harper. We'll be returning to the Colorado Territory soon. We just happened to be visiting in England when the queen asked me to do this service for you."

"You married an American, you say? Another surprise from my childhood comrade-in-arms. Sweetheart, Violet Sinclair's father was once my father's estate manager." He looked down at the prone body and swallowed. "Violet, this is my wife, Katherine. We had just arrived from Sussex when all of this bedlam occurred. She's held up well under the shock."

"A pleasure to meet you, I'm sure." Katherine shook Violet's hand, studiously looking toward the drawing room, away from both Violet and her father-in-law's covered body. Her tone indicated that shaking hands with an undertaker was far from pleasurable.

There were now two grieving family members, two detectives, an undertaker, and a dead body in the Raybourn entry hall. This was ludicrous. Violet opened her mouth to suggest that Stephen and Katherine might be more comfortable waiting elsewhere while she attended to her duties, when Mrs. Peet reappeared from the dining room carrying a wood tray.

"I found a navy linen, Mrs. Harper. Mr. and Mrs. Fairmont, would you also like some tea? I'll fetch the silver tray and be right back up."

Katherine lifted her chin. "I believe it is now Lord and Lady Raybourn, Mrs. Peet. Yes, we'll have tea upstairs in our room."

Mrs. Peet set her mouth in a grim line and scowled as she placed Violet's tray in the drawing room and returned silently to the servants' staircase to retrieve a more elegant tea service for the

Fairmonts. Katherine visibly shrank, her apparent experiment with boldness quite over. "Mrs. Harper, I hope you'll forgive me, but I don't think I can remain here a moment longer."

Violet sympathized with the new Lady Raybourn. She herself had once had a housekeeper named Mrs. Scrope, who was extraordinarily competent yet thoroughly intimidated Violet.

Stephen kissed his wife's hand. "I'll join you momentarily," he said before Katherine floated back up the stairs in a rustle of velvet-embellished satin.

"My sisters, Dorothy and Eleanor, will be coming up from Sussex. Do you remember them? They were older than we were, and far too sophisticated to be bothered with their youngest brother, far less the estate manager's daughter."

"Vaguely, but I look forward to making their acquaintances again."

Stephen glanced up the stairs. "I must join Katherine. She's in a very agitated state. We both are, I suppose. Please send Mrs. Peet up if you need anything."

Again on cue, Mrs. Peet appeared with another tea service, this time on a heavily ornamented silver tray. Stephen went upstairs with the morose Mrs. Peet a few steps behind him.

Violet was now alone with the officers. "Now if you will quickly assist me before Mrs. Peet returns, I'd like to move Lord Raybourn into the dining room."

She knelt and rolled down the blanket covering the body, maintaining her composure despite what lay before her. Poor Lord Raybourn. All that remained recognizable on the man's face was his cleft chin, a trait shared by Stephen. The rest of his face was bloodied and mangled. She looked at Hurst, certain her question was obvious in her eyes.

"Multiple shot wounds from a duck's foot volley gun we found next to his body. We've recovered three of the bullets."

"What is a duck's foot volley gun?"

Hurst reached inside his jacket and retrieved a vicious-looking weapon. "A duck's foot volley gun is a pistol with four forty-five-caliber barrels arranged in a splayed pattern and resembling a duck's webbed foot, as you can see here. It sprays a sizable area with a single shot. They're typically used by prison wardens and sea captains for defense in confrontations against a group. It's overkill for a suicide, if you'll pardon my pun."

Violet nodded. "What about the fourth bullet?"

"Pratt dug around a little for it, but couldn't find it, nor could the coroner."

More indignity for Lord Raybourn.

"Ready?" she asked.

"Langley Pratt at your service, Mrs. Harper." Pratt was far younger than Hurst and carried himself uncertainly, as if unsure whether to salute Violet, shake her hand, or bow.

"Thank you, Mr. Pratt. The service you and Mr. Hurst can provide me is to carry His Lordship to the dining room. Wait just a moment." Violet gently rolled the blanket back farther. Lord Raybourn wore an olive-green smoking jacket, so fashionable these days. She cupped his arm with one hand and applied light pressure, then did the same to his thigh and calf. Violet took the man's hand and slowly moved his fingers. They were pliable and his limbs weren't stiff, so rigor mortis had passed.

She removed the blanket and spread it out next to his body. "Lift him onto the blanket—gently, sir, he's a human being!"

Violet brought his arms to a crossed position on his chest and held them. "He's ready," she said.

She caught Hurst's head shaking as he went to Lord Raybourn's feet and Pratt picked up the blanket behind the man's head. The officers lifted the body and moved it to the dining room, with Hurst leading the way backward as Violet continued to hold Lord Raybourn's arms together.

"Slowly, Mr. Hurst. Do not jostle him any more than has already been done."

He grunted in exasperation but did as Violet requested. Lord Raybourn ended up on the linen-covered table with more of a thud than she would have liked, but at least he was no longer splayed out on the floor. She directed the men to gently ease the viscount from the blanket onto the cloth-covered table.

"Tell me, what does the coroner say about Lord Raybourn's death?" Violet asked.

"The coroner says His Lordship pulled the trigger on his own pistol yesterday afternoon. It was at close range and there are no signs of a struggle. I agree with him, as I also do not see signs of a struggle, nor can I find evidence that any acquaintances had a quarrel with him."

Violet nodded. But why would someone of Lord Raybourn's stature, wealth, and royal esteem do something as undistinguished as shooting himself? It made no sense.

Hurst continued. "I've confirmed with the family that His Lordship regularly kept loaded pistols stored about the house."

Which meant that the whereabouts of the pistols might be known to many people. "I see. Does this mean that your investigations here are concluded?"

"For the moment. We will return to interview the family members when they arrive in London. Although I believe his death to be self-inflicted, we must cover every possibility, and quickly. I want to finish with this, as we have another case to tend to."

"I'm sure your interviews will prove quite illuminating, Mr. Hurst."

"Yes, well, I should say so." Hurst was momentarily nonplussed. He and Pratt bowed to Violet and left, returning a few moments later.

"One more thing, Mrs. Harper. Please do not put any bunting on the windows or do any exterior decorating that will make it obvious that someone here has died."

"Why not?"

"The press. They will swarm around and cause me no end of irritation. I prefer to keep this quiet."

Violet frowned. "First of all, Inspector, you are saying this in front of Lord Raybourn. It is horribly rude."

Hurst's eyes bulged. "Mrs. Harper, are you even aware that this man is dead? Deceased? Gone to the after—"

"Furthermore, sir, my responsibility is to undertake for Lord Raybourn and his family. That includes not only preparing this gentleman's body, but performing services that will comfort the family. Bunting on the windows lets the world know the family is grieving, and I intend to have it installed as quickly as possible."

"Surely a small delay won't bring disaster upon the family."

Violet crossed her arms, her own irritation rising. "Nevertheless, I'll not shirk my duties to save you a small bit of inconvenience."

"Small? The press are parasites. They cause endless damage to our investigations, with their prying questions and slanderous articles posing as journalism."

"Perhaps we can agree, Inspector, that the Raybourn patriarch's gruesome death by a multibarreled pistol is a bit more inconvenient than the scribbling of a newspaper reporter. Therefore, it is the family's needs I will respect. I cannot bury Lord Raybourn yet, but there is much else I can do to serve the Fairmonts. The windows will be covered as soon as possible."

Hurst opened his mouth twice to say something, then turned on his heel once again, with Pratt right behind him. Violet heard him muttering complaints about the "Bedlamite ghoul" the queen had foisted on him.

She'd heard worse.

Finally alone, she could get now to work in making Lord Raybourn appear to be serenely at rest, which would bring great comfort to the family. As for her other duty to the queen, looking for "anything unusual," well, she was far less serene and comfortable about her ability to accomplish *that*.

8

With the heavy curtains between the dining room and the drawing room, plus those between the dining room and the hallway, pulled closed, Violet only vaguely heard Mrs. Peet come back down the stairs and pass by on her way to the kitchen, breaking out in muffled tears anew, what with Lord Raybourn's covered body having taken one step closer to interment.

Violet focused her attention on the task at hand—her craft, her livelihood. Whenever she did this, the entire world receded.

She started by removing the chairs that surrounded the oblong table, except for one that she left nearby. She retrieved her bag and set it on the chair, opening the top as wide as possible. She always began by speaking to the dead person, as it not only soothed her personally, but it enabled her to deal as respectfully as possible with the deceased.

"Lord Raybourn, I am so sorry for this terrible thing that happened to you. Who did this? Chief Inspector Hurst says you probably committed suicide, but is that really true?"

Violet folded the bloodstained blanket and placed it on the floor. Mrs. Peet would have to decide whether to wash it or burn it. Sometimes families kept gruesome mementos.

Where to begin? Violet had cared for many off-putting corpses, from poisoning victims to those ravaged by disease and accidents to those hobbled by old age. Never, though, had she been asked to prepare someone whose face was so horribly disfigured. She bent over the body and sniffed it at various points.

Lord Raybourn was already decomposing, but it wasn't intolerable yet. The queen had instructed her to delay the funeral. The only way she could possibly do that would be to embalm his body.

But many families took offense to such an idea. Although it had become common practice in the United States since the Civil War, it was still frowned upon in England as an unnatural and un-Christian practice.

Why, most people argued, would you fill a person full of chemicals and then commit the body to the ground where those toxic ingredients could leach into the earth?

It wasn't an illogical premise, especially given the concoctions some undertakers had developed—creosote, arsenic, and turpentine being just some of the foundation chemicals used in proprietary formulations. Each undertaker had his own special formula, and they were closely held secrets, Violet's method included.

She'd settled years ago on a combination of chloride of zinc, alcohol, and water. She reached into her bag and pulled out the ingredients to make a fresh batch.

The only problem was, she always asked permission from the family to embalm. But it was likely that Stephen would refuse, and then what? She didn't dare go against a family's desires, especially not one she'd known from childhood. Yet, how else could she delay the funeral? Putting the body over a cooling chest wouldn't keep him fresh for long.

"Tell me, Lord Raybourn, what am I to do? Would you mind terribly if I went ahead and embalmed you and begged Stephen's forgiveness?"

Violet shook her head. This just wasn't how she practiced her craft. She remembered Sam's tale of two undertakers during the Civil War, Hutton and Williams, who'd gone and scoured battlefields, picking up the dead and embalming them, then writing to the families and refusing to release them unless the families paid an outrageous price for the embalming service they hadn't requested. The two men had been arrested and charged but later released, their reputations in tatters.

Violet had no desire to follow in their footsteps in any manner.

"I would normally embalm you and then work on you cosmetically, but perhaps we can do this a bit in reverse while I ponder what to do. What do you say?" She returned the embalming fluid to her bag.

"Dear Lord Raybourn, your poor face. What shall I do? I suppose I must first make you clean. Such a shameful job the coroner and officers did on you."

She sought out Mrs. Peet down in the kitchen, requesting that she bring up a tub of water and several clean cloths, and leave them outside the dining room. "Please, Mrs. Peet, for your own sake, do not enter where I am working."

A tear rolled down the housekeeper's face. "No, Mrs. Harper, I won't. I couldn't bear it."

Violet saw the pain in Mrs. Peet's eyes. "I know you won't. There is something else you can do to help Lord Raybourn."

"Yes, madam, however I can be of assistance."

"After you bring the water and cloths, could you see to the clocks in the house? They haven't been stopped. I will take care of the one in the dining room."

"Of course, Mrs. Harper, where is my head? I forgot in all of the . . . difficulties."

The clock hands needed to be stopped once someone in a household died. The custom demonstrated that for the deceased time stood still, and he could start his new, eternal period of existence in which time did not exist. To permit time to continue unhampered was to invite the deceased's spirit to linger endlessly.

Violet opened the glass face to the dining room's mantel clock and adjusted the hands to twelve o'clock. She then turned the clock around and reached inside its works to stop the pendulum bob. Now time was frozen until someone came in and intentionally restarted it.

With the supplies delivered and Mrs. Peet otherwise occupied, Violet dragged them into the dining room and set to work cleaning up Lord Raybourn's head. It was awful work, and it quickly became clear that not only would she be unable to successfully clean his face and hair, she wouldn't be able to repair him enough so that visiting mourners could see him.

She threw the cloth into the now-murky water basin. "Perhaps one way I can serve you is to retrieve whatever is lodged in your face. It's unconscionable that you were probed and mauled without anyone even removing it."

Violet drew a box from her bag. She unsnapped the latch and reviewed the set of Sheffield-made metal scalpels, nozzles, scissors, and other instruments. She selected a thin tool that resembled a crochet hook.

"Please be patient with me. I promise not to take too long." Violet gently inserted the instrument into where she thought the bullet might have entered. After a few moments she realized she would have to probe deeper.

"Just a little bit more, sir. Ah, I believe I've found it." Violet drew the bullet out past the sinewy shreds of muscle and fragments of bone. She held it up triumphantly in her stained hand. "Here it is, my lord. You can rest easier now."

With that done and her hands rinsed, Violet still had her embalming dilemma. She clasped Lord Raybourn's cold, limp hand in her own as she contemplated what to do. Without even the tick-tick-tick of the mantel clock, all was as silent as a tomb.

She squeezed the man's hand and released it. "Lord Raybourn, there is nothing I can do other than ask for the family's permission and hope that they agree. I expect the queen will be furious with me if they don't, but I'll face that when it happens. I'll be back shortly."

With dread her only companion, she climbed the stairs and knocked on a closed door through which she heard murmuring voices. "Lord Raybourn? Lady Raybourn?"

Stephen's voice bade her enter. The couple was sitting at a small, round tea table, with half-finished cups before them. Katherine Fairmont still looked wan and distressed.

"Pardon me for interrupting, but I need to discuss something with you."

"Of course, please sit down, and given that I have seen you covered in grass stains with scraped knees, you must call me by my Christian name," Stephen said. "Tea?"

Violet sat in an armchair with an elaborate floral covering next to a marble-topped pedestal table. "Thank you, but no. Lord Raybourn has been moved into the dining room and made more comfortable. I recommend that he remain there until such time as the funeral takes place."

"That should just be a day or two. The family has its own mausoleum at St. Margaret's churchyard in West Hoathly. Can you arrange to have him transported there?"

"Yes. Well. Ah, I have to tell you that Lord Raybourn cannot be buried just yet."

"Whatever are you talking about? Why not? Are things . . . worse with him than we thought?"

"No, it's simply that . . . that . . . while the queen cannot honor him with a state funeral, she would like him to have as decent a lying-in as possible. She may even send a member of the royal family to pay respects."

Violet waited for a lightning bolt to strike her. When it didn't come, she felt emboldened in her falsehood.

"Lord Raybourn must therefore be preserved as long as possible, so that dignitaries can have time to visit."

Stephen frowned. "It seems unusual for the queen to be so involved in the death of one of her lords."

"You must understand, though, that the queen has become much more attuned to death since the loss of her dearly beloved Albert. The loss of a peer means so much to her now." At least that statement was mostly true.

Stephen's expression was conflicted. Katherine's face was blank, although her hand shook as she picked up her teacup again and brought it to her lips. Stephen glanced sympathetically at his wife before speaking again.

"Violet, you must understand how horrific this has been for us. Father dying so unexpectedly and so brutally, then the detectives just leaving him here like that. Now the queen—while flattering us immensely—has sent away the family undertaker and is asking us to postpone the funeral. It's a bit overwhelming. I suppose it is a grace that Mr. Crugg was replaced by someone else we know."

"I know this is very hard on you both, and I—"

"Not just on us. Dorothy and Nelly aren't here yet. They will be devastated."

"When will they arrive?"

"Dorothy will be on the six-thirty train to London Bridge tomorrow. Nelly is in London for the Season, and is meeting Dorothy at the train station."

No staff to meet the Fairmont sisters at the train station? Curious. "Is Mrs. Peet the only servant here?"

"Yes, Father only brought her, his valet Larkin, and Madame Brusse, Willow Tree House's cook, with him to London prior to heading off to Egypt. He'd planned to spend the rest of the Season in parliamentary session."

"Where are the valet and cook now?"

"We have no idea."

The valet and cook were gone? "Do Detectives Hurst and Pratt know this?"

"Yes, they've questioned us extensively, which is why my poor wife is nearly exhausted. Father took Larkin and Madame Brusse with him on his journey, leaving Mrs. Peet to manage the empty house."

"And so your father came home early for some reason, but without his two servants."

"It seems so. Do you think Larkin and Madame Brusse know something? Could they have had something to do with this? Inspector Hurst had no opinion, but I thought maybe . . ." Stephen's voice trailed off on a sob. He cleared his throat and continued. "Do you know, I do believe he suspects me of killing Father."

"You? For what reason?" Didn't the inspector think it was a suicide?

"The inheritance, of course. Do you remember my elder brother, Cedric? He went off to the Crimea in fifty-four after a rather, er, disastrous marriage, and we never heard from him again. He was declared dead in 1861 and I was made the heir. So I suppose I stand the most to gain in my father's death."

Violet shook her head. "But surely Inspector Hurst sees that is ridiculous. Not only did you love your father, I'm sure, but why would you do this all of a sudden now?"

"Especially given that he may have been dying anyway."

"Stephen!" Katherine said. "Should you speak of such things to the undertaker?"

"Of what topic other than death *should* I speak with the undertaker?"

Katherine blushed.

"It's quite all right, Lady Raybourn," Violet said. "Most people don't know what to make of the undertaker. We're used to being partly detested, partly feared, and only occasionally admired. So have no fear that you can either offend or distress me." She smiled encouragingly at Katherine. The grief-stricken frequently argued and lashed out at one another, hardly remembering later what they'd said. No need for this husband and wife to have a petty quarrel over her.

"What do you mean that your father may have been dying?"

"It's as I told the detective. Some months ago, I went to Willow Tree to visit Father, and caught him taking some pills he'd gotten from the chemist. He said he had a stomach ailment, but that I shouldn't worry, as he planned to stop for a cure somewhere along the way on his Egyptian tour. I knew he was scheduled to return yesterday, so Katherine and I took the train up from Sussex to surprise him. We arrived here to find only Mrs. Peet in residence. She was . . . was . . . standing over my father's body. I—we—were devastated. Still are."

"So if your father had taken a cure and it worked, he should have been feeling healthy, and if his illness had been exacerbated by his time in Egypt and he was possibly ill to the point of dying, what purpose would there be in killing him, as he would soon pass on himself?"

"Exactly what I told the detective. It didn't seem as though he believed me, although he said that he and that other fellow— Prigg? Plum?"

"Mr. Pratt."

"Right, that he and Mr. Pratt had other investigations to set upon, and that he wasn't sure when he'd be back."

Could Lord Raybourn have killed himself because of his illness? Did it worsen while in Egypt, making him realize he might die a painful, lingering death if he didn't put a quick end to it all?

Perhaps, but the notion didn't sit well with Violet.

There was nothing to do but plow on. "I'm so sorry, Stephen. I'm sure Inspector Hurst will soon clear your name and discover what really happened. Meanwhile, I need to ask you for permission to do something."

"Anything, just ask."

"In order to ensure I can obey the queen's request, I need to inject—I mean, I need to fill, no . . . what I'm asking you is whether you would permit me to embalm your father in order to preserve him as long as possible. I have an excellent formulation that will prevent—"

Katherine's cup clattered down into its saucer. "Heavens, no! You—the queen—can't mean to do such a thing. Stephen, really, hasn't your father been through enough?"

Stephen reached over and took his wife's hand. "Darling, please. We mustn't blame Violet."

Still clutching his wife's hand like a life preserver, he passed his other hand over his eyes. Taking a deep breath, he dropped that hand to his lap. "I don't know. I suppose it wouldn't be any more dreadful than what has already happened. Go ahead. Just . . . be careful."

"You can trust me to treat your father as if he were my very own. One last thing, though. I'll need some fresh clothes for him."

Stephen waved his hand, exhausted from the entire affair. "Talk to Mrs. Peet; she knows more about his wardrobe than I do. Speaking of which, can you recommend a mourning dressmaker? My wife and sisters will want wardrobes made. We also need some black armbands."

"Of course. Mary Cooke is very reliable. I'll have her sent to you."

"Also, can you do something to prevent every family in Mayfair from coming to gawk at my father?"

"I can have a discreet sign made to go beneath the doorbell, and will also have 'No Visitors' announced in his obituary."

"Yes, that's fine."

With permission granted for the embalming, Violet retreated downstairs to request more clean cloths and a change of clothes from Mrs. Peet, then went back to the dining room to finish taking care of Lord Raybourn.

"Sir, I am sorry for the indignity, but I'm afraid I must relieve you of these spattered garments and make you look fresh again." Violet had developed unusual strength in moving dead bodies around, typically by rolling them in one direction or another, instead of trying to lift them with her arms. With some struggle, she relieved Lord Raybourn of his clothing and folded it all into a pile. She covered his private area with a modesty cloth, and once again went through the exercise of examining his limbs and muscles in detail.

Beyond the tragedy that had befallen him, his body was in relatively good shape for his age, for he must be in his seventies by now. He had the usual nicks and scars one might expect from a man who'd had a life well lived on his estate. Many aristocrats had taken spills from their horses or been attacked by game they were pursuing.

There was one particularly nasty gash in Lord Raybourn's side. Violet traced it with her finger. "What happened here, sir? Something with a long nail had its way with you. A disagreeable falcon not in the mood for hunting, maybe?"

With her physical inspection of his graying skin complete, Violet patted Lord Raybourn's hand for comfort.

Pulling out another fresh cloth and soaking it with a special alcohol solution from her bag, she carefully but quickly wiped down the man's arms, legs, and torso as if he were a newborn babe, patting carefully around his neck and face to avoid any further damage there. "Your final toilette, sir. The odor will be gone presently, I promise. It was worth it, though, for now you are sparkling fresh."

Although a body's natural decomposition would release smells into the air, the fragrance of any lotions, ointments, or colognes added to the body wouldn't last. Occasionally, families tried to give Violet their loved one's favorite toilet water or cologne, which she could only spray on the deceased's clothing. Once the body no longer had blood flowing in its veins, there was no pulse or warmth to radiate a fragrance. Imbuing a shirt or hat with scent usually satisfied the family without her having to explain the grim reality of things.

Once again Violet withdrew her embalming ingredients and mixed them inside a dark bottle half full of water. A half ounce chloride of zinc, which was a white, granular salt, followed by a quart of alcohol. The resulting solution was highly corrosive and irritating to the lungs, hence why she only made it up in small batches when she needed it. Any leftovers were kept in dark bottles to prevent decomposition in sunlight. She capped her concoction for the moment.

From her box of tools, she removed a scalpel and two nozzles and set them on the table next to the body. She also withdrew two sets of tubing and a clear bottle.

Laying out another cloth on the floor beneath Lord Raybourn's midsection, she placed the clear bottle on top of it. She attached each nozzle to one end of each tube and laid them both aside.

Picking up the scalpel, she whispered, "This won't hurt a bit, I promise."

With a hand around his leg, Violet selected a location and quickly sliced into it with the knife, opening up a vein. In went one of the tubes, with the other end trailing into the basin.

She spoke quietly as she worked. "You know that many important people have been embalmed, don't you, my lord? Why, even President Lincoln—you probably didn't know that I live in America now—was embalmed. In fact, he, too, was embalmed in his home, the White House. You are keeping very fine company."

Working quickly now, she cut into Lord Raybourn's neck, inserting a nozzle tube into his carotid artery. She reopened the bottle of embalming fluid, holding her breath at the acrid odor, and screwed on a pump mechanism, through which she secured the other end of the tube into the bottle using a special clamp. She worked the pump several times to get fluid flowing through the tube, then held the bottle upside down in her left hand, as far above her head as she could manage.

Her right arm, scarred from an accident, could no longer bear such a position for more than a few moments.

Maintaining this position was one of her most difficult tasks when she didn't have a pole to which she could attach the bottle. However, she didn't like carting around hanging poles to her customers' homes. It was too stressful for grieving families to witness the undertaker's tools. Therefore, she had purchased the largest leather case she could find that was still manageable for a woman, and only what could be closed up inside it usually went with her.

The embalming solution quickly did its work. As it flowed into Lord Raybourn's arteries through his neck, it began pushing out his blood, which exited through the vein in his leg. Soon there was a rhythmic spattering of blood into the previously empty bottle below.

Violet typically added a tincture of red dye to the fluid to give the skin a rosy bloom. The amount of dye varied from customer to customer. This time she skipped the dye, for she knew it was impossible for Lord Raybourn to be on display for mourners and visitors.

He was just too damaged.

The best she could do was sew up the worst of it, augment his face with a bit of putty, and liberally apply Kalon Cream—Natural Number Six, perhaps?—over her work. She didn't think even the family should see him.

Once Lord Raybourn's blood was completely drained and the embalming fluid had settled in, Violet checked her work by once again probing and gently squeezing his limbs. The solution appeared to have distributed evenly.

With needle and thread, she made several stitches in the two locations she had cut open. The embalming process was now complete.

Mrs. Peet had dropped off an elegant suit on the hall table outside the dining room. The requisite trousers, tailcoat, shirt, collar, cuffs, and cravat were overshadowed by the most elegant double-breasted vest of burgundy satin Violet had ever seen. Violet exchanged it for the soiled clothing she'd removed from Lord Raybourn, as well as all of the dirty rags, then stepped back into the dining room to inspect her embalming one more time and to dress Lord Raybourn.

Embalming was an imperfect technique, since it was not in regular use. Those opposed to the practice pointed to cases where an embalming had resulted in perfectly preserved arms, face, and torso, and completely disintegrated legs.

True enough, yet wasn't the purpose of embalming to keep the body fresh while it was transported a long distance, or while grieving family members gathered around to mourn? As long as it served that purpose, why make a fuss that it couldn't preserve indefinitely?

"Indefinitely" was a word that now made Violet nervous. How indefinitely did the queen intend to leave Lord Raybourn lying out? Would Violet have to reembalm him if things dragged on too long? She'd never done that before and wasn't certain it would even work.

Violet worked quickly to cork the heavy, blood-filled bottle—whose contents she would take to an undertaker's shop later for disposal—and clean up her instruments so she could re-dress Lord Raybourn.

"My lord, it's time for me to serve as your valet and dress you. I need you to cooperate," she said, wrestling to get his arms into his jacket without jostling him too much. Arms were always so much more difficult than legs.

Once he was dressed, Violet laid a cloth on his neck and torso to protect his clothing from her cosmetic work. She cut, filled, and stitched as best she could, despite the ravages caused by the gunshots, finishing off with a liberal application of Natural Number Six and a dusting of talcum powder.

She stood straight to examine his face. No, it wouldn't do. His cheeks were still . . . uneven. She took another of Mrs. Peet's cloths and tore it into little strips, rolling each one up and tucking it inside His Lordship's cheeks. After some adjustments, his face was fuller.

Rather than sewing his mouth shut, or dragging a wire under his chin and sewing it behind each ear to keep his jaw from dropping, she put a block of wood under his chin, raising his shirt collar as high as she could and tying his cravat to hide it. After all, hadn't he suffered enough indignity over her ministrations without her probing his mouth with a needle?

With his eyes sewn shut, his lips firmly closed, and his torn flesh either sewn or augmented, Lord Raybourn resembled something of his former self.

Violet stepped back to view her work from a few feet away. She was kidding herself. Poor Lord Raybourn looked like the monster from Mary Shelley's novel.

And I am Dr. Frankenstein.

"Well, my lord," she said as she finished cleaning up. "I trust you won't arise and terrorize Londoners while I go out to find a coffin befitting your station. Pardon my jest, sir. Rest easy, I won't be gone long." She covered Lord Raybourn with a length of black crape, turned off the gas lamps, and left him in dark solitude.

Only later did she realize she'd completely forgotten the tea tray Mrs. Peet had brought up for her.

"It must be peculiar," Katherine said, putting aside her cup and picking up a shortbread bar, nibbling distractedly at it, "to be a lady undertaker. And to then be called to do service for a family who once employed yours. How well did she know your father?"

"Not that well. She might have seen him out riding, or, more likely, striding to the pond in a fury to find me as Violet and I muddied up our clothes capturing toads."

"What delightful fun, I'm sure. Will she take good care of the body?"

"I believe so. She was just the estate manager's daughter, but I suspect she still retains enough memory and respect of our family to be gentle with him."

"That's not what I mean."

"You refer to Her Majesty?"

"Of course."

Stephen picked up a smoked brown trout sandwich. "We can

hardly expect the undertaker to have enough influence with the queen to persuade her to let us get on with a burial, despite Violet's association with the prince's funeral."

"So this . . . awkwardness . . . might go on for days or weeks? Oh, Stephen, I'm not sure I can endure it."

"Sweetheart, be of good cheer. It will be done soon, I'm sure. If you prefer, I can send you back to Willow Tree while this is all sorted out. We'll bring him back there for burial, anyway."

"I don't know. It would be so cowardly of me. And what of Dorothy and Nelly? I can't simply run off before they've even arrived." Katherine cast her eyes down. "I'm already enough of a disappointment in the family."

"Never say that; you know it's not true." He swallowed the last of his sandwich and reached across the table to squeeze his wife's hand. "This nasty business will be over with shortly and then we can get on with life. Remember, you are Lady Raybourn now, wife to, well, to *me*. Is that not some consolation for your troubles?"

Katherine offered a wan smile. "It is a bit of solace, I suppose. Mrs. Peet doesn't seem to care much for it, though, does she? I wonder why she finds the thought so distasteful?"

Having discussed with the new Lord and Lady Raybourn the errand she wished to run, Violet set out to visit two old friends, Harry Blundell and William Swift. The two young men had taken over Morgan Undertaking from her when she left to go to America. Presumably they were still in her Paddington location, despite her having been gone these four years.

She was pleased to see that not only was the location still intact, but Harry and Will had retained the Morgan Undertaking name. The sign even had a fresh coat of paint on it.

"Mrs. Morgan, I mean, Mrs. Harper, how well you look," Harry said. He put out his bear paw of a hand in greeting. Violet remembered hiring him because of his great strength. Harry could practically carry a coffin alone on his shoulders.

At the sound of their voices, Will came out from the storage room. "Mrs. Harper, what a delight. What brings you back to London?" Will was very slight as compared to Harry, but had a more congenial manner with customers; therefore he tended to do all the interactions with the grieving while Harry managed behind the scenes.

Violet shook his hand. "A funeral, naturally. You both look well. I confess I am gratified to see that you've made few changes here."

Harry grinned. "No sense in mucking about with what is already perfect, is there? I guess the only change is that Will and I are married men now. Married my Emily two years ago and Will entered the matrimonial state not six months ago."

"How wonderful for you both. I should like to meet your wives while I'm in the city."

"Hah! D'you think Lydia will want to meet another undertaker, Will?"

Will's ears turned pink. "I'm sure she would be most accommodating."

"Not likely. You see, Mrs. Harper, Lydia doesn't much like Will's profession. Constantly at him to join her father's floral business and leave this 'foul and ghastly' business behind. She thinks our trade as worthwhile as that of a clairvoyant. I told him she'd be no end of trouble."

Poor Will. His marriage was probably as unhappy as hers with Graham had become. Time to change the subject and let the man be.

"Yes, well, I've been asked to manage a funeral for the queen, and naturally I wish to hire Morgan Undertaking for all of the equipage."

Will looked puzzled. "You came all the way from America to bury someone for the queen? Why didn't she just use the royal undertaker?"

"A rather interesting question. She seems to have a soft spot for me since I stepped in and handled last-minute details of the prince consort's burial. Sam and I have been in Brighton the last month visiting my parents, and the queen reached me there."

"Newspapers say she continues to grieve him and stays locked away at Windsor as much as possible."

"I'm afraid that's true. She isn't interested in much, although this particular funeral situation seems to have roused her. It's ironic, I suppose, that death is what enlivens her."

Will shrugged. "Same is true with us. How can we help you?"

In a typical arrangement with a grieving relative, Violet would retrieve her bulging book full of coffin drawings, suggested funeral plans according to the deceased's social class, and price lists, and have the relative make selections. As it was, she merely ticked items off on her fingers.

"I want an elm burl coffin with your best brass fittings, a wool mattress, and lined with the finest cambric. Something like what we did for Admiral Herbert, remember? Also, a large silver plate on top, engraved 'Anthony Fairmont, the Viscount Raybourn, Perfect Father and Friend.' Have a broken column engraved on either side."

A broken column symbolized the death of the family patriarch.

"Simple mourning cards with a quarter-inch line of black around them. Black-edged stationery for the new Lord Raybourn. Twelve pots of lilies for the home in Park Street. Enough black bunting for twelve windows. A card for placement beneath the doorbell announcing 'No Visitors.' A half dozen black armbands." Violet continued detailing the items she had discussed with Stephen and Katherine.

"What about a postmortem photograph?"

"Absolutely not," Violet said. "The deceased is in no condition for it."

"Shall we post an obituary? When and where will Lord Raybourn be buried?" Will asked as he once again dipped his pen in an inkwell and wrote furiously to keep up with Violet.

"An obituary, yes. Make sure it also states that the family isn't accepting visitors. We shan't announce his burial just yet."

"What? An important lord dies and the family doesn't want society to know about the planned funeral route?"

"It's just a temporary delay."

Will shook his head. "I presume the family would like the finest of services?"

He meant the large glass carriage with velvet curtains inside, four horses, each wearing ostrich plumes, more plumes on the four corners of the carriage, multiple professional mourners, and a long travel route to the cemetery.

"I'm sure they will eventually wish to have these things."

"Eventually? When is eventually? How odd, Mrs. Harper."

"Please, don't ask me any more for the moment. Right now I just need to see Lord Raybourn comfortably ensconced in an elegant coffin and to make sure the lying-in is done properly."

"As you wish, of course. And now, ahem, if you don't mind my asking since you are not our typical customer—will they pay?"

Violet understood his question. Aristocrats frequently pretended bills didn't exist, especially those aristocrats living beyond their means. A death was a prominent way of showing off class and wealth to the community, since carriage size, number of mourners, and the like indicated the relative position of the family. Therefore, some aristocrats would order funerals they could ill afford to ensure society was assured they were as prosperous as ever and also to ensure the newspapers would write glowing accounts of the services.

Such public accounts would enable the aristocrats to gain more credit, thus enabling them to spend more.

"I think so. My father worked for the family long ago, and so I believe the new master of the house will endeavor to keep his debt clear with me. In any case, I shall keep an eye on it."

"Very good." Will wiped his pen on a cloth and set it down, capping his inkwell.

Violet stood. "Now I'm off to see Mary Cooke. Is she also still in the same location?"

"Indeed she is."

Another reunion awaited her at Mary Cooke's mourning dressmaking shop in Bayswater Road. "Violet, dearest! How happy I am to see you. How is Susanna? And Sam? What of Colorado? Is it as wild and majestic as I read about in magazines?" Mary fluttered about, removing piles of fabrics and notions from a chair next to where she worked and adding them to an already precarious stack on the sewing table.

"I see you still work in complete disarray, my friend." Violet wasn't much of a housekeeper herself, but her workplace was always pristine.

Mary wrinkled her nose. "I suppose I am too old now to be taught how to be tidy." Mary was indeed nearly twenty years older than Violet, but looked far younger, despite her wayward husband, George, whose squat, pig-eyed expression was a total contradiction to his wife's sweet countenance. This was a second marriage for Mary, and much less happy than her first. Although presumably faithful to his wife, George had the annoying habit of disappearing for days or weeks on end whenever life served him a helping of difficult or unpleasant circumstances. Unfortunately for Mary, she could never predict what situations would send her husband running.

Violet and Mary became close not only because their relevant shops were located near each other, but because they had shared in intrigue and tragedy together.

Violet sat in the cleared chair, hopeful that none of the other heaps in the shop would fall on top of her. Her own messiness was a mere anthill to Mary's Pike's Peak. "What happened to your assistant?"

"She decided she didn't like making mourning wear day in and day out. Wanted to fashion ball gowns. Honestly, I think she just didn't like dealing with the grieving customers. It's not for everyone."

Violet nodded. "I see you've finally installed gas lighting."

"George convinced me to spend the money. I admit I was quite nervous about it. In fact, I was certain the shop would explode from a gas leak. Was this the last shop in London using candles?"

"I'm sure there are others, but I'm glad Mr. Cooke talked you into it. Is he . . . here?"

"Yes. Today he is out at the tailor's, having some pants made. Silly bear refuses to let me do it for him; says he doesn't want to waste my time on it when I could be doing paid work. I'm sure he'll be back soon and would love to see you."

"Perhaps another time. I've had a terribly long day and want only to entomb myself in blankets right now. I'm only in London for a short time before Sam and I return to America. I'm helping the queen with a funeral."

Mary gave her the same dumbstruck look that Will had. "How . . . interesting."

Violet sketched out briefly what was happening, asking that Mary visit Raybourn House as quickly as possible to outfit the women. "I was also hoping, though, that we could reacquaint our friendship for however long I will be here. I've missed you."

"And I've missed you." Mary impulsively leapt out of her chair to grab Violet's hand, jostling her table and sending the tottering pile of supplies tumbling down against Violet and all over the floor.

Violet loved Colorado, but it was good to be back in London, too.

After promising to visit Mary again soon, Violet took her leave and hired a hack to return her to St. James's Palace. She fell into an exhausted sleep inside the carriage, despite the incessant clattering of the coach's wheels and its tired springs that would have jostled a corpse back to life.

Violet awoke as the carriage came to a stop before the Tudor-fronted tower entry of the palace. Her brief nap had been refreshing, but she realized how hungry she was. How did one find food inside a palace? Or would she need to search the streets for good dining?

Heaven forbid she should be left to her own devices to cook. She might well starve to death.

A liveried footman opened the grand entry doors to the palace, then another servant escorted her to her rooms. All thought of hunger pains disappeared as she entered her apartment, for there was Sam, rumpled from travel, sprawled on a settee with his bad leg dangling over and propped up on a footstool.

He opened one eye sleepily. "You know I'll never be able to afford something like this for you on a lawyer's wages."

Violet removed her hat and tossed it onto her dressing table without a care as to straightening out the tails. "I didn't expect you to follow me here. What a lovely surprise. How did you know where I was staying?"

"I went to Windsor and talked to the master of the household."

Sam struggled to his feet, reaching for the eagle-headed cane he'd started using since his Civil War injuries, claiming to be grateful that such accoutrements were fashionable. He held out a hand. "You've been gone mere hours and already I'm starving for the sight of you."

Violet went to him to be folded in his free arm. She inhaled deeply of her husband, a habit she'd never broken since the day he'd shown up unexpectedly on her doorstep following the war. She gazed up into his face, one that was etched almost like a map from everything he had suffered during the war that ended in America just a few years ago. A scar cutting through his right eyebrow was the least of his bodily dents and abrasions. They were a perfectly matched pair of cracked vases, though, since Violet herself had suffered severe burns on her right arm during a train crash several years ago. The hideous mass of scars had faded some, but she would always have them. More troublesome was the periodic tightening she felt in the arm, and the lack of full use of it.

"More like you were starving to get away from our recovering patient. Was Mother terribly distraught that I left?"

"Not nearly as distraught as your father and I were. Actually, you departed in such a swirling vortex of activity that there was no time for her to realize what your leaving would mean to her. More importantly, this came in the post as soon as I returned from taking you to the train station." Sam pulled a letter from inside his jacket.

"From Colorado?" Violet said. "Oh, a letter from Susanna." She opened the letter and quickly read the contents.

> *Dear Mama and Father,*
> *How is Grandmamma getting along? I've only had one letter from you and I'm quite cross.*
> *The Johnson family had a tragedy. Both of their boys killed in an accident while working on the Union Pacific Railroad tracks being laid as far west as Weir. Their so-called transcontinental railroad is supposed to link up with the Central Pacific Railroad in Utah in just a couple of years. How sad that Ernest and Thomas will not live to see it. I comforted their mama as best I could as well as*

*laying out their boys, but Mrs. Johnson will never be the
same.*

*Ben has been very busy with Father's clients. I think you
would be quite impressed with his manner and everyone
says he has apprenticed well. He says he will write to you
about some pressing client matters.*

*When will you be home? I miss you, and there is so
much to discuss. Bring Grandmamma and Grandpapa
with you.*

*Mrs. Softpaws recently discovered a colony of mice in
the attic, and has taken seriously to cleaning them out. She
is quite fat now.*

Susanna went on with some newsy tidbits about the townsfolk,
then signed off with her typical curlicue signature. Violet never
knew how much a signature could make her long for home.

Except that England was home, too.

Violet lifted the letter to her nose and sniffed. It smelled faintly
of the jasmine perfume Susanna favored.

"Would it surprise you to know that I received a separate post
from Benjamin about his 'pressing client matters'?" Sam said.

"Is it . . . ?"

"Indeed it is. He wants my permission to marry Susanna. Shall I
give it?"

"Sam, be serious, of course you should. Oh, this is terrible. My
mother is improving, but now we're bound here in England until
Lord Raybourn is buried."

"Surely that will be within the week?"

"Maybe. But then there is all of that horrid travel back to Colorado."

"A steamer ship followed by a train ride?" Sam smiled and
kissed her forehead.

"And all of that bone-jarring wagon travel. Let's not forget that.
And near shipwrecks. And miscreants on railways. I do so hate
trains. I don't look forward to another perilous journey, but I do
want to hold Susanna in my arms again."

"You'll soon have a son-in-law to hold, too, and there are wedding preparations to undergo."

"True. I just hope my responsibilities here don't extend more than a few days. You don't think they would marry without us there, do you?"

"No, of course not."

"Oh, I just had a wonderful idea for a wedding present. I wonder if that doll shop I used to visit with Susanna is still in operation."

"I remember it. I bought her a miniature coach and four horses there once."

"Wouldn't it be fun to purchase something for her dollhouse to decorate it as if for a wedding?"

Sam shook his head. "You two and that dollhouse. Still playing with it even though Susanna is an adult. Now, tell me what is happening with the queen."

They were interrupted by a palace servant rolling in a tray of covered plates and a bottle of sherry.

"I didn't request this," Violet said.

The liveried footman snapped open a crisply ironed white tablecloth and covered a nearby round table. He then uncovered the dishes to reveal pheasant cooked in bacon, onion, and tomatoes; macaroni in a butter and cream sauce; sliced carrots; and a molded pudding. He transferred them to the table and moved two chairs to sit directly opposite each other across the table. His movements were deliberate and precise, as though he were giving a performance.

"The master of the household says it's the queen's orders, ma'am, to make sure you are well provided for while you're here."

"Do you mean I will be served supper this way every day?"

"Whatever meals you wish. And for your husband, too."

Violet hadn't expected such treatment, which was indicative of how important the queen felt the death of Lord Raybourn was.

Once the footman had poured their first glasses of sherry and departed, they settled down to eat. Violet found she was ravenous, having had nothing since breakfast that morning in Brighton, an eternity ago. She fell upon the meal like a wild dog.

As she wiped her fingers with a napkin and suppressed an unladylike belch, Sam returned to Violet's funeral assignment.

"So, who is the important recipient of Mrs. Violet Harper's services?"

"You won't believe it." Violet proceeded to tell her husband everything that had happened that day.

"Do you mean to say that the queen is involving you with another murder?"

"Hardly. The detectives will find out who is responsible and capture him, if it wasn't, in fact, a suicide. My work is much tamer, merely caring for Lord Raybourn's body."

"Hmm."

"Honestly, Sam, there is no danger in this at all. I have no other duties beyond what I've just said."

"Perhaps. In any case, what a full day you've had, my love, and how odd that you know Lord Raybourn. Do you think the queen was aware of this?"

Violet stretched, happily full and contemplating removal of her corset and skirts. "I don't see how. It was so long ago that my father worked for him. Which reminds me, I should write and tell him."

"I can tell him when I return tomorrow."

"Tomorrow? You aren't staying? Mother is better and I'm sure Father can manage without either of us."

"That's part of the reason I came up to see you." Sam winced as he stood from the table, went for his walking stick, and began to pace. Violet always knew that when Sam was either upset or obsessed by a topic, he hobbled back and forth across the room, frowning. He did so despite the discomfort she knew it caused him.

"What's wrong?" she asked.

"You think your work will be concluded in a week?"

"I can hardly know. The coroner declared Lord Raybourn's death a suicide, but the queen is not sure. Scotland Yard has gone on to other investigations, so now I will assist the family for as long as the queen wishes. Which reminds me, I didn't tell you that I am now faced with the unenviable task of questioning the Prince of Wales over events in Egypt."

"Why aren't the police doing that?"

Violet held up her palms. "I have no idea; she hasn't said why. The queen says it would be unseemly for her or the police to do so. But to have me do it? I'm not sure I'm up to all of this."

"If any living being is up to it, it is you. However, my greater concern is that you not get mixed up with a murder again."

"I'm sure it won't come to that."

"Well, perhaps your stay here presents no difficulty."

"What do you mean?"

Sam stopped pacing to face her. "I'm going to Sweden."

"Sweden? Whatever for?"

"I meant to talk to you about it today after talking it over with your father, but then the household was in such an uproar with your departure that I decided to wait. As you know, silver was discovered in Nevada ten years ago, and seems to be far more plentiful than what can be had from gold mines, especially given that the Colorado gold mines dried up right quick. There was a silver vein found in Summit County just five years ago, although it has yet to be fully explored."

"I knew about Nevada's Comstock Lode, but didn't realize we had silver in the Colorado Territory, too." What did this have to do with Sweden?

"I've been casually reading about it in the papers, but I've learned something that makes me think my future isn't law, but silver mining. You see, there is a Swede by the name of Alfred Nobel. He's a chemist who has invented a substance called dynamite, an improvement upon nitroglycerine as an explosive. He already has patents in the United States and here in Great Britain, and is preparing to start the British Dynamite Company near Glasgow. I want to meet with him, and possibly consider investing in a dynamite factory either here or back home."

Violet's head swam. "So you mean to be a procurer of explosives? That sounds dangerous."

Sam sat down again. "That's just it. Dynamite is far less dangerous than what has been used before. There is a fortune to be made in bringing a safe method of opening mines to Colorado, I'm sure of it. But I want to meet with the man personally before moving any further."

9

Fully rested and serene, Violet saw Sam off at the train station the next morning before returning to Morgan Undertaking to check on what supplies Harry and Will had pulled together. They were loading a coffin onto their wagon as she arrived.

Harry removed his undertaker's hat and wiped his brow with a handkerchief. "Good morning, Mrs. Harper. Unusually beastly today, isn't it? We've got your coffin and other things right here." He patted the polished box with its ornamental brass handles. "Don't have the plate for it but will have it by tomorrow, I expect. The florist will deliver the lilies directly this afternoon. Would you like to ride over with us?"

Will and Violet rode up front, while Harry wedged himself into the wagon with the funerary goods. Traffic was heavy, and Violet found herself removing her black gloves just for a little relief from the heat on an abnormally warm May day.

As they waited at an intersection for an omnibus to pass by, Will turned to Violet. "How is Mr. Harper? Is he here in London with you?"

"Briefly. He's gone to Sweden to explore a business opportunity. How is your new wife? I hope I will get to meet her before I leave."

Will reddened. "That might not be possible. Lydia is a little, er, shy, about any involvement in my work. Which is entirely proper,

Violet wrinkled her nose. "It still sounds so . . . perilous. Won't people think you've invested in a substance guaranteed to bring me clients?"

"To the contrary, I believe dynamite will save lives."

"I see. Well, it seems we both have a great deal of work ahead of us." She stood. "You say you are returning to Brighton tomorrow?"

"On the early train. I'll settle things there and head to Sweden right away so that I can be back as soon as you've concluded the funeral. We'll be back in the Colorado Territory in a jiffy."

"We have precious few hours before you leave."

Sam took her hand. "Then we'd best make good use of what time we have left."

of course. I am her husband and provider, and there is no reason for her to concern herself with what I do during the day."

Such swagger from gentle Will. Traffic cleared and he flicked the reins as he rounded into Bayswater Road.

Violet turned toward his slim profile. "Are you troubled, Will?"

He glanced back to ensure that Harry was paying no attention to them. "I'm mostly worried. Harry had the right of it when he said Lydia wants me to join her father's floral business. He just doesn't know how adamant she is about it. I must say, I find the idea appealing. There's good profit to be made in it, and I wouldn't have to deal with grieving families and coffins and all of this death apparatus. I just don't want to disappoint Harry. How will he manage on his own?"

"Undertaking isn't for everyone, but I'm sure Harry can find someone to work in the shop with him. Surely pleasing your wife is more important than pleasing your business partner."

Will grimaced. "I'd prefer to do both." He clucked his tongue and maneuvered the reins so that the horses stopped in front of Raybourn House.

Mrs. Peet greeted Violet at the door once again, her face still blotchy and swollen. Lord Raybourn must have been a benevolent master to have engendered such grief.

Mrs. Peet informed her that the new Lord and Lady Raybourn were still upstairs performing morning ablutions and having breakfast, but would be down shortly. The housekeeper then scurried back downstairs into the kitchen.

Harry and Will brought the coffin into the house while Violet unloaded a folding wood bier and several heavy canvas sheets. The men returned in multiple trips for the ice container and other supplies.

The coffin was left in the entry hall while the three undertakers silently went to work. They rearranged furniture in the drawing room, creating an empty space in the middle of the room. Harry and Will placed the deep ice chest on the floor. Violet unfolded the canvas pieces and lined the chest with them. One side of the chest dropped lower than the other, providing a gap where Will and Harry dumped in bags of chipped ice.

Violet then unfolded the bier and positioned it over the ice chest, then draped a length of black crape over it. The bier was now ready to hold the coffin. The ice chest below would keep Lord Raybourn's body cool, adding protection beyond Violet's embalming.

The two men placed the coffin on the bier. Violet opened the lid and nodded in satisfaction. It was lined in exquisite cambric linen. She gently pressed down on the mattress, which was firmly stuffed. Very good.

"I think we're ready for Lord Raybourn," she whispered.

At the dining room table, Violet removed the covering cloth, leaving Harry and Will to carry the body from the dining room table to the coffin, while Violet murmured encouragement to Lord Raybourn's lifeless form.

Once Raybourn was ensconced in his resting box, the three of them examined their work.

Harry shook his head. "This gentleman must have been in a bad way. I imagine he wouldn't be recognizable to his family."

"No, despite my best efforts, this poor man has not only suffered a gunshot blast, but is totally unable to receive family." Violet gently shook out the covering cloth and billowed it back over Lord Raybourn, letting it gently drape over him. She pulled down the coffin lid, which tapped closed with barely a sound.

Violet helped the men clean up all of their supplies in preparation for leaving. "I'll stay here to wait for the lilies. Leave behind a draining dish, will you?" Violet said. The ice chest had a spigot at one end that would allow her to drain melting ice. She would order ice as needed, refilling the chest through the lowered side. In this way, Lord Raybourn should stay well preserved—she hoped.

"Will," she said as the two men were about to leave. "I've another thought. I think it might be best if we locked the coffin. Visitors might get it into their heads to inspect him, and I'd like to avoid any disrespect to Lord Raybourn's person."

"How many keys?"

"Just one, I think."

"I'll bring a brass locking kit over tomorrow when I deliver his inscription plate. We'll take care of the window bunting now."

As the door clicked behind them, Stephen and Katherine Fairmont descended the stairs.

"Oh," Katherine said, paling to see Violet standing next to her father-in-law's new coffin now prominently displayed in the drawing room. She clung to the newel post at the bottom of the staircase.

"Hello, Violet." Stephen stepped forward. "May I see my father?"

Violet put a hand on the lid of the coffin. "Respectfully, I think it better that you don't. He is resting comfortably here as he is, but I don't think he is prepared for visitors."

Stephen frowned. "You aren't finished?"

"I am. Your father is simply not looking well enough for anyone to see him."

He blinked as he absorbed what Violet was telling him. "I see."

Behind him, still paralyzed at the foot of the stairs, Katherine put a hand to her throat. Violet continued as gently as possible. "I did the best I could, but I don't think anyone should see him. In fact, I've ordered a lock to ensure no one inadvertently lifts the lid to add a memento to the coffin. If you've no objection, I'll stay here with Lord Raybourn until the flower sprays arrive this afternoon."

"Right. Of course. Whatever you recommend. Actually, Dorothy and Nelly will be here soon. You might enjoy seeing them again. I'll ring Mrs. Peet and tell her to serve you a tray around two o'clock."

Stephen and his wife retreated back upstairs, leaving Violet alone with the coffin. She waited in the total silence to which she was accustomed in a home containing the recently deceased. It was ironic how, when time was symbolically stopped, so too was all activity.

Breaking into the stillness was the distant ringing of a bell from upstairs—probably Stephen summoning Mrs. Peet regarding a meal for her—followed by Mrs. Peet's footsteps up the servants' staircase.

Violet didn't mind being alone with the dead. Once they had been prepared, the quiet time gave her an opportunity to think. At the moment, she mostly wondered why she was even here and what sort of secret purposes the queen had with regard to Lord Raybourn. What was she to do after today, when the floral arrangements were done and there was nothing left but to plan a funeral, a funeral that she wasn't yet permitted to plan?

The detectives assigned to investigate Lord Raybourn's death would surely determine who had done this to him. Violet had no detecting abilities. Well, it was true that she had once stumbled upon the evidence of a killer at work in London, evidence that many others had overlooked or ignored, but that was just a handy piece of luck.

Besides, she'd nearly been killed herself in the process. If she were to be involved in this, who knew what would happen?

Violet shook her head in frustration. What did the queen really want from her?

To clear her mind, Violet went to the drawing room's mantel clock and examined it. An old John Harrison clock, very fine indeed, although everything in the home showed great taste and attention to detail, from the multilayered, fringed draperies to the thick and heavily patterned carpets that covered most of the herringboned wood floors, to the overstuffed, overcarved rosewood furniture. In addition to the jumble of paintings lining the stairway, there was a confusion of pencil drawings, watercolors, and oils lining most of the walls on this floor, as if the owner couldn't decide what his tastes were but desired above all things to be considered artistic, and therefore had purchased a little of everything.

Tables around the room were lined with daguerreotypes. Violet picked up frames, trying to distinguish whom she might know. Here was a recent shot of Stephen and Katherine outside of Willow Tree House. Violet remembered the unusual rust color of the house's stone, not apparent in the sepia-toned rendering.

Another photograph showed Lord Raybourn in a classic posed

shot, wearing a suit and sitting on a chair, one leg crossed over the other and his elbow on a table. Behind him was a somber-looking woman. His wife? No, not possible. The original Lady Raybourn had died long before photography was available.

More photos included one of Willow Tree House staff gathered at the front entrance, one of a hunting dog—a conceit only a wealthy man like the viscount could afford—and one of a very handsome young man, his expression studiously bored and . . . was that condescension for the camera's eye?

She set his photo down. This was none of her business, and soon—

The distant ring-a-ling of a doorbell emanating from the kitchens caused Violet to jump at its sound invading her silence. *That must be the floral deliveryman*, she thought, and retreated back to her chair next to the coffin to wait for him to appear.

It wasn't the lilies. Mrs. Peet went to the front door, admitted what sounded like two women and a man, and brought them upstairs to the drawing room. Presumably the women were Stephen's sisters, Dorothy and Nelly Fairmont.

Time had not been kind to either sister.

When she and Stephen were playmates at age ten, Nelly was a teenager and Dorothy was in her early twenties. Violet mentally calculated their ages. She and Stephen were now both thirty-six, making the sisters roughly forty-two and forty-nine.

Nelly, the younger sister, had the better of it, with her auburn hair fashionably arranged in waves with long ringlets flowing around her shoulders, and her slim and petite figure shown to perfection in her fashionable day dress. She might have just stepped from the pages of *Godey's Lady's Book*. But the smile on her face at greeting Stephen and Katherine did not reach her eyes, which were webbed with crow's feet and underscored by dark circles that had a permanence suggesting they were established long before the death of her father.

Stephen kissed his sister's cheek, commenting on how long it had been since he'd seen her, and greeted the man next to her with bluff heartiness. He then pulled Dorothy close for an embrace. Dorothy tolerated Stephen's touch, but just barely. She looked like a ragged old tomcat about to be bathed, all ten claws on Stephen's shoulder, as though she might launch off him and run yowling out of the house.

Dorothy was much taller than Nelly, almost as tall as Stephen, but did not carry herself in a statuesque way. She was frumpy and disheveled, her graying hair completely untamed by her hat. She reminded Violet of a sturdy farmer's wife, not the daughter of a peer.

Violet stood as the entourage entered the drawing room. Stephen made introductions. "Dorothy, Nelly, Gordon, may I present to you Violet Harper, the queen's undertaker? You might remember her father, Arthur Sinclair, who served as Father's estate manager for a short time."

Nelly shook her head, while Dorothy squinted at Violet, as if to bring her into focus. At least Gordon smiled at her.

"Violet, these are my sisters, Dorothy Fairmont and Eleanor Bishop. This is Nelly's husband, Gordon Bishop."

Only Nelly's husband moved forward to shake Violet's hand, pumping it up and down with vigor. "A pleasure, I'm sure. Well, not such a pleasure at the moment, is it? No, no, things are most tragic, tragic indeed."

"Really, Gordon, there's no need to unhinge the woman's shoulder," Nelly said to an immediately crestfallen Gordon. "I suppose that's Father in there?"

"Yes, Mrs. Bishop. He is resting comfortably now."

Nelly sniffed. "I suppose he really isn't doing much of anything, is he?" She began removing her gloves. "Katherine, what about some tea? It was a dreadful wait at the train station."

"Of course, Nelly dear." Katherine went to a panel on the wall between the drawing room and the dining room and tugged on one of two decorative rope pulls. Violet heard the distant ringing again, summoning Mrs. Peet for more tasks.

"Why is the coffin closed?" Dorothy asked, the size of it too large to require her to squint.

"Lord Raybourn is not really presentable for company," Violet told her.

"Isn't my brother Lord Raybourn now? Father is gone and that's that." Dorothy removed her hat and handed it wordlessly to Mrs. Peet, who had just entered and opened her mouth to ask her new mistress what service she required.

Were Mrs. Peet and Stephen the only mourners of Lord Raybourn's death? Violet was used to seeing relatives with grudges against the deceased, but they usually attempted to mask their feelings in some way, at least until the will was read. Dorothy and Nelly wore their feelings on the outside like sandwich-board men wore advertisements.

What had Anthony Fairmont done to engender such enmity from his daughters?

She had no time to ponder it, for someone twisted the doorbell again. Mrs. Peet opened it to Detectives Hurst and Pratt, who added their own hats to Mrs. Peet's arms.

"Excuse me," Stephen said to Hurst. "To what do we owe this visit? As you can see, my family has just arrived and we are mourning my father."

"Our sympathies are naturally with you, sir, but we were hoping to interview your relations as soon as possible."

"This isn't a particularly convenient time."

"Be that as it may, sir, we'll have our interviews now." Hurst stood there like an impenetrable fortress wall that Stephen was never going to be able to scale. "Perhaps we could start with you, miss." He nodded at Dorothy.

"Right then," Stephen said. "I suppose the rest of us will be upstairs. Mrs. Peet, bring the tea up, would you?" The remainder of the Fairmont family went upstairs.

Violet's tray was completely forgotten, for sure. Her stomach growled gently, to remind her that it would require attention sometime soon. For the moment, she needed to figure out how to wait for the florist while getting out of the detectives' way.

"Pardon me," she said. "I'm just waiting for flowers to arrive, but I can wait in the kitchens while you talk."

Pratt spoke up for the first time. "Mr. Hurst, maybe Mrs. Harper should stay for this. She's the queen's undertaker. . . ."

The other detective grunted. "I hardly think the Crown's request to cooperate with her means involving her in our investigation."

Pratt scratched his head. "I don't know, sir. It might speak in our favor if we let her listen in."

"Really, I can just go downstairs and—"

"Please sit, Mrs. Harper, while I think," Hurst said as he paced back and forth in front of the coffin, head down, deep in thought. Dorothy and Pratt sat down, as well. After several moments of pacing and muttering to himself, Hurst stopped and addressed Violet.

"Very well, then. Mrs. Harper, why don't you stay while we talk with Miss Fairmont. She might prefer having a female presence in the room."

Violet glanced across the room at Dorothy, whose back was hackled even as she tried to behave with perfect aristocratic boredom. Hurst adopted an air of great friendliness as he sat down in a chair next to her, a small table covered in photographs separating them. Pratt was perched on a tufted armchair a few feet away, while Violet remained across the room next to the closed coffin.

If the warmth of the day wasn't suffocating enough, the thought of being present for Inspector Hurst's inquisition was.

"First, I am sorry for the loss of your father . . . Miss Fairmont, is it? Are you a spinster?"

"Yes, I have never been married."

Pratt pulled a tattered notebook from his breast pocket and jotted down notes while Hurst questioned Lord Raybourn's daughter.

"Tell me, when was the last time you saw him?"

"The last time he was home at Willow Tree House. That would have been back in February, about three months ago. We dined together the evening before he left for London."

"How did he seem to you?"

"Seem? He was what he always is, or was. Selfish and thoughtless."

Hurst nodded. "And what made him selfish and thoughtless?"

"You obviously never met Father. He had a single-minded drive in everything. His singular goal in life was service to the Crown, and his children were merely instruments of his pleasure in making this happen. In particular, we were not to embarrass him. Any discomfiture was tantamount to treason. Some of us were blessed with Father's favor; others of us were cast aside like slops. Of all of us, I imagine Cedric had the best of it."

"Cedric?"

"Our eldest brother."

"Why did he 'have the best of it'?"

"Because he died, of course. He joined the war in the Crimea in fifty-four and never returned."

Violet tried to maintain as neutral a face as Hurst and Pratt were, but her stomach was roiling at Dorothy's contentions toward her father. Or was it hunger getting the better of her?

"Your father permitted his heir to go to war?"

"Cedric was our father's cherished boy. He did as he wanted. When Cedric's marriage soured, he decided to join the army, and Father blessed the decision. When Cedric died, Stephen became the new heir and Father anointed him The Favorite."

Dorothy's face was worked into a cross between rage and sadness. Violet feared that the merest touch might cause years of resentment to explode from the poor woman's body.

Hurst continued. "So I am to understand that you were not one of your father's favored children?"

"Look at me, Detective. Do I *look* like I have enjoyed much favor in my life, despite the fact that I am the one who remained with Father all of these years, never marrying and never having my way in anything I truly desired?"

"How have you not had your way?"

"In anything."

"For example?"

"Just as I said. Father never let me have my heart's desire." Dorothy's face was resolute, as though she'd mustered the will to tamp down all of her anger and misery in order to seem dispassionate. Violet wondered how many times she'd done that in the past.

Hurst changed his line of questioning. "Perhaps your father's death was not a suicide, and someone shot him with his own volley gun. Do you have any idea who may have wanted him dead?"

"Anyone who really knew him, I suppose."

"Would that include you, Miss Fairmont?"

"Don't be ridiculous. As long as I had lived with him, why would I want to kill him in his dotage? And why would I wait until he'd gone to London to do so? It would be far more convenient to drown him in his bath back in Sussex."

She spoke like a woman who had considered it.

"Very well, I think that is enough for now. Please make yourself available for more questions should we have them."

"I do hope you'll find the criminal soon."

"We are not firmly of the opinion that your father was murdered. He may have committed suicide."

Dorothy, however, merely shrugged. "Either way, the funeral should be in a few days and then we'll all return home."

"Actually, the funeral will be held at the queen's pleasure. Mrs. Harper is on hand to ensure that your father will be"—he glanced Violet's way—"comfortable, I believe is her term, until the funeral is held."

"I don't understand. What does the queen care when Father is buried?"

"Given your father's service to the Crown, the queen wishes the matter closed before your father is put to final rest. May I ask that you have your sister, Eleanor, come down to meet with us?"

So Scotland Yard didn't know anything more than Violet did as to what the queen's concern was in this situation. Interesting.

As Dorothy went upstairs, Violet heard a noise outside. Glancing toward the window, she saw through a parting in the curtains that the florist had arrived. She bit her lip. Should she excuse herself and meet him downstairs at the servants' entrance, or stay put? She decided that after Mr. Hurst's internal struggle over allowing her to stay, it would be rude to disappear. Mrs. Peet could handle the delivery, and she would help bring the pots upstairs later.

There was a great rustling of activity from upstairs, followed by loud whispering. Violet caught what sounded like a hushed argument, and from their expressions, Hurst and Pratt heard it as well.

Mr. Pratt made more notes, his fingers quickly becoming stained black from graphite.

Eventually, Eleanor Fairmont Bishop floated down the stairs. Unlike Dorothy, who had completely ignored the coffin's substantial presence in the room, Nelly made a perfunctory acknowledgment of her father, putting two fingers to her lips and to the coffin's lid before greeting the detectives and Violet, and then sitting in the chair Dorothy had just vacated.

"My sister said you wished to see me now," Nelly said. "I'm not sure what more I can add. Dorothy was much closer to Father than the rest of us, since she never left home."

"Would you say that they enjoyed good familial relations?" Hurst asked.

"As good as a disappointed spinster with no home of her own can have."

"What of you? What was your relationship with your father?"

Nelly shrugged. "Gordon and I lived nearby, but we didn't frequent Willow Tree House. We were busy with our own lives. We had a son to raise. We also spend a great deal of time in London. Therefore, I suppose you could say my relationship with him was quite pleasant."

"What is your son's name?"

At that, Nelly's face actually broke into sunshine, the age in her face receding into the background behind her wide smile. "Tobias. We call him Toby. He just turned eighteen and has thus far proven quite successful this Season. He's not only handsome and quite clever, but since Dorothy and Stephen have no children, he will most likely inherit one day if we can figure out how to put him in the line of succession. In fact, here is his picture."

Nelly picked up the photograph of the bored young man that Violet had noted earlier. She passed the framed picture proudly, and they all murmured accolades of his youth and good looks. Nelly kissed the picture before setting it back in its place.

"When was the last time you saw Lord Raybourn, Mrs. Bishop?"

"As I said, we saw very little of him. I suppose . . . oh, let me think. The last time we saw Father was for Toby's birthday, in January. We went to Willow Tree House and Father gave him a sporting rifle for weekend hunts. To Father's credit, he did want my son to be well accepted into society. Yes, I can say that with certainty."

"Where is your son now?"

"In our rented lodgings here in London."

"So you've been in London this entire time and just now came to join the family?"

"There was nothing I could do about Father's death, was there? Besides, someone needed to meet Dorothy at the train station with a growler cab for all of her luggage."

"And you didn't think it necessary for Tobias to join you and your husband here today?"

Nelly's expression was incredulous. "And have him distracted from his parties and horse races and all of the other festivities in London? Are you mad? There is a very limited amount of time in which to meet marriageable young ladies. Every second counts."

Hurst shook his head. "Mrs. Bishop, tell us about your husband. He's not titled like your father."

Nelly's features settled back into their previous overly ripened arrangement. "No. Gordon was my father's choice for me. A punishment for being too wild in my youth. He thought marriage to a solicitor would tame me."

"Did it?"

She opened her mouth to say something, then seemed to think better of it. "My son fills my life and in him I am very happy."

Hurst seemed content to move on to other topics. "Tell us more about your husb—"

"Mrs. Bishop, where was your son two evenings ago when Lord Raybourn died?" Violet said, without stopping to consider what she was doing.

Hurst shot her a glance of irritation, but Nelly's look was that of a coiled snake, deciding on which part of Violet's flesh to sink her fangs.

"What exactly are you insinuating about my son, Mrs. Undertaker?" Nelly's voice dripped poison.

But if this viscount's daughter thought to intimidate Violet

Harper, who had handled and charmed many a viperish family member, she was sadly mistaken.

"Insinuate? Quite the opposite, Mrs. Bishop. I am concerned for his safety. If someone desired to kill the elder Lord Raybourn for some unknown reason, might he not also seek to do away with all potential heirs in his line?"

It was tripe, but it had the desired effect on Nelly, whose concern for her son made her anxious and submissive. "You mean you think Father's death was not by his own hand? That's impossible. Please, you mustn't let anything happen to my darling Toby. Detective, you will protect him, won't you? Please, he is everything to me. What can I do to help?"

Thus was Nelly Bishop defanged.

Pratt stared at Violet, slack-jawed, his pencil fallen into his lap, and even Hurst gave her a look of grudging admiration before addressing Nelly again.

"What you can do is to stay nearby. Perhaps you and Mr. Bishop could stay here with your brother until our investigation is over? That way our job is made easier should we need your assistance in the coming days."

"Yes, yes, of course. I'll have some things sent over right away."

"Now we need to speak to your husband."

"Certainly, but what could he possibly have to say?" Nelly seemed truly baffled that the detectives would want to interview him.

"Mrs. Bishop," Hurst said gently. "He is the son-in-law of a violently killed peer. He will surely have something valuable to tell us."

"Right. Well, I'll send him down for you." With greater elegance than her sister, Nelly swept back up the stairs, where the other occupants of the house must have felt like they were being corralled up in a sheep's pen, waiting for the gate to open and release them into the field to be herded about by a Scotland Yard sheepdog.

More whispering ensued and wafted down the stairs in an incomprehensible swell. While they waited, Hurst spoke in low tones.

"Mrs. Harper, you shouldn't have interrupted my questions. I am in charge of this investigation, and your presence here is due to my good graces."

"Of course, Detective. I'm deeply sorry."

"Somehow I doubt that. Nevertheless, I admit you turned Mrs. Bishop around and I expect she'll be more agreeable from now on. As for her sister, I imagine she will continue to be shrewish. I've seen her type many times. Never married, never been the center of attention, never been doted upon. Makes a woman shrivel up. I believe we'll be concluded once we speak to Mr. Bishop. I'm still of the mind that it was a suicide, and it may be associated with Lord Raybourn's work in Egypt."

"What work?" Violet asked.

"That's what we need to explore. May even require a trip down the Nile, eh, Mr. Pratt? I think he may have been caught in something underhanded during his trip that was going to lead to public shame if it was discovered, hence he decided to end it all now. That's why we need to wrap up these family interviews, so we can begin the real investigation."

Seeing his superior's chattiness as a cue that all was well between him and Violet, Pratt said, "The attempt by someone in London to blackmail de Lesseps of some alleged corvée labor to finish the canal is the Crown's greater interest."

Hurst shot Pratt a look Violet didn't understand, but she felt a chill from it. Pratt must have caught the same cold wind, for he quickly changed subjects. "May I ask, Mrs. Harper, how you came into this trade?"

"My first husband's family owned an undertaking shop and I learned the trade from him."

Pratt flipped farther back in his notebook and began a new round of note taking. "What happened to your first husband?"

"He was killed during a crossing of the Atlantic."

"I see. And now you operate this business by yourself?"

"Yes."

"How do you come by most of your, er, clients?"

"Mr. Pratt, is this mere curiosity, or are you also interviewing me in conjunction with Lord Raybourn's death?"

"What? Oh." Pratt reddened. "Sorry, I was just wondering. We don't normally have anything to do with a body once it finally goes off to be prepared for burial. You're the first undertaker I've really known, and you're a woman at that. Makes a man interested, is all. I mean no offense, truly."

"None taken."

At that moment, Nelly's husband finally came downstairs to meet with the detectives. Pratt flipped back in his notebook to where he was previously, and the questioning began anew.

"Thank you for meeting with us, Mr. Bishop. Can you tell me anything about your father-in-law?"

"What would you like to know? Anything I can do to help, Mr. Hurst, anything." Mr. Bishop's smile beneath his long and full mustache seemed overly bright to Violet.

"How, for instance, would you characterize Lord Raybourn's disposition in the months leading up to his death? Did he seem anxious or depressed to you?"

Gordon reached into his jacket and pulled out a cigarette case, offering it to each of the detectives, who declined. He selected one for himself and put the case on the occasional table next to him. "So you believe it was a suicide?"

"We are considering all possibilities. As such, we are interested in Lord Raybourn's frame of mind. For example, he may have been under duress because he was being threatened by someone."

"I see what you're getting at." Gordon pulled out a silver fili-greed match case, struck one of the matches, and put a flame to his cigarette, puffing several times before putting the match case on top of the cigarette case, and placing them next to a large crystal ashtray. The intricately cut pattern covering the receptacle re-flected light in many colors, showing it to be much more a work of art than a utilitarian accessory.

Gordon settled back, blowing a cloud toward the ceiling. "Now that you mention it, the old man did seem fixated on something, especially in the weeks leading up to his departure from Willow Tree House to come to London. Once we heard that he'd been in-vited to go with the prince to Egypt, I assumed his preoccupation was over those plans."

"So you saw him frequently?"

"Certainly. We were family, and we have a grandson the old man doted on."

"That's a handsome case you have," Hurst said.

Gordon lifted it from next to the thick ashtray and held it up. "Isn't it? The old man gave it to me Christmas last. It's probably worth quite a few pence. This ashtray of his is one of my favorites, too. The old man had excellent taste in smoking goods."

"Was that the last time you saw your father-in-law?"

"Heavens, no. There was Toby's birthday, a dinner here and there, and Toby and I went on a weekend shoot with him so that Toby could use the new rifle the old man gave him. Bagged quite a few woodcock, indeed. He enjoyed having us around."

"I see. So you were on good personal terms with Lord Raybourn. What of your wife? How did she get on with her father?"

"Quite well." Gordon dropped his voice. "You know, between us, I think Nelly was her father's favorite. Would never let on to Stephen, of course. He's quite devastated by the old man's loss."

"Why do you think she was his favorite?"

"Look at her. She's a beauty still, isn't she? And still full of youthful spunk. What father wouldn't adore her? Even today I can't imagine why the old man championed me with her. Look at me, a poor solicitor's son, married to the exquisite daughter of the Viscount Raybourn."

"Have you a profession, Mr. Bishop?"

"Ahem. Well, I followed my father into law, and since my marriage I've taken a stab at a few investments and such, but the old man, you know, wanted his son-in-law to live more like a gentleman and he, er, helped us along a bit."

Hurst nodded. "I presume that help has disappeared with Lord Raybourn's death?"

"Hardly." Gordon tapped his cigarette against the ashtray's edge and brought it back to his lips for another long draw. "The old man assured me that we were well provided for in his will."

"So his death was beneficial to you?"

Gordon shrugged. "I'll forgive you for your understandable insensitivity. His death is irrelevant. From a financial perspective, I mean. We are quite distraught as a family. But Nelly and I were to be comfortable whether her father lived or died." He crushed the cigarette in the tray, which was so large it appeared to swallow the stub whole. "How else can I help you?"

Hurst changed course. "You don't seem the least bit worried for your son."

"Worried? For what?"

"Doesn't he stand to inherit if the new Lord and Lady Raybourn don't have children, which I imagine is quite unlikely at this point?"

"A peer's inheritance is through the male line, so Nelly would have to pull off some remarkable intrigues to make that happen."

"Your wife told us that she is desperately frightened that whoever killed Lord Raybourn might also be after his heirs, specifically Tobias."

"She said that?"

Hurst nodded.

"But that doesn't . . . he couldn't have . . . when would . . . well, then." Gordon smiled. His teeth were remarkably white for someone who enjoyed tobacco. Perhaps it was a recent habit. "I must be mistaken then. Whatever my Nelly says is correct, I'm sure, and if she's worried, so am I."

"I see," Hurst said. "You should also know that your wife intends to stay here while we seek out what happened to your father-in-law, so that she is available to assist us."

"Nelly said she *wanted* to stay here? With the rest of the family?"

"Yes."

Gordon blinked a few times but his friendly smile returned as he picked up his match and cigarette cases. "Very well, whatever Nelly wants is what I want, too. You can count on the Bishops to be on hand for whatever is necessary."

He stood, shook hands with the detectives, nodded his head in Violet's direction, and bounded back up the stairs like a hunted stag.

"You lied to Mr. Bishop," Violet said to Hurst.

"Yes, I did. You also lied to his wife."

"But yours was an outright falsehood. I was merely attempting to . . . soften her."

"You do not have a hold on cleverness, Mrs. Harper. I decided to use your own bit of trickery to unsettle Mrs. Bishop's husband. Those two are playing to some script, I'm sure of it, although whether it has to do with Lord Raybourn's death or some other aristocratic melodrama, I don't know. Assuredly, they are right now having a spat, and eventually something will come out that will be helpful. First, though, I'm going to nudge them into getting that boy of theirs over here so we can talk to him and be done with this for now." Hurst stood, ready to leave.

"Wait." Violet reached into the ashtray and held up the stub of Gordon's cigarette. "Look familiar?"

Hurst nodded. "The same type that was next to Lord Raybourn's body. What of it? It's probably a popular local brand. And Mr. Bishop said he was on very familiar terms with his father-in-law, who probably gave them to him."

"But what Mr. Bishop says directly conflicts with what his wife says, doesn't it? So if the wife is correct and they rarely saw Lord Raybourn, then it is a great coincidence that he smokes the same cigarette, isn't it?"

Hurst rolled his eyes, but snatched the stub from Violet and handed it to Pratt. "Match this up to one in Lord Raybourn's tobacco box, then go to a tobacconist to see whether it is a rare or expensive brand."

Pratt tucked the cigarette remnant into one of his pockets.

"As for you, Mrs. Harper, it is best you realize that detection is a tricky business and not something that can be engaged in on a whim."

"Did I suggest any such thing?"

"I suppose not. I think we're done here until we can do our last interview with the boy. Come, Mr. Pratt, the ancient lands await us."

The two detectives left, and Violet went downstairs to see to the lilies.

Mrs. Peet sat on a bench before a well-worn table stained with years of cut vegetables and meat juices. Pots of lilies dotted the floor, overwhelming the kitchen with their cloying fragrance. Mrs. Peet held a plucked bloom in her hand and was twisting it back and forth. Violet wasn't sure if the woman was praying or merely muttering to herself.

"Mrs. Peet?" she said. "I'm here for the flowers."

The housekeeper refocused, as if just seeing Violet for the first time. "Yes, Mrs. Harper. Are the detectives still here?"

"No, they're gone. Could you help me carry these pots upstairs? In fact, I could use your help in deciding exactly where they should go to complement Lord Raybourn's coffin."

Mrs. Peet brightened considerably at the suggestion, and the two women worked quickly to get the flowers upstairs. Except for insisting that a pot go on either end of the coffin—more insurance against any objectionable smells wafting from out of the coffin—she allowed Mrs. Peet to dictate where each plant went.

The woman seemed much cheered by the task, and, as Violet prepared to leave—would she ever be able to get anything to eat?—Mrs. Peet cleared her throat. "Er, Mrs. Harper, might I have a word? Downstairs?"

"Certainly."

Back in the kitchens, Mrs. Peet spoke in hushed tones. "I can't talk for long, as I expect the family will be wanting supper soon. Would you care for a buttered scone?"

"Heavens, yes." Violet fell on it, once again almost embarrassed by her appetite, but not discomfited enough to refuse the tangy lemon curd the housekeeper spooned out for her. She finished the treat in mere seconds.

"You wanted to talk to me?" she asked, blotting her lips with a napkin.

"Yes. It's about Lord Raybourn." Mrs. Peet sniffed and wiped away a tear as she picked up Violet's crumb-littered plate and put it in a sink.

When she sat back down across from Violet, Violet reached out and took the woman's hand. "You were very devoted to your employer, I can see that."

"More than you know, ma'am. But it's all for naught now." Mrs.

Peet exhaled a great sigh and removed her hand from Violet's, lifted an edge of her apron, and daubed at her eyes. "There's something I must tell you about his death."

"Are you sure this isn't something you should tell the detectives?"

"No, I don't trust them. You're taking care of His Lordship— and quite considerate you are about it—so you're the only one I trust. Plus, I don't think the family would take too kindly to me running about talking to the police."

"Very well. What do you want to tell me?"

"It's about what happened before Lord Raybourn died. With the cook, Madame Brusse, and Lord Raybourn's valet, Mr. Larkin. You see, we all came to London with him in February, prior to the start of the Season. When His Lordship said he was going to Egypt, he decided to take Madame Brusse and Mr. Larkin with him, to take care of him while he was away."

"But he didn't take you along?"

"No, but I have no complaints. I had my duties here and I knew he'd come back to me—I mean, to London. Besides, why would he need a housekeeper in a hotel?"

"For that matter, why would he need a cook?" Violet asked.

"Lord Raybourn was very discerning about his food. He sent over to Burgundy just to hire Madame Brusse away from some fancy place there. I expect taking her with him meant he would always have the dishes he liked. His Lordship loved Beef Bourguignon and said Madame Brusse made the best in the world. Succulent so as to melt in your mouth, he always said."

Where was Mrs. Peet wandering off to in this conversation?

"So Lord Raybourn took along his cook and valet . . ." Violet said.

"Yes, and that's just what's wrong." Mrs. Peet dropped her voice one more level. "Where are they? Lord Raybourn came home unexpectedly early, but didn't bring Madame Brusse and Mr. Larkin with him?"

"Perhaps he gave them leave to stay behind for a longer visit?

Or maybe Madame Brusse stopped along the return to visit relatives in France?"

Mrs. Peet shook her head in frustration. "Lord Raybourn wouldn't have allowed it. As I said, he's particular about his food. My cooking is acceptable, but it's not . . . French. And why would Mr. Larkin stay behind?"

"Mrs. Peet, are you suggesting that Lord Raybourn's trusted cook and valet had something to do with his death and have now disappeared?"

Violet heard a rustling noise at the top of the servants' staircase. Mrs. Peet must have heard it, too, because she looked up that way, her eyes round as biscuits. "Oh dear," she said, now speaking in nearly a whisper. "Someone must have heard me. I can stay but a moment longer. May I ask a very special favor? Might I see His Lordship one last time?"

"I don't think that's a very good idea. He's not up to visitors."

"Mrs. Harper, I know you think I'm just a housekeeper and therefore probably without feelings, but I tell you I loved that man more than anyone else in this family. I should like to clip a lock of his hair before he's buried."

"No!"

"Please, I know that he's not what he was when he was alive, but I must see him one more time. I have this"—she pulled an empty, glass-domed brooch from her apron pocket—"and I plan to curl his hair in the shape of a fleur-de-lis inside it. I thought I might even edge the inside with some blue ribbon, and if I can cut enough from his head, I'll braid the rest into a bracelet. . . ." Mrs. Peet's voice trailed off.

Violet was torn. Under normal circumstances, the housekeeper's request was perfectly benign. But Lord Raybourn's circumstance was anything but normal, and Mrs. Peet was not a family member.

Tears rolled down the woman's face. "Please," she whispered again, her voice cracking as she took Violet's hand and squeezed it.

"Very well. I suppose Inspector Hurst cannot object to it, although it's better if we don't tell him. I have to return tomorrow morning to put a lock on the coffin. I'll think of a way to get the family out of the room, then I'll unshroud him for you. Your visit with him must be very quick, do you understand? I'll inform the new Lord and Lady Raybourn about it, but I don't want the family to see us opening the coffin. You must realize that it's very irregular for me to do this."

In an overwrought show of emotion, Mrs. Peet kissed Violet's hand. "I am forever in your debt."

Violet didn't want anyone in her debt; she just wanted to wrap up this burial and go home.

Before heading back to her temporary home, though, Violet went to Oxford Street in search of the C. Laurent Fashion Doll Shop. It was still in its same location as when she last visited eight years ago, although the front had expanded into the shop next door. The doll business must be booming. Of course, the queen had been a renowned doll collector in her youth, so it was no surprise that public demand for them had grown over the years.

She was pleased to see several dollhouses in one of the shop's windows, each filled with sofas, tables, paintings, lamps, carpets, and other miniature items. The strap of bells on the door jangled as she entered. Standing behind the counter was the regal, elderly woman she remembered waiting on her back then, except there was a teenage girl with her.

"May I help you?" the girl said, as the older woman nodded approvingly.

"Good afternoon. My name is Violet Harper."

The young girl smiled, but it was the older woman who spoke. "I'm Elizabeth Greycliffe Peters, and this is my granddaughter, Lizzy, named for me, I'm proud to say."

"You have a fine business here. I have one of my own that I run with my daughter."

"Oh? What is that?"

"I'm an undertaker."

Mrs. Peters blinked several times, but she didn't let down her professional demeanor for a moment. "I see. How can we help you?"

"I purchased a dollhouse from you some years ago, the Barclay House."

"Yes, the Barclay House was a very popular model, but we stopped carrying it last year. We still have many pieces that go well inside its Regency interior."

"Actually, I'm looking for something else this time. My daughter lives in the United States, and I think she may be getting married soon. She and I spend many hours playing with her dollhouse, and it may be overly sentimental, but I'd like to purchase bride and groom dolls to send to her."

"Ah, but I adore sentimentality. My parents fell in love during the French Revolution and theirs was a wildly sentimental tale. What a wonderful idea yours is. I shall have to place an advertisement recommending such a course of action for all of my customers attending weddings. Remember that we need to do this, Lizzy." Mrs. Peters patted her granddaughter's shoulder and turned back to Violet.

"She'll take over the shop one day from my daughter, and will be the fourth generation to do so. It's good to train them early, isn't it?"

"Yes, Mrs. Peters. My daughter, Susanna, joined in my business at a very young age, and now she is running it by herself out in the Colorado Territory."

"Grandmamma," Lizzy said. "The prince and princess dolls . . ."

"Excellent idea, child. Mrs. Harper, we still have one set of the bride and groom dolls we made to commemorate the marriage of the Prince and Princess of Wales. Lizzy, fetch them from the storage room for Grandmamma."

The girl returned a few minutes later with two dolls nestled on purple velvet in a wooden box. They were large, two-foot-high replicas of the royal couple, exquisite in detail down to the princess's heavily lace-and-flower-embellished dress and long, layered, matching veil.

Violet was instantly transported back to the days of playing dollhouse families with Susanna in their London home's drawing room.

Had she just sighed aloud at the memory?

"I'll take them."

After her purchase, Violet took the doll box back to St. James's Palace and set the dolls on a chair in the middle of the room, so she could see them from almost any vantage point. They were a perfect reminder of her daughter . . . and of home.

10

The next morning, Violet was awakened by a distant scratching. What was that irritating noise at her door? She opened one eye. It was still dark out and already mid-May, so it couldn't even be six o'clock in the morning yet.

She dragged herself up, threw on a wrapper, and opened the door a crack. A footman stood there, his hand raised as if to scratch at the door again. He blushed at seeing Violet in her nightclothes and turned his back to her.

"Two men from Scotland Yard are here to see you, Mrs. Harper."

What in the world . . . ?

"I'll be there shortly." She shut the door and hurriedly put herself together before heading into the corridor and through several hallways to the staircase leading to the front entry where Detectives Hurst and Pratt waited.

"Have you no other garb but deathly black, Mrs. Harper?" Mr. Hurst asked.

"I am an undertaker, sir." She touched the brim of her hat for emphasis.

"How could I forget? I suppose you're dressed appropriately for today. You'll need that bag of yours, though."

"Why?"

Hurst raised an eyebrow. "Why do you imagine? We've had another death at the Raybourn home. We'll never get on with our other investigations now. Hurry, woman."

Violet ran back up to her rooms and opened her undertaking bag, removing the bottles of Lord Raybourn's blood and shoving them into the far reaches of the room's armoire. Hopefully, no maid would open the doors and be startled out of her wits upon finding them.

"We must make a stop along the way," she told Hurst.

"I have no need to run women's errands. This is police business."

"As is my errand, sir. I need to pick up a lock for His Lordship's coffin."

"For what reason?"

"Just in case."

Hurst grunted in irritation, but followed Violet's directions to Morgan Undertaking. Fortunately, she could already see Will moving around inside the shop, despite the early hour.

"Mrs. Harper, yet another surprise," Will said, looking curiously out the window at Hurst, who stood next to the carriage looking for all the world as though he'd like to murder someone himself.

"I'm glad you're up with the roosters, Will. Do you have the locking set and silver plate yet?"

"Yes, they're right here." Will retrieved a cotton bag from behind the counter, and pulled out a tissue-wrapped item. "This is the plate for Lord Raybourn's coffin."

It was just as Violet had requested it. Broken columns etched on either side, with the prescribed wording between them.

Will handed her the bag. "The lock set and brass nails for the plate are in here. Is something wrong? I was still planning to come along sometime today to affix the lock to the coffin."

"No, nothing's wrong. It's just more a timing issue of attaching the lock. I'd like to do so first thing this morning, so I think I'll just take it and the plate with me now. Have you some tools I can borrow?"

"I don't mind doing the work, Mrs. Harper."

Violet smiled. "It's quite all right. Have a long supper with your bride this afternoon."

Will's downcast expression as he handed over a hammer and screwdriver suggested he'd rather be securing a coffin's lock than securing his wife's affection.

Throwing in the lock set and inscription plate, she snapped the valise closed again, and went back to join the detectives. At the door, she turned back. "Will, do you still have my old sample cases? I could also use a couple of collection bottles." She would eventually need to deliver the bottles of Lord Raybourn's blood to Morgan Undertaking for disposal.

"Of course." He went behind the shop's antique counter, and from shelves behind it pulled out some glass-covered trays filled with selections of jet necklaces, rings, bracelets, and ear bobs—which Lord Raybourn's daughters would be able to wear once two months had elapsed—plus black lace fans, hair brooches, and other mourning accoutrements. He disappeared briefly into another room and returned with two thick bottles.

With the trays in hand and the bottles stowed in her bag, she went back to the carriage. She and the detectives rode silently to Park Street, Hurst refusing to say anything more about what had happened at Raybourn House.

Upon their arrival, all was chaos. Katherine was folded in Stephen's arms, crying in the entrance hall. The Bishops were arguing between themselves in front of the coffin inside the parlor. Dorothy sat stony-faced, watching her younger sister and Gordon quarrel.

Everyone was still in nightclothes except for the young stranger sitting near Dorothy. Violet recognized him from his photograph. This was Nelly's son, Tobias.

Hurst clearly recognized him, too, for he whispered, "I told you we would eventually see him here. Must admit, I didn't expect the mother to get so worked up as to fetch him right away."

Tobias drummed the fingers of his left hand on the arm of his chair. Seeing him in person, Violet realized that it wasn't an expression of condescension the young man wore, it was more like . . . irritation. As though he found his parents insufferable.

Stephen looked up from where he was comforting his wife.

"Detectives, Violet, good of you to come so quickly. Please excuse our appearance. Everything has just gone so wrong. This way, please."

Violet set her trays down on a table in the hallway, while Mr. Pratt laid her undertaking bag on the floor beneath the table, then she and the detectives went down the servants' staircase to which Stephen pointed. Violet gasped at what awaited them.

Mrs. Peet, her face red and bloated, dangled from a rope attached to an exposed water pipe running across the ceiling. She wore the same dress and apron she'd had on yesterday. Her once-arresting eyes were dull and faded, staring blankly.

"What happened?" Violet said.

"Yes, someone explain what happened to this poor woman," Hurst said, as Stephen, Gordon, and Tobias came down the stairs and into the kitchen.

Stephen spoke for the group. "We don't know. Dorothy says she woke during the night and wanted some tea and a little snack, so she rang and rang for Mrs. Peet, who never showed. Eventually, Dorothy came downstairs, figuring to chastise the housekeeper, but found her . . . as such. We've all been in such shock, as you might imagine."

"Where do you want her?" Hurst asked Violet.

"Here on the worktable," she replied. It was the same table where she'd met with an overcome Mrs. Peet just hours ago.

Stephen found a ladder in the larder, and the men worked together to cut the poor woman down. The rope around her neck was thick and required a great deal of cutting to free it from the pipe. With Hurst on the ladder sawing through the rope with a knife, Pratt, Stephen, and Gordon held on to the woman's body to capture her once she was freed. Once Mrs. Peet was down, they carried her to the kitchen worktable and laid her unceremoniously on it, with Hurst commenting insensitively that this was becoming a second profession for him. Only Tobias refrained from assisting, instead standing back to watch the proceedings, his lips moving but no sound coming out.

"First the old man, now this. What is happening to our family?"

Gordon said, pulling out his cigarette case from his jacket. "Anyone care for one of these?"

"Mr. Bishop, please. There will be no smoking here while I work on Mrs. Peet," Violet said.

"Oh, right you are." He put the case back. "Although I doubt she'd notice."

"Might I have a word upstairs?" Mr. Pratt asked Gordon. "I was wondering if you might be able to show me something among His Lordship's belongings."

The two men went back up the staircase, leaving Violet, Hurst, Stephen, and Tobias behind.

"I can't understand why Mrs. Peet would do this to herself," Stephen said. "She had a good home with the family. I know she was overcome by Father's loss, as we all are, but I can't imagine it would have caused her to do *this*." He glanced at her body and grimaced. "I had no idea she was so devoted to my father."

Hurst nodded thoughtfully. "Did you know any of Mrs. Peet's friends? Did she have any questionable associations? Were you aware of anyone new she may have met?"

Stephen shook his head. "She was our housekeeper. I have no idea how she spent her free time or whom she met."

"Right. Well, neither of you need remain down here," Hurst said. "A terrible tragedy for the family to have to witness. Scotland Yard extends its condolences."

"Thank you, Detective," Stephen said. "Toby, come."

Tobias Bishop obediently followed his uncle up the stairs, leaving just Hurst and Violet with Mrs. Peet's body.

"So, Lady Undertaker, what do you think happened here? Unfortunate suicide or do we have an unrestrained killer on the loose, intent on persecuting this house?" He smiled as he leaned against the wall and crossed his arms, as though testing her intelligence.

"Mrs. Peet wouldn't have done this to herself."

"How do you come to that conclusion?"

"Because I promised yesterday that I would open the coffin this morning for her to say a final, private good-bye to her employer."

Hurst shot up, erect. "Why would you do that?"

"She helped me carry lilies upstairs, and afterward spoke with me at this very table about her affection for Lord Raybourn. She begged me to let her clip a lock of hair."

"And you agreed to this?"

"She was quite melancholic about it."

Hurst rolled his eyes. "A woman's sensibilities. So we have an agitated housekeeper. Not the first one I've seen. You can hardly blame her—the master of the house had just died. I doubt it's of any significance. However, I must chastise you, Mrs. Harper. You planned to let this miserable woman view her employer's disintegrated face for one last moment of reverence? If she hadn't killed herself beforehand, she might have done so afterward."

"You mischaracterize what happened, sir."

"I know that you promised to do something dubious for the Fairmont family housekeeper."

"Well, Mr. Hurst, since you find my actions so questionable, I must suppose you are not interested in what I found out about the other servants."

"Which servants?"

"Madame Brusse and Mr. Larkin, the elder Lord Raybourn's cook and valet, whom he brought with him from Sussex to London. Stephen said he reported to you that they were missing, and that you questioned him at length about it."

"You have no business conducting your own interviews, but what of it? How do two servants benefit from the death of their employer?"

"You are the detective, sir, so I am sure you realize that Lord Raybourn's *French* cook was taken along to maintain the quality of Lord Raybourn's table, so it would be understandable if she stopped in France on the return to visit relatives, but why did His Lordship return without his valet, a critical member of a lord's household?"

"Mrs. Peet told you this? That the cook was French?"

"Yes."

"Was there a relationship between the cook and the valet?"

"She didn't say."

"For what possible reason would you have withheld this information from me?"

"I hardly did so intentionally. You may recall that you roused me from slumber not two hours ago, and insisted on quiet during the ride over here."

"Well . . . perhaps I was a bit forceful earlier."

"I am not your enemy, Mr. Hurst. Doesn't it seem as though we need to discover what happened to these two servants? Either they may have had something to do with Lord Raybourn's death, or are in great peril, or may have met with their own unfortunate ends."

Hurst nodded gravely. "It pains me to admit that I was wrong to overlook that bit about the cook and valet, although I can't see how two servants would benefit from the death of their master. If anything, they would be anxious to keep him from pulling the trigger on himself. Mr. Pratt and I will look into it right away. I guess we'll have to interview the neighbors and their servants. God, here comes the press. I was hoping to avoid having Scotland Yard excoriated in *The Times*." Hurst started for the stairs.

"And I shall take care of Mrs. Peet. Mr. Hurst. . . ." Violet said.

He turned as he reached the bottom step.

"There's one more thing. There was a noise at the top of the stairs as Mrs. Peet and I spoke. She seemed very frightened of being overheard. I don't know if that might be important."

He sighed. "Try not to hold back anything else from me, Mrs. Harper. And kindly don't leave the premises once you're done with Mrs. Peet. I'll see to the coroner. If he thought Lord Raybourn's death was a suicide, he won't put any extra effort into a housekeeper's death."

Once she was alone with Mrs. Peet, Violet took a deep breath and patted the woman's face. "Oh dear, what happened? I don't believe for one moment that you did this to yourself."

Violet took a pair of snips from her bag and went after the individual fibers of the rope's coil, slowly digging and clipping her way through until she finally broke through and removed the thick cord from around the woman's neck.

"Much better." She tossed the rope to the floor and kicked it out of sight beneath the table.

"I'm sorry you didn't get to say good-bye to Lord Raybourn, but hopefully you are with him now." Violet felt the woman's limbs. Rigor mortis was setting in quickly. She patted Mrs. Peet's shoulder.

"I'm going to find something clean and cheerful in your room for you to wear. I'll be back later, once this stiffening has passed, to dress you, arrange your hair, and perhaps we can do something about your coloring."

Mrs. Peet's face was scarlet from the pooling of blood caused by the cessation of air and blood flow through her head. There was no cosmetic massage color dark enough to mask the resulting flush and swelling to the housekeeper's face.

Violet took the servants' staircase all the way to the fourth floor, containing the staff living spaces. She found Mrs. Peet's room, made obvious by being the largest of the servants' quarters. Two dresses hung on hooks, one an alternate uniform and the other what must be her only day dress. Violet examined the dress, which had a light brown checkered pattern. Perfectly acceptable. She removed the bodice and skirt from the hook and went to Mrs. Peet's small chest of drawers to retrieve undergarments. As she was ready to gather everything up to take to the basement, she noticed a large trunk in the corner. It was brand new, wrapped in fine red Moroccan leather and missing none of its gleaming brass studs.

An interesting contrast to the rest of Mrs. Peet's surroundings. Overcome by curiosity, Violet knelt before the trunk. It wasn't locked. She lifted the lid. Inside were several exquisite dresses of velvet-edged satin and fine silks, separated by tissue. Beneath the gowns were three pairs of gloves, a beaded reticule, and a flat jeweler's box containing a multistrand jade necklace and matching ear bobs. The necklace must have been spectacular, resting on the woman's neck and complementing her green eyes.

How would a housekeeper, even one of a fine household such as this one, be able to afford such finery? She couldn't have afforded even one of these dresses on her annual salary. The only way she could have come into possession of them was if she were stealing them or being kept by a wealthy benefac—

Oh!

Violet rapidly worked it out in her mind. The widowed Lord Raybourn must have been having a secret affair with Mrs. Peet. Were the clothing and jewelry intended as gifts for his beloved or as bribes for her to keep their relationship a secret?

Many a servant had fallen in love with her master, only to discover that he was not constant in return.

Violet realized now that Mrs. Peet had been very much in love with Lord Raybourn. Had she done away with herself, Shakespearean style? Although hanging was not particularly romantic. Plus, a housekeeper would have reasonably easy access to poisonous substances, arsenic and the like, making a hanging a bit . . . dramatic.

Of course, Mrs. Peet probably wouldn't have realized how much damage she would do to herself through hanging.

Violet closed the trunk, gathered up the day dress and undergarments from the bed where she'd dropped them, and returned to the basement. Mrs. Peet was visibly stiff now. Violet draped the clothing on the back of a chair. "I'm so sorry for your loss," she whispered. "It must have been very hard on you to carry your secret and not be able to grieve openly when Lord Raybourn died. I do wonder, though, did he love you as well as you loved him?"

Violet retrieved the drawstring bag containing the locking kit, inscription plate, and tools from her undertaking bag and went up to the first floor. Toby sat morosely in the drawing room, idly thumbing through a copy of *Punch*.

"Mr. Bishop, excuse my interruption, but I need to affix a lock to your grandfather's coffin," Violet said.

Toby waved a hand toward the coffin.

"Are Mr. Hurst and Mr. Pratt still here?"

Without looking up, Toby replied, "No, they left together on important business, I'm sure."

"What of your parents?"

"They've gone off to see their solicitor about something. Uncle Stephen and Aunt Katherine took Aunt Dorothy with them to see a service about getting some temporary help. They went through your trays and left a list of which pieces they wanted. I've been left alone."

Violet noticed that the coffin lid was slightly ajar. Had morbid desire and desperate longing gotten the best of Mrs. Peet, and she had taken it upon herself to lament her loss outside of Violet's presence? Perhaps seeing Lord Raybourn in such a state was too much for her to handle, as Hurst had suggested? Violet had a sickening feeling of guilt, but cast it aside, since such action seemed uncharacteristic of Mrs. Peet. Or was it?

Violet shook off all thoughts and worked as quickly as she could to attach the latch and hasp, sliding the lock through and firmly clicking it shut.

What maid would want to work in a home with corpses located on two floors?

She pocketed the key for herself, having a strange feeling that she shouldn't give it to anyone in the family unless they demanded it.

Standing on tiptoe, she aligned the silver plate to the center of the widest point of the coffin, where Lord Raybourn's shoulders lay, and gently tapped the brass nails into it. With this finished, she put her tools into the cloth bag and turned to leave, only to find Toby staring steadily at her, the magazine tossed onto a table.

"You aren't the family undertaker. What happened to him?"

"I am here on behalf of the queen, who regarded your grandfather highly and wished to provide undertaking services as a gift to the family."

Toby's expression was inscrutable. "I see."

"May I sit down?"

Toby waved a hand again, this time at a chair covered in a green fabric decorated with an airy peacock feather print.

"You must be quite affected by your grandfather's death."

Toby shrugged. "I didn't know him that well."

"Surely you visited regularly with him?"

"My parents trotted me out for display during school term breaks and at Christmas, but I never spent any real time with him. Mums didn't care for the old man much."

"Why not?"

Another shrug. "Why does she do anything she does? Mums is a rather pent-up piece, in case you hadn't noticed. Always hysterical about something. It wouldn't surprise me at all if she did off with my grandfather because he took her to task over her fits. I do my best to avoid her, a near impossibility, believe me. Father dotes on her every outburst. I'm in London looking for a wife, or so my parents tell me. My hope is to find one who is not only the opposite of my mother, but is a girl that my mother detests. I couldn't be completely happy otherwise. Actually, the qualities I really want in a wife are . . . but it's not my tribulations you care about, is it?"

Toby looked directly at Violet, his gaze steady and sad.

"May I ask you some more questions?" she said.

"Do you know how many times I've heard that? Every curiosity seeker masquerading as a mourner accosts me in the streets and has dozens of questions about my grandfather's death." He shook his head. "But you're not a curiosity seeker, are you, Mrs. Harper? Go ahead. I suppose it helps pass the time until I can leave this tomb and get to more important things. Really, can't we just bury the old man and be done with it? And now Mrs. Peet is downstairs." He shuddered. "I just want to get back to my own activities and away from all of . . . this."

"I understand."

"I guess the bright spot in it all is that with Grandfather gone, my mother might abandon all of her grand plans for me, enabling me to do what I want. Especially if Grandfather has left me something substantial."

"What would you do with your inheritance?"

"I suppose I'd use most of the money to further some interests I have. I would also buy Aunt Dorothy her own place; that would be a kick."

"Why so?"

An actual smile flitted across the young man's mouth. "Poor Aunt Dorothy. They say she's always been a bit homely. She always desperately wanted to be married and mistress of her own household. When an offer for her finally came, my grandfather scotched it. Something about the man's family being associated with the Metropolitan Board of Works, involved in the flow of sewage out of London. They were rich as Midas, though, and I can only imagine the estate he would have purchased for his wife. Mums said Aunt Dorothy never forgave the old man for it.

"Aunt Dorothy tried to act as mistress of Willow Tree House, but Mrs. Peet ruled there with a firm hand, and my grandfather seemed content to let the housekeeper have her way. So my aunt has never had a husband, nor a home to call her own. Sad, really."

"I'm sure things have been difficult for all of you." Violet used her most soothing undertaker's voice.

"Especially Uncle Stephen. He was the one who loved the old man the most."

"Except now he is the heir to your grandfather's fortune."

"I doubt he cares much about that. Uncle Stephen is as loyal as a collie."

Their conversation was interrupted by the return of Hurst and Pratt. Seeing Violet and Toby in conversation, Hurst gave her a quizzical look. "Mrs. Harper, might we have a word?"

Toby stood. "Have your word here. I need to find something to do that doesn't involve corpse-sitting." Lord Raybourn's grandson strode out of the house, his relief at escaping the house's gloom emanating from him.

Hurst and Pratt joined her in the drawing room. Violet had never before had so many unpleasant conversations in the presence of a coffin.

"I see you've locked the coffin," Pratt said. "Why so?"

"To prevent anyone from having a look during visitations. Lord Raybourn isn't fit for it."

Hurst arched an eyebrow at her but said nothing.

"Do you do this often?" Pratt asked.

"Not often, no. Lord Raybourn is a peer, making him special, and, of course, he is in gruesome condition."

"Right. So, your profession must also include techniques for making gruesome corpses presentable. Have you ever been involved in waxworking? Making prosthetic limbs?"

Violet hesitated to answer such a question. Inspector Pratt was very close to inquiring about her professional secrets.

"You seem fascinated by Mrs. Harper's profession," Hurst said. "Perhaps you should consider a new job as a mourner or grave digger."

"It was just a question," Pratt mumbled, taking out his notebook and pencil.

Hurst ignored him. "I see you were in deep conversation with the Bishops' son. Did you learn anything?"

Violet told the two detectives about her conversation with Toby.

"So his aunt is a bit irritable. It doesn't necessarily mean much. Not enough to hold up our other investigations into what occurred in Egypt."

Violet didn't like the insinuation that the twin deaths at Park Street were a distraction.

"Does this mean you will ignore these two murders?"

"Two likely suicides, you mean." He stroked his chin. "Perhaps it is not so bad that the queen is delaying the funeral, since it keeps the entire family under one roof while we conduct our other inquiries. Do you know how you can prove valuable to us, Mrs. Harper? Encourage some hostility among the Fairmonts. If someone should happen to be keeping a secret, he is more likely to break down and do something foolish under the anxiety of familial disputes."

"It seems to me that someone keeping a secret is more likely to commit another crime that way," Violet said.

"Which would be quite foolish, would it not?"

"But you've already got—"

"Before we go, you may be interested to know that we interviewed neighbors. Not much information to be had there. We talked to Lady Cowgil and Lord and Lady Wetherden, who live on either side of here. Both were very cooperative, undoubtedly seeking information from us, but had very little to share. They didn't hear the gunshot, were unaware of His Lordship's trip to Egypt, and did not know enough about his personal affairs to be aware of any bad relationships he might have."

"Did you speak with any of their servants?"

"I saw no need. Both Lady Cowgil and the Wetherdens were anxious about when they could pay their respects, I think mostly in order to get a look at Lord Raybourn, so it is probably best that the coffin remain locked."

Pratt cleared his throat and nodded pointedly at Hurst, who scowled. "What is it? Oh yes, the cigarette. Go ahead, it was your uncovering."

"I took the stub to a well-known tobacconist in Haymarket, who told me that it was one of their own exclusive brands, and quite expensive. Not surprising, of course. They deliver boxes of them regularly for Lord Raybourn.

"When I went upstairs with Mr. Bishop earlier, I asked him if he knew where Lord Raybourn's tobacco box was. At first, he pretended not to know whether Lord Raybourn had a special storage place for his cigarettes, then he said he had no idea where it was. When I suggested that Mr. Hurst and I would conduct a search for it, he suddenly remembered that it was in Lord Raybourn's study, which is attached to His Lordship's bedroom.

"He followed me up and I opened the tobacco box to find it full of one particular kind of cigarettes, with only two empty slots. I asked him when Lord Raybourn had given him the other one. Mr. Bishop said that he buys his own, that he and his father-in-law had the same taste in tobacco, but Mr. Bishop was nervous for sure. His hands shook and his eyes did the dance of the guilty—"

"The dance of the guilty?" Hurst interrupted him. "For heaven's sake, Mr. Pratt, stick to facts."

"Ahem, right. So he made up some excuse about his wife needing him and would I pardon him and he bundled out of there faster than a—well, it was quick."

Violet nodded. "So you think that Mr. Bishop had had some kind of secret meeting with Lord Raybourn upon his return, one in which his father-in-law offered him one of his prized cigarettes, and that something transpired between the men resulting in Mr. Bishop murdering Lord Raybourn."

"That's Mr. Pratt's idea. Or, he and his father-in-law simply enjoyed the same brand of cigarettes. You can never tell with the aristocrats. They can have hearts of stone or hearts of goose down. What would be your own theory, Mrs. Harper?"

"I haven't one. I can only say that Mr. Bishop seemed genuinely fond of his father-in-law."

"I've seen men kill for nonsensical reasons. In a case I solved a few years ago, a man threw another from Waterloo Bridge because he lost his bet over a cricket match. I don't think heated passions are confined to the lower classes. Let that be a lesson to you."

"Yet you say you don't think Lord Raybourn was murdered, by Mr. Bishop or anyone else in the family."

"What I'm actually saying is there is enough doubt he was murdered that I don't want it to delay Mr. Pratt and myself from looking into Lord Raybourn's affairs in Egypt. That's where I think the real mystery is."

After the detectives left, Violet checked through the accessories trays and totaled up the Fairmont purchases for Will's ledger, then went back downstairs to tend to Mrs. Peet. Her eyes were still open and now her jaw hung slack as though in a perpetual scream.

Violet reached out a hand to Mrs. Peet's hand. Still stiff, but gradually relaxing.

"Do you want me to wait to prepare you?" Violet asked softly as she dug out her undertaking bag, dropping in the cloth bag of tools.

As she was about to depart, she heard a knocking at the rear door. Who could that be? Perhaps some deliveryman? Or a florist dropping off a spray of camellias for the family? Violet stepped through the butler's pantry, scullery, and larder to answer it, finding a housemaid in the stairwell, one hand behind her back.

She couldn't have been much more than a teenager. Despite the warm day outside, the young woman shivered. She seemed startled to see someone not in a uniform at the door. "Excuse me, my lady, I thought to speak with . . . with . . . another maid, perhaps? I brought this for Mrs. Peet." She produced a handpicked bouquet of pink-and-white apple blossoms from behind her back.

"Those are lovely, Miss—?"

"Rebecca, madam." The girl curtsied.

"I am just the undertaker, Violet Harper. How may I help you?"

"I heard about Mrs. Peet. These are for her."

How in the world had news traveled that quickly?

"Thank you. They will be much appreciated."

The girl gave no indication that she would leave, instead peering over Violet's shoulder at what might lie beyond.

"Is there a message I can pass on to the family?" Violet asked.

"Oh no, madam, I would never presume to think the family would have a care what I thought. I was just wondering . . ."

"Yes?"

"Well, if perhaps I might be able to say good-bye to Mrs. Peet properly. We've all been talking and we agree that we never saw her as the type. She was very kind to me. More than once did she help me carry carpets in and out for beating. She even . . . protected . . . me once."

"Protected you from what?"

The girl's eyes grew wide. "I shouldn't have said that, madam. Forgive me. May I see her, God rest her soul?"

"I'm not sure it's a good idea. She's not really ready yet."

"Mrs. Harper, I know what she did to herself and I know she won't look normal. I grew up on a farm and have strangled and chopped the head off many a hen. I can endure the sight, I promise."

Violet wasn't sure about that—a dead human being was a far different sight from slaughtered dinner—and she might have made a mistake by giving in to Mrs. Peet's demands to see Lord Raybourn's dead body, but the girl reminded her of a young Susanna, so she let her in anyway. True to her word, Rebecca didn't act mortified at all to see Mrs. Peet stretched out on the table, but merely gazed sadly at the housekeeper.

"Do you think she felt a lot of pain?" she asked. "It's always so quick with the chickens."

"It's hard to know," Violet said.

"She must have been very brave to do this to herself, don't you think? To deliberately put a rope around your neck? To be so brave and yet so sad at the same time." Rebecca shook her head.

"You said that Mrs. Peet once protected you from something. What was it?"

Rebecca bit her lip. "It was more like some*one*, Mrs. Harper. Would have lost my honor had she not stepped in. Some men think any housemaid is theirs for the taking, don't they?"

"Was it Lord Raybourn?" Violet asked gently.

Tears filled the girl's eyes. "I mustn't talk about this. I promised Mrs. Peet I wouldn't." She laid the bouquet on the housekeeper's chest and fled the house.

Violet turned back to Mrs. Peet. "What other secrets were you and Lord Raybourn hiding? Did you discover Lord Raybourn making advances on Rebecca and kill him in a fit of anger? Was the subsequent guilt too much?"

Violet put a hand to the side of Mrs. Peet's face and gently pressed. Rigor mortis was passing. "Are you ready now for your beauty treatment?"

As with Lord Raybourn, Violet washed Mrs. Peet's body, assembling the needed materials from the kitchen and scullery. How ironic that mere days ago, Mrs. Peet had gathered these items up for Violet herself. Unlike her employer's preparation, Mrs. Peet wouldn't receive an embalming treatment. Instead, Violet focused first on washing the body, then set to work on improving the housekeeper's appearance as much as possible through cosmetics and other artifice.

Something had to be done about the eyes. Violet pushed the woman's lids down with her thumbs, but they refused to stay shut. Should she sew or glue? She'd sewn Lord Raybourn's eyes shut, but in this case . . .

From her undertaker's bag, Violet retrieved a small brown bottle and an eyedropper. After undoing the bottle's seal, she inserted the eyedropper and filled it, then gently squeezed glue along the lid edges of first Mrs. Peet's right eye, then her left eye. Violet then put her supplies down and gently pressed the lids shut on each eye, using the thumb and forefingers of both hands. Those arresting green eyes would never be seen again.

Satisfied that the lids would remain closed, Violet took out a needle and spool of wiry thread. She threaded about eighteen inches of the filament and stitched an end from a spot behind one ear, down around the chin, then back up and behind the other ear, making several more stitches and tying off the thread. This was another method to prevent the jaw from gaping open. Some undertakers used "invisible" stitches inside the mouth to lock the gums together, but Violet preferred to invade the body as little as possible. With a high-collared bodice or shirt, no one would ever notice what Violet had done.

Violet studied her handiwork. "Just a bit of cosmetic massage will cover it all up, won't it?"

She retrieved her tray of tinted creams and brushes, holding up various jars to the light drifting in from the transom windows. "I think you need Deep Beige Number Seven, which will help cover some of the remaining bruising on your face."

She unscrewed the pot and swirled a brush in it, then applied it to the woman's face with an artist's eye for symmetry and precision, being careful to daub extra cream along Mrs. Peet's eyelids to cover a couple of drops of congealed glue that had seeped out. She also applied the cream heavily to the woman's neck to mask the rope burns in case her clothing would not cover them, as well as more lightly to her shoulders and the tops of her hands.

Having given her as near to a fleshlike appearance as possible given the circumstances, Violet pulled out another tinted pot, this one of rouge, which she brushed heavily across the woman's cheeks and lips, and more lightly on her forehead, chin, and hands. "Now it almost looks as if blood is flowing through your veins. Your appearance is so much better. Now for the finishing touches."

Violet shook out the dress she'd selected for Mrs. Peet, examining it and looking down at the body, wondering how long it had been since the housekeeper had worn this dress. She'd gained some weight since she'd purchased it.

With the usual struggle it took to do it by herself, Violet replaced Mrs. Peet's undergarments, omitting a corset, an item far too difficult to lace up and tighten on a cooperative human being, much less the leaden weight of a corpse.

Mrs. Peet's dress was even less accommodating.

"No worries, I know just the thing that will have you looking like a society debutante."

Using a pair of scissors that had fallen to the bottom of her bag,

Violet cut a slit down the center of the back of both the skirt and the bodice. She put Mrs. Peet's arms through the armholes and laid the skirt across her midsection, then, turning her over to one side, then the other, brought the back sides of the dress together as closely as possible.

Time for more needle and thread. This time she selected a heavy cotton thread from her bag, and used large zigzag stitches to loosely connect the ripped edges of the dress. Violet gently brought Mrs. Peet down on her back again.

"Now, why don't we arrange your hair back into place? Lucky for you, I remember just how you wear it."

Violet brushed Mrs. Peet's coarse, graying hair back and tucked in a variety of pins to hold it still.

Violet stepped back once more. "You look lovely, Mrs. Peet. Ready for a fancy tea or a ride through Hyde Park. Just one more thing."

Violet wrapped Rebecca's bouquet in Mrs. Peet's hands and used more thread to tie her fingers around the flowers. "I don't think anyone can see a bit of this thread, and now you appear peaceful and relaxed."

After cleaning up and repacking her undertaking bag, Violet patted the woman's shoulder. "I'll leave you here to rest, but will be back soon with your coffin and some other things to prepare you for your big day."

Back upstairs, Violet found Stephen and Katherine in the drawing room, huddled together over Lord Raybourn's coffin. Katherine was trembling while Stephen soothed her. "I'm sure he didn't suffer, sweetheart. You must stop thinking about it."

Violet cleared her throat.

"Ah, we didn't know you were here," Stephen said, disengaging from his wife as they both turned to the undertaker. "Mrs. Cooke was here earlier with patterns. The women were quite pleased with her. She said she has some partial-mades that she can finish off by tomorrow. Can you pick them up?"

"Of course."

"And now I presume you wish to discuss Mrs. Peet?"

"Yes. Actually, I would like to talk to you about her funeral."

Stephen held up a hand. "Whatever is proper for someone of her station, we'll cover. I trust your judgment. She was actually a distant family member, you know."

"She was?" Was Violet wrong in her deduction that the house-keeper and Lord Raybourn were having an affair?

"Yes, but a cousin several times removed from my mother. A part of the family practically unknown to us. We've never really acknowledged her as other than a servant."

Violet nodded. "In that case, then, perhaps you would like to upgrade to a tradesman's funeral. It would show further respect without recognizing her as a member of the family."

"Yes, yes, that's fine."

"To what cemetery should I direct her remains?"

"I don't know. What do you think, Kate? Should we inter Mrs. Peet back at St. Margaret's?"

Katherine's eyes were red-rimmed. "She would have liked that. She loved Willow Tree House and the surrounding area."

"That settles it, then. I presume the queen will allow us to bury our housekeeper?"

Violet made another trip to Morgan Undertaking to drop off the trays and to order a pine coffin with an unbleached cotton lining, a thin mattress, and iron fittings, along with a tin inscription plate—all items appropriate for a tradesman's funeral—for Mrs. Peet.

"Mrs. Harper, we must show you our new carriage, meant just for trade funerals," Harry said, escorting her around the block to the mews where the carriages were kept. Still smelling of a thick coat of fresh black paint, the carriage was mostly enclosed, with just a small window on either side of it. Unlike with aristocrats, people didn't care to see who was inside the funeral carriage of a tradesman.

"I think this will do quite well for Mrs. Peet," she said.

After the stop at Morgan Undertaking, Violet returned to St. James's Palace. A royal carriage stood in the courtyard, its driver erect and unblinking, like a propped-up corpse awaiting photography.

Stationed outside her apartment was a footman holding a summons from the queen to come to Windsor.

Violet sighed as she quickly changed out of her undertaker garb and into something a little more presentable for being in the queen's presence.

At Windsor, she was led to the usual room where she met the queen. This time, the queen sat behind her immense mahogany desk, whose top shone from regular waxing. Sitting behind it, Queen Victoria managed to be both regal and sorrowful. To one side of the room, next to the great, yawning marble fireplace, stood an older, serious-looking man, his graying hair in wavy tufts around his ears and what looked like a permanent scowl etched upon his brow.

Violet curtsied once again. "Your Majesty," she said.

"You may rise, Mrs. Harper. How is your husband?"

"Well, thank you, Your Majesty. He has just departed for Sweden to meet with a man named Nobel, who has invented a safe explosive called dynamite."

"A safe explosive? Can there be such a thing? What is the purpose of this dynamite?"

"My husband believes it has good application for silver mining back in the United States."

Victoria shuddered. "Does your husband intend to bring this explosive to England?"

"I don't know whether—"

"One must think carefully about handling dangerous substances."

"Yes, my husband is—"

"You know, we have survived more than one assassination attempt. What if our attackers had access to this explosive you speak of? Why, we might be dead. Although we would then be lying peacefully next to Albert at Frogmore, away from the cares of ruling. . . ." The queen's gaze went to some unknown spot behind Violet.

The tufty-eared man cleared his throat, which brought the queen out of her reverie.

"What? Yes, yes. Mr. Gladstone, this is Mrs. Harper, the undertaker of whom we have spoken to you. Mrs. Harper, I'm sure you know of Mr. Gladstone as our prime minister."

"Mrs. Harper." Mr. Gladstone inclined his head toward Violet but did not move from his position. "The queen has told me of your work during the prince's funeral. Well done."

"Thank you, sir. It is an honor to meet you."

"Mrs. Harper, Mr. Gladstone, be seated." They each sat on matching chairs across from the queen's desk. The arms were covered by black velvet protectors edged in cream lace.

"I've asked you here, Mrs. Harper, to discuss how you are faring with the Raybourn family. As prime minister, Mr. Gladstone has an interest in our esteemed Lord Raybourn, too."

"Has Scotland Yard spoken to you?" Mr. Gladstone asked.

"Yes, sir."

"What is their assessment?"

"They believe it was probably suicide. Chief Inspector Hurst says they have leads to follow regarding Lord Raybourn's activities in Egypt."

A look that Violet couldn't begin to fathom passed between the queen and her prime minister.

"Very good," Gladstone said. "And so you have prepared Lord Raybourn, I presume?"

"Yes. I put a lock on his coffin, as well. You should know—"

"Have all the family arrived?"

"Yes, but the housekeeper—"

"What need was there for a lock?"

"His physical condition precluded viewing, in my professional opinion. Which leads me to—"

"Has anyone in the family insisted that the funeral proceed?"

The queen tapped her fingers on the desk. "Mr. Gladstone, it would seem Mrs. Harper has something important to say. Perhaps we should let her do so."

"Eh? Yes, yes, quite right, Your Majesty. What is it, Mrs. Harper?"

Violet explained that Mrs. Peet had been found hanging in the kitchen, and that she didn't believe the housekeeper had done it to herself, any more than Lord Raybourn had. Another strange look passed between Victoria and Gladstone.

"What was the family's reaction to the housekeeper's death?" Gladstone asked.

"They are shocked, of course. Mrs. Peet was a distant, impover-ished relative who had been running the household for many years. I also think it possible that she was having an affair with Lord Raybourn."

The queen put a hand to her chest. "Are you quite certain? That would have been scandalous on Lord Raybourn's part."

"I'm not entirely sure, of course, but I do believe it to be true."

"What has happened to our kingdom? We expect our trusted men to be beyond reproach. At least Lord Raybourn was widowed, but carrying on with his servant is so unseemly."

Violet doubted the queen was surrounded by many men who were beyond reproach.

"Yes, Your Majesty. If I may inquire, is there any impediment to proceeding with Mrs. Peet's funeral?"

"I shouldn't think so. What did the detectives say?"

"They believe her death to be a suicide, a response to her utter devastation over her employer's death. If you have no reason for Mrs. Peet to remain aboveground, I'd like to bury her, if it pleases Your Majesty. I've not embalmed her, so it is imperative that she be buried quickly."

"Yes, by all means, see the woman to her rest. Of course, she is a suicide, so she can't be buried in sacred ground. Were you plan-ning to put her in a pauper's section somewhere?"

"The family has agreed to inter her in their churchyard in Sussex."

Victoria shook her head. "We do not think it wise to allow the family members out of London for a funeral."

Violet blinked. *How am I supposed to explain this to the family?*

"But, Your Majesty . . ."

"Surely it is not that important that a housekeeper be buried on the family estate, is it? Tell them our gratitude in doing this small thing will be deep and unending."

"And what of Lord Raybourn . . . ?"

The queen shook her head again. "We are not yet satisfied with his situation. He is sufficiently preserved, is he not?"

"Yes, madam."

"Mr. Gladstone, perhaps it might be prudent for you to pay your respects to the family."

"I am yours to command, Your Majesty, but might it not be better to wait and see what our other sources have to say on the matter?"

"Perhaps you're right." The queen sighed. "It is so hard to know the right course sometimes. When our dear prince was with us, he always knew what to do. He would have been bold and confident in this situation, I am sure. Why must we go on alone? It is so unfair. We are singularly blessed, though, that everyone surrounding us continues in expressing their admiration and grief for the prince consort."

Gladstone shifted uncomfortably in his chair. "Yes, we all dwell on the prince's many remarkable qualities on a daily basis. Sometimes I am so overcome as to not realize that my valet hasn't remembered my armband."

"Perhaps you need a new valet. Our staff knows to lay out clothes for our dear Albert each day as though he had never gone. It is their homage to his memory. Mr. Gladstone, please leave us for a few moments. We wish to speak with Mrs. Harper alone."

Violet made a mental note to never enter the queen's presence again without wearing some piece of mourning wear, and prepared to be berated over it. What actually happened was even worse.

"We have arranged for you to visit our son at Marlborough House, Mrs. Harper. He is in receipt of a private message from us, indicating that you will be arriving this afternoon to question his activities while in Egypt."

"What activities, madam?"

"We wish to know what sort of devious involvements he may have had. How close to Lord Raybourn was he? Did Bertie share any secrets with Lord Raybourn or vice versa? Our son knew that Lord Raybourn was there at my behest, so it is possible that something untoward happened between them."

"Your Majesty, surely you aren't suggesting that the prince is responsible for—"

"No, no." The queen sighed again heavily. "Yet we are sure he was up to his typical failings. We need to be sure those failings didn't impact Lord Raybourn in any way."

With the undertaker gone, Victoria rang a bell to have Gladstone brought back to her presence.

"As I was saying before the undertaker's arrival, Your Majesty, it would appear that we have some blackmail on our hands."

"What? Did you say 'blackmail'? Who could possibly have reason to blackmail the Crown?"

"It isn't blackmail of the Crown itself, but of the Crown's interest. In order to meet the completion deadline later this year, corvée labor was quietly reinstituted last year. They were to do hand digging alongside all of the dredging equipment, in case any of the machinery broke. The project cannot withstand even a single day of idleness.

"Commissioner Henderson says that Monsieur de Lesseps has received several letters intimating that some person unknown will notify all of the British presses of the corvée labor being used, unless he is paid quite a substantial sum."

"Why don't they arrest the man?"

"He is keeping himself quite hidden. They believe he has genuine, firsthand knowledge of the corvée trade. See here."

Victoria took the message Gladstone held out to her. "Hmm, yes, we see. How very troublesome."

"Monsieur de Lesseps didn't want to bother Your Majesty with it directly, in case it could be handled discreetly without disturbing you."

"Yet here we are with the matter in our lap."

Beads of sweat accumulated on Gladstone's considerably wrinkled forehead. This was a delicate political nightmare for them both, but Victoria refused to perspire so heavily and obviously over it.

"The question is whether we should be personally involved or not."

"Begging Your Majesty's pardon, I have already requested that Scotland Yard contend with it. You can let the commissioner know that it is of utmost concern to you that the blackmailer be caught, but that you will let justice work on its own timetable. I will add a message to confirm that Parliament, too, will leave the work of finding this cretin to Scotland Yard."

"Pray it is soon. If word gets out that Britain is condoning the use of slaves when we just abolished the practice not forty years ago, well . . ." Victoria shuddered. "Maybe Monsieur de Lesseps and Isma'il Pasha have some sense about them and are providing the workers due compensation. We must not give more benefit to an anonymous blackmailer than to de Lesseps and the Egyptian viceroy without more facts."

"We could weather the storm, Your Majesty, but I agree—the sooner this is resolved without public knowledge, the better."

Victoria dismissed her prime minister and sat alone in the silence with her own thoughts. Was it a mere coincidence that her son was in Egypt just as this blackmailing scheme started? What might it have to do with Lord Raybourn's death?

What could she have Mrs. Harper discover, without the undertaker realizing she was doing it?

11

Violet returned to St. James's Palace, where she had a letter from her father awaiting her, which she read while sitting down to veal collops, boiled tomatoes, and spinach dressed with cream. What joy it was to have food simply appear like this. The letter expressed shock at learning from Sam that Lord Raybourn had been killed, and shared gossipy tidbits about the Fairmonts.

> There was always bad blood in the family. I remember great rows between Lord Raybourn's eldest son, Cedric, and the younger, Stephen. Lord Raybourn always tried to mediate between the two. The two boys each wanted what the other had, whether it be a toy or a favored word from their father. I never understood it, but then, I never had boys.
>
> Be careful of the younger sister, Eleanor. She fancied herself a journalist as a girl, but Lord Raybourn thwarted her, pushing her into marriage with a milksop. She and her husband were married by the time we came to the estate, but I remember His Lordship telling me of the arguments he would have with Eleanor when she returned for visits. I doubt she ever gave up her desire to be a newspaperwoman.
>
> Lord Raybourn was a kind employer, but he was

perpetually in a battle with some of his children. How fortunate I am in you, dear daughter.

Mother sends her love. With Samuel off to Sweden, I confess I am adrift without him. Almost wish I'd gone to Sweden with him to talk to that Nobel fellow, although I suppose your mother needs me. Never breathe a word of this to her, but lately I have been longing for my carefree bachelor days, not that I would trade her—or you—for the world. I would just like a few days without a carping convalescent.

Violet smiled as she folded the letter. How she would miss her parents when she returned to Colorado, although it would be good to get back to Susanna. To think that a bedraggled little orphan she'd found sleeping in a coffin eight years ago had become her apprentice, daughter, friend, and was now on the verge of transforming into a married woman.

Which reminded Violet that a critical question Sam should ask Benjamin Tompkins was whether he would object to Susanna continuing to work with Violet in her undertaking shop once they were wed. Violet could never agree to losing Susanna from the shop, unless Susanna actually wanted to leave.

A servant scratched at her door and entered at Violet's beckoning. As an experienced and dutiful palace worker, the man tried to keep his face bland as he notified Violet that the prince would now see her, but as she followed his gaze around the room, she realized why he seemed to be hiding a look of dyspepsia.

Violet's housekeeping skills were already on full display. Clothing lay scattered about as though intended for the dustbin, and her personal papers, books, and newspapers covered every available surface.

Perhaps he would think better of Violet if he knew that at least her cavernous undertaking bag, sitting proudly near her bed, was thoroughly organized. Every embalming fluid bottle, tinted skin cream jar, syringe, and cutting tool was ensconced where it belonged.

Or perhaps he wouldn't think better of her.

At least the poor fellow was unaware of the bottles of drained blood tucked deep inside the armoire. He might faint dead away.

"I am ready to escort you when you are ready, Mrs. Harper," he said stoically, before stepping outside to wait.

Violet had no idea what to wear to visit the Prince of Wales, who was a reputed connoisseur of feminine beauty and aesthetics. Perhaps she would command more respect if she wore her customary undertaker's garb. Yet, to do so might be offensive to the high-spirited prince.

In the end, she chose a dusky blue skirt and jacket edged in pearl gray. She hoped it conveyed confidence, and not the utter terror she felt.

Marlborough House, the Prince of Wales's residence in London, was directly across from St. James's Palace, but it may as well have been ten miles away, as long as the walk seemed to Violet.

The St. James's Palace servant handed her over to a Marlborough House servant, who took the letter of introduction the queen had written and escorted her inside.

Originally built for Sarah Churchill, the Duchess of Marlborough, the residence had been renovated over the past decade to suit the entertaining style of the Prince of Wales and his wife, having gained another full story and reputedly a new range of rooms on the building's north side.

The home wasn't nearly as imposing as Windsor, yet Violet had never been more intimidated. She drew a deep breath for courage as she stood in the massive, gray-veined marble foyer, and she could smell the distant notes of sawn wood, glues, and the peculiar odor of freshly unrolled Turkish carpets.

One of those carpets lined a wide staircase of matching marble tile leading up five steps to some sort of gilded, over-tapestried salon beyond it.

Another liveried servant came to escort her through a series of tall paneled doors, finally arriving in a drawing room wallpapered, carpeted, and draperied in apple green. Seated on a cream-colored damask settee was Albert Edward, the Prince of Wales. For all of his reputation as a great lover of women, he was not particularly handsome, with the same protruding eyes he shared with his mother.

On a nearby chair covered with pale stripes sat a beautiful, reserved woman of maybe twenty-five years. This must be the Princess of Wales, Alexandra of Denmark. The princess smiled so warmly in greeting at seeing Violet that all of the undertaker's butterflies fluttered away.

The prince, however, scowled as Violet rose from her curtsy. "My mother sent you?" he asked without preamble.

"Yes, Your Highness."

"Were you responsible for this?" He removed a folded paper from underneath a lamp on the table next to him.

"I'm sorry, Your Highness, I don't know what that is."

His expression stated quite plainly that he didn't believe her.

"This is my mother's wish—excuse me, command—that I not only entertain you, but that I make haste to Raybourn House as quickly as possible to pay my respects over that wretched man's death. Why would the queen berate me over someone so inconsequential?"

"He is a peer. . . ."

"Yes, yes, I realize that. But she doesn't send me roving about to visit every deceased peer's home as though I might bring them back to life."

"Sir, I had nothing to do with Her Majesty's desire for you to visit Raybourn House. I am merely here upon her wishes."

"To interrogate me?"

"No, simply to ask you a few questions." Good Lord, in her anxiety, Violet had forgotten to develop a list of questions. The butterflies angrily beat their way back into her stomach.

"Who are you, exactly, Mrs. Harper? Why does my mother regard you so highly that she sends you in to question me?"

Violet folded her hands in front of her, hoping it looked meek and submissive.

"I am an undertaker, Your Highness, and I—"

"An undertaker?" The prince nearly exploded out of his seat. As it was, his eyes were bulging even more than before. "The queen not only distrusts me so much that she has me secretly interrogated, but she also despises me enough that she sends in one of these black crows that pick corpses clean of money, valuables, and dignity?"

Princess Alexandra moved to the settee and placed a hand over her husband's, speaking in a soothing voice. "Bertie, my love, please calm down before *you* need Mrs. Harper's services. I don't think she wishes you ill. She looks harmless enough, doesn't she? In fact, she seems quite kind. Why don't we see what she has to tell us?"

Albert grunted but relented. "I suppose you're right, Alix. How much harm can a woman do? Go on, Mrs. Harper, tell me more about why my mother feels it necessary to persecute me."

"Your Highness, I am merely an undertaker, but I was present for your esteemed father's funeral. I believe the queen trusts me for discretion because of my work with the prince consort, and she merely seeks a quiet resolution to what may have happened to Lord Raybourn."

The prince leaned forward, staring intently at Violet. The stale smell of tobacco floated forward with him.

"Wait, I do believe I remember you. You yelled at all of the mourners as we gathered up for the march down to Windsor Chapel." He sat back again, a smile flitting across his face. "You grabbed my walking stick and pounded it on the floor for attention."

Violet reddened. "I can be bold where propriety and the outcome of a funeral are concerned, sir."

"A dark day my father's funeral was. Nothing has been the same since. Mother has practically abdicated the throne, except for special little projects that interest her. She blames me for his death still, you know. Says he would never have been sick and died if he hadn't visited me at Cambridge in the rain a few weeks before he died. Doctors say it's rubbish; my father was ill long before that. But Mother insists it was his rush to see me and chastise me for what she called infantile behavior that did him in."

"I am sorry for your loss, Your Highness."

The princess reached over for her husband's hand again. "Mrs. Harper doesn't blame you for it, though."

"No, I suppose she cannot. His death was a tidy bit of business for her. It's the journalists, priests, and undertakers who profit the most from tragedy, isn't it? You had the great fortune not to be present for my father's funeral, Alix. If you think the queen is absorbed in her grief now, you should have seen her eight years ago."

"But we were married less than two years later, remember? I do recall how very . . . somber . . . things were." The princess smiled again at Violet. "Mrs. Harper, please forgive my husband's ill temper. There has been so much sadness in the family and the prince now wants only to immerse himself in pleasure so that he isn't reminded of his sorrows."

The prince's eyes were full of affection for his wife. "You understand me well, Alix. Unlike my mother."

"But we must be patient, right, my love? The queen will eventually come around. In the meantime, it is an easy thing to please her by entertaining Mrs. Harper's questions."

The princess was a born diplomat. Violet's admiration for the woman was deepening by the second.

"I suppose you're right." Albert leaned back on the settee and sighed heavily. "All right, undertaker, what do you wish to know about the cursed Lord Raybourn?"

Indeed what *did* Violet wish to know? What would Inspector Hurst ask first?

"So Lord Raybourn was a member of your entourage to Egypt?"

"Yes. My mother added him for her own purposes. Surely you already know that."

"Right. Of course. Did you spend much time with the viscount?"

"As little as possible. He was a stuffed old prig, really. Rarely joined in on fun and entertainments. Raybourn said he was there to negotiate the opening ceremonies of the Suez Canal with the Egyptian viceroy, but those negotiations took an extraordinarily long time. Frankly, Mrs. Harper, I think he had some other scheme. Perhaps something illegal or unsavory. I'm guessing my mother would be disgusted by him if she knew the truth. Alix, a smoke, please."

Alexandra rose and crossed the room to a table beneath a large pastoral painting of Sarah Churchill wearing a flowing red dress. As graceful as Marlborough House's original owner looked in the painting, the princess held herself with much more poise.

Violet watched as Alix pulled several selections from an inlaid mahogany tobacco box. The princess then went to the ornately carved fireplace mantel between two windows of the room, and lifted an odd glass cylinder with a metal top from the mantel. It was as Alix was returning to the prince that Violet observed what she'd originally thought was an old pianoforte in a corner, except that it wasn't at the right height. In fact, it almost looked, well, like a coffin on a table.

"Your Highness, is that a musical instrument you've picked up on your travels?"

"What? Oh, not quite, Mrs. Harper, although it is certainly a souvenir from my time in Egypt. Would you like to see?"

She followed him to the oblong box, which contained . . . it couldn't be.

"What do you think?" he asked.

"Is this a human form carved of wood?"

The prince laughed for the first time. "No, it is actually a human. They are the remains of some ancient Egyptian, mummified thousands of years ago, but without his linen wrappings, which we removed."

Violet's butterfly wings were beating rapidly again. "You removed his wrappings, sir?"

"Yes, it was great fun. Several members of my traveling party uncovered gold trinkets and statues from the wrappings, and I won the body itself. Makes a striking piece for this drawing room, doesn't it?"

Violet had to sit down, lest she be ill. "Yes, Your Highness. Will he be buried?"

"No. Once I tire of him, I'll send him off to the British Museum. I considered giving him to my mother, but I don't think she'd appreciate him." The prince lifted the glass cylinder to his cigar, and flicked a metal lever on top of the jar. Almost instantly, a jet flame hurtled from a tiny nozzle next to the lever. Violet jumped and reflexively let out a squeal.

"Sorry, dear lady. This is my Döbereiner's lamp. Amazing what a little zinc metal and sulfuric acid can combine to do. Some say it isn't safe because it's a hydrogen flame, but it is certainly memorable."

Alexandra returned the lamp to the mantel and went back to the settee, but Violet wasn't finished with the mummy, despite her wildly beating heart. "Your Highness, doesn't this man or woman deserve a decent Christian burial?"

Albert drew deeply on his cigar and blew upward. "He perished thousands of years before Christianity, but I imagine he already had a decent burial, full of fanfare and ritualistic nonsense. For all we know, he spent thousands of years in a pyramid, surrounded by servants and all the comforts of life. Quite decent, wouldn't you say?"

"Except that now he is quite exposed and in a most undignified position."

The prince blew another cloud of smoke up toward the plastered ceiling. "Mrs. Harper, are you here to ask questions or to critique my antiquities collection?"

"My apologies, Your Highness." Violet followed Albert as he returned to his place next to Alix. She tried furiously not to think about the mummy but to concentrate on questions.

"So Lord Raybourn was in Egypt to negotiate opening ceremonies, but you think he may have been there for some other reason. Do you have any idea what else he may have been doing?"

"He spent almost all of his time with Isma'il Pasha, the viceroy. It is my belief that they were concocting something having to do with the canal that was outside of the opening festivities."

"Was Monsieur de Lesseps a part of these discussions?"

"Not that I could tell. Alix, did you ever see de Lesseps join them?"

The princess shook her head. "Never."

"Other than going behind closed doors with the viceroy, did he exhibit any other peculiar behavior?"

The prince considered this. "He always seemed to have a telegram to dash off to someone. At first I assumed it was a steady stream of reports to my mother about me, but now I'm not so sure."

Whom could Lord Raybourn have been contacting, and about

what? Names flitted through Violet's mind: Mrs. Peet, Stephen, the queen. He could have had any number of reasons to send messages to any of them. But constantly?

"Did Lord Raybourn have his cook and valet with him?"

"Yes. Madame Brusse was practically a third arm to him. He would eat no local cuisine. He even refused the roasted, stuffed pigeons we were offered at the viceroy's palace, insisting that only Madame Brusse could prepare his food. The viceroy was offended, but said nothing. Raybourn missed out on a divine dish, not to mention the grilled eggplant and *roz moammar*. Remember, Alix? That divine rice cooked in cream?" The prince patted his stomach at the memory.

He was not yet thirty years old, but already suggesting a future paunch, unlike Alix, who was thin and corseted to the point of rib breakage.

Why would a British diplomat sent to negotiate with an Egyptian diplomat be so offensive as to refuse to eat in the Egyptian's own residence?

"Is it possible that Lord Raybourn was fearful of being poisoned?"

Albert shrugged. "Why would anyone bother to poison him? He was bound to expire from his own tediousness at some point."

If the viscount feared being poisoned, he clearly had that fear before leaving London, hence why he took his own private cook with him. Any aristocrat might take a valet along to assist with shaving, dressing, and undressing, but a cook was more unusual.

"Did Lord Raybourn split off from your party once you arrived back at Dover? Or were you on the same train together for part of your return to London?"

Albert looked at her incredulously. "Are you suggesting that I should have kept notes on what any of dozens of people were doing when they debarked the ship?"

"No, no, of course not." What a muddle Violet was making of this. "So Lord Raybourn came back with you via ship, but you don't know what happened to him once you docked."

"I didn't say that at all. I have no idea whether he was on the ship. We also had port calls in Constantinople, the Crimea, and

Athens. He could have debarked at any of these places and not re-turned. As I said, Mrs. Harper, I was not conducting an inventory of who sailed with us, and spent much of my time in my private cabin with my wife. Isn't that right, dear?"

Alix nodded in agreement, self-consciously putting a hand to her own stomach.

"I guess all we really know is that Lord Raybourn returned to London, died almost immediately upon his return, and neither his cook nor his valet were with him," Violet said.

"Unless one of them helped to dispatch him," Albert replied.

And, as with any of the other members of Lord Raybourn's household, what reason could they have possibly had for doing so? Why would either of them want to see Mrs. Peet dead?

Every time Violet thought about things, she got more twisted than a knot of black bunting.

When she took her leave of the royal couple, the princess fol-lowed her down the hall, both pairs of their shoes clacking along the black-and-white-tiled hallways. "Mrs. Harper, I hope you don't think too poorly of the prince. He has been suffering from undue pressures."

"No, Your Highness, I don't."

"I do hope you will inform Her Majesty that he was most coop-erative with you. You see, I want nothing more than peace in the family, for this and future generations. It is most important to me. Do you understand?" She lightly patted her stomach again.

"Your Highness, I understand you perfectly."

12

Will and Harry delivered Mrs. Peet's coffin the next morning through the servants' entrance, helped Violet transfer the woman into the coffin, then placed the coffin back onto the table. Violet directed that the coffin remain down in the relative ignominy of the kitchens, as it would never be appropriate for a servant's corpse to share space with her aristocratic employer's.

Violet propped the coffin lid open and picked out some dying stems from Rebecca's posy, ensuring it still looked fresh.

Will and Harry headed back out, but a few moments later, a rapping at the door revealed that Will had returned.

"Did you forget something?" Violet asked.

"No," he said, removing his tall hat and tapping it against his thigh. "I was just, ah, wondering if you might—might possibly . . ."

"Will, what's wrong?"

"It's my Lydia, you see. She's threatening to move back with her parents if I don't do something."

"About your profession, you mean?"

"Yes. She says she wants me to do something more respectable."

"A common grievance about our business. But she knew you were an undertaker when she met you."

Will cast his eyes down and brushed away invisible lint from his trousers. "Yes, but I think she always had designs on fixing that problem."

"I see." Violet shuddered to think of Sam preventing her from doing her life's calling. "What is it you want me to do?"

"I was just wondering if . . ." The man looked pained.

"Speak plainly, Will."

"I thought perhaps you might like to buy me back out of Morgan Undertaking."

"What? I'll be leaving London for Colorado as soon as these two burials are finished. What use do I have for an undertaking shop here?"

"Do you really think the queen will let you leave? There's no real reason for her to keep you here to attend to Lord Raybourn's funeral. Any number of competent undertakers could have been dispatched—including the royal one if she was so concerned—yet she pulls you from your mother's deathbed for it. Imagine how many dozens of funerals will be lined up for you outside Windsor as soon as you're done here, each one an opportunity for the queen to discuss her darling Albert's own service with you."

"Will! We shouldn't talk about the queen that way."

"Yet you don't deny it."

"I merely haven't thought about it. It's a silly notion."

"Is it?" Will put his hat back on his head and a hand on the door latch. "Promise to consider it, Mrs. Harper? I'll give you very favorable terms."

"But I won't be staying—"

The door clicked shut behind him, leaving Violet alone with Mrs. Peet once more.

She decided to check on Lord Raybourn's flowers and the ice chest before leaving. The chest would need draining and refilling with ice soon. Except for Toby, the entire family was gathered in the drawing room talking, and Violet was obviously interrupting.

"My apologies, I just wanted to remove any wilted stems . . ."

"Go ahead," Stephen said. "We were just noticing the undertaking wagon driving away. I presume Mrs. Peet is taken care of?"

"Yes, her coffin is open downstairs if you'd like to see her."

The look of distaste that passed across everyone's face provided a stark answer. Violet plucked a drooping lily from one of the pots surrounding the coffin. The room was utterly silent except for what she was doing and she felt all eyes upon her as if she were an intruder.

Turning back to the group, she said, "The queen has approved Mrs. Peet's burial, so I recommend that we plan to inter her tomorrow at Highgate Cemetery."

"Right charitable of Her Majesty to let us bury our own servant," Dorothy said.

Violet ignored her. "Was she Anglican or Nonconformist?"

"Anglican, I'm sure. But wait, I thought we were going to bury her back in Sussex," Stephen said.

"The queen wishes that everyone stay in London while the investigation of Lord Raybourn's death proceeds."

The room erupted in protest, with Dorothy leading the charge of disparaging comments toward Queen Victoria.

This was familiar territory for Violet, who was used to families squabbling over funereal details. She moved to a section of floor not covered by carpet and sharply rapped her leather-covered heel on it twice.

"Since Mrs. Peet doesn't seem to have any relatives beyond who sits in this room, I see no need to delay. I'll visit the cemetery director this afternoon and arrange to have space made for her in the Anglican section. He need not know she was under suspicion of suicide, which would complicate her ability to be buried there. A modest gray obelisk gravestone would be appropriate, I think. May I assume you wish a direct routing to Highgate?"

Her command of the situation had the desired effect. Everyone's head turned to her as the authority on the matter. Mrs. Peet was, after all, just a servant, and not a popular one at that.

"Yes," Stephen said. "We've already got embarrassment enough, what with Father staged here indefinitely and two detectives wandering about at all hours. Too bad we can't bury the woman in the dead of night. Pardon the pun."

In fact, might it not show Mrs. Peet a modicum of respect *not* to be dragged through the streets like a show animal on parade for curiosity seekers to gawp at?

Violet pursed her lips. "We could perhaps do this discreetly."

                        *   *   *

With the family's approval, Violet coordinated a midnight burial, even enlisting Hurst and Pratt to assist, along with Will and
Harry, in stealthily removing Mrs. Peet's coffin under cover of
night, carrying her out the door feetfirst—an old custom intended
to ensure the deceased's spirit did not look back into the house
and beckon another family member—loading her onto a hearse,
and paying the cemetery director and a minister extra to do their
part via the light of lanterns in a consecrated section of the cemetery. Soon Mrs. Peet disappeared into one of many two-foot-by-
six-foot openings in the ground, with Stephen, Gordon, and Toby
the only mourners present. None of the family shed tears at her
departure.

That left just Lord Raybourn in earthly purgatory.

The next morning, Violet stopped by Mary Cooke's dress shop
to pick up the Fairmont women's black dresses, gloves, fans, and
hats. How would she ever manage to carry it all back to Park
Street? She stopped worrying about it as she took a closer look at
her friend's face. Mary's eyes were swollen, and she unsuccessfully
blinked back tears.

"What has happened?" Violet asked, taking her friend's hand.

"It's George. I am such an old fool," Mary said.

"Is he gone again?"

"Yes, he said he was off to Switzerland to buy watch parts, but
I'm not so sure. Couldn't he just order them, as I do fabric? Why
must he leave the country?"

An excellent question.

"Did he say when he would return?"

"A few weeks. Does it take so very long to buy gears and
springs?"

"Perhaps there is a special supplier there that he wants to meet
with. We need to get your mind off of this. Why don't we go to
Hyde Park tomorrow? We can stroll or maybe row out on the lake.
After all, I won't be in London much longer."

Mary's face cleared. "What a lovely idea; let's do it."

With a plan to meet at the park the next day, Violet took the clothing, carefully laid flat in muslin bags, to the Fairmont home. She noticed a piece of bunting dangling loosely from one of the windows and made a mental note to ask Harry to come by and reattach it to the sill.

She was greeted at the door by a nervous, garishly red-haired young woman in a maid's uniform. Her left eye wandered back and forth as she spoke.

"Louisa, from Mrs. Hill's agency," the maid said in response to Violet's inquiry as she took the bags from Violet's hands. Her tone implied she was not happy with her assignment with the Fairmont family.

Violet waited in the drawing room with Lord Raybourn while Louisa notified the family of her presence. Dorothy came down to meet her. Taking in the stack of mourning clothing and accoutrements, Stephen's sister said, "I doubt our mourning will be all that serious."

Before Violet could respond, the maid admitted another visitor up to the drawing room. Violet and Dorothy stood together, blocking the view of the coffin.

"Miss Fairmont, 'tis Ellis Catesby to see you, from *The Times*." Louisa bobbed and disappeared down the hall.

Standing before them was a middle-aged man in a rumpled suit, with bloodshot eyes. His fingers were even more ink-stained than Mr. Pratt's. Violet's initial thought was the man was a drunkard, but she quickly realized he was someone who probably never slept. Mr. Catesby looked pointedly around them at the coffin.

Dorothy's eyes narrowed. "What may I do for you, Mr. Catesby?"

"I'll only take a moment of your time, Miss Fairmont. And your name, Miss—?"

Violet looked to Dorothy, who replied, "This is Mrs. Harper, our undertaker."

"Ah, indeed, indeed." Catesby took a worn notebook from his jacket and scribbled away in it. "Important to have the family bonemaster about in times like these, eh?"

Dorothy drew herself to full aristocratic imperiousness. "Times like what, exactly, Mr. Catesby?"

"Times of grief and sorrow. Made worse with all of the gossip."

"What sort of gossip?"

"About Lord Raybourn's . . . misfortune, of course. I have it on good authority that he was murdered by his housekeeper." Catesby tapped the side of his nose.

"Who, exactly, told you such a thing?" Dorothy looked like a volcano spewing ash in anticipation of a full-blown eruption.

"Can't reveal my sources, now, can I, Miss Fairmont?"

"What tangle of foolishness is this, Mr. Catesby?"

"We're preparing a special story on Lord Raybourn. It's going to outsell any story we've done thus far this year. A peer attacked by his servant—imagine the sensation it will be! I'm surprised the story has stayed so quiet, what with all the black crape on the house practically announcing it. This will make me famous."

"I hardly think that it is our responsibility to feed the newspaper's scandal furnace, much less to make you famous. What do you want with us? I've a mind to call the police."

"Apologies, apologies. It's in the family's best interest that I'm here, to make sure I tell your side of the story."

"Our side?" Molten lava was making its way to the surface. Perhaps it was best if Violet intervened.

"Mr. Catesby, the family is under a great deal of duress, as I'm sure you realize. I suggest you wait until after—"

"Ellis!" Nelly Bishop glided down the stairs in a dark blue gown, a stark contrast to the animated expression she wore. Her leathery face was magically transformed into something almost resembling joy. "I thought I heard a familiar voice. I've not seen you since . . . since a long time ago."

"But you—"

"So sorry you are seeing us in such a state of unhappiness. What brings you here?" Nelly smoothed her skirts before offering Catesby her hand. What was turning this Fairmont sister into such a coquette?

The reporter bent over Nelly's hand, then held up his notebook. "I've been assigned to report on your father's death, may God rest his soul. The tittle-tattle is that he was cheating at faro and was murdered by the injured party in the card game—scandalously, his servant. I thought it might be best to hear the family's side of things."

"Pure nonsense, you can be sure, Mr. Catesby. My father was a pillar of society, a regular Greek column—you can quote me on that—and would never stoop to such a thing."

"Of course, of course. After all, look at his lovely daughter. Only a man of impeccable standards would have raised such a vision of perfection."

"The years have not tempered your gift of flattery, have they? Very well, you should know the truth of things. I'll spare my sister the inconvenience and grant you an interview myself. Won't you join me upstairs?"

The reporter eagerly followed Nelly out of the room. Dorothy's face was so mottled that Violet feared she would soon be preparing another body. With only a muttered, "My sister will ruin us all," Dorothy thanked Violet for delivering the mourning clothing and showed her out.

As Violet stepped into the street, she was accosted by a tall, lanky man of indeterminate age who looked malnourished, as if he'd been living in the streets or in a workhouse for some time.

"You a member of that family?" he asked as he grabbed her elbow, nodding his head at the Fairmont home. His breath reeked of liquor.

Violet wrenched out of his grasp. "How dare you touch me and inquire about my business?"

"Miss, if you belong to that family, your business is my business. Who are you? One of the sisters?"

"Who are *you*, may I ask? Other than a complete stranger to me." She saw his dark eyes for the first time, which gazed at her with an intensity that may have been hatred or desire, it was impossible to fathom.

"I'm a friend of the family. I need to know if the new Lord Raybourn is home."

"He is not, although I don't see how it is a concern of yours." Violet marched off toward the omnibus stop, but the man pursued her.

"I need to speak with him, but without anyone around. Tell him James is staying at the Tavistock Hotel."

"Leave me be," Violet said, running the last few steps to the omnibus, which had just drawn up and was ejecting passengers.

She had planned on returning to her lodgings at the palace, but perhaps it might be wise to stop at Scotland Yard first to talk to the detectives about recent events.

Irritated that Hurst dismissed her encounter in the street as the work of a random drunkard, Violet returned to St. James's Palace to rest. An envelope covered in Sam's familiar scrawl awaited her. How had he managed to get a letter to her so quickly? She tore it open with eager hands.

> *Ulvhälls Herrgård*
> *Strängnäs, Sweden*
> *Sweetheart,*
> *I am safe in Strängnäs, a short train ride from*
> *Stockholm, despite a torturous trip—didn't we just*
> *complete one calamitous sea voyage not long ago?—yet*
> *found myself so anxious to meet with Mr. Nobel that I*
> *hardly took the time to change my clothes at the hotel before*
> *heading to his residence.*
> *I already find the man fascinating.*
> *He has studied in both Paris and the United States,*
> *even collaborating with John Ericsson, who designed USS*
> Monitor.

How well Violet remembered that ship, whose captain had intercepted her first husband's ship during the Northern blockade of the Southern states.

> *His family owned an armaments factory for some*
> *years, and provided armaments for the Crimean War, but*
> *went bankrupt later. Nobel subsequently devoted himself to*
> *the study of explosives, especially nitroglycerine. He*
> *developed a detonator in 1863 and a blasting cap in*
> *1865. He is really quite brilliant.*
> *He performs his experiments aboard a barge on Lake*

*Mälaren, so as not to destroy any nearby property should
an experiment go awry.
    Unfortunately, his brother Emil was killed in a
nitroglycerine explosion a handful of years ago in 1864.*

How dangerous was this substance, then? Was Sam considering
investing in something that might kill him? Violet couldn't bear
the thought of losing him.

*Nobel is committed to his life's work, though, and has
relentlessly pursued it. As I mentioned before, he has
invented an explosive called dynamite. He mixes
nitroglycerine with silica to make it, then adds one of his
blasting caps so that the dynamite can be more safely
detonated by lighting a fuse. Tomorrow he will take me to
his newest factory to demonstrate how it works. He assures
me that it will easily blast through many layers of rock.
There are many exciting possibilities with Nobel's
invention, and I plan to be in front of it all, dearest wife.*

Violet rubbed her forehead. What was Sam getting into? It was
no use worrying about him, for there was nothing she could do except get Lord Raybourn into the ground as soon as possible. She
wrote back to Sam, giving sketchy details about the ongoing investigation into the viscount's death and the new tragedy of the
housekeeper. She omitted any mention of the man in the street, to
keep Sam from worrying.

Violet was worried enough for them both.

To occupy herself with something else, she firmly affixed a bonnet to her head and walked six blocks to a bookshop. She wandered
pleasantly about the shop for nearly an hour, before finally settling
on a book of memoirs by Mr. Barnum, the American circus man.

This should relieve her mind of her troubles, for a short while,
anyway.

"Your Majesty." The servant bowed as he offered the queen a
silver salver with a folded note on it.

Queen Victoria took the note and nodded, the signal for the man to depart, before opening it.

> *Have conducted search that you requested.*
> *Identification made and package to be sent from Egypt as*
> *quickly as possible. Await your direction on notifications*
> *to be made.*

The queen tossed the note into the fireplace grate, where it would be incinerated when the evening's fire was lit. The situation was just as she thought it was.

No notifications would be made. This was information Victoria would keep to herself for the moment.

13

The following morning, Violet returned to Park Street to tell Stephen of her encounter with the man outside his home. She was greeted again by an ashen-faced Louisa, whose eye was roving back and forth frantically, and found the family already in a major uproar in the drawing room. Toby sat in a chair, studiously examining his nails, while his parents, Dorothy, Stephen, and Katherine stood in a loosely formed circle, like bare-knuckle fighters each waiting for a chance to hit an opponent.

"... did this deliberately, knowing the shame it would bring upon us. How dare you revel in such tripe?" Stephen threw a newspaper to the ground.

"I say, that's no way to talk to my wife," Gordon said, reaching for Nelly's hand. Nelly disengaged from his fingers and fussed with the sleeve at her other wrist, arranging a black handkerchief that was peeking past the end of her sleeve.

"I did nothing deliberately. In fact, I did nothing at all," she said.

"Isn't it just like you to present yourself as the perfect princess?" Dorothy said. "You forget that I saw you escort that reporter upstairs to your room to give him a private interview. His lurid 'facts' in this story could have only come from you. Ah, here is Mrs. Harper. She witnessed your wantonness, too."

Violet wondered if she looked as pale as Gordon Bishop did at the moment. Toby looked up from where he was seated and gave her a lopsided, see-what-I'm-enduring grin before returning to his fingernail analysis.

"Good morning, Lord and Lady Raybourn, Mr. and Mrs. Bishop, Miss Fairmont, Toby. I've come to see Lord Raybourn, but can see that I am interrupting—"

"Not at all. You can testify to what I just said. Tell them you saw Nelly take that reporter, that Mr. Catesby, upstairs to dazzle him with concocted stories." Dorothy was nearly cackling over the joy of her revelation.

Violet picked up the newspaper.

VISCOUNT RAYBOURN BRUTALLY SLAIN IN MAYFAIR!!

By Ellis J. Catesby

Anthony Fairmont, the Viscount Raybourn, has been viciously murdered in his London residence. Shot in the head by one of his own pistols, he was discovered at the bottom of the first-floor staircase by his devoted housekeeper, Mrs. Harriet Peet.

Devoted to her employer in many ways, it would seem. The Times has learned from an exclusive source that Mrs. Peet had an intimate relationship that surpassed that of master-servant. Such was the power of their love that mere days after Lord Raybourn's murder, Mrs. Peet hanged herself in the basement, leaving behind a note explaining her anguish over losing her secret lover.

Violet looked up at Stephen. "What note?"

"Pure literary license by the reporter. Or by my dear sister."

Nelly stamped a foot in anger. "I said only the most innocuous things to Ellis. He would never betray me."

"You shouldn't have said anything worth betraying," he replied.
"I didn't. He is . . . embellishing the facts."
Violet continued reading.

> Her lamentations are surely shared by the vis-
> count's remaining family, although a constant
> vigil on their Park Street address has revealed
> little activity of note, save the comings and go-
> ings of two inspector detectives and a lady
> undertaker.
> This raises questions. Why so much police
> investigation at the Raybourn home unless they
> suspect a household member of having shot
> Lord Raybourn? Why have they not made an ar-
> rest? And of what need is the constant atten-
> dance of the undertaker? Why has there been
> no funeral held for either Lord Raybourn or
> Mrs. Peet?
> Our source confides that the housekeeper
> may have discovered something about her
> beloved master that sent her into an uncontrol-
> lable rage against him, and her suicide was the
> result of her subsequent regret.
> Are there other dark secrets hidden in the re-
> cesses of Raybourn House's finely carpeted
> drawing room and its walnut-paneled study?
> Be assured, this reporter will continue to keep
> a watchful eye on developing events.

"I see," she said, carefully folding the newspaper so that the
headline was hidden inside before handing it to Stephen. "Journalists need to sell newspapers, of course. I've read many a dis-
torted account of funerals I've managed. When my first husband
died as the result of very bad judgment on his part, the papers
went wild accusing me of all sorts of improprieties and conspira-
cies on his behalf. Assuredly, they will eventually tire of it and
move on to other more sensational topics."

"Thank you for the encouragement, Violet, but you must understand that my father was a peer. Such stories can ruin a family's good name permanently. It is no one's business what sordid past he may have had. My sister exercised very poor judgment with that reporter."

"Stephen! I did not—"

"Oh, Nelly, of course you did," Dorothy said. "You've always sought to be at the center of the universe, haven't you? You even found a way to use Father's death to your advantage."

"Now, Dorothy, you needn't be jealous of my wife." Gordon tried unsuccessfully again to reach for his wife, who deftly stepped aside and yanked the newspaper away from Stephen.

"Of course she should," Nelly said, her voice dripping with hatred. "Hasn't she always resented me as the more successful of us two? After all, I am married and have a son, not to mention that I don't look as though I have drunk too much sour milk."

This familial clash had to stop lest they destroy themselves before the newspapers had a chance to do it.

"Pardon me, Stephen, but I came by to tell you about a disturbing incident that happened to me when I left yesterday," Violet said.

This got everyone's attention.

"A man grabbed me in the street and wanted to know if the new Lord Raybourn was home. I confirmed nothing. He said to tell you that James is staying at the Tavistock Hotel."

"James?" Stephen said. "Did he leave a last name?"

"No."

"Do any of you know this James?" Stephen's family responded to him with looks of puzzlement.

"Toby, is this one of your friends playing a prank?"

"Why would one of my friends wish to accost an undertaker? Seems like awfully bad luck to do such a thing. She might smother you in a winding sheet while you sleep or nail you shut in a coffin."

"Toby, darling, please. Not everyone is able to understand your clever wit," Nelly said.

Toby shrugged and went back to his nails.

"Did he say anything else, Violet?" Stephen asked.

"No, although I didn't quite stay around to have him abuse me further."

"No, of course not. I suppose we should have Inspector Hurst call around so you can tell him about it." Before Violet could protest, Stephen rang a bell and Louisa appeared. He asked her to make tea for the assembled group and then fetch the detective from Scotland Yard.

Once again, Toby found an opportunity to slip out without stating where he was going.

Violet had little time to ponder Toby's whereabouts or the Fairmont family discord, for soon there was a commotion outside that demanded everyone's attention. They all crowded at the window to see a large carriage, emblazoned with the royal coat of arms and pulled by four horses wearing red plumes, clattering to a stop in front of Raybourn House and people out in the street gathering around to see who would emerge from it. The liveried driver sat stoically up front, atop a gold-fringed red cloth covering his seat.

Violet was unsurprised to see Albert Edward step onto the red velvet steps the footman extended out from under the carriage. The prince's bored expression was obvious.

"I can hardly believe my eyes," Stephen said.

As the prince leisurely made his way to the front door with his walking stick, acknowledging the accolades of people in the street, the family members hastily arranged themselves, while the maid furiously plumped pillows and straightened pictures before fleeing to the entry door to await His Highness.

Violet was certain the girl was trembling at the thought of encountering the heir to the throne of England.

Violet quickly inspected Lord Raybourn's flowers and blew across the top of his coffin to eliminate what few dust particles were there. "I'll go upstairs, then," she told Stephen.

"No need. The prince knows you now, doesn't he? Might as well stay."

The prince entered grandly, as princes do. He didn't carry the air of authority that his father had, but then, Albert Edward did not share any royal duties with Queen Victoria.

Violet, Katherine, Nelly, and Dorothy all swept into curtsies, while the men bowed. Once introductions were made, Albert Edward stated the intent of his visit.

"I wish to extend my sympathies to the family over your father's death." He nodded toward the coffin. "May he rest in peace and may you all be succored and strengthened."

"We are grateful for your visit, Your Highness," Stephen said. "May we offer you some spirits? Perhaps a glass of brandy?"

"Ah, no, I cannot stay. Important meetings to attend, you see."

"Of course, Your Highness. Very understandable."

Gordon brought forth his cigarette case, and Nelly whispered harshly under her breath at him. Chastened, he started to put the case back in his jacket, but the prince stopped him. "Are those from Fribourg and Treyer?"

"Quite right, sir. Would you like one?"

The prince's bored expression was replaced with desire. "Don't mind if I do. Perhaps a drop of brandy *is* in order, Raybourn."

Stephen nodded to the women. "Ladies, if you don't mind . . ."

It was their cue to exit and leave the menfolk alone. Violet was surprised when Nelly invited her to join the others in her room to visit. However, they were in the room mere seconds before Nelly suggested creeping back down the stairs to listen to the conversation.

"That would be eavesdropping," Dorothy said.

Nelly rolled her eyes. "Of course it would. I have to make sure Gordon doesn't say something ridiculous. Besides, we have the Prince of Wales in our home and I am not about to stay in my room and miss anything."

The women moved slowly down the stairs, going as far as they could without being seen. Each sat on her own stair, with Nelly leaning forward eagerly to listen and Dorothy frowning in disapproval.

"This just isn't done," she whispered to her sister.

"Hush, I can't hear," Nelly replied, waving Dorothy away.

Katherine shot Violet a worried look. Violet shared her apprehension over what they were doing.

As they settled down, male conversation drifted up to them. Violet imagined the men were seated by now, with the prince facing away from the coffin.

". . . honor you have done to this family. We have avoided society condolence visits as much as possible, but we happily welcome Your Highness's visit."

"Yes, well, your father was naturally an esteemed member of our expedition. Quite helpful with the local government. Tragic about his death. The Princess of Wales is quite devastated, too, and asked me to send along her regards. I've hardly slept since finding out."

"So very kind of you, Your Highness."

"Yes, a true diplomat. Many a time did I seek his advice."

Now it was Violet's turn to roll her eyes. The men lowered their voices and it was difficult to hear anything until Gordon asked a question.

"Scotland Yard thinks my father-in-law's death was at his own hand, but that doesn't seem quite right, does it? Yet, it's quite puzzling to us as to who may have wanted him dead."

"Idiot," Nelly hissed. "Speaking to the prince of such things."

"Perhaps an Egyptian followed him back to London, Mr.—Bishop, is it? Yes, I'll have another." There was rustling and the sound of a match flaring. "He ruffled more than a few feathers while he was there."

"How so, Your Highness?" Stephen asked.

The prince exhaled loudly. "Not intentionally, mind you. But he was a very . . . curious man. Always questioning what others were doing and seeming suspicious about it all. Was forever scribbling in a journal. The Egyptians wondered if he was spying on them."

That was some information the prince had forgotten—neglected?—to tell Violet.

"I must say, these are excellent. Turkish?"

"Yes," Gordon said. "Pure. No American blending."

"No wonder they're so smooth. I'm used to cigars, you know. These small sticks are fascinating. I must pick some up for myself."

"Lord Raybourn enjoyed them, too. Very few tobacconists carry them. Did he smoke them while in Egypt?"

"Not that I can recall. Of course, the Egyptians were generous with the hookah, and we had no need to supply our own tobacco."

The conversation moved from there to a discussion of the merits of Andalusian brandy versus that from the Armagnac region of France. How quickly they had forgotten the serious topic of Lord Raybourn's untimely demise and possible murder, with his earthly remains within arm's reach.

Violet shook her head in disgust. There was no more information to be gleaned here. She took her leave of the other women to head down the rear servants' staircase into the kitchens, where she spent an hour attempting to puzzle out whether the prince had accidentally or purposefully omitted the information about Lord Raybourn not getting on well with the Egyptians. Or perhaps he was merely inventing the story in front of Gordon and Stephen. But if he was, why? How was telling Lord Raybourn's heirs that the family patriarch was a busybody of any benefit?

She had many more questions to add to her ever-expanding list.

The detectives arrived late the following morning as the family was finishing breakfast. Stephen welcomed them.

"Lord Raybourn, thank you for sending a note to us regarding your strange visitor," Hurst said.

Was he referring to "James" or the Prince of Wales?

He turned his penetrating stare to Violet, who had also arrived early to check on the elder Lord Raybourn's body. "Why didn't you come to us straightaway about this, Mrs. Harper?"

"I tried to tell you—"

"Surely you realized that Inspector Pratt and I are vastly more qualified to find your assailant than the Fairmont family, who are still managing their grief." Hurst was at his pompous best in front of a big audience.

"You dismissed my—"

Hurst ignored her and looked at Stephen. "Women and their hysterics, eh, my lord?"

Stephen didn't respond.

"Now, Mrs. Harper, I'm sure you understand the importance of reporting crimes to the police."

"Which I did. And I don't believe he did anything that would constitute a crime, Inspector. He was merely rude," Violet said.

"Best to let us judge that. I don't make recommendations for burial clothing, do I?"

"No." Violet's teeth ached from gritting them. Surely this funeral could take place soon and she could return home with Sam, leaving behind this bullying inspector and the battling Fairmonts.

Stephen rescued Violet. "You may be interested in knowing, Inspector, that a newspaper reporter was here earlier, poking about. This is the result of his visit." Stephen handed him the previous day's newspaper.

Violet could have sworn she saw steam blasting from the detective's nostrils. "Reporters! They are the greatest scourge the earth has ever known. Worse than a cholera outbreak. A bigger blight than—"

"Yes, we already know firsthand how duplicitous and irritating they can be." Stephen took the paper back from Hurst.

Violet busied herself around the coffin while Hurst calmed down and asked the family more questions about who "James" might be and Pratt scribbled notes. They asked no questions about the prince's visit, which suggested to Violet that Stephen hadn't mentioned it in his note.

She pulled several more stems that were browning, and once again blew away some dust settling on the coffin's lid. The family's minimal household help was quickly beginning to show.

What was this? With her back to the family, Violet examined the lock. There were scratch marks on it. Someone had been tampering with it. But who?

She started to turn around to make mention of it but stopped. Perhaps someone in the family had brushed up against it. Or the new maid had acted with curiosity. She might have even let in a curiosity seeker who had fiddled with it.

Why give Mr. Hurst an opportunity to mock her further? Perhaps she could simply figure this out for herself.

Once the detectives were gone, Violet took her leave of the

family so she could meet Mary Cooke for their trip to Hyde Park. As she stepped into the street, she noticed a boy selling newspapers on a corner. He looked to be a mere ten years old. His brown knickers were torn and his hands and face were filthy from ink. She purchased a fresh edition of *The Times* from him.

She immediately regretted it.

The headline, written once again by the detestable Ellis Catesby, trumpeted the prince's visit to Raybourn House, but was less than flattering about it.

> . . . we can but be grateful that our dear Princess Alix was not dragged into that den of horrors and misery. The question remains, why would the Prince of Wales demean himself by attending to a family tainted by murder?
>
> Never fear, dear reader, we can answer it for you. The Viscount Raybourn was a known crony of the prince's during his recent sojourn to Egypt. What sinister goings-on were there in the land of harems and hookahs that resulted in Lord Raybourn's death? Were his activities in Egypt so highly inappropriate and inflammatory in nature that even his housekeeper couldn't live with the shame after his death? Rest assured we will pursue this to whatever sordid conclusion there is. . . .

Violet couldn't read any further. She hoped no one in the family would see the day's paper, but did it really matter if they did? A spiteful neighbor would surely bring it by. Well, there was nothing Violet could do about it now. She took it with her to her meeting with Mary.

Originally an enclosed deer park, Hyde Park was the largest royal park in London and had been open to the public since the time of Charles I. It had also been the home of the Crystal Palace Exhibition of 1851, the prince consort's most notable accomplishment during his short life.

As Violet passed through the Grand Entrance into the park's southeast end with Mary, she remembered the visit she had taken to the Exhibition with her parents, and having been overwhelmed just by the magnificent glass pavilion on the south end of the park that had held the event. Alas, the structure was gone now. The public complained about its continued presence after the Exhibition, so the architect purchased it and removed it to Sydenham Hill in Kent.

Without the glass palace, though, the Serpentine River, a man-made body of water snaking through the trees and walkways, took its rightful place as the highlight of the park.

Mary still had a cloud of misery surrounding her, and the casual walk through the park's winding pathways did nothing to revive her. Instead, she seemed to shrink from the throngs of people taking advantage of the cloudless, warm day.

"Why don't we hire a rowboat and take a closer look at the swans?" Violet pointed to the long-necked, snow-white birds, with golden beaks framed in black, floating on the Serpentine as though they hadn't a care in the world.

Most likely they weren't dealing with errant husbands or dead bodies that couldn't make their way into the ground.

Mary offered a wan smile for a particularly big cob as he floated past their rented boat in search of a female. How was it that the birds glided along so easily, barely making a ripple in the water, while Violet was straining with the oars to keep up with them?

Violet showed the newspaper article to Mary, who offered sympathetic noises. "Such dreadful things the newspapers say. It reminds me of what they said about you when Graham disappeared."

"I know. Except I'm sure the viscount's family is used to only appearing in the newspapers for announcements about parties they've attended, marriages they've made, and heirs they've birthed. This will send them reeling."

She paused rowing, letting the boat drift along where it would. Mary leaned back and closed her eyes, dipping her fingers into the water over each side of their small craft. The noise of people talking and shuffling along graveled paths receded from consciousness as the two friends moved with the breeze. Violet's eyelids grew heavy and she'd nearly fallen asleep with the oars across her lap, when Mary interrupted her pleasant nap.

"I read once that something dreadful happened in this lake about fifty years ago."

Violet opened one eye. "How dreadful?"

"It had to do with the poet, Percy Bysshe Shelley. It was in 1815, no, 1816—or was it 1817?—no, no, I'm certain it was 1816. His first wife, the one before Mary Wollstonecraft Godwin—you know, the one that wrote that frightening novel about the hideous creature produced by a scientific experiment that goes awry—"

"Yes, I know. What about his first wife?"

"Oh yes, her name was Harriet. She was pregnant, and committed suicide by drowning herself in this very lake. You see, Percy and Mary were already an item and traveling off to Geneva together, with Mary already calling herself 'Mrs. Shelley.' I'm sure the poor woman could hardly stand the scandal of it all."

Violet thought about Mary Cooke's roving husband, and understood why the story was compelling to her friend. "How very sad."

"But that's not the most remarkable part. Only six years later, Percy himself drowned in a sudden storm while sailing along the Italian coastline. Isn't that peculiar?"

It was. They rowed awhile in silence, and soon Violet drifted off again. When Mary next spoke, it was with surprising forcefulness.

"I do believe George intends to leave me for good."

Violet's eyes flew open. "What are you saying?"

Mary swirled her fingers in the water. "Things are . . . missing. A pearl necklace, a cameo brooch, and a sapphire ring Matthew gave me have disappeared from my jewelry casket."

Matthew was Mary's first husband, who had died years ago of a tumor on his brain.

"I also had some extra money hidden beneath a floorboard in the shop for emergency purposes. I'd saved nearly thirty pounds. It's gone."

"Maybe someone broke into the premises."

Mary's expression was that of a child who has realized that the mongrel puppy she adored really has died and would not be joy-fully licking her face or chasing sticks ever again.

"I have to accept that it was George. Everything went missing just before he left this time, and he has not written at all. Is there another conclusion?"

Violet could think of nothing to cheer her friend. They contin-ued to drift until Mary finally took her fingers out of the water and held them up. They were completely shriveled.

"They look like my heart," she said.

Poor Mary. Violet sympathized with her situation, but what could be done about it?

The two friends remained in companionable silence as Violet rowed back again, each caught up in her own thoughts about death and betrayal.

Mary rubbed her hands together. "Enough feeling sorry for my-self. I've had a lovely time. Shall we do it again?"

The women agreed to meet again in another week's time to once again rent a boat on the Serpentine, with Mary promising to bring crumbs along to feed the swans.

Mary was so cheered by the idea that Violet did not voice her doubts that she would still be in England by then.

Violet was about to relieve herself of her front-lacing corset when a palace servant knocked at her outer door. Violet quickly re-assembled her bodice and skirt, but by the time she was ready to answer the door, she found merely an envelope that had been slipped under it.

It was from a Mrs. Young, requesting that Violet meet her the following morning in the crypt of St. Paul's Cathedral, by Sir Christopher Wren's tomb.

> . . . for privacy, of course. I am well acquainted with
> the viscount's family, having been a close family friend for
> many years. I know that you are more than just an
> undertaker to them, and since they are refusing society
> visits, I thought I might share some vital knowledge about

> *Lord Raybourn that you could take back to the family. I*
> *cannot speak to the police, as this information would*
> *prove embarrassing to me if made public.*

Was this a prank, or was it possible that this woman had valuable information about Lord Raybourn's murder? Violet supposed the crypt at St. Paul's was safe enough, given the number of tourists that would surely be there. It was unlikely that this woman truly knew anything. She was probably just a curiosity seeker who had figured out a unique way to ferret out gossip about the family.

Violet chose to leave early the next day for St. Paul's, to spend time in quiet contemplation among its various chapels. She eschewed her normal undertaker's garb, instead choosing a burgundy-and-black outfit, appropriately somber yet not mourning.

At the appointed time, Violet took the staircase down into the crypt. Originally off-limits to visitors except for those attending interments, the crypt had been open to tourists since Lord Nelson's body had been buried down there in a fantastic black tomb more than fifty years ago. The cathedral's crypt was a rabbit's warren of hallways with tiny chapels jutting off them. The air had the peculiar stillness common to underground burial chambers. It was familiar and oddly comforting for Violet, and she supposed she was the only person down here actually breathing deeply to capture the atmosphere in her nostrils.

She went in exploration of Wren's tomb, her heels clacking against the stone floor and the noise reverberating off the stone walls and ceiling. The floors were punctuated by flat grave markers, giving the observer details about the birth and death dates of whoever was located beneath the metal slab. After some searching, she found it in an alcove with a barrel ceiling above it. A spiked gate created a private enclosure for Wren's tomb. No one was inside. Violet stepped through the opening at one end of the fencing to wait.

She examined Wren's tomb. Upon it was inscribed, LECTOR, SI MONUMENTUM REQUIRIS, CIRCUMSPICE. *Reader, if you seek his monument, look about you.*

Violet smiled. Wren certainly deserved his reputation as a master architect for his designs of St. Paul's, parts of Hampton Court, the Royal Observatory, and countless other buildings he created after the Great Fire of 1666.

After studying the inscription, she turned to examining the tomb itself, wondering what funerary practices were used upon the great man. Was he embalmed? How long did he lie in state before burial? What was his coffin inside the tomb made from?

Violet eventually grew bored of the mental exercise. Where was Mrs. Young? A couple carrying a guidebook approached the tomb. Violet looked at them hopefully, but they quickly moved on.

Had the woman decided not to come at the last moment?

Violet glanced at the watch pinned to her bodice. It was half an hour past the appointed time. She waited another half hour, then gave up and returned to her lodgings.

Yet another envelope waited for her under the door when she returned. It was an incoherent ramble from Stephen, demanding to know what she'd done with his father's body and when did she plan to inform the family of it?

Now thoroughly confused by the morning's events, Violet quickly changed into her undertaking attire and hired a cab to take her straight to Park Street.

"Has something happened?" she asked, removing her hat and gloves and handing them to Louisa.

"They's in the drawing room, madam," was all the maid said, making Violet even more unsettled.

As usual, the Fairmont family was in an uproar, except today the fury was reserved for Violet. She felt as though she'd been placed against a wall, and five members of a firing squad were aiming weapons at her heart. At least Toby wasn't there.

"I see you received my note," Stephen said as she entered the drawing room. "Pray tell, what made you decide to abscond with the coffin?" He waved a hand toward the empty bier. One of the lily pots was knocked over; there was a dark stain on the carpet from spilled water.

Violet hardly knew what to say. "Your father is gone?"

"Obviously," Dorothy said. "Your men said you instructed them to take the coffin."

"My men?"

"Yes. Said they were from your shop and you were having him buried today. I didn't know what to think, but since you're the undertaker . . ."

"But I no longer have a shop in London."

"Leave it to Dorothy to foul up a perfectly simple situation," Nelly said. "Perhaps the word 'no' was in order, dear sister."

Dorothy pointed a finger at Violet. "She's the one who is the queen's favorite and therefore dictates our own lives."

Gordon joined the fray. "I say, if the queen was ready for the old man to be buried, wouldn't it be right to have a chat with us first?"

"Please." Violet held up a hand. "Can someone tell me what happened here? I did not have Lord Raybourn taken away."

Stephen looked at her incredulously. "You mean to say that another undertaker got confused and picked up our family member by mistake?"

"I'm saying no such thing. I'm merely saying that something quite unprecedented has occurred and I'm trying to make sense of it. Please, Miss Fairmont, when did this happen?"

"This morning. Just a few hours ago. Louisa admitted two men in matching wool frock coats. I thought they were a bit seedy-looking, but they said they were here at your behest, and that you wanted Father's body taken back to Sussex for burial."

"It wasn't Will and Harry? The ones who have been with me before."

"No."

"You didn't question their legitimacy, then?"

"And why should I do that, Mrs. Harper? We all know that you are at the queen's command and therefore we are at your mercy. I assumed the queen finally decided it was time to end Father's long repose in the dining room."

"I'm at a loss."

"Violet, are you telling us that you had nothing to do with his removal?" Stephen asked.

"I'm sorry to say it, but I believe Lord Raybourn has been stolen."

The room was silent, except for a single gasp from Katherine. Violet didn't know what to do next although she now understood Mrs. Young's purposes.

"I think you need to know what happened to me this morning. I received a note from a Mrs. Young, requesting that I meet her at St. Paul's Cathedral, at Mr. Wren's tomb, because she had information for me regarding your father's death. I can see now that she— or whoever it was—was merely trying to ensure I wouldn't be attending to the coffin so it could be more easily spirited away."

Dorothy shook her head in frustration. "The papers mock us, our neighbors loathe us, and now complete strangers are persecuting us. When will this end?"

Violet sympathized with the woman's feelings. "Unfortunately, sometimes bad things happen to dead bodies. Would you like me to report this to Inspectors Hurst and Pratt?"

"I suppose it is the only thing we can do. Not that they have provided a moment's help to our state of affairs, have they? And the press will go simply wild with this, won't they? Thanks to Nelly, they're already slavering over the situation. Imagine tomorrow's headlines."

"Stephen, I've already told you I didn't—"

"Yes, Nelly, you've told us over and over." Stephen closed his eyes for a moment. When he opened them again, he looked directly at Violet. "The police are as bad a lot as the journalists. They take notes and nothing productive comes of it. They are worse than useless. But you can move about inconspicuously with your undertaker's bag. After all, it is only natural for an undertaker to make inquiries about a dead body. For the sake of my father's honor, will you find him for us before he is desecrated? Help us get our father buried properly?"

Five pairs of eyes were upon her again, but were no longer brimming with loathing. Katherine and Nelly were nodding. Dorothy's face was still sour, but no longer accusing.

What choice did she have? If the queen discovered that Lord

Raybourn was missing, Violet's reputation with Victoria would be destroyed. Without a body, there could never be a burial, and without a burial, Violet would never make it home to America.

Yet, the family was asking her to work behind the backs of Inspectors Hurst and Pratt. What sort of trouble might she be purchasing for herself? If only Sam were here to advise her.

Of course, if she simply discovered where Lord Raybourn had been taken and immediately reported it to Scotland Yard, there could be no harm done, right? It wasn't as though she had to personally confront a criminal or haul Lord Raybourn's body back to the premises. All she had to do was find him.

Remembering her father's great affection for his one-time employer, and sympathizing with this family's plight, Violet took a deep breath.

"Yes, I will help you."

14

Violet's first stop was Morgan Undertaking, just to be sure that Will and Harry hadn't been involved in Lord Raybourn's removal. As she suspected, they were flummoxed at the suggestion.

"You gave us no such guidance, Mrs. Harper. Why would we do this? I don't even know where the family churchyard is," Will said.

"I didn't think you would. I just thought it best to make sure someone hadn't led you to believe they were acting on my behalf, or I hadn't somehow led you astray in the viscount's funeral plans."

The other undertaker rubbed his chin. "What plans?"

Indeed.

Violet asked him for a current edition of *Funeral Service Journal*. With the publication in hand, she returned to St. James's Palace to pore through it, tossing aside the gloves, corset, and other personal items that had managed to wander onto her chair and desk.

There were more than two dozen undertakers in London. How was she to decide which ones to visit?

More important, what question should she ask? "Did you steal the body of a peer this morning from Mayfair?" didn't seem appropriate. Undertakers were a secretive and sensitive lot, both by the nature of their work and because the public frequently held them in such low regard. Any question Violet could possibly ask would be construed as an attack on the profession.

She herself would feel the same way if presented with questions that had even the slightest hint of impugning her good name.

In the end, she decided she would work in as narrow a radius as possible around Park Street, visiting those undertakers and asking if they knew anything. If she didn't learn anything, she would expand the bands of her search.

Violet realized that an undertaker not on her list was the one whom she'd encountered when she first arrived at Raybourn House. Of course, how could she have been so blind as to have overlooked him? Mr. Crugg, who had accused her of spiriting the Fairmont work away from him. He was as angry as if someone who had dropped an urn on his foot.

But to steal a body for spite seemed more senseless than what the lowliest undertaker would do, didn't it?

She went there first.

The man's shop was filled with many of the overwrought tricks and devices that Violet loathed. Prominent in the center of the display area was a sample safety coffin, fitted with bells that a prematurely buried occupant could ring to alert the outside world that he was not actually dead.

Mr. Crugg also offered Franz Vester's recently invented burial case, another absurd item permitting a person buried alive to climb out of his upright coffin and go up a ladder through a wide tube to the ground's surface.

Edgar Allan Poe's works had done much to stir the public anxiety for such things, and Mr. Crugg was profiting from it. Unfortunately, these fears were distributed across the classes, and unscrupulous undertakers tried to convince everyone from the poorest chimney sweep to the richest member of the House of Lords to buy any number of ridiculous contraptions.

Her rival undertaker's displeasure at seeing her upon arriving was palpable. "Have you come to pilfer more customers?"

"I am not in the habit of pilfering customers, Mr. Crugg. However, I have come to investigate a theft, that of Lord Raybourn's body."

Was it a theft? Or was it more aptly termed a kidnapping? She wasn't sure what you would call the taking of a dead body. A corpse snatching?

Mr. Crugg's expression was at first puzzled, then a great smile settled upon his face, eventually resulting in laughter, most inappropriate in a place that served the grieving.

"Oh, that is perfect irony. The woman who stole a body from me now finds that same body stolen from her. I would happily reward whoever did that. Complimentary funerals for him and his entire family. Richly deserved." Mr. Crugg's laughter rolled into a coughing fit.

Violet remained still as the man recovered himself from his own wit. "I am certain you find this amusing, but assuredly the family does not. In fact, there is some question as to whether you might have been offended enough by your removal from Lord Raybourn's funeral that you devised his kidnapping yourself."

Mr. Crugg's amusement quickly ceased. "What? That's preposterous."

"Is it?"

"Of course it is. I may have been put out by being ousted by not only a chit of a woman but by someone who has never buried a single member of the Fairmont family, but that doesn't mean I am so unethical as to steal a body!"

Violet wasn't quite sure about that.

"Where were you this morning, Mr. Crugg?"

His eyes narrowed. "A detective inspector, are you? I've no responsibility for answering your question, but if you must know, I was burying Mr. Thomas Little, headmaster of a boys' school, who died after a tumble down the stairs into the school basement when he went after some cricket equipment. As dark as a crypt down there, and a fine mess he was for me, too."

He noticed her skeptical look.

"I can give you Mrs. Little's address for verification," he said, going to a desk and scrawling on a piece of paper. "But assuredly, I was too busy to worry about Lord Raybourn's body. Besides, what on earth would I do with it? Go to the trouble of having a burial at my own expense? What would be my gain?"

"The satisfaction of ruining my own good name, to start. A lesson to families about not daring to allow your dismissal, perhaps? An exercise in flouting the queen's authority?"

Mr. Crugg sputtered. "What you say is slanderous. I don't care if you are a woman, I'll haul you into court, Mrs. Harper. I'll not have my honor impugned."

Violet swept her arm to indicate the various coffin samples in the room. "You impugn your own honor with your crude and seedy artifices for taking advantage of people in mourning. Good day to you, sir."

Violet didn't stop until she was a block away from the shop, then leaned against a lamppost, worn out from the interaction. Mr. Crugg was contemptible, but did that make him a body thief? She looked at the address he'd given her. It was in Holborn. She'd visit Mrs. Little in the course of visiting other funeral people.

Violet spent two more days on interviews. As she expected, she was met with frowns, scowls, and the occasional, "How dare you?" Not even her own status as an undertaker made the path smooth for her.

A visit with Mrs. Little, a short woman with a strange bald spot on one side, confirmed Mr. Crugg's claim that he was conducting the headmaster's funeral at the time Lord Raybourn's body was taken.

Not that it prevented him from hiring someone else to do it for him, which he must have done, since Dorothy didn't recognize either of the men who showed up to take Lord Raybourn. Yet for all of Mr. Crugg's bluster and irritating manner, she had to admit she wasn't certain that the reasons she'd presented to him for wanting to steal Lord Raybourn were really valid.

Violet stopped at Twining's tea shop along the Strand, located near the last of her undertaker visits. While sipping a cup of black tea and nibbling at a watercress sandwich, she spread her papers on the table in front of her, hoping she might discern something of value from her sparse notes.

There was nothing.

She asked herself obvious questions, hoping to divine an answer. Why would someone steal an embalmed body? Was Lord Raybourn stolen by the same person who had murdered him? If not, did the thief know the murderer? How was it that two different crimes had been perpetrated on poor Lord Raybourn?

Moreover, what of Mrs. Peet? Her death was most certainly not a suicide, although now that she was buried and gone, no one would give her a second thought. What of that neighbor's maid? Rebecca, wasn't it? A nervous little thing, but she'd implied that there was an immoral undercurrent in the house. What was it? Perhaps she should talk to the girl again.

The Fairmont family was a puzzle in and of itself. The sisters harbored great resentment for their father, Gordon was a milksop who had few interests outside of pleasing his wife, Toby was an enigma, and Katherine was a skittish colt. Stephen was the only placid, composed one currently residing at Raybourn House.

The queen and Gladstone sat across from each other over Victoria's favorite desk, a mass of papers between them. Victoria frowned at what she was reading.

"You obtained these from Scotland Yard?"

"Yes, Your Majesty. They are reproductions of the blackmail letters de Lesseps received. Commissioner Henderson thought we'd be interested in seeing them ourselves."

Victoria continued reading, amazed at the blackmailer's audacity.

> *I know everything about your scheme to finish the canal with slave labor. I will sail to England with one of these workers and tour with him to show the British people your callous disdain for human life in your quest to join the two seas.*

How utterly outrageous. Did Britain not have enough problems without some lunatic parading a paid actor through the kingdom to spew slander and lies? She picked up another letter.

> *My temper is sorely tried. I expect to receive notice of payment shortly, else my voice will see your project destroyed, much as Pharaoh once saw Egypt destroyed by plagues when he refused to listen to Moses.*

"He is quite the theologian," Victoria said.

Gladstone chuckled, despite the gravity of the situation. "It's almost as if he sees himself on some sort of moral crusade, except that money is at the forefront of his mind."

"Shouldn't it be a simple thing to find him? Can't the delivery of the messages be traced?"

"It's a curious thing. The blackmailer had an elaborate system set up involving the passing of notes through a series of boats along a stretch of the Suez Canal near Port Fuad. They use some intricate combination of hand signals and lamps that was never decoded. It appears that he is using the same method in London."

"What a ridiculous scheme. Can't the police merely post some men along the Thames?"

"It's not quite so simple as that, Your Majesty. The blackmailer appears to be using some, er, unsavory characters for his messages. The riverbank teems with them, and they move in the shadows, so it is hard to figure out who is a messenger and where along the river he will be picking up or dropping off a message."

Victoria frowned. "Has Monsieur de Lesseps considered paying the blackmail amount?"

"He refuses to do so, madam, on principle."

"Yes, we suppose a blackmailer is like a rat. Once it has discovered a good feeding source, it never leaves and brings in friends to join him. What are these papers here?"

"Commissioner Henderson also sent these along. The detectives assigned to the case discovered them."

They were a series of telegrams between Lord Raybourn and a Gordon Bishop. There were many of them, dated during the period that Lord Raybourn was in Egypt.

"It looks as though Mr. Bishop was asking His Lordship to purchase items for him," she said.

"Scotland Yard believes it may be code for something underhanded. For example, here Mr. Bishop instructs Lord Raybourn to spend twelve Egyptian *gineih* for three Pea Blue butterflies and four Yellow Pansies. Scotland Yard has researched, and says that butterflies do not thrive in Egypt, therefore 'Pea Blue' and 'Yellow Pansy' probably stand for something else."

"Such as?"

"They aren't quite sure. Possibly antiquities."

15

xhausted and without a single genuine hint as to what may have happened to Lord Raybourn's body, Violet returned to [Ra]ybourn House to report on her futile search. The entire family, [in]cluding Toby, gathered in the drawing room to hear what little [sh]e had to say. She'd hardly opened her mouth to speak when [the]re was a loud banging at the door, followed by Hurst, Pratt, and [an]other police officer barging in. They quickly stomped up the [sta]irs, the officer dangling handcuffs from his hand. Hurst planted [him]self firmly with both legs spread apart and hands balled on his [hip]s, like a Roman centurion about to announce the taking of bar-[bar]ian lands.

"Gordon Cyril Bishop, you are under arrest for the murder of [An]thony Fairmont, the Viscount Raybourn. You will be remanded [t]o custody and held to answer criminal charges against you. . . ." [Vio]let was too shocked to hear the rest of what he said.

[Mr]. Bishop rose, pale and speechless. A cigarette dropped from [his] lips, scattering ash down his front before landing on the carpet. [Ke]lly bent down and picked up her husband's stub, depositing it [in] an ashtray as the officer attempted to put the manacles on Gor-[don]'s wrists.

"Is that really necessary?" she asked. "You don't know what [you]'re doing, anyway. Gordon is as harmless as a ladybird beetle."

"Procedure, Mrs. Bishop," Hurst said.

"That isn't illegal."

"It is if they are being poached from archaeolog
stolen from museums."

Victoria nodded. "More embarrassment for us. Do
sioner Henderson know what we know about Lord Ra

"No, Your Majesty, I thought it wise to keep close
that until we see what Scotland Yard unearths."

"We've not told Mrs. Harper, either. We shouldn't
this investigation into disorder."

"Which reminds me, Your Majesty, have you receiv
tion of the . . . situation . . . yet?"

"I have, which makes me wonder what in heaven's r
happening here? We do so wish our dear Albert were
care of things."

"We all do, madam."

"Just a moment here." Gordon laughed nervously. "What is all of this? On what grounds do you presume to arrest me?"

"We have been investigating Lord Raybourn's activities in Egypt. It seems he was regularly sending telegrams to you, sir."

"What of it? I'm his son-in-law."

"It was the nature of these telegrams, some of which we've copied down." Hurst waved a hand to Pratt, who read from his notebook.

" 'Find some Tigers and Diadems. They are worth whatever price I must pay.' And here is another: 'Shipment received. Several pieces missing. What happened?' Most interesting is this one: 'Must discuss poor shipments upon your return. Insist that money be returned.' "

Gordon's face was pale. "Inspector, this is not what it appears. I've been expanding my butterfly collection, and my father-in-law and I were merely discussing an investment into some unusual samples from Egypt. Few knew it, but there are more than fifty varieties in that country, although I'm most interested in obtaining a Baton Blue. It's the world's smallest, you know." Gordon held up his cuffed wrists to display his thumb. "Smaller than my nail. Lives exclusively in a special thyme plant that grows around Mount Sinai. Difficult to find and capture, as you might imagine, and you have to pay old Bedouin women to venture up into their habitats. That's what our correspondence was about."

"Butterflies! What man collects insects?" Hurst said.

"I can show you my collection. Nells, would you retrieve one of my mounting boards?"

Nelly started to go upstairs, but Hurst stopped her. "I don't care whether you are collecting butterflies, spiders, or cockroaches, Mr. Bishop. It's no answer to the communications we have between you and Lord Raybourn. Your defense was a cleverly invented answer, I'll give you that."

"This is madness," Nelly said. "Gordon has never so much as stepped on a cat's tail. Besides, he loved my father. More than I did."

Gordon smiled, despite being bound and surrounded by Hurst, Pratt, and the police officer. "That's right good of you, Nell."

"Mr. Pratt," Hurst said. "If you would be so kind as to show Mr. Bishop what else we have."

Pratt produced a small package from his jacket and unwrapped it. Inside the paper were two cigarette stubs. Holding the paper flat in his hand, Pratt showed the group the stubs. "This one is the one we found next to Lord Raybourn's body. This other one is what Mr. Bishop was smoking the other day."

"Two crushed cigarettes and you've declared my husband guilty of killing my father?" Nelly said.

"That's not all, Mrs. Bishop," Pratt said. "I visited Fribourg and Treyer, tobacconists who have served the royal family, and your father, for many years. It is their label you can see right here." He pointed to a small, decorative band of blue around the stub. "This is one of their exclusive ones, made of pure Turkish tobacco uncut with anything else, produced only for Lord Raybourn."

"So my father gave my husband a cigarette. I still don't understand what the fuss is about."

"Lord Raybourn's tobacco box is special. Not only does it have a lock on it, but each cigarette lies in its own wooden depression. Therefore, once we broke into it, we could easily see that there were just two cigarettes missing. We found one next to his body. The second one was smoked by Mr. Bishop."

"Again, so my father gave my husband a cigarette. What of it?"

"You are failing to follow, Mrs. Bishop. Lord Raybourn was home only briefly—mere hours—before he was killed. In the interim, he went to his tobacco box, and retrieved a cigarette for himself and Mr. Bishop. Can we not therefore deduce that Mr. Bishop was the last person to see him alive? And if he was the last to see him alive, he most surely knows something about the man's death."

Nelly was speechless, as was the rest of the family. Gordon licked his lips but was silent.

Inspector Hurst pointed to the new stub Nelly had put in the ashtray. "I believe that's an identical blue marking band."

Nelly picked it up. "Yes, so?"

"If I go up to Lord Raybourn's study, will I find a third cigarette missing?"

"Maybe, but it doesn't signify anything."

"Except that your husband was more than likely the only other person in the household who knew of Lord Raybourn's hiding place for his box. Weren't you the least bit curious to find the lock broken, Mr. Bishop?"

"I . . . I . . ."

Stephen said, "Inspector, it's impossible that my brother-in-law could have done this. As Nelly said, he's the most gentle of creatures."

"Even the nicest of dogs will wrap its jaw around your wrist if cornered or threatened. I can hardly use such descriptives in determining whether to arrest someone, can I?"

Violet ventured in. "Inspector Hurst, isn't this a bit premature? After all, we don't—"

The detective held up a hand. "Thank you for your considered opinion, Mrs. Harper, but kindly leave the detection to those at Scotland Yard who make a profession of investigating such matters."

The detective's audacity was beyond comprehension. A few days ago he didn't even think Lord Raybourn had been murdered. Now he was strutting about in the Fairmont drawing room, making an arrest.

"It isn't my intention to interfere with your investi—"

"Then please do not. Thank you very much." Hurst waved at Pratt and the police officer, who escorted Gordon out.

It was just then that Hurst noticed the empty bier in the drawing room. "What have you done with Lord Raybourn?"

"He was—" Violet began, but Stephen interrupted her.

"We moved him down to the kitchen. It was too much for the family, what with not knowing how long he would be forced to remain here."

Hurst frowned. "But you've left everything except the coffin up here."

Stephen struggled with an answer.

"It's my fault," Violet said. "I sent my men over to move the coffin and didn't give them specific instruction to send everything downstairs. I stopped by to take care of it myself."

"Right, then." Hurst followed the other men out of the house. Violet marched after him.

"Inspector," she called. Hurst turned back, annoyance emblazoned on his face, but she plowed on anyway. "It seems to me that your arrest is based on the flimsiest of evidence. You cannot possibly think he can be found guilty of murder because he may have shared a cigarette with Lord Raybourn."

"You have much to learn about detection, Mrs. Harper. Let's say that Mr. Bishop did not murder Lord Raybourn. Someone the viscount knew did do it, and I'm fairly certain Mr. Bishop knows something. A few days without his special cigarettes, glasses of brandy, and fine clothes should sharpen his memory a bit and make him cooperative. Butterfly hunting, indeed."

"So you have changed your mind about Lord Raybourn's death being self-inflicted."

"I am not a man who cannot change his mind. And now I will use all of my powers for justice."

Violet shook her head. "Your methods are heartless. I would never do such a thing to Mr. Bishop."

"Which is why I am the detective and you are the undertaker."

Violet watched helplessly as Gordon Bishop, still handcuffed, was jostled and pushed into an open wagon with "Metropolitan Police" painted on the side.

Poor Mr. Bishop. How humiliating this was for him, to be unceremoniously shoved into a police wagon in front of all of his Mayfair neighbors.

The papers would be in a feeding frenzy now.

Violet returned to Raybourn House, where she found Nelly collapsed into a chair, with Katherine fluttering over her. Dorothy was rigid and unblinking, as if completely unaware of what went on around her, while Toby had apparently fled upstairs.

"As I said before, Violet, the authorities are worse than useless," Stephen said, taking her by the elbow and leading her to a corner of the adjoining dining room. "Don't worry about Gordon. I'll contact the family solicitor straightaway to see about things. You were about to tell us what you'd found out from the other undertakers."

"Unfortunately, nothing of any value. I went around London,

meeting with the city's undertakers, to see if they knew anything or were even possibly involved. I even saw Mr. Crugg—"

"What?" Stephen's frown made Violet question the wisdom of having gone to Mr. Crugg's shop.

"—but I am of the mind that he isn't guilty."

"You suspected him of stealing the coffin out of our home?"

"He was very angry when I . . . when the queen dispensed with his services."

"Yes, but to suggest that the man who has been burying Fairmonts for more than thirty years would reduce himself to such common criminality, well, really, Violet."

"I'm not an actual detective, Stephen. I am merely taking the steps I think most logical."

"Yes, of course, you're right. I apologize. So what is your next course of action?"

Violet debated whether to voice her next suspicion. Surely it couldn't be true. But she had no other idea at the moment. "I am wondering if perhaps . . ."

"Yes?"

"If perhaps he was taken by a resurrectionist man."

"Violet! That's even more fanciful than the idea that Mr. Crugg took him."

"Isn't it possible, though? Doctors and medical schools constantly need fresh cadavers for dissection. The newspapers just published their piece on your father and Mrs. Peet. For all we know, they wanted both bodies but were only able to get your father."

"But my sister said they only asked about Lord Raybourn."

Right. Maybe Inspector Hurst was right about her. Violet was not proving to be an apt detective thus far.

Think, Violet, think.

She stewed over the situation over a meal of baked carp back at her rooms. What line of reasoning should she pursue next? Whom should she talk to? Who would even talk to Violet Harper, a lady undertaker?

She pushed the food tray aside and got out her notes again. She scanned them once more, unsurprised that they still didn't reveal anything, then made a list of every thought she'd had about the Raybourn situation.

After all, Mr. Pratt constantly made notes and presumably he and Mr. Hurst solved many crimes. They weren't going to be very happy that Violet was Stephen's new "detective," especially now that Hurst had seemingly concluded the case. She could imagine the inspector swelling up like one of the wild turkeys she'd seen in America, and verbally pecking her to death over it.

1) Is it possible that the kidnapping of Lord Raybourn's body is unrelated to his murder?
2) Why was Lord Raybourn brutally shot, instead of merely poisoned? A crime of passion? And was he afraid of being poisoned?
3) How is Mrs. Peet's death connected? Not a suicide. Was their relationship somehow a contributing factor to their murders?
4) Gordon Bishop cannot possibly be guilty, can he?
5) What of the other siblings? Should I interview them?
6) Is it a stranger? An associate of Lord Raybourn's we don't know? How do we find him?
7) Who was the man who accosted me in the street?

The more she wrote down, the more questions she had. When she finally had the list complete, Violet drew a fresh sheet of paper to her and made a secondary listing of what actions she could take based on those questions. Reviewing this second list of activities, she selected her first task for the next day: to interview Rebecca, the maid at Lady Cowgil's residence next door.

By the time she was done, the back of her head was throbbing. She took a Beecham's powder and lay down with Mr. Barnum's book to help her sleep, but it was of no use. She put the book down and turned to prayers to calm her mind. Tomorrow would be a long day.

*   *   *

Violet's morning was not off to a promising start. She went to the rear servants' entrance of Lady Cowgil's home and was greeted by a young boy covered in ash, presumably from cleaning fire grates. He scampered off and retrieved the housekeeper, a frazzled woman who quickly informed Violet that Rebecca was no longer employed at the Cowgil residence.

"Was she dismissed or did she take another position elsewhere?"

"I'm sure it's not for me to say, ma'am." The woman stood resolutely in the doorway, to let Violet know that she wouldn't be invited in.

"Did her departure have anything to do with the goings-on at Raybourn House?"

"Pardon me, you said you were the Fairmonts' undertaker? Why is a maid of this household of such interest to you?"

"She might know something about the Raybourn housekeeper's death. She paid her respects not a week ago and I was of the impression that she knew something about the family."

A shadow of alarm flitted across the woman's face, but she quickly concealed it. "I'm sure Lady Cowgil can tell the new Lord Raybourn more about it than I can."

In other words, it was none of Violet's business.

The housekeeper began ushering Violet away, but Violet refused to be bullied.

"Can you at least tell me when she left?"

The housekeeper sighed. "Three days ago."

"Of her own accord?"

"Yes. I have a good mistress; she doesn't throw her servants out on a whim, like some lords and ladies do."

"No, no, of course not. I'm sure Lady Cowgil is the kindest of employers." Violet adopted her softest undertaker tone. "And she is rewarded with the most competent of staff, made evident by your fierce devotion to the family."

"Yes." The housekeeper stared beyond Violet, as if in thought. "I was just making tea. Would you care for a cup?" She left the doorway and retreated into the kitchen, a signal that Violet had met a certain level of approval.

Over spiced cakes and steaming cups of tea made with leftover leaves, the housekeeper finally opened up.

"I'm Mrs. Dennis. I've been with the family for more than thirty years. I hope they'll pension me off when my day comes that I can't work anymore."

"May that be many years from now."

"There's never been a breath of scandal coming from this house, and not likely to be any now. Lady Cowgil would never tolerate happenings such as what is going on next door."

"Is that why Rebecca is gone?"

Mrs. Dennis poured more tea for herself and dropped four cubes of sugar into the cup. Lady Cowgil might be a kind employer, but she would probably have sharp words over her housekeeper using so much of a precious commodity.

"In a way. With Lord Raybourn's death and then Mrs. Peet's, my mistress was concerned that Rebecca's connection next door might lead to trouble here."

"What connection is that, Mrs. Dennis?"

The housekeeper dropped her own voice to match Violet's. "Lord Raybourn's valet, Mr. Larkin, he was a bit of a bad sort. Took a liking to Rebecca and was overly attentive to her. Mrs. Peet once caught him cornering Rebecca in this very room when she came by to share a recipe with me. I was out shopping at the time. Rebecca said later there was quite a row over it, with Mrs. Peet nearly boxing his ears off, and Mr. Larkin never bothered poor Rebecca again. When we heard he went to Egypt with Lord Raybourn, it was sighs of relief all around here."

"Lady Cowgil didn't complain of Mr. Larkin's behavior to Lord Raybourn?"

"No, she wanted to maintain peace between the families. I'll tell you, though, Mrs. Harper." Mrs. Dennis leaned in closer to Violet. "I always wondered myself if Mr. Larkin didn't go off with Lord Raybourn to avoid any future consequences of his behavior. Now that we know he never came back, I think he escaped and went to some foreign country to live in disguise." Mrs. Dennis tapped the side of her nose. "That's what criminals do."

After more pleasantries, Violet realized she wasn't going to learn anything else of value.

"Thank you kindly for the tea and cakes," Violet said, giving Mrs. Dennis her sweetest smile as she left. At least the mystery surrounding Rebecca was cleared up. She marked the task from her list and examined the rest of it. Perhaps she should drop by the Raybourn House to interview the family members, provided that Stephen would allow it.

Stephen and Katherine were in the dining room with Nelly, who was weeping over the remains of her poached eggs. An empty place setting indicated that Dorothy had already eaten and left.

"Pardon my intrusion. I can return again later," Violet said.

Stephen waved to Dorothy's vacated seat. "Please, sit. We have plenty to share. I've arranged for Pye's Dining Rooms to deliver meals until we can, well, sort out everything and hire permanent staff."

Violet took a plate and served herself a helping of oysters and bacon from a steaming silver salver, then sat down at the dark mahogany table next to Katherine and across from Nelly. Stephen sat at one end, between the other two women, talking of inconsequential things.

It was difficult to eat while watching Nelly sniffling and pushing egg scraps around on her plate. Violet tried to focus on what Stephen was saying, as he read from the newspaper about a current legal trial.

". . . so Mr. George gave the hair wash to his wife, who used it and ended up losing her hair and having a scalp disorder. He has sued the manufacturer, whom he said represented the hair wash as 'fit and proper to be used for washing the hair.' Mr. George says that Mr. Skivington, the manufacturer, owes a duty of care to the people using their products."

Violet frowned. "Mr. George himself was not injured by the hair wash?"

Stephen scanned the article again. "No, it was only used by his wife."

"Then how could Mr. George sue Mr. Skivington? He wasn't injured."

"The court allowed it."

"A third person has sued a manufacturer and may win?" Katherine said. "You don't really think that will happen, do you?"

"Yes, I think he may actually win the case. If he does, it will be the first time a third party is awarded damages for a manufacturer's false representation of a product."

Nelly slammed down her fork. "How can you speak of such foolishness? What difference does a silly lawsuit make to our lives after everything that has happened inside these four walls?"

"Nells, you know Mr. Hall is doing everything he can to extricate Gordon," Stephen said. "He is one of the best solicitors in London, but we must be patient."

Nelly wiped her mouth and threw down her napkin, covering her uneaten remains. "You be patient. I plan to do something. Gordon may be completely feeble-minded, but he's still my husband and a member of the family. No one else seems to have noticed."

"Nells . . ." Stephen said helplessly as she trounced out of the room and upstairs. Katherine kept her head bowed over her plate, as though embarrassed by her sister-in-law's behavior.

An uncomfortable silence ensued, but Violet realized this was her opportunity. "Might I talk to her? I am accustomed to dealing with those in all forms of grief."

Stephen nodded his head. "Nelly was always . . . headstrong and volatile. Our family troubles have made her even more unruly. If she'll talk to you, you have my blessing."

"Actually, this brings me to the real purpose of my visit. I thought that perhaps, with your permission, I could talk to everyone in the family to try and put together the pieces of what may have happened."

"What's the point of that? No one in the household had anything to do with it."

"But someone may have heard or seen something that he doesn't realize was significant."

"You would certainly be better at it than the inspectors." Stephen looked at Katherine, who looked up from her plate and nodded. "At least you won't go around randomly arresting people."

"Very well, then. Nelly's on the next floor in the room over this one. I suppose you'll start with her?"

"Yes."

"Well, Kate, I guess we'll fall under the undertaker's watchful eye."

This actually elicited a smile from Katherine. "Be kind to me."

"Will you talk to Gordon?" Stephen said.

"I suppose I could visit him. Where is he?"

"Newgate."

Violet made a mental note of it before heading upstairs and tapping on Nelly's door. At a subdued "You may enter," Violet went in. The room was in typical bedroom fashion for the upper classes, with its floral wallpaper, Wedgwood on ledges of varying heights, interspersed with pastoral, romantic pictures on the walls, and heavy, layered draperies on the windows that faced the rear yard. The draperies were artfully drawn back to allow both sunlight and fresh air through the open windows, but Violet knew that by October they would be drawn down to tightly cover the windows, thus preventing any smuts from drifting in from the coal-choked atmosphere of London in winter.

Nelly sat with her back to Violet at a writing desk that had been turned into a vanity table. It was littered with perfume bottles, talcum boxes, brushes, and combs. An ornate tabletop mirror sat in the center of it all, a witness to the disarray. In the reflection of the mirror, Violet saw Nelly turning a pair of gold cuff links over in one hand.

"Yes, what is it?" she asked, looking up into the mirror at Violet.

"Forgive my intrusion, Mrs. Bishop. I was wondering if I might offer any help?"

Nelly turned around in the wheeled, deep blue lady's slipper chair, still holding the cuff links. "Have you the key that opens my husband's cell? No? Then do you have a powder I can take that will put me in a trance from which I would never have to wake?"

Violet sat down at the foot of the bed, putting her within two feet of Stephen's distraught sister. "I don't have a key, but maybe I can help you remember something vital that will prove Mr. Bishop's innocence."

"No, it's impossible. Gordon is such a terrible old fool. I warned him not to bother with Father's cigarettes, but he saw no harm in it."

"So you knew about your father's hidden tobacco box?"

"Of course. It wasn't that great a secret."

"And your husband does collect butterflies?"

"Yes. I don't know why he enjoys it. He soaks the dead bodies in gin to soften them up so he can spread their wings without them crumbling, then he pins them to a board and labels them. It's repulsive." Nelly shuddered.

Could a man whose most aggressive activity was pinning butterflies to a board possibly be guilty of murder? Furthermore, could a woman who found pinning butterflies abhorrent possibly have anything to do with murdering her father?

Surely no one in the family had anything to do with Lord Raybourn's death, but Violet had to be sure.

"Was there something between your husband and father beyond the collecting of butterflies?"

"Nothing beyond the ordinary between a man and his son-in-law. Gordon was quite grateful to be brought into the family. He was a barrister's son, not really called to the law but feeling that he had to do it to please his own father. He lives to please everyone around him. My father 'discovered' Gordon through some financial transaction and decided he would be a good match for me. That he would settle me down into domestic felicity."

"But he didn't?"

Nelly shrugged. "I don't know. We rub along, I suppose." She smiled tremulously. "Do you know, Mrs. Harper, how much I envy you? Even though your profession is peculiar, to say the least, you have freedom. You come and go as you please and make your own decisions for all to see. What I do I must do in secret.

"I've always thought that I share much in common with Gordon's ridiculous butterfly collection. They are simple creatures, unmindful of their predators as they merely seek joy in traveling from flower to flower. But they are caught, unawares, stuffed into a box and left to die, then are eventually pinned to a board by a proud collector who wants the world to see what he captured. My wings have been pinned down for years. I just wish I'd been able to . . ." Her voice trailed off as she stared down at her feet.

"What do you wish you'd been able to do?" Violet asked, again using her softest undertaking voice.

Nelly looked up. "What? Oh, nothing. Cobwebs of the mind. I suppose if I wished anything it was that I had been born the eldest boy."

"That's an odd wish. Why?"

"Because my eldest brother, Cedric, had a grip on my father's heart that could not be pried off, simply because he was the heir. Even later, poor Stephen was just a pale substitute for Father's hope in Cedric. Yet Father never understood what a sniveling rat Cedric was. You know I wanted to be a journalist?"

"Yes."

"Father was aghast. He said it was wholly unsuitable and unseemly for the daughter of a viscount. He was right, of course, but I didn't care and pursued it in secret. Ellis helped me, publishing my articles under an assumed name. I was happy to see my work in print, even if Ellis and I were the only ones who knew who had actually written the pieces.

"Unfortunately, it was impossible to keep secrets from Cedric. I don't know how, but he discovered the identity of 'Montgomery Fairchild.' Instead of joining me in my intrigue, he went straight to my father, who was apoplectic over it. Even twenty-five years later, I remember the look of satisfaction on Cedric's face as Father chastised and humiliated me over it.

"Father took it into his head that I needed to be married, and quickly. Cedric encouraged him in it, despite my protestations that I didn't wish to marry yet. So I found myself rushed to the altar with a dull weakling, facing a mind-numbing existence of utter boredom.

"I hated Cedric from that moment on, for ruining my greatest desire for no reason other than to see me disgraced. In fact, I was quite happy when Cedric died in the Crimea. It was a just end for him. I can't say that Father's death upset me much, either."

"I'm sorry, Mrs. Bishop. I suppose my social status didn't hamper me as much as yours did you. I've had some strange looks from people who don't understand a woman wearing undertaker's garb, but I've learned to ignore them. I can't remember a time when I wasn't doing what I love."

"You're a strange one, Mrs. Harper. How can a woman love to prepare dead bodies?"

"I don't know. I like to know they are cared for in their most intimate moment. That someone loved them right up until the moment their coffin was sealed away forever."

"I understand now why the queen had you in attendance on the prince."

The two women sat in silence for several moments. Violet wanted to fold the woman in her arms, but knew it would be highly inappropriate to touch the viscount's daughter, even if she was now married to a commoner.

Finally, a single tear rolled down Nelly's face. "Ellis has offered to hire me openly at *The Times* again if I want it, to write under my own name. I've been toying with the idea, but there's so much scandal on at the present that I think Stephen's heart might burst if I did it. Anyway, how can I even think of it while Gordon rots in a jail cell?"

"Mrs. Bishop, does Mr. Catesby know more about the family's situation than he should?"

Violet's question seemed to make Nelly tense, for she began worrying the cuff links in her hands, rubbing them back and forth. One fell from her palms to the floor.

Nelly bent down to retrieve the cuff link. "I don't think—"

At that moment, a projectile smashed into the vanity mirror, spraying shards of glass all over Nelly's back, the desk, and the floor. Nelly bolted upright, sending more glass tinkling down to the carpet. "My God!" she gasped.

Instinctively, Violet crawled backward on the bed, but her voluminous skirts didn't allow for much movement. After a few seconds to gather her wits and realize that Nelly was unharmed, Violet ran to the open window and leaned over the sill. There was no one in the garden. She looked up and down the alley between the Raybourn garden and the rear of the home behind it. Other than a severely dressed nanny showing her two young charges how to play marbles, there was no one else in sight.

She ducked back into the room. Nelly stood, trembling, and held out a piece of paper that looked as if it had been crumpled up, then smoothed out. "This was tied around the . . ." She pointed back at the desk, where a rock lay beneath the shattered mirror frame. A perfume bottle had also been a victim of the impact, and was now on its side, dribbling its jasmine-scented contents to the floor.

Violet took the note from Nelly's outstretched hand.

> *Your dear papa is safe with us. He will return unharmed for a payment of three hundred pounds. You will be instructed in three days' time where to bring the money, to be in sterling. The papers say you will be meeting with your solicitor for the will reading tomorrow, so we are generously giving you time to obtain your inheritance. Our generosity will be retracted if you choose to search for us meanwhile. Do not force us to prove this.*

The writing was that of an educated man or woman.

"They plan to kill us," Nelly said.

"The note only says they will give us more instruction about how to retrieve your father. It would seem they only want money."

"They want retribution. They've already tried to assassinate me with this stone. What if I hadn't been bent over when it came through? I've been a rotten wife to my husband all these years, and first Father is killed and now Gordon is jailed. Now they're coming after me."

"Mrs. Bishop, who are 'they'?"

"The ones who will kill me. I have done terrible things, and now I will pay for them. 'Retribution is mine, sayeth the Lord.' I will suffer now, I know it. What of Toby? My boy must be protected."

Eleanor Bishop was breaking down before Violet's eyes.

"Mrs. Bishop, please be calm. You won't be hurt, nor will your son."

Nelly's eyes were frantic and she grasped Violet's forearms with both hands. "Can you promise me this? How will you ensure it? You mustn't leave the house. Mrs. Peet's room is empty now; you can stay there."

"I'm not sure I can—"

"Promise!" Nelly shook Violet's arms.

"Very well, I suppose I can stay here until we recover your father's body."

Nelly almost instantly calmed down. "I think I should like some tea now. Ring the new maid, will you?"

By the time Violet returned to let Nelly know that tea would be up shortly, Stephen's sister was curled up in a ball on her bed, a childlike smile on her sleeping face.

Violet wondered what was making the woman so mercurial.

With Nelly dozing, Violet sought out Stephen once more to tell him of the rock incident and his sister's request.

"A stone thrown through the window? Doesn't that seem rather juvenile? A bit of trite drama more suited to the pages of a novel?" he said.

It was an excellent point. Why would a serious kidnapper resort to silly chicanery like this? Something else to puzzle out.

"We should report this to the police," she said.

"Must we? Maybe we can just quickly pay it and have the whole sordid thing done with. Furthermore, we are complicit in not informing Inspector Hurst of the missing body, which will more than likely bring us a scolding rather than any sound answers."

"But your father's kidnapping may have something to do with his death. They might release Mr. Bishop if they believe there is another suspect."

"True. Then by all means, we should inform them."

Violet first went to St. James's Palace to pack her few belongings for a stay at Raybourn House. She briefly considered writing a note to the queen to inform her of this location change, but in the end decided the monarch would not be particularly concerned with such a detail.

After arranging for her things to be delivered, she walked to

Scotland Yard to see Inspector Hurst. He nodded impatiently at seeing Violet, and waved to another man, who escorted her to a small room devoid of anything within its oak-paneled walls except a round oak table, three chairs, and a gas chandelier in the ceiling with white globes covered in years of dust.

He joined her several minutes later and dropped heavily into one of the other chairs. "What is it, Mrs. Harper? I've already had a visit from the Fairmont family solicitor."

"I'm sure they were concerned with securing the release of a cherished family member. However, I am here with information that should make you consider your arrest of Lord Raybourn's son-in-law to be premature."

"Do you indeed? And what is this special information?"

Violet handed him the note, saying, "The family has asked me to stay on the premises until Lord Raybourn's body is recovered."

"What?" Hurst bellowed. "Lord Raybourn's body *recovered?* What in heaven's name are you saying?"

Violet proceeded to explain that due to the uninvited publicity already thrust upon them, the Fairmonts decided to have her discreetly visit the other undertakers, thinking that it was simply a mix-up. It was only now that it was clear that the body was snatched and that prior to this she didn't think it necessary to concern Scotland Yard, who had far more important matters on their hands.

Violet knew the explanation of her actions stretched credulity, but then again, hadn't she learned this tactic from Hurst himself?

Once Hurst simmered down from his rolling boil and composed himself, he scratched at his chin as he read the crumpled note. He had at least a day's growth on his face. Had he become too busy detecting crime to care about his appearance?

Finally, he looked up, having apparently charted the path forward. "It seems to me, Mrs. Harper, that we can make a bargain."

"What sort of bargain?"

"It's not often that I can get an inspector installed directly into a crime scene like this. Not that I consider you detective material, but you could certainly redeem yourself by serving as eyes and ears for Scotland Yard and reporting back whatever you learn. In return, I'll see to it that Gordon Bishop is released soon, although he will remain under suspicion."

"But what about the ransom note? Isn't that proof enough that Mr. Bishop isn't guilty, or at least that there is some doubt about it?"

"Perhaps, perhaps not. I can't be sure this isn't part of some sort of prank. In fact, the family themselves may have been behind it in order to dupe you. As I said, Mrs. Harper, things are almost never what they seem to be. Someone is always harboring something. Even if Gordon Bishop isn't guilty, if I hold him long enough, whichever family member is in the shadows will eventually venture out and do something foolish. Then, snap! I will have the guilty party."

"But what if the guilty party is a complete stranger, or someone outside the household?"

Hurst scratched his chin again. "My instinct tells me that isn't true."

"But you cannot imprison a man based upon your instincts! It's immoral."

"This is why I do not like women mucking about in investigations. Their sensibilities are perpetually offended, and they don't understand the value of duplicity. Mr. Bishop is in the comfortable section of Newgate. He can pay for whatever creature comforts he wishes. You must understand that detection is grimy work, Mrs. Harper. However, I do see that you can be useful to us in this particular situation."

The detective brought to Violet's mind many a doctor and coroner she had met before. It took a certain type of man, full of self-conceit and arrogance, to be successful in these professions.

What choice did she have in his offer? She couldn't possibly return to Park Street and tell the family she'd turned down a glorious opportunity to have Nelly's husband freed. One thing she vowed, though. Inspector Hurst would develop respect for her by the time this was finished.

"Might I visit Mr. Bishop?"

"You wish to enter a jail?"

"No, not especially, but I do want to visit the innocent man you've arrested."

"You've a tart tongue, Mrs. Harper. Very well. Mr. Pratt?"

Violet accompanied Langley Pratt to Newgate. Despite Pratt's effort to keep her confined to an outer area away from any actual cells, she found it dank and depressing. She was asked to wait while Gordon was brought in from yard exercise. Pratt arranged for her to meet with the prisoner in a private room.

"No more than fifteen minutes, right, Mrs. Harper?" Pratt left Violet alone with Gordon Bishop.

Gordon was disheveled and still wore the clothes he had been arrested in the previous day. His face was shadowed with beard stubble. "Kind of you to visit. Haven't heard yet from my Nells. I'm afraid I'm not at my most elegant at the moment." He touched his cheek stubble as though in disbelief that it existed.

"She's worried sick about you, Mr. Bishop. I had to see Inspector Hurst and he made a special arrangement to permit me to see you, and now I can comfort her that you're sound. Have you no uniform or other clothes?"

"I'm not a convicted prisoner, so I only have what I came in with. This is dratted embarrassing, but can you get me some clothes, food, and money? And I'm sure the old man, bless his soul, wouldn't mind if we nicked a few more of his Turkish cigarettes."

"Of course. I'll bring it all tomorrow. Perhaps Mrs. Bishop will come with me."

Gordon smiled wanly at Violet. "Can you imagine my Nelly in a place like this? It's not really fit for a woman like her, is it?"

Violet said nothing. He was probably right.

"So to what do I owe the honor of this visit, Mrs. Harper? Presumably it isn't to see me in my fallen state."

"No. I wanted to make sure you are . . . unharmed."

He nodded. "How ironic. The family's new undertaker is ensuring I'm still alive. Isn't that a bit removed from your profession?"

Violet dropped her voice. "The detectives rushed you out so quickly it was difficult to know what was happening. I thought I might inquire as to whether there was something more between you and Lord Raybourn that wasn't mentioned. Anything that might further explain the nature of your correspondence."

"Truthfully, I am a butterfly collector, and my telegrams back and forth with my father-in-law only concerned the collection. I'm afraid some of them got quite testy, as I kept receiving crushed specimens. But it was certainly no reason to murder a man I respected and loved."

Violet agreed. It seemed impossible that Gordon Bishop's telegrams referred to something subversive.

But if they did, the Fairmont family members would be subject to public shame and ridicule for the rest of their lives.

And Gordon Bishop would earn his gray prisoner's uniform.

Violet's belongings were already stacked in Mrs. Peet's old room by the time she returned to Raybourn House. She carefully combined the housekeeper's few underclothing items into one drawer in the chest, then laid her own clothing in the remaining drawers. She didn't touch the trunk full of Mrs. Peet's fancy gowns.

She examined her surroundings when she finished. It was a far cry from St. James's Palace, for certain. The luxurious down bedding atop an overstuffed mattress against an elegantly carved headboard was replaced with an iron bedstead covered with serviceable muslin sheets and a dingy blanket. Instead of an intricately woven Turkish carpet, her feet would settle down each morning directly on a worn wood floor.

At least the bride and groom dolls had made it here unscathed.

Not that it mattered. The moment Lord Raybourn's body and murderer were found, Violet and Sam would be on a ship bound for America, dolls securely packed in their luggage.

She stepped into the hallway, intending to find Stephen and let him know that she was installed in the house. However, as she began her descent to the floor below, she heard angry voices coming from Nelly's room.

"... can't believe you aren't doing more. After all, we've kept *your* secret for years now." Nelly's voice rose on the word "your."

"It was best for everyone that things not be publicized," Stephen replied.

"Best for you, perhaps. So first we had to worship at the altar of

Cedric, and now we must bow down to whatever is best for Stephen?"

"Nelly, darling, we're all having a difficult time—" The voice was soft; it had to be Katherine.

"Be quiet, you stupid cow. You're of no help."

"Nells, that's enough. Kate is trying to be kind." Stephen's tone was even but with a rumbling underpinning. It was a warning, but Nelly ignored it.

"I have sacrificed everything my entire life: a career, a husband of my choice, everything a waste except for my darling Toby. You, however, have reaped rewards for having the good fortune to be born your father's favorite son. Or, rather, to be his favorite after Cedric died."

"That's unfair, sister. Father always tried to work in everyone's best interests—"

"Except mine. Had it not been for that old beast's constant manipulation, I would be a woman of independent means, as free in my life as Mrs. Harper is in hers."

Violet restrained a mild laugh of amusement. Here she was, relegated to the servants' quarters of a squabbling family, hoping that their patriarch's dead body would soon be recovered and his killer identified, so that she might finally have permission from the queen to go home.

Free, indeed.

Dorothy couldn't contain herself. "And what of me? The famed Fairmont Spinster, without even a son to dote on. At least Father permitted you to be married. And Gordon isn't so bad. I'd have called it a fine day if Father had picked him for me. You're an ungrateful snob, Nelly, and always have been." Dorothy was loud and shrill.

"Hah! As if even a mouse like Gordon would have looked twice at you after meeting me. But isn't that just selfish old Dorothy, worried about her own marital status when my husband has been arrested—*arrested*—for no good reason and now sits rotting at Newgate. But don't worry, dear sister, I have no real venom for you. I blame this on Stephen. Don't you think it's time you shared your secret?"

"Why? What bearing could it possibly have on Father's death or disappearance?"

Nelly's voice dropped lower. Violet crept down several more stairs in order to hear her. "It would show that you are a liar and a bit of a . . . thief, wouldn't it? You might not want Inspector Hurst to know that about you, but I imagine the inspector would be very interested in it."

Someone gasped. Violet wasn't sure if it was Katherine or Dorothy.

"You are trying me, Nelly. Be very careful with what you choose to bandy about to the police. Any secrets we keep are merely for the good of the family. Since you are a member in good standing of this family—for now—I advise you to keep your simpleminded blathering to yourself."

Violet heard a couple of grunts and a sound as though a chair was being rolled along the floor. Had Stephen just pushed Nelly into the same slipper chair she'd been in when Violet visited her? The sound of footsteps in the room drove Violet back up to the servants' floor. She waited until everyone dispersed before heading back downstairs again and seeking Stephen out.

He was in his father's study, grinding a fist into his palm as he stared out the window.

"Excuse me, Stephen?" Violet said. She had no idea how explosive his mood might be after what had just happened.

"For heaven's sake, what is it? Oh, Violet, sorry, do come in. Louisa said your things arrived earlier."

"Yes, I was just upstairs unpacking and thought I'd find you to let you know I'm here. Since I've already spoken with Mrs. Bishop, I thought I might talk next to Miss Fairmont."

"As you wish. You don't need to—"

Stephen was cut off by Nelly's screech, which pierced through the air like a cat whose paw has been caught underfoot.

"What the deuce . . ." Stephen ran out of the room and down the stairs, with Violet on his heels.

Gordon Bishop stood in the drawing room, clutching a babbling Nelly, who could scarcely contain her train of thought.

"Why did they release you? How did you get home? Your suit is so very crumpled; we must have it pressed. Did they feed you well? I'm sure we have something left over from dinner. Were they cruel to you? Toby will want to know straightaway that his father is home."

Gordon was completely unable to get a word in edgewise, yet reveled in his wife's attention. For a man who had just spent time in a cell with others he undoubtedly considered his inferiors, Gordon Bishop glowed like a full moon.

"I see Mr. Hall finally had some influence," Stephen said, clapping his brother-in-law on the back.

"He must have. All I know is that an officer came and released me without explanation, told me to go home."

So Inspector Hurst had lived up to his end of the bargain. Now Violet would have to live up to hers.

16

Stephen Fairmont, the new Viscount Raybourn, gave his wife a reassuring squeeze on her elbow as the family settled in on an overcast morning to hear Mr. Hall read from the will.

Poor Katherine was just exhausted from the entire ordeal. Her constitution wasn't as strong as, say, Nelly's. Nelly sat several seats away, her face nearly obscured by the fashionable black hat she was wearing. Where did she get such a hideous thing? The flowers on the brim were large enough to attract a swarm of bumblebees.

As impassive as Nelly was, Gordon was sitting forward eagerly in a freshly pressed suit, while Toby sat away from his parents at the back of the room, with his nose in a book.

Why so disinterested? The boy was certain to inherit quite a bit from his grandfather.

Dorothy's usual sour expression was unchanging. She probably assumed that Father would be as kind to her in death as he had been in life. Stephen resolved to use some of his inheritance to help make her independent.

Mr. Hall cleared his throat noisily, as if a bumblebee from Nelly's hat had flown over and gotten caught in his throat.

"We are all saddened by the loss of Anthony Fairmont, the Viscount Raybourn," he began. "It is my duty and honor, as the family solicitor, to inform you of the dispensation of Lord Raybourn's worldly goods."

The solicitor covered various minor bequests to friends and colleagues, followed by gifts to various Willow Tree estate servants. Madame Brusse and Larkin, who had disappeared somewhere with Father down in Egypt, were given thirty pounds each.

"Now I will read the more, er, significant bequests."

How odd. Father didn't mention a small legacy for Mrs. Peet. It was almost as if he knew she wouldn't survive to receive it.

Mr. Hall outlined specific monies and items for Dorothy and the Bishops, all of whom nodded happily. Ironically, Father left his entire tobacco collection to Gordon, who seemed fully recovered from his short imprisonment. What would Father say if he knew it had been responsible for nearly destroying his son-in-law's life?

"For my eldest son, Stephen Francis Fairmont . . ."

Naturally, Father passed Willow Tree estate and its contents not otherwise bequeathed to Stephen. He stood.

"Thank you, Mr. Hall, I prefer not to belabor all of Father's holdings in front of my siblings."

The bumblebee rattled around in the solicitor's throat again. "I'm sorry, Lord Raybourn, but I'm not quite finished with your father's bequests."

Stephen frowned but sat back down. What else was there?

"As I was saying, 'The property known as Willow Tree and its surrounding acreage, plus all furnishings and goods not otherwise assigned are hereby willed to Stephen in accordance with English law and tradition. The property known as Raybourn House, plus all furnishings and goods not otherwise assigned, are also willed to Stephen. The remaining cash and securities I own not otherwise assigned, including my interests in the Great Western Railway and Union Bank of London, I leave to my dearest friend and companion, Harriet Peet."

Stephen blinked. Did the solicitor just say that his father was leaving the bulk of his cash to *the housekeeper?*

Thank God she was dead.

He immediately regretted that uncharitable thought. Was everyone else as shocked as he was? He turned again to look at his other family members, just in time to witness Dorothy pitching forward to the floor in a dead faint.

* * *

Violet joined the family for a relatively peaceful, if peculiar, dinner that day. The Fairmonts were probably the first aristocratic family in England to have their undertaker sharing their supper table with them.

The food delivery from Pye's was piping hot and fresh, and conversation focused on Lord Raybourn's will.

Poor Dorothy, she had a blackened eye and her lower lip was swollen from a fall in the solicitor's office. Her appearance was even more forbidding as a result.

As discussion about the devastating will faded, a pall of gloom descended over the dining room table, impacting everyone except Toby, who seemed to find the entire situation mildly amusing.

Not even Violet's suggestion that Mr. Bishop was looking well after his stay at Newgate elicited any significant comment, other than Nelly's offhanded "He was happy to return to his insects."

Now that the excitement surrounding Gordon's arrest, imprisonment, and release was wearing off, replaced by other, more pressing news, Nelly was returning to her normal self.

As they finished off cups of baked lemon pudding, Louisa entered the room with a sealed note in her hand. "Sorry, my lord. I just found this pushed through the mail slot with a message that I must give it to you right away."

Stephen attempted to remain calm as he opened the note, but his glance at Violet across the table told her that he shared her own fear: that this was from Lord Raybourn's kidnappers.

He scanned the contents quickly and dropped the note to the table. He spoke quietly. "The money is due in two days. They will let us know tomorrow where to drop it off. What a penny dreadful this has become."

Violet pushed her plate away without comment, lifted her skirts, and ran for the hallway, scurrying quickly out the front door. She clutched the porch railing, looking right and left in Park Street from her perch seven stairs up from the hive of activity. Although there was little carriage traffic in this genteel neighborhood, there were plenty of people moving to and fro, including the young boy hawking newspapers in the street itself, as well as a flower seller encouraging wealthy men to buy a bouquet before returning home to their wives.

Violet did not see anyone suspiciously running away from Raybourn House.

Not that the note couldn't have been delivered by anyone she saw in the street below her. Perhaps the newspaper boy had been paid to deliver it.

She went to where the same grimy boy was selling newspapers and purchased a copy of *The London Illustrated News* from him.

The boy insisted that he had not delivered a note to the Raybourn home, nor had he noticed who had done so. Violet gave him an extra halfpence, which he happily pocketed.

The flower seller said the same thing, so Violet returned to the house, now carrying both a newspaper and a bouquet of fragrant peonies.

She had no idea the detection business could be so costly.

Back inside, the family members had apparently been revived by dessert or the note, for they were arguing over how to pay the upcoming ransom. With Mrs. Peet's death mucking up the remarkable contents of the will, Lord Raybourn's accounts would not be turned over in a timely enough way for the kidnappers, so something else had to be done. Violet listened quietly from the hallway, and quickly determined that the battle was ranging between Dorothy, Nelly, and Gordon, who thought the ransom was entirely Stephen's duty, and Stephen, Katherine, and, surprisingly, Toby, who felt that it was a family responsibility and that some household items of value should be sold to pay the ransom.

Violet had never been more grateful for her own familial harmony. She even missed her mother's complaining in light of what was going on inside this home. Rather than listen in on the Fairmonts' continued warfare, she went up to her own room and wrote a letter to Sam, inquiring as to when he would return from Sweden and letting him know of her new living arrangements.

She took a break from her writing to look out the window to the street scene below. As she watched traffic go by, Toby left the house. At the bottom of the steps, he looked both ways as if worried that someone was watching him, then headed south on Park Street to a destination unknown.

As she finished up her letters, she heard the servants' bell ringing repeatedly. Eventually, there was a tap at her door from Louisa.

"Mrs. Harper, Mrs. Bishop asks to see you."

Putting aside pen and paper, Violet went down to Nelly's room. Gordon's wife greeted her with a smile. "Please, have a seat. Would you like some?" She poured steaming tea into a fragile cup with a gilded rim, placed it on a matching saucer, and handed it over to Violet.

"Sugar? Milk?"

"No, thank you."

Nelly added four cubes of sugar to her own cup and stirred vigorously. "How is your tea?"

Violet sipped, confused as to why she was here. "Lovely."

Nelly nodded as she took her own taste. "How are you getting on up in Mrs. Peet's room?"

"Well enough. It's not St. James's Palace, of course."

"No, I suppose it isn't. There are no other bedrooms available in the house, though, and you're the undertaker. . . ."

Violet smiled. She was like a governess. Not a servant, but not quite respectable, either. "I'm not used to such finery, anyway. It's rather wasted on me."

"Oh, that's good to know. I mean, not that finery is wasted on you, but that you don't mind." Nelly took another long swallow from her cup, as though dragging out the moment until she decided what to say next.

"How are your investigations coming along? Have you any idea yet who may have killed my father and stolen his body?"

"It may not have been the same person. Or persons."

"No, of course not. Do you have any suspects, though? Isn't that what they say in the detective novels?"

"None that I know of. It's difficult to fathom why someone would take a corpse and hold it for ransom. Such things are normally done with living people of great importance to their families. You'd think they would have kidnapped Lord Raybourn *before* he died, not after."

Nelly raised an eyebrow. "If they'd done it while my father was still alive, Dorothy might have insisted that the kidnappers keep him."

"You would have paid the ransom, though, wouldn't you?"

Nelly poured herself more tea, another delay as she considered her response. "He is my Toby's grandfather, so, yes, I would have been as insistent on retrieving his living self as Stephen is about getting back his dead self. Listen to us, such morbid creatures. It's all this black we're wearing. I don't know how you don such bleak attire each day."

"It comforts my customers."

"I suppose so. Personally, I'm ready to move on to lilac or mauve. Or at least gray, although that color always makes me look sallow. I wish gray could be completely eliminated from half mourning. I should write—" Nelly stopped and sipped.

"Yes?" Violet said.

"I should write a book to rival *Mrs. Beeton's Book of Household Management*. I would call it *Mrs. Bishop's Book of Happy Living*, and I would recommend elimination of all traditions and customs that are boring, oppressive, or ridiculous."

"Mrs. Bishop, I must confess something to you."

"Of course, what is it?" Nelly's eyes lit up as though she were about to receive a state secret.

"I hate Mrs. Beeton."

For the first time since they'd been together under the same roof, Violet heard peals of laughter ring from Nelly's throat. "How is it that you can hate the highly regarded Mrs. Beeton?"

"That woman has caused me no end of trouble in my life. When you write your book, Mrs. Bishop, you should also eliminate all onerous housekeeping tasks, too."

Nelly tapped the side of her head. "I'll remember that. Well, if you don't have any suspects yet . . ."

This was Violet's cue to depart. "No, but I do have a question for you. I was wondering what you know about Toby's . . . activities."

"What activities?"

"Where he goes at night, whom he sees, that sort of thing."

Nelly frowned. "Toby is actively pursuing a wife and a place in society. I imagine he is at clubs, dances, and sporting events."

Violet nodded but said nothing.

"Why do you ask this? Are you accusing my little darling of something? You don't suspect *him* of having anything to do with my father's murder or kidnapping, do you?"

Nelly was quickly becoming a tigress defending her cub. Violet understood it; she'd developed claws many times herself during Susanna's youth.

"Not at all. I just found it curious how often he goes off by himself. I'm sure you're right that he's pursuing his ambitions."

Nelly was mollified. "Would you like a gooseberry scone? Louisa picked them up from a bakery this morning."

Violet took the plate upon which the scone was presented, and also accepted the lemon curd Nelly offered. She felt as though she was being rewarded for good behavior, and it troubled her.

The following morning, all eyes were on Violet as another royal carriage drove away, its driver having delivered a message to her. The queen's note felt like lead in her hands and she dreaded opening it. With the family waiting expectantly, though, she couldn't very well retreat to her room to read it.

The note's content and tone were what she had feared. She offered a wan smile to the Fairmonts.

"The queen has asked to see me."

"Will you tell her what has happened?" Stephen asked.

"I don't really have a choice. I cannot lie to the Queen of England."

"No, no, of course not."

What Violet didn't share with the family was the queen's pique at having learned through the household staff at St. James's that

Violet had moved to Raybourn House. Victoria had not given her permission for it.

Perhaps Violet should have written that note to the queen, after all.

She arrived at Windsor with the weight of dread having transferred from her hands to her stomach. Was she in for a royal tongue-lashing? The queen's morose, never-ending soliloquies about the prince consort she could manage, but to endure the queen's rage? Her sharp temper was legendary.

A servant wearing a black armband led her to the queen, who sat reading with a black-and-white border collie napping at her feet.

"Mrs. Harper," the queen said flatly, as Violet curtsied before her. Was it Violet's imagination, or did the queen wait a few extra moments before allowing her to rise? She was glad she had thought to add jet ear bobs, a necklace, and a bracelet to her black dress to acknowledge Prince Albert.

"You may sit." Violet chose a chair across from the queen. Victoria wore her usual black, softened only by a trim of white lace at her neckline. The queen opened her mouth with, "We understand you took it upon yourself . . ." but stopped when the dog raised his head, opened an eye, and examined Violet.

She must have passed an initial inspection, for he scrambled to his feet and lumbered over to sniff her. His coat was a sleek ebony with large white patches on his muzzle, chest, and paws. After a couple of snuffles, he licked her hand, then dropped back down at the queen's feet.

The queen's mood instantly lightened. "Why, Sharp, do you approve of Mrs. Harper? Sharp is our favorite dog. He's quite faithful and gives us such comfort now that we live alone as a widow. There are few companions who can understand grief the way a dog can."

The door to the room opened suddenly, without even a cursory knock or scratching. Violet jumped at the booming voice saying, "What ho, here's the laddie. How am I supposed to check on the new clutch of partridge eggs without ye, boy?"

It was Mr. Brown. Sharp must have been of one mind with his mistress about the man, for he went bounding up to Brown, playfully grabbing his arm and shaking it. Brown wrestled with the dog for a few moments before giving him a hand signal to stop. Sharp obediently sat next to him.

"What have we here, wumman?" he asked. "Both of ye in somber black; it's like a gathering of crows."

Violet couldn't believe the man's audacity, but the queen was unfazed. "You remember Mrs. Harper, don't you?"

He peered at Violet. "Your husband's undertaker. I guess that means you'll not be wanting me around for a while so you can stew in yer gloomy broth."

"It won't be for long."

"I'll take Sharp with me, and when I return we'll have a little tarot reading, won't we?"

"Yes indeed, Mr. Brown. We'll have your favorite oatcakes and Brie cheese brought up, too."

He left with the collie close on his heels.

"Really, Mrs. Harper, we do insist that you stay for Mr. Brown's reading and have one done for yourself. His interpretations are simply remarkable. We feel so close to our Albert when Mr. Brown spreads out the cards. Surely there is something troubling in your life that could use supernatural attention."

Be careful, Violet thought. *Don't offend the queen.*

"I suppose what troubles me the most, Your Majesty, is what happened to Lord Raybourn."

The queen's expression was guarded. "Yes, that is a mystery for us all, but with so many people working diligently on that, might it be best not to trouble the supernatural world with it? Not just yet."

"As you wish, naturally."

"Which is really the purpose of your visit here today, isn't it? We wish to know what you've learned about Lord Raybourn's death."

Violet took a deep breath. "Unfortunately, Your Majesty, I have some difficult news. . . ."

She explained about Mrs. Peet's death and Lord Raybourn's subsequent kidnapping and Gordon Bishop's arrest and release. To her surprise, the queen remained passive and did not rail against Violet for making such a botched mess of everything.

In fact, it was quite the opposite.

"Quite informative. Yes, we are quite interested in this. You say that the kidnappers will return his body in two days' time?"

"Presumably. The family is waiting for news about where to deliver the ransom money and where to pick up the coffin."

Victoria nodded thoughtfully. "Has there been an epidemic in London of thieves spiriting away coffins and holding them for ransom?"

"I don't think so."

"Then why now? Why Lord Raybourn in particular? It seems to us that the answer to this question will lead you to him, Mrs. Harper."

"I've assumed it was someone connected with his death."

"That could be so. Or it could be someone with other intentions entirely."

The door banged open. Mr. Brown had returned with a panting but exuberant Sharp. He carried with him a small wooden box.

"Will ye be having Mrs. Harper stay for our reading today?"

"Yes. We've told her about your remarkable talent, and she is most anxious to see it for herself."

For the next hour, Violet sat patiently while the queen's ghillie shuffled, dealt, and manipulated the cards, which were longer than playing cards and covered with colorful pictures of maidens in filmy dresses, young men in medieval dress, swords, and chalices. It seemed as though any card with a picture of a man on it was interpreted to be the queen's dead husband with a message for her life. The queen clasped her hands together in eager anticipation each time Brown shuffled the deck, asking her what question she wanted answered and then laying out a spread of seven cards.

At first frustrated by Brown's obvious chicanery, it slowly dawned on Violet what he was doing. Each subsequent reading saw the queen's manner become more and more relaxed, and soon she was even smiling and laughing.

So the mystery of Brown's attraction for Victoria was solved. He eased her mind about her husband's death through this entertaining activity, allowing her to forget her sorrows for a short time.

Violet felt a glimmer of respect for Mr. Brown.

When it came to her turn, she asked for a reading about her daughter, Susanna. As she expected, Mr. Brown found that Susanna was very happy but missed Violet greatly. A tidy, satisfying answer.

Once the queen tired of the game, Violet rose to make a final curtsy before her departure. Victoria had apparently not forgiven Violet entirely, despite Sharp's slobbery approval, for her final words were, "We expect that you will move back to St. James's as soon as practical."

The Fairmont siblings had decided, after much disagreement, that they would discreetly sell some of the silver from the house to raise money, rather than go to a bank for a loan, since it would raise society's eyebrows as they wondered why the inheritors of the wealthy Lord Raybourn would need to borrow money when all they had to do was wait a short time. Why stir up the gossip papers?

Violet was quickly realizing that all three siblings had been kept generally impoverished by their father, which led to this particular crisis of none of them having the funds to satisfy a kidnapper.

Was impoverishment a motive for murder?

The final note arrived the next day. It instructed Stephen specifically to go to Westminster Bridge with the ransom money early the following morning, at which point he would receive further instructions for recovering the body. The note warned against bringing the police.

"What insipid and banal idiot is behind all of this?" Stephen asked.

"Someone reading too many Wilkie Collins novels," Gordon

said. "Shall I go with you? They certainly can't accuse me of being the police."

"Hmm, I think it might be better for Violet to come. That way she can . . . attend to the body if need be. You don't mind, do you, Kate?"

"Of course not."

"Violet, have your undertaker bag prepared at dawn."

17

Stephen silently handed Violet into the driver's seat of the funeral carriage that used to be hers but now belonged to Morgan Undertaking, then came around to the other side and climbed into the passenger seat. Violet smiled to think of how inwardly mortified Stephen must be, an aristocrat riding on a funeral carriage through Mayfair, past Buckingham Palace, and on to Westminster. But if he was truly embarrassed, he gave no outward sign of it. He was also silent on the topic of his father's will.

The morning was like so many London mornings, the air thick with swirling fog at their feet, making the other carriages and pedestrians resemble specters floating by. It was even worse at Westminster Bridge, where fog settled over the bridge in such a blanket that it was nearly impossible to see what was in the murky Thames below.

What was unmistakable was the putrid stench of the river, full of sewage, animal carcasses, and who knew what else. It wasn't as noxious in the morning as it would surely be later in the day, and not nearly as pungent as it would be as London inched toward July.

Westminster Bridge spanned from one side of the Houses of Parliament over to Lambeth. Violet pulled the carriage over at the base of the bridge, near the clock tower whose workings were affectionately known as Big Ben after Sir Benjamin Hall, who oversaw installation of the great bell in 1859. As if in greeting, the clock struck its chime for the quarter hour.

"Ironic, isn't it?" Stephen said as he helped Violet out onto the pedestrian path and tied up the horses to a post.

"What do you mean?"

"We've been summoned to a bridge painted green to match the leather seats in the Commons, when my father was in the House of Lords. You'd think they'd have had us come to Lambeth Bridge." He pointed to a scarlet-painted bridge that crossed the Thames nearby, its span starting on the other side of the Parliament building. "The seats in the House of Lords are red leather. Perhaps they're making a statement. Maybe the kidnapping is political in nature."

"Had your father done something controversial?"

"No, but you know how these crazed labor rioters are. Maybe it looked like a way to bolster their cause."

Violet was doubtful. "It seems an odd thing to do."

"You can never tell with these vagrant types. Regardless, it will all be over soon." He held up the coin-laden bag, secured with twine. "What do we do? Stay here on the one end? Walk to the center of the bridge?"

"I recommend that we stay here. Whoever it is will come to you."

There was little foot traffic this early in the morning, but plenty of boats were out, made visible only by their glowing lanterns cutting through the fog. Despite the warmth of the morning, Violet felt a shiver creep up her spine. There was something not quite right with what was happening here. She looked straight down over the parapet. It felt as though she were floating, hovering over an abyss. She stepped back.

She felt a sharp jab in her back. She turned, and a cloaked figure thrust an envelope in her hand before disappearing in the direction from which she and Stephen had come.

"Wait! Who are you?" Violet called, running after him.

"Violet, where are you off to?" Stephen caught up to her in just a few steps and took her by the elbow. "What are you doing?"

She held up the envelope. "A man just shoved this into my hands."

"Who was it? Did you recognize him?"

"No. It happened in just a second."

Stephen opened up the envelope and read from it. " 'Go to the center of the bridge. Look for a steam launch to pass under bearing a man standing at the prow with his fists crossed on his chest. Drop the money down to the boat. You will receive further instruction on where your father's body is located.' And so the ridiculous subterfuge continues. Why not just walk straight up to me for the ransom money? Alas no, the feeble-minded idiots have not finished leading us on their merry chase."

They walked to the center of the bridge. The sun was rising, but not enough to penetrate the mist. "How will we ever be able to see which is the right boat?" Violet said.

"If they want their money, they will undoubtedly make themselves known."

Violet gripped the rail. The sooner this was finished, the sooner she could recover Lord Raybourn and hopefully leave London.

A whistle blew from somewhere below, its sound mournful and despondent. Several lanterns began glowing from the same location, revealing a steam launch approaching the bridge. Yet another lantern was lit, and the form of a man standing at the prow became visible. His arms were crossed on his chest, his hands curled into fists. He did not look up.

Violet turned to Stephen, who nodded wordlessly. He tossed the bag down, and Violet leaned over the rail, watching to ensure the money made it into the boat. It struck the deck with a jangling thud.

Now what would happen? Violet and Stephen stayed at the bridge rail several more moments, unsure whether they were supposed to wait for another signal there, or return to Park Street for yet another message.

The boat was almost completely under the bridge now. Violet stood on tiptoe and leaned over just a bit more, to be sure there was no other signal or sign being emitted from the steam launch. It was so difficult to see through the fog, despite the rising sun. Perhaps this was to be one of the days where the fog would stay—

From nowhere, she felt strong hands shove her between the shoulders, rolling her over the rail. She flailed wildly, but managed to throw her right arm over the metal railing. Thoroughly unused to supporting her own entire weight against gravity, her damaged arm howled in resistance, the pain radiating up her arm and through her shoulder, threatening her tenuous grip on the rail. She dangled perilously over the Thames, and knew she wouldn't survive a fall.

She tried to scream, but had no strength for it.

"My God, Violet!" came Stephen's voice from above her. She felt his hands clamp around her arm and the nonsensical thought flashed through her mind that she would be mortified if Stephen could feel the ridges of her scars through her sleeve.

"I have you," he said. "Give me your other arm."

With great effort, she lifted her other arm up to him. He began pulling, and when he had enough leverage, put an arm around her waist as he brought her slowly back over the railing. Violet stood, but just barely, so badly were her legs shaking.

"What happened? How did you stumble over the rail?"

"I didn't. Someone pushed me."

"Pushed you? I didn't see anyone. Of course, it's still so damnably thick out here. Are you all right? Even in this baffling vapor you look as a pale as a corpse. Oh, sorry."

Violet gave him a weak smile. "I'm fine, just a little weak-kneed. I don't understand why someone would have pushed me. It's quite beyond a schoolboy prank. I might have died."

"If whoever it was had been a few moments sooner, you'd have ended up in the boat."

An interesting point.

"Can you walk now?" he asked. "We may as well return to the carriage, since it doesn't look as though there will be any further notes delivered."

"But . . . shouldn't we look for whoever did this? He might still be nearby."

206 Christine Trent

"Will you recognize his hands when you see him? Do you think he will greet us, tip his hat to you?"

"I suppose not."

"Come." He held out an arm. "Let's go back to Raybourn House to wait."

Violet took his arm, but was unsettled. Stephen seemed unconcerned that she'd just been attacked. In fact, someone had attempted to murder her. Why? Was it one of Lord Raybourn's kidnappers? But why would they want to kill his undertaker? Or was this connected again to Lord Raybourn's murder? If so, how?

A dreadful thought rose in the back of her mind. If Stephen was unconcerned about the attack, was it because he was responsible? Had he himself pushed her? She tamped the thought down. It was too ludicrous to consider. After all, they had been childhood friends, and now she was helping him find his father's body.

No, it was a foolish notion and without foundation. Besides, he'd had plenty of other opportunities to hurt her if he were so motivated.

The sun was finally piercing through the fog as Stephen once again handed Violet up onto the driver's seat. An envelope lay there. Violet held it up for Stephen as he joined her on the seat.

"From our friend, presumably," he said, taking it. "Perhaps he pushed you so we wouldn't notice him at the carriage."

The carriage had been entirely too far away from the center of the bridge for them to see him in the murky fog. Violet made no comment.

"It says we will find the coffin in the cold store building at the Smithfield meat market."

"At Smithfield! How did they manage to move a coffin in broad daylight all the way from Mayfair to Smithfield?" Violet said.

"You're the undertaker. How would you do it?"

Violet thought. "St. Bart's Hospital is near there. I suppose I would pretend I was headed there."

"A good assessment, I should think. I recommend we take Victoria Embankment."

This road had recently opened, and was intended to provide

congestion relief in the Strand and on Fleet Street. It commenced at the base of the bridge across from Parliament. "I agree."

Violet guided the carriage out into traffic. Soon they were racing along the Embankment—to the extent traffic would allow—which ran parallel to the Thames. At Farringdon Street she turned north toward the meat market, passing within a couple of blocks of St. Bart's. St. Paul's dome was visible to the east, towering over everything as it had done for two centuries.

They came nearly to a halt as they approached the market, as the road became clogged with men driving cattle into the central entrance. The stench was overpowering, as cow dung competed with the droppings of the passenger-carrying horse carriages. The cattlemen were shouting unintelligibly at their herds and cracking whips over their heads. They had clearly already been at this for hours, long before the average Londoner arose.

"Smart of them to keep this downwind on the east side of London. And imagine what this looked like before they built a railway tunnel beneath it for primary animal transport," Stephen said.

Violet looked at him in surprise. How unusual for an idle aristocrat to have a working knowledge of something as pedestrian as a meat market.

Violet managed to find a place to park the carriage, then she and Stephen went in search of the cold store. Stephen tossed an extra coin to the boy who offered to watch the equipage, and who pointed out the cold store entrance, which led to an underground network of lockers for storing carcasses. They went from locker to locker, hunting through the slabs of beef and pork, not sure whether they were looking for a coffin, or perhaps just Lord Raybourn's embalmed body.

Hours later, fatigued and perspiring despite the chilled lockers, they admitted defeat. There was no body or coffin anywhere inside the cold store. They returned to the carriage, dejected.

"I don't understand," Stephen said, running a hand through his hair as Violet took the reins. "They took the money *and* kept the body. Isn't there some sort of kidnappers' code that prevents that?"

Now that sounded more like an aristocrat's view of humanity, imagining a world that wouldn't dare betray him.

"There is no honor among thieves," Violet quoted.

"A pestilent lot of mongrel dogs, aren't they? You don't suppose they were down inside the cold store, watching us on our futile pursuit, do you?"

She shook her head. "I don't know. I haven't a single idea as to what is in their minds."

Watching Stephen's profile, though, she had that dreadful, queasy feeling again. Impossible, she told herself. Men like Stephen Fairmont did not kill their fathers, nor did they kidnap their fathers' bodies for no reason.

Did they?

Violet sat in her attic room at Raybourn House, a large book in her lap propped up as a table as she wrote a letter to her parents, telling them of her exploits thus far, but omitting any mention of her near fall from Westminster Bridge.

As she blotted the letter dry, she heard the loud ringing of the doorbell in the hallway outside her door. What a cursed life a servant led in a rich household, having all manner of summons—front doorbells, servants' entrance bells, ladies' handbells—all going off riotously day and night both in the basement and the servants' quarters. At least she'd learned not to jump each time one of them sounded.

Violet folded her letter and slid it into the envelope, then took it downstairs to add to the mail tray.

A man sat in the drawing room, so tall and cadaverously thin that his knees jutted up and out from the chair in an awkward way. Louisa intercepted Violet as she dropped the letter, along with a penny for the post, into the tray.

"Mrs. Harper," she said, her voice low and her eyes cast down. "This 'ere's Mr. Godfrey, a friend of Mr. Fairmont. The late Mr. Fairmont. The dead one."

"You mean the viscount?"

"No, ma'am, the elder brother, that one what perished in the war. There's no one else home right now, so I thought you might speak wi' him?"

"Of course, if I can help."

"Mr. Godfrey?" Violet said, extending a hand as she entered the drawing room. He rose, and proved himself to be even taller and thinner than Violet suspected. He looked as if he might be on war rations, and his nose cut out sharply from his bony face like a short bayonet. He looked familiar. "I'm Violet Harper, a friend of the family, staying here temporarily. Everyone else is out. May I help you?"

He took her hand and eyed her clothing. "I see you, too, are in mourning for the late Lord Raybourn?"

"Actually, I'm the . . . yes, I'm in mourning with the family."

He released her hand. "I was hoping I might speak to Lord Raybourn's son. Stephen, I believe his name is? Do you know when he'll return?"

"I don't. Again, might I assist you?"

They sat down. He rested spidery hands on his jutting knees. In that moment, she realized how she knew him.

"You're that man," she blurted out.

"That man?"

"You accosted me outside of this home not long ago. You reeked of spirits and demanded that I tell Lord Raybourn you were waiting for him at your hotel."

A light of recognition dawned in his eyes and he was immediately apologetic. "Ah, that. I'm greatly sorry. I'm afraid I was in my cups at the time. Mrs. Bagwell at the temperance society always tells me I'll come to no good end that way. I suppose I'm too used to free living. When my notes were sent away unanswered, well, I took matters into my hands."

Violet nodded her forgiveness. She was already mentally widening her circle of suspects who might have attempted to push her over Westminster Bridge, although she couldn't imagine why he had a motive to do so.

"My name is James Godfrey. I'm a friend of Cedric Fairmont,

Lord Raybourn's eldest son. We served together in the Crimean War." Godfrey paused, as though considering whether to continue.

Violet encouraged him. "It must have been terrible what you endured against the Russians, and you, too, have experienced a loss in your friend. I know the family was also most grieved by his death on the Crimean Peninsula."

He clasped his hands together on his knees. It looked as though a giant arachnid had curled up and died in his lap. "That's just it, though. Cedric isn't dead."

18

Violet sat stunned, but was saved from struggling to make a co-herent response by the return of the Fairmont siblings and their spouses. Stephen, Katherine, Dorothy, Nelly, and Gordon arrived in reasonably high spirits, having just gone for a drive through Regent's Park. It was a highly improper activity for a family in recent mourning, but most family deaths didn't encompass quite so much tragedy. It was good to see them all smiling.

Violet introduced James Godfrey to them, and he repeated his statement about Cedric being alive. Their rare jubilance was terminated in a mere moment. The stream of Fairmont revelations seemed to never cease.

"Pardon me, did you just say my brother is still alive?" Dorothy asked. "That can't be. He's been dead for at least thirteen years. We never heard from him again after he left for the Crimea. He was formally declared dead by the courts seven years later. He's *dead*." She said it with emphasis, as if repeating it would make it so.

"I'm sorry, ma'am, but that isn't so."

"Speak up, then, man. What are you talking about?" Stephen said. "What do you mean he's still alive?"

"I first met Cedric on a ship bound for Sevastopol on the Black Sea. We ended up serving together in the disastrous Battle of Balaclava in October of fifty-four. During those dark hours, he told me of his family and his time at Willow Tree House."

Showing little respect or pity for his past service and suffering,

Nelly, in a sharp mood now, couldn't control her tongue. "What else did he tell you?"

"I'm not sure what you mean."

"Hmmph," Nelly said, arms crossed.

"Cedric was promoted to lieutenant, and managed to secure me as his batman. He nearly died when we made the charge on the Russians. I was one of the lucky ones, coming out unscathed. He took a terrible wound to the thigh, though. They wanted to take his leg, but I wouldn't let them. Spent weeks tending to him on the floor in what they called a hospital. Blood and excrement everywhere, despite the wood shavings thrown down to absorb it all. Rats as big as small dogs coming by on occasion to inspect Cedric's leg, to test whether he was weak enough to be gnawed on as a snack.

"Cedric was an officer, so he was upgraded to a bed as soon as one was available. He might have gotten well sooner, but then cholera ran through the camp. I risked infection to make sure he was well. Cedric told me later that he was forever indebted to me for my loyalty and friendship."

Godfrey pulled a cigarette from inside his jacket. "Do you mind?" he asked as he lit it. He leaned back, closed his eyes, and blew a great plume of smoke toward the ceiling. He was quiet several moments, as if gathering his thoughts as to what had happened next.

"Even after he recovered, Cedric was never quite the same, here." Godfrey touched his temple with the cigarette between his fingers. "Got in a few scrapes he shouldn't have, and I always talked him out of doing anything too foolish before he got into trouble with his own superiors. When the war was over, he decided he didn't want to go home, but instead wanted to start his life anew. As I said, he wasn't quite . . . right.

"I accompanied him to France, where we joined the *haut bohème*. Cedric's aristocratic status enabled us to live a more privileged lifestyle, although we certainly embraced the unconventional, vagabond lifestyle after being so long confined to the rules and discipline of the army. Even more, we embraced the, er, generous nature of the women we met there."

Godfrey flicked ash into the crystal ashtray.

"Alas, our money eventually ran out, even though we adopted the poverty of the regular bohemians. Cedric tried his hand at painting and selling his oils in the streets, while I attempted—quite unsuccessfully—to publish a memoir of the war. In due course, we decided we hated poverty more than we loved the kindhearted and affectionate women, so we traveled a bit more, sampled what else the world had to offer, and returned to England."

"When was this?" Dorothy demanded. "Are you telling me that Cedric is here *now?*"

"Indeed, madam. We arrived a few months ago and parted ways. On pleasant terms, of course, but in the way that friendships will sometimes do. I've taken on odd work here and there, but haven't quite found my legs, so to speak. I read that old Lord Raybourn had died, and thought I'd come around to pay my respects if Cedric was here, but I wasn't sure if he'd ever returned home or not. I sent a few letters, but they went unanswered."

Katherine looked at her husband. "We never received them."

Stephen patted her shoulder but addressed his own gaze to Godfrey. "And so what made you decide to land on our doorstep, despite getting no response to your letters?"

Godfrey ground out his cigarette in the ashtray. "I came to the conclusion that after our run of poverty in France, he would be unlikely to stay away from his father, since old Lord Raybourn would be the one to fix all of his money problems. Cedric didn't really have a reason to return to England unless it was to reunite with his family, did he?"

Stephen's face was as white as a shroud. "But Cedric didn't reunite with us."

Godfrey frowned. "That doesn't make sense. He must have shown his face to his father. This certainly dampens the purpose of my visit."

"Which is . . . ?" Dorothy said.

"I was hoping Cedric might see his way to, er, rewarding me for my services during the war, as he promised. I showed the man a great deal of loyalty during his convalescence, and now he has surely inherited a great fortune. A few pounds sterling would be greatly appreciated."

"You intended to blackmail my dead brother?" Nelly said.

"What? Of course not. First, he isn't dead. Second, I have nothing with which to blackmail him. I just hoped he'd remember an old friend. I see now my hopes were misplaced."

After letting them know that he had recently moved into new lodgings so that Cedric could find him if he showed up, Godfrey left. The room exploded in fear and anxiety, with everyone talking at once.

"How could Cedric possibly be alive?"

"How dare he hide from his loving family!"

"This isn't right, no, not right at all. I say, it seems a rather nasty trick if it's true."

But it was Katherine, her voice barely a whisper, who asked the most pressing question of all. "Did Cedric kill your father to hurry along his inheritance?"

"Impossible!"

"Ridiculous! He's still dead by all accounts. How could a dead man collect an inheritance?"

"I'd kill Cedric myself if he were here right now."

"He must have figured he'd never be caught because he was presumed dead, and now he plans on somehow returning and blackmailing us," Nelly said.

Dorothy gave her a look of disdain. "Blackmail us over what, you nitwit?"

"There are plenty of secrets in this house."

"Hah! As if you wouldn't run straight to the newspapers if you had hold of a single juicy morsel."

"I never—"

Violet cleared her throat loudly to interrupt the squabbling. "Pardon me, but may I suggest that if your elder brother is alive, we should find him? It would clear up many questions."

"Yes, of course you're right," Gordon said. "After all, we don't know this Godfrey brute from any other street person. He may have read the old man's death notice in the papers, which surely included a note about Cedric's death during the war, and decided to capitalize on it. How difficult would it be to make up such a story? Tending to Cedric on a hospital floor, indeed. He probably did intend to blackmail the family. Or garner false pity, and reap some rewards from the disbursement of the will. You are clever as always, Nells." He gazed adoringly at his wife.

"I'll go to Scotland Yard with this revelation tomorrow," Violet said. "Hopefully, we can determine the truth of Mr. Godfrey's story, and, if it's true, it will lead us to Cedric."

Stephen couldn't contain his disdain. "A lot of good that will do. The police couldn't find someone if he was hiding inside their overcoats."

After supper, Violet spent an odd evening in the drawing room with the entire Fairmont family, except for Toby, who showed up just as supper was served and went upstairs as soon as he finished wiping his mouth with his napkin. In total silence, everyone sat at his own activity. The sisters read books, Stephen had a newspaper spread in his lap, and Gordon surrounded himself with trays of pinned butterflies as he flipped through an illustrated guide to the winged beauties.

Violet sat quietly with her lists, reviewing them and crossing off things that no longer seemed relevant, as well as adding in information about Godfrey's unexpected visit. It felt productive, but wasn't actually getting her any closer to an answer regarding the whereabouts of Lord Raybourn's remains, or whether it was a suicide or murder. There were no interruptions, save a friend of Toby's. With barely a nod to acknowledge the family, the friend scurried up to Toby's room.

When she could no longer keep her eyes open, Violet decided it was as good a reminder as any that a night of sleep would work wonders on her mind's prowess, which seemed utterly devoid of cogent thought these days.

She said good night and went upstairs, but once again found herself pausing on the stairs leading up to the attic rooms. Toby and the friend were talking, and what Violet overheard was disturbing.

". . . have your uniform yet?" the friend said.

"Yes, I'm to be made lieutenant in his army."

"Already? Training is two years."

". . . special dispensation . . . my family's position."

The friend grunted. "Naturally . . . outpost you'll join?"

"Someplace far from here, I hope."

Whose army was Toby talking about? Was he involved in some sort of insurrectionist movement? Bored young men were easily led into the worst sorts of societies, most of them sounding perfectly idealistic, but ultimately proving to embrace wretched, ill-conceived notions.

Violet's heart sank to think that Toby might be involved with a group that might lead to his own injury or death—or to that of others.

She continued slowly up to her room, completely mystified over what to do about it.

A few minutes later, Violet heard Toby see his friend out. Despite sensing the impropriety of snooping, she hurried to her window overlooking the street below, in the hope of learning more about what they were up to. The gas lamps illuminated the street in a shadowy way, casting erratic light on people scurrying to and fro. Even in a quality neighborhood like Mayfair, it wasn't wise to spend much time in the streets after dark.

Her attention was captured as she saw Toby's friend leave Raybourn House and step into the street. He was almost immediately approached by a man who stepped out from somewhere in the shadows beyond the reach of the streetlamps. The two entered into earnest conversation.

Violet extinguished her own lamp and pressed her face closer to the glass in order to see more clearly.

What in heaven's name . . . ??

It was James Godfrey talking to Toby's friend. The two were arguing—no, wait . . . they were merely enthusiastic. How did Godfrey know Toby and his friend? What could they possibly have to discuss? Had Toby been aware of Cedric's existence long ago? If so, why hadn't he told anyone? The young man was full of secrets, for sure.

The two men clasped hands and parted ways. Violet lit her lamp again, and sat down on the bed in her most unladylike fashion, chin in palm and elbow on knee, in order to think. Despite her determined appearance, her thoughts were a scrambled mess as she reflected on the conflicting possibilities.

One thing she did know: Mrs. Peet had certainly had an interesting view down on the aristocratic world.

The next morning, Violet rose early in order to make amends with Hurst by keeping him informed in a more timely manner on new facts. Inside the same interview room where she had spoken with him before, Violet laid out for Inspector Hurst everything that had occurred in the past few days, from the bridge incident to the futile coffin hunt to James Godfrey's unfortunate visit. Hurst nodded periodically as he listened, as though Violet had said something of vital significance.

"The puzzle has more pieces than I thought. It would seem you are now one of them, Mrs. Harper."

"I can't imagine why someone would want to harm me. I've been thinking it over, trying to make sense of it all. Stephen believes whoever it was only intended to distract us from returning to our carriage too quickly. But I wonder, is it possible that whoever pushed me at the bridge thought I was someone else?"

"If true, the only person it could be is Stephen's wife. What other woman wearing mourning would reasonably be out with him at dawn?"

"You're right, of course. I can't imagine why someone would want to harm Katherine."

"My instincts tell me that you were a specific target, Mrs. Harper, but we can't rule anything out."

"Is there anything you *have* ruled out?"

Hurst scowled. "We've so little to go on. Of course, the queen's interference created this additional affliction of the kidnapping, since Lord Raybourn was not buried promptly. So the primary question is, who killed Lord Raybourn? Secondarily, who killed his housekeeper?"

"So now you don't believe she committed suicide, either?"

Hurst cleared his throat. "Ahem. She may have; it's impossible to say."

Hurst continued. "Our third question is, who kidnapped Lord Raybourn's body? Our last and most puzzling question is, why was he kidnapped? The answers to these questions might point to one person or several people. There may also be circumstances we do not yet understand. For example, his kidnapping may have nothing to do with him personally."

Violet struggled with impatience. The detective was sermonizing on what she already knew. The interview room's door opened and Inspector Pratt entered. "Sir, I've written up the details of our visit with the theater owner whose ticket seller was murdered—oh, Mrs. Harper, a delight to see you."

Hurst motioned for him to take the other chair in the room. "Mrs. Harper has just informed me of some interesting happenings in connection with the Lord Raybourn case. Mrs. Harper?"

She repeated for Pratt what she'd told Hurst.

"She and I were about to discuss some possible theories we have to explain the tragedies."

"Did you tell her about the resurrectionists?"

"I was about to do so. Mrs. Harper, in your line of work, I'm sure you've heard of resurrectionists?"

"Yes, it was one of my own thoughts. I visited as many undertakers in the London area as I could to see if any of them might have been involved, but never discovered any information of value."

"Of course, such men don't seek ransoms for the bodies, as they have ready buyers."

"Lord Raybourn's body wouldn't have been much use to a resurrectionist, since he was embalmed. It makes good dissection difficult. But the kidnapper wouldn't necessarily have realized he'd been embalmed."

"Unless he was taken by one of these bizarre religious cults. We've been watching the Order of the Golden Dawn closely. They incorporate Egyptian motifs into their rituals. An embalmed body might be preferable to them."

Violet had never heard of such a cult.

"Conversely, it may have been an elaborate prank," Hurst continued. "It wouldn't be the first time some porridge brain cooked up such an idea."

"If this was a prank," Violet said, "it was elaborate in the extreme. They had to secure a hiding location—which was clearly not the cold store at Smithfield—where no one would find it. A coffin is no easy thing to hide. And to what end? A bit of money? Some notoriety? Moreover, if this was just a prank, why haven't they told us where to find the body?"

"Perhaps they aren't finished blackmailing the family. I admit, it's been a most peculiar case. I never expected it to require so much attention, but we have no further progress from our informants in Egypt so we may as well focus our minds on it."

The three of them stayed in the room another hour, turning over one theory after another, with no firm conclusions made. As Hurst rose to signal that their meeting was over, he said, "Is there anything else you wish to tell me?"

Violet thought about the argument she'd overheard among the siblings, where Nelly said something about keeping Stephen's secrets. What did she mean by that? Reference was made to these secrets again today in front of Mr. Godfrey.

Not to mention Toby's clandestine behavior.

Some instinct cautioned Violet not to reveal the information. *It will keep*, it whispered.

"Not that I can think of. I'll come back as soon as I know more."

"I think perhaps Mr. Pratt and I will go round to see this Mr. Godfrey. Just to pay a friendly visit, if you will, to discern where Cedric Fairmont might be hiding. Would you care to come along?"

This was the friendliest the inspector had ever been. "I would very much like to come."

Hurst's massive presence intimidated Godfrey's landlord enough that he immediately gave them access to his tenant's rooms.

"This shouldn't take long," Hurst said, looking around at the sparsely furnished room with few belongings. "Look for anything whatsoever that connects Godfrey to Cedric Fairmont."

While Pratt went through various drawers and Hurst inspected wall and floorboards for anything loose, Violet examined Godfrey's mattress and bedding. It reeked of spirits and sweat. She wondered if he was so thin because he was malnourished. He would come to a bad end one day if he didn't cease being an inebriate.

After feeling around in his pillowcase and the bedcovers, Violet lifted up one side of the mattress. Tucked underneath was a packet of envelopes. She extracted them and scanned through them. A letter from a law firm, several bills, an advertisement from a tailor, and . . . what was this? She tossed the other envelopes onto the bed and opened one that had neither an address nor postage on it, so it was possibly a letter that had merely been handed to someone.

> *James, I believe our time has come. Fleur is plaguing me; I can hardly get away from her carping about marriage. I should never have told her I was the son of a viscount. It's as though she looks at me hoping she'll find my eyes have turned into diamonds and my teeth into pearls that she can pluck and sell. I must get away from here. What say we return home? I have an idea, actually.*

The letter was undated.

"Inspector, you may be interested in this." Violet held the note out to Hurst.

"So Godfrey was telling the truth," he said, after reading it and handing it to Pratt. "At least in broad terms. Mr. Pratt, I believe you and I will wait here for James Godfrey's return so that we can have a little chat with him. Mrs. Harper, it's best if you don't stay."

Violet gladly left the men to their police work, having no desire to witness what might happen later, but an unhappy thought pained her the rest of the day.

Was it possible that Cedric Fairmont returned to England, hoping to secretly reestablish relations with his father, but was perhaps rebuffed? Maybe Cedric eventually killed his father in rage, either for rejecting him or for refusing him money.

Or maybe Violet's imagination had the better of her. She needed a hot cup of tea, a few hours of light reading, and a good night's sleep to clear her mind. Tomorrow was her scheduled trip back to Hyde Park with Mary, and surely the world would seem brighter and clearer after a day with her friend.

The day was chillier than it had recently been as Violet and Mary made their way across the parade ground, where English kings and queens had once reviewed their troops, into Hyde Park and to the boat rental pier. Occasional puffy clouds, tinged with gray, dotted the sky. They seemed to want to pour down a good English rain, but it was as though the clouds felt they weren't numerous enough to produce a soaking rain, so they were merely biding their time for an eventual onslaught. As a result the cloud cover was enough to prevent the sun from warming them.

As Violet once again settled into her role of rower, maneuvering the craft around the small island set in the lake near the boat launch, Mary brought forth a loaf of stale bread, breaking off small pieces and tossing them out to the eager swans, whose long necks ricocheted back and forth as they targeted the yeasty tidbits and gobbled them down. The trees all along the edge of the water, carefully planted to suggest a casual wildness, induced a sense of tranquility, despite the multitudes of people all along the pathways crisscrossing the park on either side of them.

"Shall we go all the way to the Italian Gardens?" Violet asked, referring to the other end of the winding lake, where an ornately sculpted garden with multiple fountains, walkways, and statuary beckoned visitors to stroll about.

"Yes. Do you suppose we could secure the boat there and walk around?"

"An excellent idea."

Violet continued rowing until she reached the Serpentine Bridge, which crossed the lake and created a divider between the part known as the Serpentine and the far narrower portion called the Long Water. Carriage traffic thundered overhead as they passed beneath the bridge. Violet estimated that she had another quarter of a mile to row through the Long Water before reaching the Italian Gardens. After a brief rest, she continued rowing.

A group of four boats approached, filled with reveling young men joking, splashing water at one another with their oars, and being generally unaware of everything around them. Violet guided her own craft to the right, next to the tree line on shore, to enable the band of carousers to pass them without upsetting their own craft.

She struggled to stay away from the other boats, as well as to avoid getting caught up in the wiry brambles and fallen limbs that were prevalent along the edge. The water was shallower here, so she laid one oar down in the boat and used the other to try and dig into the soft earth beneath them, in an attempt to anchor them.

A red squirrel in an overhanging branch above the two women chattered angrily, as though chastising the revelers, as well as Violet and Mary, for disrupting his peaceful existence. A couple of acorn hulls dropped into the boat from above.

Mary looked up. "Forgive us, Sir Squirrel. We'll be out of your way soon."

The other boat group had passed by. Violet lifted the oar out of the soft earth to reposition it to push off the bank. She drove it back under the water and was met with resistance. She'd hit something that was not merely slippery, algae-covered earth. She tentatively stuck the oar back in the water.

"What's wrong?" Mary asked.

"I'm not sure. There seems to be some sort of strange undergrowth here. I can't get a firm hold on—"

Suddenly, Violet felt whatever it was loosen from underneath her oar, then, as she watched, the undergrowth rose to the surface. Except it wasn't undergrowth.

It was a body.

Mary shrieked and clamped a hand over her own mouth, her eyes wide in terror. Even Violet, as used to corpses as she was, felt a moment of fright. One didn't go rowing in a lake expecting a dead body to make an appearance in broad daylight.

Breathing deeply to calm her own pounding heart, Violet said, "We must get help, but we don't want to alarm anyone in the park. We'll continue to the Italian Gardens and find a guard or bobby."

Mary nodded, removing her hand from her mouth and staring at Violet to avoid looking down at what was a foot away from her.

Her undertaking instincts taking control, Violet looked over again to examine the poor soul who had managed to drown himself in the Serpentine, beginning at his shoeless feet. Drowning suicides were not that uncommon.

The body was in relatively good shape, suggesting the man had been underwater less than a day. He was dressed in some sort of military uniform, the jacket of which was unbuttoned and floating loosely around his torso. It was what she observed next, though, that caused Violet to cover her own mouth to prevent herself from screaming.

Just as with Mrs. Peet, a rope was burrowed into the flesh around his neck, and his face was bloated almost beyond any human recognition.

Almost.

It took Violet only a few seconds to realize at whom she was staring, whose body she'd been inadvertently poking.

It was James Godfrey.

19

Once she'd found a bobby to notify about Godfrey's body and had dropped a shaken Mary off at home, Violet took a hackney straight back to Raybourn House for a cup of tea to settle her nerves. Toby and his friend were in the drawing room, a decanter of sherry between them.

"Mrs. Harper, this is Adam Farr." Farr stood to greet her, his blond hair perfectly combed, beard neatly trimmed, and suit crisply pressed. It seemed incongruous that a warmonger would look so tidy.

Next to the sherry decanter were several patches, each with a different insignia on it. One had a single star on it, another contained a red bar, and a third displayed a silver crest with an "S" inside of it.

Violet knew little about military insignia, but these obviously represented some sort of rankings and were intended to be sewn onto a uniform.

Farr noticed Violet's gaze, and scooped up the patches in one hand, swiftly tucking them inside his jacket without explanation.

"We were actually just leaving," Toby said. "So feel free to use the drawing room."

Violet watched out the drawing room window as Toby and Farr went outside, once again heading south down Park Street. Were they going to the same place Toby had gone before? She should have attempted to question Farr about his relationship with Godfrey. Was this young man somehow involved in Godfrey's death?

What were Toby Bishop and Adam Farr really up to? Perhaps it was time to tell Toby's father what she'd overheard and seen regarding his son, although she found it unlikely that Gordon Bishop would be any more willing to hear anything ill of Toby than Nelly had been.

The tea settled Violet's stomach, but not for long. Her thoughts had become such a jumble it was as though she were walking through a cemetery at midnight without the aid of a lantern, and was perpetually bouncing off gravestones and the edges of crypts, bruising herself without benefit as she whirled about in a daze.

Didn't the detectives in stories usually gather information and quickly deduce what had happened and why? Shouldn't events be getting clearer, not murkier?

Violet knew what might help: writing letters to her parents, Sam, and Susanna. She spent a quiet evening doing so, being careful to sanitize events differently for each recipient—her parents would have been particularly upset over her involvement in an investigation—so as not to cause undue concern.

As Violet sealed up the last letter, one for Susanna, a thought occurred to her. How would a criminal "sanitize" the events involved in his schemes? Tell a story that resembled the truth, wasn't too far off from it, but vastly altered everyone's understanding of it?

Had someone in the household been sanitizing Violet's perception of events since she'd been here? If so, how was she to ever figure out who it was?

The following morning, Violet went to Scotland Yard to see Inspector Hurst. By now he must know about Godfrey's death, and she wondered whether he and Inspector Pratt had ever confronted him at his lodgings beforehand. Before she could reach their offices, she ran into them in the hallway.

"We were just about to send for you," he said. "We've found Lord Raybourn's body thieves. They were students at St. Bart's

Medical College. One of them hoped we might offer a reward after his 'employer' refused to pay for taking the body. What kind of muttonheads is St. Bart's turning out, that they think the police would offer a reward to a body snatcher?"

Violet frowned. "Do you mean to say that one of their professors offered to pay two young men to steal Lord Raybourn's body?"

"No. They refuse to say who it was. One of them did let slip that they dealt with an intermediary, someone who had ink-stained fingers."

Like a journalist. But surely Ellis Catesby couldn't possibly be involved in this. What motive would he have?

"When we picked the student up and realized he was likely one of the kidnappers, we, er, convinced him to tell us where Lord Raybourn's body is, and we'd like you to come along to confirm its identity and to tidy him up if necessary. No sense in upsetting the family with it yet."

The three of them boarded a police van. "Where is Lord Raybourn?" Violet asked.

"Underneath Blackfriars Bridge, at the north end. I suppose it was the nearest place to St. Bart's to dump a body in water. Mrs. Harper, is something the matter?"

Violet felt weak from everything she was learning. This was to be her second encounter—in less than a day—with a murdered body floating in water. It was also the second time in mere days that she would be involved with Lord Raybourn's kidnappers at a bridge. Blackfriars Bridge wasn't that far from Westminster Bridge.

This time, she had no intention of being pushed over the pedestrian rail.

Blackfriars Bridge was newly erected, having been rebuilt to replace the crumbling old stone bridge that had stood upon the same location, and was recently opened by Queen Victoria herself. Violet and the inspectors left the coach and raced onto the pedestrian footpath of the bridge, stopping periodically to look over the parapet to search for Lord Raybourn in the water below. The rail on this bridge was so low it was dizzying. The effect was aggravated by the lethal stench of the Thames. Violet clutched the rail tightly each time she stopped.

"Inspector, look there!" Mr. Pratt was pointing back toward the base of the bridge. There was some sort of bundle afloat next to one of the bridge's piers. They all dashed back off the bridge and down the embankment, with Violet nearly tumbling headfirst down the rough slope to the water, despite Hurst's best efforts to support her.

It stank worse than any rotting corpse down here, threatening to knock Violet unconscious. Mr. Pratt reached the edge of the water first, and waded out to the first pier. A long rope had been tied around the pier, with one end of it securing a figure wrapped in rough burlap.

What an unfitting end for a viscount so respected by the queen.

Pratt retrieved a knife from his pocket and cut the rope, dragging the body out of the water and onto the shore, taking special care to bring him as far under the bridge as he could to prevent gawkers from watching over the bridge's parapet.

With Violet and Hurst at his side, Pratt cut away the burlap that had been wrapped around the body, secured at its ankles, waist, and neck with more rope strands. After he'd cut away all of the burlap, he looked up at Violet, who nodded.

This was definitely Lord Raybourn. She recognized her own handiwork with the cambric shroud that still covered him.

"Let's be certain, Mrs. Harper," Hurst said. "Unwrap him."

Pratt moved aside so that Violet could drop to her knees in the soft earth and take a closer look at Lord Raybourn. She gently loosened the body from the soaked cloth, revealing his repaired face and his torso, still dressed in his vest and tailcoat.

Stephen was going to be devastated to know how his father had been treated.

She sat back and nodded again. "It's him."

As the two detectives moved to pick up the body, though, she noticed something peculiar. "Wait just a moment," she said.

They laid him back down. Violet put her hands to either side of Lord Raybourn's face, attempting to examine him through her repair work. Like Godfrey, he hadn't been in the water for very long, or else his double layers of wrapping had protected him from fish and other sea scavengers. Or perhaps the embalming had somehow repelled aquatic creatures.

His eyes were sewn shut so she couldn't look at them again, but she ran a finger over the telltale Raybourn cleft chin and down his neck. Violet undid his shirt and once again reviewed the various nicks and scars Lord Raybourn had picked up from life on an active estate. She touched one angry-looking welt that she'd assumed was from a hunting hawk or falcon.

Or was it?

Her stomach churning, Violet felt along the body's legs, pressing gently through his trousers. She felt a depression from some sort of puncture wound in his thigh.

Cold realization hit Violet like a February rain, damp and bone chilling.

Dear God, how could I have been so blind?

She looked up at Hurst and Pratt, who were staring at her questioningly. "Gentlemen, as I look at this body again from a different perspective, I now realize something that I was too naïve to have seen before."

She hesitated. What a glorious fool she was.

"Yes?" Hurst said.

Violet sighed. "This isn't Anthony Fairmont, the Viscount Raybourn. It's his long-lost son, Cedric."

She'd never seen Inspector Hurst speechless before. "How have you determined this now? After he has been soaking in water?"

"Do you see the multitude of scars on his body? I've seen such things many times on bodies where the man was active in country life. They come from deep animal scratches, tool injuries, that sort of thing. This particular one"—she pointed to the welted ridge—"I assumed was probably the result of a cantankerous sporting falcon. Perhaps he fell off a horse while jumping or hunting.

"But now, combined with the dimpled mark in his chin, which the Fairmont men share, and the knowledge that Cedric was alive

"His face was nearly obliterated by a gunshot wound, Commissioner."

"Yes, but you took care of repairing him personally. You should have noticed if anything was amiss."

"Perhaps you've never sewn together the features of someone who has been the recipient of a blast from a volley gun. It's a difficult job, and one not likely to render a man's original appearance. And although I'm quite certain you've never provided such a service before, I'm equally as certain you've witnessed the damage that can be done by such a death."

"Mrs. Harper, right now my primary concern is the damage being done to Scotland Yard. You've made us look foolish to the citizenry, and I can only imagine what the queen thinks."

"No doubt I will be the one to bear the cross of her displeasure, Commissioner, so I hardly need your lecture, although I don't see why the burden of the body's identity rests with me and not Scotland Yard."

Henderson retreated from Violet after that, and turned to the business of discussing the various possibilities resulting from the murder victim being Cedric, not Lord Raybourn. As usual, Pratt retrieved his worn notebook from his jacket and took notes.

The four of them were soon all talking at once, each with differing opinions and theories.

Finally, Hurst held up a hand. "Mrs. Harper, didn't you tell us that Eleanor Bishop resented Cedric because he prevented her from scribbling for a newspaper? Perhaps she killed him when he showed up so unexpectedly, in a fit of rage over realizing he was still alive. With his face half gone, everyone thought it was the father, and she was pleased to encourage that illusion."

"That's impossible. Cedric was found wearing his father's smoking jacket."

"Yes, part of her plan to pass him off as the father."

Henderson nodded. "A very problematic scheme, but a brilliant one if she could get away with it. Until Lord Raybourn actually showed up, assuming he's still alive."

Why was Scotland Yard so determined to find one of Lord Raybourn's heirs guilty?

as recently as a year ago, as well as the thigh wound I car
through his trousers, I now believe this to be him. This scar-
the others—are probably wounds sustained in the Crimean W

Hurst passed a hand over his eyes. "This is quite a new d
opment, Mrs. Harper."

"It pains me to no end to admit to it at this late hour."

"I have a thousand new questions to consider."

"As do I."

He grunted. "Very well. Let's get him to the police van, the
have much to discuss back at Scotland Yard. I believe Con
sioner Henderson will want to know about this."

"As will the queen." Dread and loathing gripped Viol
though she'd just encountered a ghost. Except the ghost was
Raybourn, and he was presumably alive.

Commissioner Henderson stood and paced as Violet, Hurst
Pratt sat at the interview room table. All three of them reeked o
trid water and offal. Violet's dress, which had been muddied n
from the waist down, clung stiffly to her like the fish breading
the previous evening's meal. Henderson, though, took no noti
the trio's bedraggled condition. "So you've just discovered tha
body was, in fact, not Lord Raybourn at all, but his *son?*"

"Yes, sir," Hurst said.

"Despite the fact that he was embalmed by an undertaker
professed to actually know the supposed victim in question."

Hurst looked pointedly at Violet and raised his eyebrows.

"Yes," Violet said. "You must understand, Commissioner,
Lord Raybourn was always a very strong and vigorous man. C
versely, Cedric was a man who had experienced the ravages of
making him look older than he truly was. The Fairmont men
share a physical trait, a dimpled chin, which further lent cred
to his identity. In addition, I assumed it was Lord Raybourn
cause I was *told* it was him, and I had no reason to believe ot
wise."

"Surely, Mrs. Harper, you could have simply recognized th
wasn't Lord Raybourn by looking at his face."

Violet cut into Hurst's theory. "First, I'm sure Mr. Bishop and his son will vouch for Mrs. Bishop's whereabouts on the day Lord Raybourn was murdered. Second, she—"

But Hurst was warming up to his theory. "Oh, yes, I'm sure her husband and son would indeed vouch for her whereabouts. Don't be naïve, Mrs. Harper. It's simple enough for any criminal to convince a family member to protect him. Threats, bribery, cajolery— all effective tools a wife could use on her husband and son. Eleanor Bishop had the greatest motive of all the family members for killing her brother."

"But Stephen never said that Mrs. Bishop was on the premises prior to the murder. Stephen himself was seeing her for the first time since they came to London for the Season. If she didn't know that Cedric had returned, what was she doing at Lord Raybourn's London home? And how did she visit without Stephen's knowledge?"

Hurst shrugged. "Perhaps he sent her a note to let her know. He was hoping for a confrontation with her over her relationship with that reporter, Ellis Catesby."

"As I said, though, it is impossible to think that Mrs. Bishop committed the murder."

"Why is that?" Hurst's expression was that of someone who had made up his mind, and no amount of threats, bribery, or cajolery could cause him to change it.

"Because she is a middle-aged woman who has probably never performed a back-breaking chore in her life. It is simply ludicrous to think that she could have maneuvered the dead weight of her brother to put a jacket on him. I struggle with such tasks myself, and I do them routinely."

"You know, Inspector, she does have a point," Pratt said without looking up from his notes.

"Only a minor one. Mrs. Bishop could have had her husband help her dress the body. He probably escorted her there for the visit, things turned ugly as relations between family members do, she shot her brother, and now the husband is helping her cover it up. No wonder now that he hardly resisted arrest when we took him."

The commissioner resumed his pacing. "I follow your line of thought. So not only did she murder her own brother, she must have killed James Godfrey for fear he would somehow figure out it was his friend lying in the coffin, not Lord Raybourn."

Hurst picked up the thread. "It also explains the housekeeper's death. Didn't you tell us, Mrs. Harper, that Mrs. Peet wanted a last look at Lord Raybourn?"

"Yes, but—"

"Mrs. Peet must have mentioned it to Mrs. Bishop, who couldn't risk the housekeeper sticking her nose in the coffin and realizing who *wasn't* in there."

Pratt put down his pencil. "So you think the woman murdered three people? Seems like excessive violence from a society lady, doesn't it?"

Hurst's chest expanded. "That's because you don't have as much experience with criminal investigations as I do. Continue to observe, and I will turn you into a great detective."

"What of the theft of Cedric's body?" Henderson asked. "Do you think Mrs. Bishop was behind that, or was it something else entirely?"

"Obviously she panicked, and paid those two cretins to take the body to make sure no one would ever know it was her brother."

"And the ransom demand?"

"Her way of paying them."

Henderson frowned. "But they eventually gave up the body."

"More than likely, there was some altercation—maybe they thought they could extract even more money from the viscount's daughter—and when she wouldn't pay, they exposed the body."

"A neat theory, Inspector. I'm impressed," Henderson said.

Violet wasn't. Hurst's analysis left too many unanswered questions in Violet's mind. She thought about the conversation she'd overheard, when Nelly said she had been keeping Stephen's secret. Did this secret have anything to do with Cedric's death, or was it totally unrelated? And was a decades-old grudge truly enough to make a sister slay her own brother? Nelly was selfish and spoiled, but did she have a murderous heart?

Then there was the scene at Westminster Bridge. Was Nelly the one who came from nowhere and pushed her over? For what reason would she want to kill Violet?

I'd already supported the story that the body was Lord Raybourn's through my undertaking work. Why get rid of me? Unless she thought I was someone else? But whom else could she possibly want to kill?

Violet reflected on the moment when she felt strong, rough hands at her back. The image of Stephen's face rose in her mind again.

No, impossible.

As impossible an idea as that of Nelly having gone on a murderous rampage, all because she was mad at her presumed-dead elder brother.

"Inspector," she said. "Your theory neglects one important aspect of this case."

"Which is?"

"You haven't explained what happened to Lord Raybourn in the first place. That's whom the queen is most interested in."

"For reasons she has never shared."

Violet couldn't argue with that.

Hurst rubbed his hands together. "Commissioner, I believe we are ready to make an arrest. One that will stick this time."

Henderson nodded. "Mrs. Harper, you may wish to report to the queen that Lord Raybourn is perhaps not dead after all. Or, if he is, we have no idea where he might be. Meanwhile, Inspector Pratt and I have a visit to make to Raybourn House. I expect we'll extract a confession rather quickly."

"Inspector, I must protest," Violet said. "It seems as though you are conjecturing—"

"Once that's done, Mrs. Harper can return to the United States, which is her singular goal in all this. Correct, dear lady?"

"Not at the expense of an innocent woman going to jail!"

Hurst shook hands with Commissioner Henderson and signaled to Pratt that it was time to leave. Outraged, Violet followed them.

* * *

"How much longer do you think the undertaker will need to stay here?" Dorothy asked over glasses of chilled champagne to finish off their dinner. "You seem to have regained your senses, Eleanor. Isn't it time to send her packing?"

Nelly glared at her sister. "I find comfort in having her around. Besides, she's an old friend of Stephen's, and it's not as though Mrs. Peet's room is being used anymore."

"Comfort! Two people have died since that woman entered our lives, Mrs. Peet and that Godfrey creature. Who knows when one of us will be next?"

"Surely you aren't suggesting, dear sister, that the undertaker brings bad luck?" Nelly said.

"What do you think? Our father's body stolen, a servant's death, the arrival of a blackmailer, more death entering the household . . . Honestly, it has been Bedlam having her here."

"Now, Dorothy, I hardly think we can lay that at Violet's feet," Stephen said, setting aside his drained glass. "She has been quite helpful, moving in to soothe Nelly's fears and willingly staying in Mrs. Peet's old room after having luxurious accommodations at St. James's Palace."

"That makes her all the more suspicious, doesn't it? Doesn't she have her own husband to return to? Why would anyone give up royal quarters just to pacify a hysterical woman?" Dorothy said.

"Such blithe words from someone who couldn't possibly know what it's like to have your husband snatched away from you and thrown into a dank and grimy prison cell. What with your perpetually unwedded state," Nelly said.

The barb landed as intended, directly into Dorothy's heart. She clamped her lips together.

"It wasn't so bad," Gordon said, pouring both his wife and Katherine more champagne. "I shared a cell with just one other chap, and he was only there for vagrancy."

"Honestly, Gordon, consider my point of view. I was the one worrying myself ill about you."

"Of course, Nells, dearest. I shouldn't be so selfish."

"Speaking of selfish, I think it's time we ask Toby to stay home from all of his social activities while this mess is sorted out. He isn't here nearly enough and I do miss him so."

"I'll talk to him tomorrow."

Nelly offered her husband a rare smile.

A commotion outside interrupted the family discussion. Stephen went to the window and drew back a curtain. "It's Violet and Inspectors Hurst and Pratt. They seem to be arguing. I've never seen Violet so livid before. And look at her, she's positively filthy. I wonder what's wrong now."

20

Violet was granted another audience with the queen, and was happy to flee Raybourn House, which had become a five-story mausoleum since Nelly's arrest. Stephen and Katherine stayed locked away in their rooms, with Katherine's pitiful sniffling audible at all hours. Toby vanished from the house altogether, without even a word to his father as to where he was going. Not that Gordon would have noticed, as he spent his time in a state of near insensibility, sitting in chairs with his legs crossed, staring at nothing.

Dorothy's sharp tongue was now like a knife, cutting and wounding anyone in her path. Violet witnessed the lack of humility firsthand, as the maid, Louisa—already tense and jumpy over the endless number of tragedies occurring to the family—spilled a bit of sherry at the dining table. Dorothy berated the poor girl as though she'd dropped a thousand-year-old Chinese vase.

The family was near to breaking apart.

So despite the fact that she was probably due for verbal lashing and crucifixion herself, Violet was almost glad to be at Windsor, away from the fragile atmosphere of Park Street.

At the castle, she was told that the queen was riding at the Great Park, and was taken aboard another carriage for the mile's journey to where Queen Victoria, sitting sidesaddle on a sturdy pony, was with Mr. Brown. He walked along to her right, the reins in his left hand as he guided the animal along a grassy trail. Sharp, the ever energetic border collie, pranced about, occasionally nipping at the horse's heels as if guiding him back to the herd.

The queen was dressed in customary black, although for her ride she'd donned a pair of tan kid gloves, the only spot of color in her ensemble.

The driver helped Violet out of the carriage and drove off a respectful distance to wait, while Violet approached the queen and curtsied.

"Mrs. Harper, we were just visiting our daughter, Princess Helena, at Cumberland Lodge here in the park. Such a dutiful daughter, staying close by even after marrying her husband. She recently produced another son. Our dearest Albert would have been delighted. Please rise.

"Your timing is fortuitous. We were thinking of stopping at Frogmore to visit Albert on our way back to the castle. We would be pleased to have you join us."

Violet had overseen Albert's reinterment from Windsor Chapel to the specially built Frogmore Mausoleum in 1862. On that day, she had joined the queen in a private mourning session next to the prince's tomb.

Victoria signaled to Brown, who arranged the queen's skirts as though he were her lady's maid ensuring she looked dignified enough to hold court.

It was terribly awkward to address the queen as she sat regally erect on a pony, especially when the animal splattered droppings behind him, which they all studiously ignored. The pony's actions did serve to quiet Sharp, who decided a nearby rabbit was much more interesting, and took off after it in a happy lope.

"Actually, Your Majesty, I'm afraid I've come with bad news for you."

"Indeed?" Not the queen nor her pony nor Mr. Brown moved an inch. Was it necessary for Violet to receive her punishment in front of the queen's ghillie?

"Yes. I have made a great error in judgment. You see, Lord Raybourn's body is—well, *isn't*—actually Lord Raybourn."

That earned Violet a majestically raised eyebrow.

"And who, exactly, is it?"

"His son, Cedric, whom the family believed had died in the Crimea."

The queen nodded slowly, as if trying to absorb what Violet said. Violet was still trying to absorb it all herself.

"Well, 'tis a fine turn of affairs, ma'am," Brown said. "The lass embalmed a man she thought was his father, and dinna know what she did."

Violet felt fiery heat climbing up her neck to her face. This had to be the most embarrassing moment in all the days of her livelihood.

Brown continued, "I wish you'd let me have her do up my wicked cousin, Robert. I'd tell everyone it was some town drunkard who fell into the River Dee and be done with the man, I would."

To Violet's surprise, the queen laughed. "Mr. Brown, you are very naughty."

The ghillie looked over at Violet and winked.

"What has Scotland Yard to say about it, Mrs. Harper?" Victoria asked.

"They believe that Eleanor Bishop, Cedric's sister, killed him and played along that it was her father. She has been arrested."

The queen frowned. "That doesn't seem logical, does it?"

"No, Your Majesty."

"Unless the sister is crazed. Does she seem unbalanced in her mind to you?"

"No, Your Majesty."

"I see. Well, it does complicate things a bit to have the son involved. We are glad you've come to tell us this. Return when you have more news."

That was all? No royal temper tantrum? No castigation for incompetence? No lamentation over where Lord Raybourn might be? Praise God for Mr. Brown, who seemed to keep the queen in a harmonious state. Violet vowed to defend him against any suggestive comments made by any Briton in her presence. She could have danced her way back into London, but confined herself to a train.

* * *

The queen and her ghillie slowly made their way north to Frogmore, so that the queen could have a quiet visit with Albert at his tomb. Strange that the undertaker didn't want to go along, but instead wanted to rush back to London.

Of course, everything was strange these days, ever since Lord Raybourn had gone missing. But now they had an answer, didn't they? This latest turn of events might prove very interesting to her prime minister.

"Mr. Brown, I'll need to see Mr. Gladstone right away."

"Yes, ma'am, I expect you will." He clucked his tongue. "Come on, Lochnagar," he said, and led the pony back to the castle.

Violet returned to a nearly empty house. All the remaining family was out, and the beleaguered maid departed for shopping errands shortly after Violet's arrival.

The quiet and solitude were a relief. In her room, she sat down on the floor with her old lists and reread them, crossing off items that had been resolved. That done, she drew out a fresh piece of paper, a bottle of ink, and a pen, to begin a new list.

Why kill Cedric Fairmont? Either revenge or inheritance . . . or some other reason?
Why was Mrs. Peet killed?
Who killed James Godfrey? Why?
Did Eleanor or Gordon Bishop really play a part in what happened? What of Toby?
Where IS Lord Raybourn?

Having finished her new list, and calculating that she had twenty-eight wholly unanswered questions about the mysterious doings in the Fairmont family, Violet decided a quick nap was in order. She tossed her lists on top of the pile of papers accumulating on the chest of drawers. Really, she should separate the funeral documents from her personal letters and her growing number of lists.

Murder lists, she supposed she should call them.

Hadn't she been frustrated when her deceased husband, Graham, used to stack newspapers and vendor bills together? Even in her worst housekeeping days, she never let herself become a sloppy record keeper.

Sleep beckoned. She'd worry about the papers later.

Before she could even think about dropping her head against the pillow, a doorbell rang. With no one else home, Violet supposed it was up to her to answer it. She glanced out the window and saw that it was Toby on the front stoop, waiting to be let in.

She hurried down three flights of stairs and let him in. "Mrs. Harper, why are you answering the door?" he asked.

"I believe I am the only one here."

"Oh. Well, I'm just here to pick something up. Tell Mother and Father I won't be in for dinner, will you?"

Violet realized this was her moment. While Toby was in his room, she went back to her own room for her reticule, then waited until she saw Toby step down into the street. He was headed south again. Violet ran down the stairs as fast as her skirts would allow, and followed Toby Bishop to wherever it was he was perpetually disappearing.

Would it be the home of a revolutionary? The back of a seedy tavern? An abandoned warehouse converted to a secret barracks? She had no idea, but she had to find out what he was doing, and whether it had anything to do with his grandfather's disappearance and his uncle's death.

21

Toby walked casually through Mayfair, whistling, down toward Hyde Park Corner. From there he hired a cab heading east. What was Violet to do now?

She attempted to follow the hackney on foot, since traffic prevented it from traveling too quickly, but she soon realized that she had no idea how far he intended to travel. So she picked up her own hack at a nearby taxi stand, and, feeling rather foolish, asked the driver to follow Toby's. "The one with the broken lamp on it."

"Husband been visiting his mistress, what?" the rough-shaven driver asked from his perch behind and above the enclosed passenger seat. "Goin' t' follow him to her place, is ya?"

"No, I'm—never mind." Violet climbed in, sat against the torn leather seat, and let the driver think whatever he wanted to think, as they drove along Victoria Embankment. Soon they were in Whitechapel, and although the main thoroughfare was not particularly squalid, the warren of dark side streets branching off Whitechapel High Street suggested poverty and suffering that had trampled its occupants down for generations. The children sitting in doorways had particularly vacant looks that made her shiver. Violet instinctively moved to the center of her seat.

The driver rapped on the window to Violet's left. "Madam, I'm not going too much farther in than this. Likely t' have the brass lamps stripped off the carriage and to be beaten to death for my boots, as well. T'isn't a fit place for a lady, neither."

She knew it was dangerous, but she'd come this far and had to know what Toby was doing, although at least now she knew he was up to nothing virtuous.

"Please, just a bit more. Look, they're stopping there, at Thomas Street."

"I'll go there, but no farther."

When he stopped, Violet paid him and asked if he'd wait. "Not likely," he said and hurried off.

Now Violet was alone. Well, her nerves would simply have to settle down. She continued after Toby, who was walking nonchalantly past heaps of trash and debris that served as multi-storied living quarters for a variety of rats and vermin. People stared at Violet in curiosity, but no one bothered her.

It seemed so much darker here. Did the sun forget to shine in Whitechapel?

About halfway down the street was a break in the bleak rows of sooty brick buildings, opening surprisingly onto a small cemetery. In the center of the cemetery was a large red-, blue-, and yellow-striped tent, an incongruous spot of happiness in the middle of the misery.

Toby headed straight for the tent. Violet stayed some distance behind, but she needn't have bothered, for he was quickly enveloped in the crowd of poor and bedraggled men, women, and children under the tent's roof. Violet made her way to one corner of the tent, whose pole was lashed to a headstone so old the name was obliterated from it.

Now she saw that a man, probably forty or so years old and wearing a carefully groomed chin beard, stood on a dais with a woman—presumably his wife?—and was shouting at the people inside.

No, he seemed to be whipping them up with enthusiasm.

Wait a minute. No, the man was preaching the gospel. He was an open-air evangelist.

What was Toby doing *here?*

As if to answer her question, Toby approached the dais, which caused the man to stop what he was saying. He and his wife warmly greeted Toby, then pulled him up on the dais, to be introduced to the milling crowd. Violet slipped under the tent to hear more clearly.

Once she was inside, she saw a banner hanging from the rear tent wall. It read, "Christian Revival Society."

Violet was thoroughly confused. How could Toby, who was apparently associated with some sort of insurrectionist movement, also be attracted to a missionary working in an abysmal part of London?

"My friends, some of you remember our good friend, Tobias Bishop." The preacher clasped an arm around Toby's shoulders as his wife smiled approvingly. "He's fed you soup and bread each week the past few months, and has faithfully shared the good news of Jesus Christ with you. Tobias has proven himself a worthy soldier in God's army, and I am proud to tell you that today he has been promoted to lieutenant. The new uniform he will receive is the mark of his rank in ministry work."

Applause was scattered and lukewarm. "Where's Mrs. Booth's soup?" someone called out. The woman onstage nodded to her husband and stepped down to a table containing a large cauldron. She began ladling out a yellow broth into metal bowls. Toby and the preacher jumped down to help distribute the soup bowls to those gathered under the tent. Some accepted the broth gratefully, others yanked it away, slurped it up, and demanded more.

Toby and his fellow missionaries remained smiling.

What was this Christian Revival Society? Violet knew that many churches were involved in reaching the wretched members of society, but she'd never heard of this group before. Perhaps it was time to make her presence known.

"Mrs. Harper!" Toby said as she approached. "How did you know I was here? Have you come to join us?" He handed her a bowl full of steaming broth, which she automatically passed on to a toothless woman with rheumy eyes. In her haste to ingest it, the woman dribbled some of the soup down her chin, so Violet took the bowl and gently tipped it up so that the woman could safely drink it all.

"I confess I'm not sure why I'm here," she said, handing the empty bowl back to Toby and accepting a fresh one to hand to a shoeless little boy. "I followed you out the door to see where it is you've been going in secret. Here I am in a place I never imagined you'd be."

Toby laughed. It was the first time Violet had seen him do so. He signaled to the preacher, who joined them. "Mr. Booth, may I present Mrs. Violet Harper to you? She is, well, believe it or not, she has become my family's undertaker. She has also been investigating my family's problems."

"William Booth at your service. Welcome to our ragtag little army of God's soldiers. Are you a good cook?"

"Hardly. I'm mostly handy with a scalpel and cosmetic massage creams."

"Well, I'm not sure those are useful for saving souls, but we can use every willing body we can get. I'm sure my wife can put you to work. Catherine, this is Mrs. Harper. She wants to help."

Violet said, "But I'm not here to—"

Her protestations were to no avail. Next thing she knew, she was hauling another kettle out from behind the tent and ladling more soup into bowls. She passed a surprisingly pleasant few hours this way, and in snatches of conversation with Toby learned that he had been visiting the Christian Revival Society for months in secret, for fear of his parents' reaction. His parents wanted him to learn to be a gentleman, settle down to an appropriate wife, and spend his time on leisurely pursuits of high society using his grandfather's money.

Toby, however, wanted something more. "My parents' world is mind-numbingly useless. Here, I can make a difference in the world. The East End might not seem the place to do so, but truly, Mrs. Harper, if you can't make a difference by sharing love with society's unlovable, then where can you do so?"

Violet couldn't argue with that. In a strange way, undertaking was frequently the care and love of those who hadn't been particularly lovable in life.

She stayed and worked with Toby until he was finished, so that he could escort her back to Raybourn House. She accepted Mr. Booth's invitation to attend a future society meeting, and, on the way back to Park Street, promised to exercise discretion with Toby's parents concerning his activities.

She also asked the question that had been burning inside her for hours. "I saw your friend, Mr. Farr, leave Raybourn House recently. James Godfrey was waiting for him in the street, and the two had quite an animated conversation. What is your connection to the man?"

"You mean the tall, gangly gent? The one you found in the Serpentine?"

"Yes. How do you know him?"

"I don't. Neither did Adam. He thought Adam was a member of the household, and came running up ranting about Uncle Cedric and the Crimea and Egypt and payments due. He demanded to know Uncle Cedric's whereabouts, which, of course, no one knew at the time. Adam entertained him because he assumed the man was a family friend. When he told me about it later, I was quite surprised."

Everything about the situation surprised Violet. Nothing made sense so far. Would the pieces ever come together? At least Toby could be eliminated as a suspect in the murder of his uncle. No man so genuinely dedicated to a Christian mission to feed the poor and save souls was likely to be a murderer.

Toby dropped Violet off, saying he would continue on with the cab to Adam Farr's lodgings for a visit. Except for distant banging downstairs in the kitchen, the house was still quiet. Violet was glad for the peace, as she'd just had an exceedingly long day, starting with a visit to the queen's elegant royal palace and ending in one of the worst streets of London.

She picked up Mr. Barnum's book again and settled atop the bedcovers and pillows to read. She awoke with a start as the book crashed to the floor. Once again, she'd fallen asleep while reading, but without the benefit of having Sam around to gently remove the book from her hands and put it away.

Making her realize she hadn't had a return letter from him in days.

Sam's letters were like a sweet balm, reminding her of both

their past and present together. It was almost like picking up a bottle of Sam's spicy-scented cologne, unstopping the container, and
letting the pleasantness waft over her before putting it away and
letting her thoughts remain on days gone by with her steadfast
husband.

Violet frowned and sat up. Letters. Days gone by. What was it
her father had said?

Heart pounding, she jumped up and went to the chest of drawers, snatching up the mound of documents and tossing them on
the bed to sift through them. A copy of *The Times* with Ellis
Catesby's piece in it, the bill for Mrs. Peet's funeral, one of Violet's
many lists . . . Where was it?

She thumbed through her letters from Arthur Sinclair. There.

With shaking hands, she once again tore open her father's letter,
written just after Violet had arrived in London.

> *The two boys each wanted what the other had, whether*
> *it be a toy or a favored word from their father.*

As the words popped off the page in a stunning, glaring explanation of what had transpired in the Fairmont family, Violet realized who had been responsible for Cedric's death.

The question was, what should she do about it? Who would believe it?

22

Violet's first instinct was to run to Scotland Yard and tell Inspectors Hurst and Pratt. But what proof did she have? She'd be no better than Hurst, finagling a theory to fit her notion and running wild with it.

No, she needed evidence.

Violet grabbed all of the papers from the bed and straightened them back into a vague impression of neatness on the chest. She crept into the hallway and went to the top of the stairs, pausing to listen for sounds in the household.

It was as quiet as an abandoned crypt.

Violet made her way down a flight of steps. She heard nothing from the bedrooms on this floor. Down another flight and all was still silent except for the swishing of her skirts. She softly opened the door to Lord Raybourn's study, its masculine interior lined in walnut and the acrid smell of tobacco smoke still lingering in the air.

If it was anywhere, it would be here. Hurst would most certainly have overlooked it, because it would have meant nothing to him.

Under the watchful eye of a marble bust of Lord Nelson perched on an elegantly carved stand in one corner, Violet started at the most obvious place—Lord Raybourn's desk. The top was bare except for a tobacco box, a gas lamp, and an old daguerreotype of a woman, framed in silver. The woman's clothing suggested the keepsake had been taken about thirty years ago. The deceased Lady Raybourn, perhaps?

Surely Mrs. Peet hadn't been appreciative of having to see it every day.

Violet went to the desk drawers. Surprisingly, none were locked. She searched through them as quickly as possible, while trying not to disturb anything. All of the drawers were as tidy as the desktop. Thinking back on Mr. Poe's detective stories, she attempted to think like C. Auguste Dupin, who would put himself in the mind of the criminal to logically deduce what he would do next.

The murderer would either destroy the evidence, or hide it very, very well.

She got on her knees and crawled under the desk, looking for any hidden compartments that were sometimes built into furniture. Nothing. She climbed back out and stood, hands on her hips, as she looked around the room. Almost nothing was out of place in here. Either Lord Raybourn was as immaculate as Violet was not, or else Mrs. Peet—or someone else—had swept the place clean after his death . . . or disappearance.

Two overstuffed chairs flanked a table with a chess set on it. It looked as if it had been abandoned in the middle of a match. She lifted the chair cushions and patted the arms and sides of each chair, wondering if evidence might have been secreted inside the furniture. Violet dropped to her knees once again and felt up under the chairs. Nothing.

Detection is hard work, she thought as she hauled herself back up to a standing position, using the chair's dense arm for leverage. She should abandon this, report her suspicions to Inspector Hurst, and go back to being a simple undertaker.

Quit grumbling and finish what you've started.

Violet turned to the set of bookcases lining one wall. Leather-bound volumes were artfully arranged, both upright and on their sides, with decorative bookends, statuettes, and framed pictures interspersed on the shelves among the books.

Perhaps it was inside one of the books. But how could she ever manage to finger through all of them to find it? It would take hours.

Violet took several steps back and studied the shelves. How would Dupin approach this?

Violet Harper, you've become addled. Why would you want to imitate a fictional character, for heaven's sake? You should try to think like Inspector Hurst.

She shuddered. Perhaps not.

It was then that she noticed that a clock on the bookcase was still running. It certainly wasn't impossible that stopping the clock had been neglected in the midst of the household's chaos, but the clock was the only objet d'art that sat atop a thick book that lay on its side. All other art pieces sat on the shelves by themselves, and were not placed on the leather bindings.

Violet lifted the clock from its resting place. It looked to be some kind of French piece—intricate, gilded, and impossibly heavy. She lugged it to the desk and placed it there, then returned for the book. It was larger than most of the other books in the bookcase. The spine said it was a world atlas. Taking it from the shelf, too, she returned to the desk and sat down to flip through it.

The book was full of colorized maps of sections of London, the remainder of England and Great Britain, as well as parts of Europe. It must have cost Lord Raybourn a small fortune to procure it. She nearly forgot what she was looking for as she got caught up in the detailed drawings.

As she turned a page near the back of the volume, though, she found a letter, tucked between Poland and Prussia. Violet's heart started pounding again as she opened it.

> *My darling Kate,*
> *It has been long since I've held you in my arms and I am anxious to see you, although you no doubt wish to stay tucked away at Willow Tree House. Please come join me in London at Raybourn House. Not only do I miss you, I have something very important to discuss.*
> *Hurry, my darling,*
> *Your loving husband*

Violet now had the evidence she required. She needed to go to Scotland Yard right away with it, but just then the door opened and Stephen entered. "What are you doing in here?"

Violet looked down at the desk, where the clock, open atlas, and letter lay, all trumpeting out exactly what she had been doing.

"Oh, my dear friend, you should have left well enough alone and just continued to do the task I set out for you—convincing the queen to proceed with the burial. I knew Scotland Yard was too impotent to do anything, but I mistakenly thought you were, too."

Violet held up the letter. "Why would you keep this? It incriminates you."

Stephen shook his head sadly. "No, it protects me."

"But it demonstrates that—"

"I know what it says, but what you don't understand is that—"

At that moment, Katherine Fairmont entered the room, her pale face brought to life by a deep green satin bonnet and matching dress. Violet was reminded once again of Mrs. Peet's eyes.

Katherine's own eyes narrowed as she saw Violet sitting at the desk. Violet rose and stood before the evidence spread in front of her.

"Stephen, what is she doing?"

"I believe she came in looking for something to read and accidentally stumbled—"

"I do not think she 'stumbled' at all. I told you that asking her to look for Cedric's body would bring us nothing but trouble, Stephen."

"We had to get him back, Kate, to bury the sordid past you were ensnared in."

"How has that turned out? Your little undertaker friend is standing here accusing us. Dear God, I just can't take this anymore. My nerves are too brittle for it." Katherine's pupils were pinpoints, and she began trembling.

"Sweetheart, there's no proof. Stay calm. Everything will be fine."

Katherine put both hands to the sides of her head. "I need another one of my powders. Get one for me, will you?"

"Of course."

As soon as Stephen left the room, Katherine dropped her hands to her sides and turned on Violet.

"Mrs. Harper, have you nothing better to do than stalk this household? I've tried my best to be polite to you, but all you've done is harass and persecute us. You are driving this family to the brink of destruction."

"I don't understand, Lady Raybourn. Or, rather, it's still Mrs. Fairmont, isn't it? I have only tried to get to the bottom of what happened to your father-in-law and brother-in-law, as your husband asked me to do."

"No! The only request Stephen made of you was to find Cedric's body. We needed it back before anyone discovered it wasn't my father-in-law inside. You made everything else your business."

"So Stephen told you that he'd killed his brother to protect you from him?"

"Of course not. James Godfrey was the one who killed Cedric. All was fine until the queen decided to insert her extra-regal nose into our affairs, thus bringing you into our lives. Why couldn't everything have just proceeded in a normal fashion?"

"It is hardly normal when your brother-in-law is murdered, Lady Raybourn. Or, should I say, when your husband is."

Katherine's eyes dulled. "Oh yes, I suppose he was that, too. Unfortunately for Cedric Fairmont, he returned to London to lay claim to me again. Imagine the hilarity and scandal that would have ensued had society discovered Stephen had married a bigamist."

"Surely people knew you'd once been married to Cedric."

"Not really. I was only seventeen and had not yet had a Season. Cedric was a mature man of thirty-six, and he kept me at Willow Tree House while he traipsed around Sussex, bedding down every nubile creature he could find while I waited for his wandering eye to heal. Lord Raybourn arranged our match. How he must have hated me to toss me into that lion's den of a marriage."

It would seem that Lord Raybourn had a talent for flinging his children into unsuitable matches. Most would call his own secret match with Mrs. Peet unsuitable, too.

"Stephen was very sympathetic to my plight, and was a great

comfort to me in those days. Cedric eventually became bored with his existence—or maybe he ran through every willing woman in Sussex—and decided to join the war effort. He didn't even discuss it with me, his wife. He merely abandoned me. About a year after Cedric's departure, with no word from him, Stephen and I naturally grew to love each other. We were of an age, and Stephen was nothing like his older brother. When Cedric was eventually declared dead, it left Stephen and me free to marry."

Surely this was the secret Nelly told Stephen she'd been keeping all these years.

"I had no idea Cedric was still alive until I received his letter asking me to come to Park Street. Stephen was in London for business at the time, so I assumed it was from him."

"Didn't the handwriting suggest it was from Cedric?"

"Cedric was *dead*, remember? And it looked reasonably close to Stephen's. I had no reason to suspect otherwise. I came to London, and was startled to find Cedric here, lounging about in my father-in-law's smoking jacket and puffing on a cigarette, as arrogant as he was the day he left Willow Tree House for the Crimea."

"Did you argue?"

Katherine folded her arms around herself, as if warding off a chill. "You cannot imagine how we argued. It was a dozen years of pent-up anger on both sides. He laughed about his ability to imitate Stephen's handwriting and referred to me as a willful dupe. I called him the most depraved and dissolute of men. I'm embarrassed to think of it now. When I realized he might become violent toward me, I fled the house.

"In the street, I saw a man that I now realize was James Godfrey. I watched as Godfrey climbed the steps into the house. A few minutes later I heard a bang in the house, but over the sound of street traffic it was hard to tell exactly what it was. Godfrey left moments after that."

Violet shook her head. "Why would Godfrey kill his wartime friend?"

"I've wondered the same thing. I think it must be that he asked Cedric for a reward for services rendered while Cedric was injured and ill, and Cedric refused. Godfrey was probably incensed out of his mind and reacted in fury. When he later calmed down, I imagine the guilt of it drove him to kill himself."

"But . . . that means that he murdered his friend, then came around looking for Cedric, claiming he was still alive."

Katherine nodded sadly. "Stephen and I have spent many hours puzzling that out. Why do such a thing? We can only figure he was greatly interested in the Raybourn family fortune, and invented a way to partake of it."

"I don't understand. Why didn't you report this before? It would have cleared up many things."

"As I said, the damage would have been extensive. We didn't want my marriage to Cedric dragged through the newspapers for public ridicule. When Mrs. Peet assumed Cedric was my father-in-law, it occurred to us that it was no bad thing to let everyone think the same thing and later work out the details of what would happen when my father-in-law returned home. It pains me, though, to imagine she killed herself thinking it was Lord Raybourn shot dead."

Stephen's and Katherine's foolish behavior seemed to be an enormous problem, but for the moment Violet needed to get down to Scotland Yard.

"Darling, there you are." Katherine turned to Stephen, who had just returned with a glass filled with a chalky-looking fluid. She drank deeply from the glass before setting it down on the desk. "That will make things better, I'm sure. Mrs. Harper and I were just discussing Cedric's unfortunate demise."

"You told her everything?"

Katherine nodded.

Stephen smiled. "I'm glad you understand, Violet. I should have known you would. You're almost a part of the family now."

With a few murmurs of sympathy, Violet managed to extricate herself from Lord Raybourn's study. She hurried upstairs and packed her reticule with her father's and Cedric's letters, and went as quickly as she could to Scotland Yard.

She was shown into the paneled room where she usually met

the detectives. They were both there, with Hurst reading from various pieces of correspondence spread all over the wood surface, while Pratt scribbled notes from Hurst's dictation.

Pratt broke into a smile at seeing Violet. "Ah, Mrs. Harper, you're just in time. We've discovered some communications that we think—"

As usual, Hurst blustered past his colleague. "How can we help you, Mrs. Harper? We're quite busy at the moment. We believe we have finally solved our blackmailing case."

"Congratulations, sir," she said. "How did you manage it?"

Hurst was happy to share the results of his expertise. "We intercepted a blackmail note and traced the paper through its watermark to Wright's Stationers here in London. Only one customer had purchased this particular paper in the past few months, a Mr. Smith, which is most likely a false name. Mrs. Wright gave us Mr. Smith's address. We were just completing our notes and plan to go see him. So, what is it that you want?"

She pulled the folded missive from her reticule. "I have a letter that I found in Lord Raybourn's study. It shows—"

"The viscount's personal effects don't interest me at the moment. I am on the verge of solving a complicated blackmail scheme that is of great importance to the Crown. I imagine whatever you have to show me can wait until we return." Hurst stood. "Mr. Pratt, come."

The paned glass inset rattled inside the door as it shut behind them. Violet blew out a breath in frustration as she shoved the letter back into her reticule. Chief Inspector Hurst was positively the most colorless, humorless, foul human being she'd ever known . . . and she'd worked with hundreds of corpses.

One moment he dismissed her, the next he thought she was of use to Scotland Yard, then once again he circled around to find her worthless. She wondered if he was married to some poor, unfortunate soul. If not, it was certainly of no surprise, and much to the relief of all womanhood. How could any woman tolerate his—

Wait, what was this?

Violet sat in the chair Pratt had just vacated and picked up the piece of correspondence from which Hurst had been reading. It was one of the blackmail notes, promising curses and scourges upon Monsieur de Lessep's head if he did not comply with the blackmailer's demands.

She read it again. And again. Then she pulled out Cedric's letter and laid it alongside the blackmail letter.

The handwriting was the same.

Cedric Fairmont, heir to Lord Raybourn, was engaged in a common blackmail scheme? Could that really be true? Was this why he was murdered? Was Godfrey involved in it with him?

It still made no sense. Godfrey said that the two of them had gone from the Crimea to France before they'd returned to London. They were never in Egypt.

Unless Godfrey was lying. With him dead also, how could they ever know the truth of things?

And if Lord Raybourn had gone to Egypt—and was presumably still there—to negotiate on Britain's behalf for the Suez Canal, how could it possibly be a coincidence that his son was involved in blackmailing the man in charge of the project?

Violet grasped the edge of the table to maintain her balance, so much was her mind reeling. Finding a clean scrap of paper in the mess on the table, she scrawled out a note to Inspector Hurst, explaining what she'd realized about Cedric.

Another thought leapt into her mind. If the stationer's information was correct, the two detectives were probably now at Cedric's lodgings, where they would presumably find no one.

For surely that wasn't where Lord Raybourn was. No, it wasn't possible. He couldn't have been in collusion with his eldest son. What interest would Lord Raybourn have in a blackmail scheme against the Suez Canal's mastermind?

She suddenly very much wished that Sam were here right now to advise her.

Stuffing Cedric's letter back in her reticule, Violet went back to Raybourn House and retreated to her room. Perhaps it was time to pack her belongings, to return to St. James's Palace, or, preferably, Brighton. Scotland Yard had its blackmail scheme under control, and no matter who murdered whom, all concerned parties were dead, so what was the point of Violet remaining in London? Besides, once Hurst realized the blackmailer was no longer among the living, he could then focus on the Raybourn House fiasco, and would then naturally push her aside. The queen would have to approve her departure, of course, but why wouldn't she?

She opened drawers and began removing her things, piling them on the bed to put in her luggage. She eyed the stack of papers on the chest, and knew that they needed sorting before she packed them. Abandoning her clothes, she began going through the papers once again. One of Sam's letters dropped to the floor. She knelt to the ground to pick it up, and noticed another letter that had disappeared just out of sight under the chest of drawers.

Violet grimaced at her own sloppiness as she reached under the furniture for it. Except it wasn't addressed to anyone she knew and was in an unfamiliar handwriting. Putting Sam's dropped letter on top of her stack of papers, she examined the other letter. It was addressed to a Marjorie Eckworth in Birmingham.

Was it a letter from Mrs. Peet that had never been mailed?

She tapped the letter against her wrist, considering. Should she open it? It seemed disrespectful of poor Mrs. Peet, and yet, what if there was something noteworthy in it that might illuminate poor Mrs. Peet's fate? The notion of the housekeeper having committed suicide had never settled well in Violet's mind.

No, the letter must be opened. "Please forgive me, Mrs. Peet," she whispered as she broke the seal. The letter was dated the day the housekeeper had been found in the kitchen.

> *I have avoided my sad news for as long as possible, but must now tell you that my employer, Lord Raybourn, has died. Shot in the head. They say he killed himself, but I know that he had much to live for and would never have done it.*
>
> *I wish to live far from London and Sussex, away from these dreadful memories. If you and Raymond will permit it, I would like to stay with you until I can find another post in Birmingham. Your city is growing quick, I hear, so surely there are posts for good, clean, honest housekeepers. I'm sure the family will give me a good character reference.*

Once you reply that he has agreed, I will submit an
advertisement to the Daily Post for a situation wanted.
Please let me know soonest, dear sister.

Violet's heart stopped beating for several seconds. This was not the letter of a woman who planned to kill herself, yet Mrs. Peet was dead mere hours after she wrote these words.

Shoving aside a pile of clothes she'd stacked on the bed, Violet sat down and reread Mrs. Peet's letter. If Mrs. Peet hadn't committed suicide, then she'd been murdered. And if she'd been murdered . . . why? What did she have to do with anything? Surely she wasn't involved in the blackmail scheme or Cedric and Godfrey's relationship. She must have known that Katherine was once married to Cedric, but what of it? Did Mrs. Peet know something else, some secret in the family that would devastate them if it got out?

Maybe Mrs. Peet wanted to escape to Birmingham because of this secret.

Retrieving her own notes and list of questions from the chest of drawers, she sat back down again, spreading the papers out on the stacks of clothing and willing something to jump out at her.

Nothing did. It all really came down to one question, didn't it? Who would benefit from Mrs. Peet's death? But the housekeeper had nothing, just a couple of worn dresses.

Except for the trunk of finery across the room.

But, once again, what did that have to do with anything? It wasn't as though someone had killed Mrs. Peet and stolen the clothing, had they?

Violet went to the trunk and opened it. Everything was still there.

So there was no monetary gain to be had from Mrs. Peet's death. What were other reasons someone might kill another person? Jealousy. Anger. Fear. To silence someone. What else? For the first time, she actually wished Inspector Hurst were here so she could discuss it with him.

Perhaps he was done with his futile search for "Mr. Smith" and had returned to Scotland Yard. Now tucking Mrs. Peet's letters into her bulging bag, she went downstairs. To her surprise, both

Stephen and Katherine were standing in the drawing room with luggage around their feet.

"Oh, hello, Violet. How fortunate we are to see you before we go," Stephen said.

"You're leaving?"

"For a short time. What with all of the scandal about to break about Cedric and Godfrey, on top of my father's disappearance, I thought it best to take our leave out of the city for a while until it all simmers down."

"But what of the rest of the family?"

"They can all do as they wish. My concern right now is to weather the storm and preserve the Raybourn title and reputation."

Tick.

Like a clock gear, something turned into its correct place in Violet's mind.

"What if your father returns home while you're gone?"

"He'll have the rest of the family around him. In fact, Nelly can explain her duplicitous behavior to him, since she is probably at the root of much of what has gone wrong."

Tock.

"Where will you weather the storm?"

"We plan to take the five o'clock to Winchester. Katherine has a friend there."

Tick tock.

Katherine tapped her husband's arm. "Come, Stephen, it will take time to get to Paddington Station. Traffic is just beastly this time of day."

"Right. If you will excuse us, Violet—"

Tick tock. Tick tock. Tick tock.

Violet refused to move. "I'm sorry, but it seems like there are many things you should be handling on behalf of your family. Arranging for permanent servants here at Raybourn House, comforting your sisters, seeking out what has happened to your father, as just a few examples."

Stephen frowned. "Violet, I do believe you are stepping outside your authority. I asked you to find my father, which you have not done, not to set yourself up as the judge of how I conduct my affairs."

"It is as you say. However, there is something important you don't know. I found a letter in Mrs. Peet's room, a letter written to her sister that she obviously intended to post but never had a chance to do. It shows that Mrs. Peet had no thought in her mind of doing away with herself. Do you have any idea who may have wanted to kill Mrs. Peet, Stephen?"

"Kindly remember that you are a guest in my home, Violet. Of course I don't know who would have wanted her dead."

Violet turned to Katherine. "But you do, don't you, Mrs. Fairmont?"

Katherine wrinkled her nose. "Killed her? I'd always assumed the grief over Lord Raybourn's death drove her to her demise."

"Mrs. Fairmont, I deal comfortably with dead people on a daily basis, but have little tolerance for deceitful living ones. Why did you kill Lord Raybourn's housekeeper?"

Katherine opened her mouth to argue, but closed it again, her mind working furiously behind her eyes. Even in this deplorable moment, Katherine Fairmont was beautiful, like a delicate china vase. Violet could hardly believe what she was accusing this striking woman of doing.

"I find it difficult to believe that someone who sullies her hands with blood and putrefaction should consider herself the arbiter of justice. You have no understanding of what I have suffered, Mrs. Harper."

"Kate, stop talking," Stephen said.

Katherine paid no attention to him. "I told Stephen that hiring you to find Cedric's body would lead to disaster, but he insisted that keeping you under his close eye would make you more manageable."

"You knew it was Cedric's body in the coffin all along, because you killed him."

Katherine rolled her eyes. "Maybe you should stick to undertaking rather than disparaging innocent, grieving loved ones."

Mrs. Fairmont was sadly mistaken if she thought she would intimidate Violet through sarcasm. She'd been through quite enough with this family already.

"You're right. Had I figured it out sooner, you would have been languishing in Newgate all of this time, instead of reclining on a sofa while both your sister and brother-in-law were imprisoned. In fact, you might even be hanged by now."

Katherine's eyes grew wide and she clutched her throat. "Never!"

"Ah, but they don't hang women anymore, do they? So you'd just be lounging about in your gray prison dress, hoping that Mr. or Mrs. Bishop will have forgiven you enough to bring you some extra food."

"Violet, please, that's enough," Stephen said. "You're needlessly frightening my wife, who hasn't done anything wrong."

Katherine continued to ignore Stephen, her attention fully focused on Violet.

"I don't plan to go to prison, Mrs. Harper. What court would convict me after what I've been through?"

"What, exactly, have you been through?"

"First, Mrs. Harper, you must understand what enormous strain we'd been under, what with Cedric threatening to expose us as bigamists."

"But you weren't bigamists, not really. You had no idea he was still alive."

"Yes, but I'm sure the newspapers would have seen it that way. You've already seen what they've done to us. He also bragged that he planned to make us all miserable, one at a time. I don't know what happened to him after the war, but he came back an even worse man than the one he was when he left.

"With Cedric formally declared dead, I knew Stephen and I were in no way bigamists, but Cedric was quite unmoved, saying that he would work diligently to embarrass and disgrace both his brother and me. He intended to drive us into poverty and make us social pariahs. Because, of course, his humiliation of me wasn't complete when he left for the war."

things to him, that windy old hen, Mrs. Peet, returned from shopping through the servants' entrance. We left the house before she could find us with him.

"Fortunately, when we returned we discovered that the housekeeper had assumed Cedric was her employer. There seemed no point in disabusing her of the notion, did there?"

"So you killed Mrs. Peet to keep her from identifying Cedric later on."

"Of course. Once you said you were going to open up the coffin for her to weep over him one last time, I couldn't possibly risk her realizing that it was Cedric. So her death is really *your* fault, Mrs. Harper, for agreeing to reopen the coffin."

Violet nodded at the woman's audacity, and made a mental note that the next time she was asked to open a coffin so someone could clip a lock of hair, she would never, ever agree to it, no matter how many tears flowed. "You didn't do it by yourself."

"No, I had to enlist Stephen to help me hoist her body up after I knocked her unconscious. Poor dear man has a queasy stomach."

But he had a perfectly composed face when he lied. "Stephen, was there any truth at all to your statement that your father was possibly dying of a stomach ailment?"

He reddened. "Who can really say what illnesses someone has?"

Violet shook her head and turned back to Katherine. "You hired the kidnappers, too, in order to prevent anyone from ever identifying Cedric."

"Yes, although those nitwits nearly destroyed everything. They thought they could blackmail me for more money after we agreed on a certain amount for their services. I refused to pay it, and they refused to return the body. We couldn't have Cedric's body roaming the countryside somewhere, waiting to be discovered as not being Anthony Fairmont. If only you hadn't embalmed him, time would have naturally solved our problem. That's why Stephen encouraged you to find him, although I knew it would come to no good."

"I do not care for being played as a dupe, Mrs. Fairmont."

Katherine shrugged. "It couldn't be helped. And anyway, you weren't harmed."

"Mrs. Fairmont, I'm sure he didn't consciously plan to h
ate you in your marriage."

Katherine laughed, the sound like a sharp bark. "I congr:
you, Mrs. Harper, on being the one person who thought so
Cedric. Of course, you only met him once he was dead, so
that."

Violet was silent.

"I suppose I remind you of Queen Catherine of Aragon, i
first to Prince Arthur, then marrying Henry VIII when his
died."

Except that Violet suspected Katherine was more likely
Anne Boleyn's fate, not her namesake's.

"I wanted to protect the family. Not just myself and S
but the others. Gordon Bishop is a yapping puppy, but di
serve to be ruined. Stephen's sisters are, well . . . even de:
pose they would be quite unpleasant, yet I still couldi
Cedric to tear us apart.

"Cedric lured me with the note I thought was from
After our terrible row, I'd been crying, so I excused my:
the study to find a handkerchief and instead went in sear
of Lord Raybourn's pistols. He kept several tucked ar
house. Fortunately, the one I laid my hands on was one o
deadly. He thought it was a great secret hidden from ever
foolish old beetle-brain. With the pistol behind my bac
told Cedric I was going to talk to Stephen about the
which he found uproariously funny. 'Yes, my brother
great help to you,' he said, and left the room. That w:
knew he had to go. He was almost at the bottom of the
I was just a few steps behind him. I said his name softly.
to me, and I pulled the trigger, hoping that the powde
fresh inside and that it was loaded with shot. It was,
more than happy to see him fall to the ground, his face

Katherine's eyes widened and she stared off in the
she smiled at the memory. Now talking as though in a
continued, "I rather panicked after that and don't
much. Stephen came home shortly thereafter, and as

Violet could hardly believe this was Stephen's meek, reserved wife. The enormity of what she had done seemed to have little impact on Katherine.

"You pretended to be Mrs. Young, the woman who invited me to St. Paul's crypt, to keep me away from the house long enough to kidnap the body."

Katherine nodded and sat down. Stephen also sat, but Violet was too anxious to do more than pace as the tale unraveled.

"So the blackmailing notes associated with the body came from you, not the actual thieves?"

"Yes. I hate to be prideful, but they were a masterpiece, weren't they? I had the ransom money delivered in the same way in which Cedric demanded it from Monsieur de Lesseps."

"He told you he was behind a blackmailing scheme against the builder of the Suez Canal?"

"He couldn't help himself. Cedric was bitter and angry about much more than me. He told me all about his failed little project in Egypt that led him back here. James Godfrey lied when he sat here telling us that after Crimea, the two of them spent time in France before returning home. He left out the detour they took in Egypt, finding and managing corvée labor for the canal. They knew the project was coming to an end, and Cedric came up with this new plan for making money. When the blackmailing didn't work out, he decided to come home and torture me."

"It seems as though Cedric would have profited more to come home and reconcile with Lord Raybourn."

"Now you are beginning to understand the manner of man Cedric was."

"What did you hope to accomplish by imitating his blackmailing technique?"

Katherine seemed disappointed that Violet didn't immediately appreciate her brilliance. "So that the theft of Lord Raybourn's body would seem to be Cedric's doing."

"But Cedric was dead. You killed him."

"No one knew that until you discovered it."

Violet remembered something else. "The newspapers reported that Mrs. Peet murdered Lord Raybourn. . . ."

"Clever of me, wasn't it? Ellis Catesby was besotted with Nelly, but she was too loyal to the family—and why, I ask you?—to tell him anything. So I visited him with a delicious story he couldn't resist. I even told him Nelly sent me with it. He enthusiastically printed it without checking a single fact."

Katherine's callousness was chilling.

"I presume you also killed James Godfrey?"

Katherine nodded.

"Let me guess. You murdered him because he could also properly identify Cedric's body," Violet said. "But how were you able to get his body to Hyde Park without anyone noticing?"

"You obviously have no idea what sort of services a titled name can purchase, Mrs. Harper. The same sort of man who would steal my father-in-law's body for me is also perfectly willing to provide a late-night sea burial for my late husband." Katherine laughed sharply at her own joke. "Although one has to be careful to hire different workers so as not to arouse too much suspicion."

Godfrey was a sad case, but didn't deserve what happened to him. This madness had to cease.

Violet slipped to the floor before Katherine's chair, covered both of the woman's hands with her own, and adopted her best undertaker's voice, low and comforting. "Mrs. Fairmont, surely you realize you must turn yourself in to Inspector Hurst. Running away will not save you."

Katherine put her hand to her neck again. "I'll not be locked up with a bunch of prostitutes and thieves. I don't belong there. People who are in jail are either stupid or poor."

And which one are you, Mrs. Fairmont?

"Perhaps if he understands the circumstances, he will plead for you at court."

Although Violet wouldn't be particularly upset to see Katherine locked up forever.

"You must be mad. I've seen what that man does to innocent people, whisking them off like falcons picking up field mice. Imagine what he'll do to me. And Stephen."

Violet looked at Stephen while still covering Katherine's hands, which were now trembling. "Stephen, you are culpable, too. You assisted in Mrs. Peet's and James Godfrey's hangings, and you have been aiding Mrs. Fairmont every step of the way. Why didn't you put a stop to it?"

Stephen didn't answer. He was gazing at his wife, tears in his eyes.

Violet tried again. "Mrs. Fairmont, if you don't go to the authorities, Mrs. Bishop might remain imprisoned forever . . . or even worse may happen to her."

"I'll not be hauled off to Newgate like Gordon and Nelly were," Katherine said, eyes blazing. "I'd sooner fling myself from Westminster Bridge."

Violet caught Stephen's eye, and knew from his guilty look that Katherine had been present the day they had taken the ransom money to the bridge. But had Stephen known that Katherine planned to push Violet? It didn't bear thinking about any longer.

"You cannot be serious. You would let your husband's sister rot in jail?"

"As if either Nelly or Dorothy ever saw me as anything other than a tramp. In their minds, I ran off with Stephen the minute Cedric's back was turned. They've always hated me for that. Dorothy despises me even more because I was next in line to become chatelaine of Willow Tree House."

Was Katherine not aware of Mrs. Peet's involvement with Lord Raybourn?

"I must insist—"

"You'll do no such thing! You're just an undertaker. What power do you have over me? None." Katherine's voice was shrill and her eyes were those of a panther who had just found her prey.

"I don't mean to imply—" Lost in her desire to discover the truth, it was only now that Violet realized she was naïvely trying to convince a rabid animal to allow itself to be caged. Too late.

"I could kill you, you know." Katherine's voice was now subdued and dangerous. Violet feared she was about to be pounced on, and there was nowhere for her to run. Not that her skirts would have permitted it, anyway. She began backing away from Kather-

ine, with the intention of breaking for the door, despite the en-
cumbrance of her skirts. The rabid animal pounced.

"Katherine, don't," Stephen said. It was the last thing Violet
heard before her head exploded into a thousand stars and she collapsed to the floor.

23

Violet was being shaken violently. Where was she? Why was she on the floor? The carpet was rough against her face. She rose to one elbow and stopped, the pain to one side of her head blinding her against moving any farther. Someone was shouting her name over and over.

"What do you want?"

"Mrs. Harper, can you hear me?"

She moaned. "Leave me be."

"Mrs. Harper, you need to wake up."

She opened one eye. Inspector Hurst loomed over her.

"What happened to you?" he asked.

"Katherine Fairmont struck me with something." Gordon's favorite ash receptacle lay broken in two nearby. She reached up to touch the spot on her head where the pain was radiating. A throbbing lump the size of a mourning bell was building. She was probably fortunate she hadn't been killed.

But that wasn't what was important. Blinking away the pain, Violet said, "Why are you here?"

"We went to Mr. Smith's lodgings."

"They belonged to Cedric Fairmont," she told them.

"How did you know that?"

"It doesn't matter now. Go on."

"We found notes and letters proving conclusively that he was in charge of the Suez Canal's corvée labor for a period of time. His friend James Godfrey helped him."

Violet nodded, despite how much it hurt to do so.

"We returned to Scotland Yard and found your note, and I was convinced that something was decidedly wrong in this household. The door was open and I found you . . . like this. Can you stand?"

"I think so." Violet struggled to her feet as Hurst held out a hand to help her. She felt an attack of nausea as she stood upright, but it soon passed.

"Inspector, I know everything. However, the crucial thing right now is that Katherine Fairmont was responsible for the deaths of Cedric Fairmont, Mrs. Peet, and James Godfrey."

Hurst was incredulous. "That demure woman? Impossible."

"Nevertheless, it's true, and her husband aided her. They said they were going to Paddington Station for a train to Winchester."

"Can you walk?"

Violet nodded.

She must have looked like an asylum escapee, as wobbly as she was on her feet, clutching Inspector Hurst for balance. Luckily, there were several taxis waiting at the stand in nearby Upper Brook Street.

Violet's head cleared and the pain receded some as they rode the mile and a half to Paddington. During the ride, Violet told Hurst what had transpired at Raybourn House prior to her unfortunate encounter with the ashtray.

"I'll have Eleanor Bishop released as soon as possible," Hurst said as their taxi came to a stop.

Paddington Station was an architectural marvel, having opened thirty years earlier. Its massive, multibarreled roofline with an intricate mesh of glass and metal provided glorious natural light to those walking along the many concourses that guided passengers to any number of train tracks.

The noise inside the station was deafening, as trains came screeching in to spew riders and then gobble up more before chugging back outdoors.

"How will we find her?" Violet said with a hand to her head.

The pain returned from raising her voice to be heard over the cacophony of the station.

"We need to find a timetable."

Violet pointed. "Over there?"

They ran—she limped—to a board listing dozens of train departures. "Here it is," Violet said. "There's another train in about ten minutes on track four."

Paddington was one of the most well-used stations in London, and it was with difficulty that they managed to push through the crowds and arrive at the right track within a few minutes. Passengers milled about waiting, some reading newspapers while surrounded by luggage, others peering down the track as if by doing so they could will the train to arrive sooner. Children were scolded by their parents for playing too close to the edge.

Paddington's overall clamor reared up terrifying memories in Violet's mind of her own train crash. Her right arm began tightening in an almost visceral response to the chaos.

"I see them!" Hurst said. Violet followed him to where Katherine and Stephen stood, apart from everyone else and with their backs to them, a traveling bag clutched tightly in Katherine's hand as she imitated those who were glancing down the track in order to hurry the train.

Stephen frowned at seeing them, but Katherine was positively livid. "Why are you alive?" she demanded.

"My apologies for disappointing you, Mrs. Fairmont," Violet said.

"You should be far more disappointed to see me, Lady Raybourn," Hurst said. "You will not be boarding that train. You have a new destination."

"You can't stop me. I'll . . . I'll scream that you're attacking me."

Hurst pulled a pair of handcuffs from his jacket. "If you create a disturbance, I'll be forced to use these. It would be a shame for a society lady to be escorted out this way."

Katherine turned her wrath on her husband. "Stephen, what are you going to do to protect me from this dunderheaded duo? I'll not be taken!"

Stephen cupped his wife's cheeks in his hands. "Kate, don't be hysterical. We must be rational." He turned to Hurst. "What can you promise us, sir? What if I confessed to the crimes? Will you let my wife go?"

"Impossible, my lord. Your wife is the guilty party in the murders, and I'll be arresting you on related crimes. Lady Raybourn, you are under arrest for the murder of Cedric Fairmont. You will be remanded into custody and held to answer criminal charges against you—"

"No! I . . . I . . . claim sanctuary. I'm going to the cathedral in Winchester to claim sanctuary. I'll live out my days in a nun's cell."

Violet wasn't sure that sanctuary was still possible. Wasn't that a medieval system?

"I'm sorry, Lady Raybourn, but I'm tired of your hysterics. If you don't willingly come with me this moment, I'll take you by force." Hurst tapped the handcuffs against one wrist for emphasis.

"It's no use, my love," Stephen said. "We're both going to go to Scotland Yard and turn ourselves in. I'm guilty of many crimes myself for having helped you with yours."

"Why are you so anxious to do her bidding?" Katherine said, pointing to Violet. "Are you lovers? Do you wish to be rid of me?"

"Don't be foolish. I want you to be safe."

"That's what Cedric used to say, all those years ago. That as long as I was safe, I shouldn't worry about anything else he was doing."

Instead of cajoling, Stephen tried another tactic, which was to shake her sternly. The effort wore him out and made Katherine even angrier.

"Remove. Your. Hands. Sir." Katherine bared her teeth in a way that frightened Violet into taking several steps backward. Even Stephen was startled into letting her go. He returned to pleading with his wife.

"Kate, darling, please. Enough of this."

Violet wasn't prepared for what happened next. Katherine lifted her bag and swung it around full force, striking Stephen on the back of the head. Caught completely unawares, he pitched sideways, grabbing on to his wife as they both flew off the concourse, directly into the path of the five o'clock to Winchester.

Violet Harper knew personally what happened when the great metal beasts, snorting steam and bellowing their presence, came into conflict with human bodies. The train was always victorious.

She turned her head reflexively as other patrons on the platform screamed and pointed. She had no desire to relive the horror of mangled and burned corpses, especially of two people she knew, one of whom had been a childhood playmate.

Even an undertaker had her limits of endurance.

24

B ack at Scotland Yard, Violet sat in Commissioner Henderson's office, along with Inspectors Hurst and Pratt, and a newly released Nelly Bishop, who sat trembling and crying as she listened to Violet tell the story of Katherine's actions, which had culminated in the death of herself and Nelly's brother. Once Henderson had been briefed on the day's events, Nelly revealed even more secrets surrounding the case.

"I couldn't have imagined that the stone that came through my window was initiated by Katherine. It's simply too fantastic to even consider. I truly thought someone was out to kill me."

"Why would someone want to do that?" Pratt asked as he handed Nelly a handkerchief.

She daubed at her eyes. "Because I was trying to expose them. You see, I told you, Mrs. Harper, that I had hoped to return to journalism one day, but in reality, I was already writing for Mr. Catesby under an assumed name. It was gratifying work. I was almost like you, Mrs. Harper, except that I had to do my work in secret. Lately, I'd been working on an investigation of baby farming—"

"The Mrs. Flood case? The baby farmer? You were the reporter on that?" Hurst asked.

Nelly's cheeks pinked. "Yes. Were you following my work?"

"Good Lord, woman, you nearly ruined me with your constant interference and nosing around."

Hurst's accusation sent Nelly into fresh tears. The poor thing wasn't used to Hurst's centurion ways.

"Inspector," Violet said, "I'm sure she was only trying to help your investigation. Weren't you, Mrs. Bishop?"

Nelly nodded as she rubbed her nose with the handkerchief. "I just wanted to do something meaningful."

Commissioner Henderson stood. "I think we have everything we need. Mrs. Bishop, I apologize for your unwarranted detention."

As the group left Henderson's office, and Hurst and Pratt escorted Violet and Nelly out, Hurst leaned over and spoke quietly to Violet.

"It pains me to admit it, Mrs. Harper, but you were mostly right about things on this case."

"Actually, it was you who was largely correct about motives; you simply missed who was the guilty party."

"Hmm. I suppose I must extend my thanks, though."

"Why, Inspector, is that a note of respect I hear in your voice?"

"Absolutely not. Why would you think such a thing? I reserve my respect for Fortuna, who apparently blessed you with several rounds of good luck."

Violet smiled and tucked her arm into his elbow. "I think one day we might be friends."

"Huh, not likely." But he didn't shrug her off as they walked out of Scotland Yard together.

25

Violet was snuggled against Sam at St. James's Palace, where she'd moved back the moment she was able to leave Raybourn House. He'd returned from Sweden the previous evening, full of news about the potential impact of dynamite on mining operations. Violet had hushed him with her lips, and assured him that all of their news could wait until morning.

Now with the sun trying valiantly to send its rays through the heavy draperies, Violet was finally willing to talk about something not involving her husband's embrace.

She rose to one elbow. "There's so much to tell you."

"In a moment. First, I have something for you." Sam rose and went to a piece of his luggage that was already buried under Violet's clothing from the previous day. He returned with a small, square wooden box, wrapped in a velvet bow.

"For what I hope becomes a collection," he said.

Violet untied the bow and saw that the lid had a daisy inset in marquetry on it. "How very pretty."

"That's just the wrapping."

She pulled off the lid to see what was inside. Cushioned on cobalt-blue velvet lay a spectacular antique watch, its beauty not in the typical form of an intricately filigreed back, but in the large face with heavily carved copper hands that had patinated to a milky green.

"It's fantastic," she breathed.

"I found it in a jeweler's shop in Stockholm. It was made by Erik Wellenius in the mid-eighteenth century."

"It's completely different from my Margaret Fleming watch, but just as beautiful." Sam had purchased her the antique Fleming watch as a mourning gift long before they were married. "I adore it."

"Now, wife, tell me what has happened since I've been gone."

Violet proceeded to outline for him the events of the past couple of weeks. Sam listened attentively, not breaking in until she told him of her near-death experience at Westminster Bridge.

"Why didn't you tell me of this in your letters? I would have come straight back from Sweden."

"That's exactly why I didn't tell you. Besides, it was over and finished; what could you have done?"

"I could have done my job as your husband and protected you."

Violet smiled. "I love when you get outraged on my behalf."

"Honestly, woman, every time I let you out of my sight you get attacked by lions, thrown from bridges, and murderers come after you."

"All coincidental things."

"Right. Finish your story."

She did, with Sam once again interrupting her as she described the blow to her head and the horrifying scene inside the train station. "Trains seem to hold rotten luck for you, sweetheart."

"But they are an amazing conveyance. I suppose their ability to shrink distances makes them worth their risk."

"Once the transcontinental railroad is finished, we'll be able to ride from coast to coast in America at forty miles per hour. Except that . . . never mind, go on."

"Well, the queen summoned us all to Windsor, where I finally met Lord Raybourn once again. The queen had maintained admirable secrecy about him as the truth at Raybourn House revealed itself in its own time. On the eve of Bertie's departure, the viscount had been directed to stay in Egypt, in order to negotiate favorable shipping rates for England on the Suez Canal. Monsieur de Lesseps and other European countries would have been furious to learn that Great Britain's shipping terms would be better than those of France and the rest of the continent, so not even the

Prince of Wales knew that he was staying behind. The queen and Mr. Gladstone didn't want an international incident over it.

"That's why the Crown knew Lord Raybourn could not possibly have been dead in London, unless he returned without permission and without his task completed. The queen found that to be highly unlikely, given her high trust in his abilities and loyalty, so she sent someone off to Egypt to set eyes on him and bring him home. The entire reason she asked me to assist her was to confirm whether it was indeed Lord Raybourn's body in the coffin. It was her intent to set me on to discovering who it really was if it wasn't Lord Raybourn.

"Not only that, the Crown had Scotland Yard chasing down de Lesseps's blackmailer, another sticky situation. If other European countries had the impression that Britain had a hand in slavery, long abolished here, well, one can hardly think of the consequences. Much to Lord Raybourn's dismay, Cedric Fairmont was the blackmailer."

Sam grimaced. "An unfortunate turn of events for the esteemed Lord Raybourn. Yet, a neat trick the queen pulled off to get to the bottom of things without compromising British interests. What I don't understand, though, is why he didn't send word to Mrs. Peet to let her know of his plans to stay behind."

Violet thought back to Lord Raybourn's red-rimmed eyes and cracked voice as he spoke of his housekeeper. "He was under strict instructions to tell no one, and didn't even permit Madame Brusse and Mr. Larkin to write to their own families about the delay. Of course, he was devastated by the tragedy unfolding in his absence."

"Wasn't there some kind of scandal involving the maid next door, what was her name?"

"Rebecca. Mr. Larkin confessed that he was rather, er, aggressive in his attentions toward her. Mrs. Peet intervened with a ferocious verbal bite that cured Mr. Larkin of showering any other neighboring servants with unwanted attentions."

Sam laughed. "I wish I could have met the old girl. She must have been quite a character."

"She had the most remarkable eyes, a shade of green that simply, I don't know, *sparkled*. They were incongruous to her plain personality. It was so heartbreaking to see them faded and to have to close them a final time." Violet shook her head to clear the memory.

"How is the rest of the family adjusting?" Sam asked.

"Well, Dorothy Fairmont was agape over her father's own admission that he had cared for his housekeeper. In fact, she made a strangling noise that caused us all some concern. Eleanor Bishop acted resigned, as though her father was confirming a truth she knew but didn't want to hear. Her husband and son seemed quite overjoyed to see Lord Raybourn again.

"Both Dorothy and Eleanor were revived, though, by Lord Raybourn's announcement of his intention to change his will in their favor."

"How so?"

"He stated that he was sickened and dismayed over what had happened in his absence. He condemned both Stephen and Katherine for what they did, not only to Cedric and Harriet Peet, but to an innocent stranger like Mr. Godfrey. Lord Raybourn said, though, that he himself had also committed great crimes against his family, and wanted to rectify them.

"First, he apologized to Nelly for preventing her from pursuing her own interests. He referred to journalism as a wharf-rat's business, but admitted that he should have let her have a go at it instead of marrying her off right away, thinking marriage would calm her down."

"Gordon Bishop couldn't have been too pleased with that."

"He didn't seem to mind. He said, 'It's quite all right, old chap. I certainly got a good bargain, having dear Nells at my side all these years. And I don't think I've been such a bad lot for her.' And Eleanor didn't shrug off her husband's touch for once."

"Very accommodating of her."

"Sam, you're teasing again. Anyway, Lord Raybourn announced that he was rewriting his will, leaving Nelly all of his business interests in a railroad and a bank. He wants to leave Willow Tree House to Toby Bishop."

Sam frowned. "Can Toby inherit the title under English law?"

"I don't think so. It has to pass through Lord Raybourn's male line of descent. A shame, really. I think Toby would make a fine viscount one day.

"For Dorothy, whom he had always blocked from marrying, Lord Raybourn made Raybourn House hers to manage for the rest of her life. Lord Raybourn himself plans to live there quietly, in the last place he shared with Mrs. Peet."

"Seems fitting. But I'm a bit confused. If Lord Raybourn's will was already read out and the estate disposed of, how can he declare himself to be the possessor of his properties once again?"

"An excellent question. Especially since the inheritor of everything, Stephen Fairmont, died without issue. You're the lawyer. How would it be done?"

Sam shook his head. "The family will be wrangling in court for years."

"There's more. The queen decided to lift Lord Raybourn to an earldom, in celebration not only of Lord Raybourn's critical and successful negotiations in Egypt, but of a new royal arrival in several months' time. Princess Alix is with child."

"An elevation that will probably die out with him, unless Lord Raybourn should happen to remarry and father another son. Regardless, it seems like a satisfactory ending after so much heartbreak."

It was. After the queen's pronouncement, the family was huddled in a circle, chatting amiably as if the decades of wounds had never been opened. Such was the way of families. Bitter enemies one day, staunch allies the next. Blood ties were both bitter and sweet.

"So, wife, what did you think of Lord Raybourn?"

"For a man who had wreaked such havoc on his children, he was quite unassuming. Gentle, in fact, as though he'd be loath to turn a mongrel out on a chilly night and would instead offer the beast his own bed to sleep in. His gray hair was thick, as were his matching mustache and beard. He looked to me to be concealing a great deal of sadness."

"He's lost everything dear to him. A son, a daughter-in-law, a son he thought was previously dead, and his betrothed. All because of Cedric's bitter store of bile." He kissed her shoulder. "And Katherine's. Perhaps now the queen's own grief will be minimized by what she has witnessed with Lord Raybourn."

"Actually," Violet said, "I have some tremendously good news to report about that. The queen has finally decided to end the requirement for black armbands in her presence."

"And to think that only eight years have passed since the prince consort's death. She has bounced back admirably."

"Sam, don't tease. I worry for her. Sometimes people need a longer mourning period than a year or two, but for the queen it seems to be her permanent way of life. I do have to credit Mr. Brown, though, for lifting her spirits. Maybe it is his influence that has caused her to at least stop forcing everyone around her to continue in mourning."

"Who is Mr. Brown?"

"A close personal servant that the prince consort hired before his death. The queen's 'dear Mr. Brown' seems to be the only human being alive who can make her laugh. There are rumors circulating that she is actually having an affair with him."

Sam frowned. "Do you think she is?"

"No, it's preposterous. She may have lifted the mourning requirement for everyone else, but she is still in black garb every day and talks of Albert incessantly. In fact, I think the reason Mr. Brown enjoys so much success with her is because he indulges her ruminations about her dead husband. He is also curiously blunt in a way that never seems to raise the queen's ire."

"Maybe all good husbands can learn lessons from him."

"Perhaps I can invite him here to train you."

Sam responded by tickling her mercilessly for several seconds.

Gasping for air, Violet said, "Oh, stop. Speaking of invitations, I forgot something important. The queen invited us to attend the Suez Canal opening ceremony in November."

"In Egypt?"

"Yes, we can travel as part of the Prince of Wales's retinue, although I told the queen we might be unable to make another trip back from Colorado so soon."

"Besides, I'm not sure a humble old war veteran is fit for such dignified company."

"You're fit company for me, and I'll personally horsewhip anyone who suggests you aren't fit for royalty."

"I do love when you get outraged on my behalf."

"My outrage is reserved for only two things: those who would speak ill of you or Susanna, and those who don't show proper respect for the dead. Now, husband, do tell me about Mr. Nobel."

"Our encounter was a great success. He is obtaining multiple patents for his dynamite, which is a cheap and effective way to blast open silver mines. There are dynamite factories opening here in Great Britain, mostly to the north in Scotland, and I'd like to meet with some of them. Perhaps I can make an arrangement to exclusively purchase their dynamite and ship it to the United States."

"Samuel Harper, are you saying you're not ready to go back to Colorado yet?"

"Well . . . if you don't mind, I'd like to stay just a while longer. You can travel with me, now that the Raybourn situation is resolved, or wait for me in Brighton, or—what is so funny?"

Violet dropped back upon the pillows, tears of mirth running from the corners of her eyes. "Oh, Sam, the queen has summoned me again. She wishes for me to attend to her on another matter. It's something to do with her 'dear Mr. Brown.' I believe she wants me to quietly investigate without arousing the alarm of Scotland Yard."

Sam was now turned on his side, his cheek propped against his fist, his elbow on his pillow. "So neither one of us wants to go back home yet?"

"It would appear not. In fact, Will wants to sell me back his share of Morgan Undertaking, and I'm wondering if I should take him up on it. I suspect we may be in London for the foreseeable future. I also think that Mary Cooke needs me. George has been less than . . . devoted. He's run off to Switzerland, ostensibly to purchase watch parts, but Mary doesn't think he will return."

Sam sighed. "I'm not surprised about him. Susanna will be furious when I tell her we're staying longer."

"Balanced by what I'm sure will be my parents' boundless joy. I purchased a pair of dolls for Susanna from a shop she loved as a child. Perhaps she can visit us here and I can present them to her."

"An excellent thought. I'll write to her with the idea."

"Later. You have other duties to attend to right now."

After weeks of horror and death, it was a pleasant afternoon indeed at St. James's Palace.

AUTHOR'S NOTE

Several of the events and people in this book are real and deserve a mention for the reader.

Lieutenant Colonel Sir Edmund Yeamans Walcott Henderson (1821–1896) was appointed commissioner of police in 1869. He was greatly loved by his men for doing away with petty regulations, such as the ones that forbade officers to vote in elections or to grow facial hair. He also worked diligently for pay increases for his men, started a registry for habitual offenders, and introduced special "schoolmaster sergeants" to increase the literacy of his constables. Henderson was responsible for making significant strides in the growth and organization of a professional detective force, and was made a Knight Commander of the Bath in 1878.

However, his achievements were overshadowed by a police strike in 1872, a police corruption trial in 1877, and the mishandling of the Trafalgar Square Riot of 1886. Upon this last event, Henderson resigned permanently from his position.

Queen Victoria's closest confidant following the death of her husband, Albert, was **John Brown** (1826–1883), a Scottish outdoor servant (*ghillie*) who became a close personal servant of the queen's. He was known for his competence and the complete trust Victoria placed in him. He also inspired jealousy and resentment in those who believed Brown was entirely too relaxed and informal around the sovereign.

This bitterness spawned rumors that Brown was the queen's lover, a position that is still speculated upon today. I don't personally think there is any truth in it, not only because she was in open mourning for Albert the remainder of her life, but because Victoria was acutely aware of her position in life. An open dalliance with a servant would have gone against every principle and scruple for which she railed at her children, her ladies-in-waiting, and her cabinet ministers. Queen Victoria was *proper* to a fault, and even if she'd decided to succumb to a dalliance, I don't think it would have been in such a brazen manner.

At the opposite end of the queen's favorability spectrum was **William Ewart Gladstone** (1809–1898), prime minister on four separate occasions, with the first time during 1868–1874. Gladstone was known for his oratory, constant reform plans, and his rivalry with Conservative Leader Benjamin Disraeli, as well as his poor relationship with Queen Victoria. Although the queen wasn't fond of Gladstone, he genuinely admired her.

Also despised by the queen was her son, **Albert Edward ("Bertie"), the Prince of Wales** (1841–1910), and later King Edward VII. Victoria never forgave him for what she perceived as his role in her husband's death, when the prince consort visited an errant and unruly Bertie at Cambridge during a particularly damp and chilly week in 1861, despite all indications that the prince consort had been ill for at least two years before his death. Although Bertie dutifully married the beautiful and charming **Princess Alexandra ("Alix") of Denmark** (1844–1925), and proceeded to provide six children to the House of Hanover, he never fully regained his mother's trust.

Alfred Nobel (1833–1896), for whom the famous Nobel Prizes are named, was a Swedish chemist, inventor, and armaments manufacturer who held 350 different patents, of which dynamite was the most famous. In 1888, Nobel's brother Ludvig died while visiting Cannes, and the newspapers erroneously reported it as Alfred's death. The obituary, with its condemnation of Nobel's invention of dynamite ("The merchant of death is dead"), deeply troubled him. Determined that he should not be remembered as someone who became rich by devising ways to kill more people faster, in his will he set aside the bulk of his fortune to establish the five Nobel Prizes. The first three prizes are for physical science, chemistry, and medical science. The fourth prize is literary, and the fifth is awarded to the person or society that renders the greatest service in reducing standing armies or promoting peace. I imagine Nobel had no idea what a lasting impact his prizes would have on the world.

The **Suez Canal** was the brainchild of **Ferdinand de Lesseps** (1805–1894), a Frenchman with a varied and distinguished diplomatic career before successfully completing a waterway linking the Mediterranean and Red Seas, effectively connecting East and West with dramatically reduced sailing distances.

The concept of a canal was taken up by Egypt as early as the second millennium B.C. Remnants of an ancient west–east canal were discovered by Napoleon in 1799. The French general contemplated the construction of another canal, running north–south to join the Mediterranean and Red Seas, but his project was abandoned after his engineers mistakenly concluded that the Red Sea was more than thirty feet higher than the Mediterranean.

It was de Lesseps, with his friendly relationship with the Egyptian viceroy, who finally pushed through construction of a canal open to ships of all nations. The Suez Canal Company came into existence in December 1858, with work beginning in April 1859.

The excavation took ten years, with Egypt providing **corvée labor** during part of the project. Unlike slavery, the worker under a corvée labor system is not owned outright, and is generally free in many respects except for how he labors. Corvée labor extends back to many societies' ancient times, and was used as recently as prerevolutionary France. In ancient Egypt, specifically, peasants were seized to help in government projects, such as in the building of pyramids and assisting during Nile River floods. Peasants were also sentenced to corvée labor for non-payment of taxes (an interesting twist on debtors' prison).

Great Britain loudly protested the use of corvée labor for the Suez Canal project, as they had officially outlawed slavery in 1834. Corvée labor was no longer being used on the project by the time I include it in late 1868.

De Lesseps was a powerful and wealthy man, and was nearly like a king in Egypt, cheered everywhere he went. Unfortunately, he overestimated how much traffic would be using the canal by tenfold, so that within two years of the canal's completion, he was booed everywhere he went. Today, more than fifty ships per day travel the 120-mile route, amounting to eight percent of the world's shipping traffic.

Britain purchased Egypt's shares in the Suez Canal in 1875, as the African nation was desperate to raise money to pay off its own debts.

As a footnote to de Lesseps's career, it is interesting to note that he also attempted to dig the Panama Canal in 1879, but the project was thwarted by epidemics of malaria and yellow fever, insufficient capital, and financial corruption. The project was picked up by the United States in 1904.

The reader may wonder why Violet doesn't use formaldehyde as an embalming agent. Formaldehyde was conclusively identified in 1869 when August Wilhelm von Hofmann mixed air with methanol over a heated platinum spiral as a metal catalyst, with formaldehyde as the resulting product. Unfortunately, its preservative qualities were not noted until 1888, so any embalming in this time period would have been performed with ingredients such as alcohol, bichloride of mercury, creosote, nitrate of potassium, turpentine, and zinc chloride.

Toby Bishop joins William Booth's **Christian Revival Society**, which was founded in 1865 as the North London Christian Mission. In 1878, Booth reorganized the mission, basing it upon a military structure and becoming its first general. Booth expressed the organization's mission in terms of the "three S's" that best described their work with the down-and-out, ranging from alcoholics to morphine addicts, to prostitutes and other "undesirables" of polite society: "first, soup; second, soap; and finally, salvation."

Booth's group became known as the Salvation Army. Today the organization has a presence in more than a hundred countries, and is famous for its iconic bell ringers in front of shops during the Christmas season.

A couple of small liberties I took with the historical record are worth pointing out.

Violet and Stephen travel along Victoria Embankment on their way to Smithfield meat market. This road, built both to relieve congestion in the Strand and Fleet Street and to provide London with a modern sewer system, was not actually completed until 1870, the year after the story takes place.

Also, I have Violet picking up a copy of *Funeral Service Journal* from Morgan Undertaking, in order to investigate other undertakers. This journal did not actually begin publication until 1886.

SELECTED BIBLIOGRAPHY

Beeton, Isabella. *Beeton's Book of Household Management* (Facsimile Edition). London: Jonathan Cape Limited, 1968.

Brett, Mary. *Fashionable Mourning Jewelry, Clothing & Customs.* Atglen, PA: Schiffer Publishing, 2006.

Karabell, Zachary. *Parting the Desert: The Creation of the Suez Canal.* New York: Alfred A. Knopf, 2003.

May, Trevor. *The Victorian Undertaker.* Oxford: Shire Publications, 1996.

Nicholson, Shirley. *A Victorian Household.* London: Barrie & Jenkins, 1988.

Picard, Liza. *Victorian London: The Tale of a City 1840–1870.* New York: St. Martin's Press, 2005.

Shpayer-Makov, Haia. *The Ascent of the Detective: Police Sleuths in Victorian and Edwardian England.* New York: Oxford University Press, 2011.

Underwood, Peter. *Queen Victoria's Other World.* London: Harrap, 1986.